S0-AES-122

# LOVE HEAR MY HEART

## Sonya T. Pelton

**ZEBRA BOOKS**
**KENSINGTON PUBLISHING CORP.**

ZEBRA BOOKS

are published by

Kensington Publishing Corp.
475 Park Avenue South
New York, NY 10016

First printing: March, 1990

Printed in the United States of America

*For my mother, Johanna,
who always delighted in
beautiful, jewel-colored
dresses.*

*"What the heart once heard,
the heart can never forget."*

# Part One

"Love enters through the eyes."
—*Arab Proverb*

# Chapter One

Slowly the black shores softened to twilight gray and the river emerged from undefined darkness. The first birdcalls sounded.

As the wreaths of white mist slowly dissolved, the light strengthened and the Missouri captured the pinkish-gold of waking sky and the verdant greens of trees and brush along the banks. The air stirred.

A fresh morning-scented breeze blew to the slim, quiet figure watching the sun burst forth roseate and gold to bathe everything in its lambent light.

The town finally came awake and the occupants began to stir, rise, and breakfast in the invading sunshine of a Missouri spring morning. Clerks opened their River Street stores, and soon the splint-bottomed chairs were occupied by whiskered old men tilting back against paint-chipped walls.

The day was glorious with expectancy, especially to the beautiful, willful blonde still waiting at the breakwater levee, her gaze roving longingly over the great, wide Missouri.

The rising sun gilded the Madonna-like features now upturned eagerly for the touch of morning warmth and lit the silver fire in blond strands that were usually plaited into a single fat braid that hung over one shoulder. Today her hair swung free.

It was nine o'clock when a plume of dark smoke appeared above the point, presently followed by the first sight of the huge floating "palace" coming around the bend, so tall in the air, so light in the water. The sidewheeler's flag gallantly flew from the jack staff, seen intermittently between great volumes of the darkest smoke roiling and tumbling from towering black stacks.

Swallowing past the lump in her throat, her incredibly long lashes lifted high over her big blue eyes in excitement, her lithe body galvanized into action, Cassandra St. James snatched up the muslin folds of her yellow-and-green striped dress. For a moment she dared herself to remove the false front bodice that made her dress appear childish, her small breasts flatter than they really were. Actually, even if she were to remove the "secret panel," her breasts would not look all that much bigger. She was small everywhere, and no matter what she did with her childish clothes, altering them in the privacy of her room, nothing could transfer her body into generously luscious curves, nothing short of a miracle.

Cassandra stepped daintily around little freight piles scattered about the levee and then hurriedly clambered over the town drunk asleep on the skids. Her stride was innocently, faintly provocative as she moved swiftly, her eyes trained on the handsome captain of the steamboat lifting his tanned hand to his men.

"Father . . ." She breathed the word with an air of reverence. She constantly worried about him, for stories abounded in which people perished in steamboat disasters. Classic accounts described the drowning of scores, the hurling of bodies across banks; many lingered on, horribly burned, while others were never to be found. If Papa should ever die—

The humid air felt like velvet flower petals against Cassandra's skin as she walked faster now, watching as the giant wheels came to a sudden halt, churning the water to pearls of foam.

*Mama says to walk like a lady, not gallop like a horse,* Cassandra tried to remind herself, slowing down a little. Oh, fiddle, she thought, it was such a waste of time trying to comport oneself as the proper lady when one wanted to run free as the wind. Or, if that were not possible, then to do the second best, which, to her way of thinking was to sew up beautiful dresses for the French aristocracy, to run a boutique all one's own! This was her fondest dream.

Now the *River Minx* wallowed closer, came to rest at last. A wild scramble ensued as "St. Looey" passengers pressed forward to get ashore. Cassandra grinned lopsidedly, wondering what all their haste was about. She would rather be in St. Louis than here in this small Missouri river town situated far below that bustling city.

"Cassandra! Is that you?" a deep male voice called out to her, the tall man breaking through the crowd.

"Papa!" Cassandra flung her slender body into Monte St. James's arms. "I have been watching for hours. I am so happy you are finally home again."

Monte laughed deep in his throat. "I have always

11

come home, Cassa. Were you afraid I wouldn't this time?" He stroked the waist-length, angel blond hair floating about her slim shoulders while he peered curiously into blue eyes surrounded by thick black starry lashes. "My Lord, while I wasn't looking, you have become a true beauty."

Monte studied his daughter. She was already a stunning young woman, no doubt about that. Many a male heart beat faster when gazing upon her dainty, ethereal beauty, he knew, and they would soon be drawn to her like bees to a honey pot. But there was only one man who could handle her fiery, adventurous spirit, he decided. His pilot and business partner, Sylvestre Diamond, of the French Diamont family of St. Louis. The only problem was that Monte's wife, Melantha, had other plans. Her longtime dream had been to make Cassandra acceptable to the wealthy Kirby family, to have her wed her distant cousin, Harlan Kirby. However, Monte was afraid that her reckless nature would someday get her into trouble before her wedding date could arrive. If only she could set her eyes upon the golden Sy. Sylvestre Diamond—now there was a man's man.

An impish look crossed Cassandra's face. "I have always been here, Papa. Is it possible that you have overlooked me because of my short stature?"

"Short? I wouldn't exactly call you that, Cassa. You are merely dainty, but not short by any standards."

"You would realize, Papa, I am lacking a few inches if you were to set me beside the younger women of our town or those in St. Louis, or anywhere for that matter." She giggled softly. "By today's standards of tall, buxom young women, *small* is not modish."

"Oh, not at all, Cassa. You see, next to any young female, you would stand out as the shining jewel, all the others dull, unpolished rocks."

Her smile was filled with unbounded joy. "Am I really polished, Papa?" She pouted prettily. "Melantha does not think of me in such glowing terms. She calls me vain—and willful." *But I am not all that wild,* she thought, wishing she could reveal her secret that Letty, her black maid, had taught her in private all there was to know about stitching up fancy clothes for fancy folks. No one knew this, not even Melantha—or so she thought.

"A beautiful brat . . ." Monte interrupted Cassandra's musings, playfully pressing her slightly upturned nose. He hugged her fiercely to him as they began to ascend the hill, feeling her young breast against his side, knowing she was developing at a rapid pace . . . knowing also that she harbored a secret from him. Maybe more than one, he decided, afraid as most fathers were, of losing their daughters to the wrong man. No ice maiden his girl, she would make some fine man a fiery catch.

"Has Sylvestre Diamond accompanied you on this trip?" Cassandra inquired about her father's business partner whom she hadn't seen in what seemed like ages.

Monte St. James felt a twinge of conscience, but mostly joy at this moment. Ever since he'd first introduced his daughter to Sylvestre Diamond, watching him play so gently with his Cassa, indulging her every whim and pleasure, knowing in his heart what Sy did not realize himself, he'd believed that these two were meant for each other, that no other man would treat his only daughter with the highest regard and respect, that in Sy's arms was where Cassa belonged. For a split second, he wondered if he was wrong about everything, then he told himself that, no, even if he should perish before that time, these two willful, stubborn souls would find each other. He only wished that he did not have the feeling that he would not live to see it.

"Accompanied?" Monte snorted belatedly, following his musings. "That is hardly the word, Cassa. Sy does not *accompany,* he works like he can't get enough of it. Pilot, yes, he does that for me"—he wondered about that sometimes—"but he also captains his own boats, too, you know."

"Honestly, Papa, I do not recall much about that in our old conversations. Does Sylvestre pilot well?"

"Indeed he does. Pilot is the grandest position of all, with a princely salary of two hundred and fifty-three dollars a month. On him depends the safety of passengers and crew, day and night. Sylvestre's is a rare ability, part long training, part detailed knowledge of an unbelievably complicated subject. He has to depend on memory, on years of accumulated skills, and on informed guesswork, for the river is a fickle lady and the pilot must take chances at every point." Monte paused to peer down into his daughter's wide, inquisitive eyes. "Sylvestre is also my business partner, Cassa."

"Since when, Papa?"

"Can we discuss all this later, darling?" He smiled secretly. "I have a surprise for you."

Cassandra cocked her bright head. "Is it in that brown-wrapped package?" *Oh if it was only a new dress from St. Louis, for she loved new fashions from*

14

*there, and especially anything velvet.*

"In just a while you'll see. First I must tell you some good news. Sylvestre Diamond is coming to dinner. At least that is what he said while a gorgeous redhead at the levee caught his eyes, then again"—he grinned roguishly—"he might have forgotten all about the invitation."

Cassandra's tawny-dark brows rose in the air. *"Which one?"* she inquired saucily.

"Ahh, you are growing up, minx, that you are." He chuckled. "So, Captain Sy has finally caught your eye?" he asked hopefully.

"Hmm, I hope he comes to dinner" was all Cassandra offered. But she was recalling the many happy Christmases they had spent with the Diamond family in St. Louis so long ago. Those warm, cheerful occasions were not to be forgotten. When she was a little girl, Sylvestre Diamond had just entered his teenage years. She had been struck by a statue of David in a school picture book and had likened Sylvestre to the strong, muscled figure ever since, blushing furiously when she gazed downward at the leafed private parts, then snapped the book shut with a bang.

As daughter walked with father, she envisioned the golden Sy. Could he really be all that interested in flirtatious women especially ones with red hair? She felt suddenly jealous of the one who had caught his golden eyes ... there was even a tinge of iridescent green in the slanted orbs, too, if she remembered correctly. His deep bronze skin he had inherited from the Choctaw Indian ancestry of his father, the pale hair from his mother, whose lineage boasted the bold French aristocracy who had landed in the lush

15

plantations of the South and had drifted westward into Missouri. Aside from this, she could not recall much more history of the Diamont family, for it had been a long stretch in time since she last visited Diamondhead Plantation.

Though Sylvestre Diamond was almost ten years older than she, Cassandra knew he would always remain in her heart as her dearest childhood friend. She only wished he were not so distant of late, in body as well as in . . . what, spirit? He was a mature man now, and something had changed drastically in their relationship. Possibly a new love, or many, had kept his time occupied, and perhaps Sylvestre would not come to dinner after all but find his pleasure elsewhere.

Monte St. James cast one more glance back at his boat, looking on her with pride. The *River Minx* was a sidewheeler, especially built for the Missouri River, though she often plied the Mississippi as well. She drew only three feet of water, but could carry three hundred tons of freight and a little over two hundred passengers to their destination.

Now Monte's teal-blue eyes shifted to the bluff top where the St. James house sat like a massive sea chest upon a shelf, with two stories of soft pink brick, the house boasting deep, arched windows trimmed with artistic limestone carvings. There was a magnificent view of the river from the house and Monte remembered well the evenings when Melantha, his second wife, whom he'd married not long after the demise of his first, had often spurned his husbandly advances and left him staring out at the dark river, wishing his beautiful fair-haired Emmaline back in his empty arms. He had had this house built especially for

Emmaline and he could not find it in his heart to reveal to Cassandra who her true mother had been. Perhaps he was a coward, he should have told Cassandra long ago. Too late now. She was almost eighteen. She would hate him. So would Melantha, and her "headaches" would come even more often.

When they reached the bluff, Melantha appeared in the doorway of the house that was now bathed in sunlit pink. Thirty-four years of age, she was tall and slender, with huge, motherly breasts, though she had never had a babe to nurse from them, could never, for she could not conceive, at least not in the seventeen years she had been wed to the virile Monte St. James.

Black hair was drawn severely back from Melantha's pale, heart-shaped face, full lips smiling decorously as she presented a smooth cheek for her husband to kiss. "Welcome home, darling." Then Melantha turned to her "daughter." "Cassandra, you must walk like a lady, not shift about like an excited schoolgirl. You have to grow up someday." Melantha shifted her gaze over the bodice of the childish dress, suspiciously eyeing the tight threads that did not quite match the original stitching of the dress. *So*, she thought, *the girl has been sewing in her room at night with that black maid of hers when I expressly ordered her to study her old schoolbooks, to read them all over again, to play her harp which was gathering dust in the drawing room!*

"I did not hear your answer, Cassandra."

"Yes," Cassandra simply said, having seen where Melantha's sharp eyes had rested.

"Yes what?" Melantha stood with her hand on a shapely hip.

17

"Yes, *Mother.*"

Cassandra longingly eyed the package her father had brought her, while her mother curiously eyed the same. "Papa has brought me something from St. Louis." She accepted the package. "May I open it now?" she asked as they drifted into the house, where the rooms were dominated by Melantha's precious Italian furniture, the other daintier pieces of French influence pushed to the corners to gather dust. "Please?" Cassandra slowly whirled to face her father, ignoring Melantha's hard gaze.

"Go ahead, love," said the doting Monte St. James.

Without waiting for Melantha's approval, Cassandra tore open the large package, and out tumbled a turquoise dress with a gay little bonnet to match. "Velvet!" she cried rapturously, her fragile hands caressing the soft folds of material, the cocky feather of the hat. "How I have hoped for a velvet dress. I love it. I love *you!*"

Cassandra hugged her father, while at the same time feeling something cold stabbing into her back. Then she heard the imperious voice a second later: "Velvet is much *much* too old for a child of seventeen."

Defiantly avoiding the ominous voice, Cassandra continued to rhapsodize over the dress. "It matches my eyes almost perfectly."

"Your eyes are not blue-green," Melantha interjected. "They are blue, as blue as the sky!"

Turning from the dreamy stars in Cassandra's eyes, Melantha put a disapproving eye on her husband. "Cassandra has spent the last two weeks in front of her mirror. And if she is not doing that, she is wasting precious moments of study or practicing the harp by

18

lingering out in the shade with that good-for-nothing maid of hers, or playing childish games with Letty's daughter. That black child has to go. Why, Cassandra has even been teaching *it* to read and write her letters."

Monte looked at his wife in surprise. "Dulcie is not an *it*, Melantha. She is only a bit slow and childish for her seventeen years."

"They are both useless as far as I am concerned, and all Cassandra does in her room with Letty is stitch, stitch, stitch. I can almost hear the needles going in and out of the cloth all during the night. Then they tear all the stitches out of the cloth and they start all over again. Dumb, dumb!"

"Melantha!" Monte thundered, his deep blue eyes wide with incredulity at her cold, hard words. "Letty is a fine woman, and, as you know, she has been with me for a long time. In fact, she and her husband, Ol' George, accompanied us from Georgia—" *Along with Emmaline,* he did not add, not in front of the curiously watching Cassandra.

Ol' George, Cassandra sighed inwardly, recalling the many stories she had listened to in the pale light of the moon as Letty recounted them, the jasmine surrounding them giving a magical, mystical quality to the night and the black tale-spinner weaving her wondrous web of gold. Letty was full African, but her daughter was so pale and creamy she could almost pass for white. Ol' George had been a Mandingo, but he had loved Dulcie as if she had been his own babe. Letty had softly, almost without emotion, told her of the white plantation owner who had kept her as a slave, made her heavy with child before Master St. James saved her from a life of cruelty and abuse by paying good money

19

for her and Ol' George. *How could Melantha speak so cruelly of her favorite people in the whole world and call them dumb! It wasn't true . . . it just wasn't!*

"Dulcie is mulatto," Melantha said, always harboring feelings of enmity toward the child and her black mother, even though Letty had gently welcomed her as Monte's new bride years back. "Few planters are willing to trust a black woman and her educated half-Nigra child around their womenfolk."

"What has that got to do with anything?" Monte stormed violently, defending Cassandra's devoted servants.

"Well . . ." Melantha sniffed again, eyeing the turquoise dress oddly, unaware of two liquid-brown eyes staring curiously out from behind the curtained French doors. "If our daughter is to marry into the wealthy Kirby family . . ." She shot her husband a look that dared him to defy her in this—"then she must go to them with dutiful servants, not those two pitiful creatures she has taken under her wing."

Cassandra's mouth was gaping. *Two pitiful creatures!* Why, Letty and Dulcie were anything but! In fact, they were the light of her life, and where her mother had failed to give her sufficient love, Letty had made up for it with generous hugs and offers of encouragement, not to mention the stimulating conversation from both Letty and bright-eyed Dulcie, whose young mind already showed promise of better things. *And if I have anything to do with her learning, Dulcie will not suffer or become mistress to a cruel plantation owner!*

"Let's get back to speaking about *our* child. I say Cassandra is much too vain, always dreams about material things, and I mean that literally. Clothes, clothes, that's all she's got her mind on. She should be praying the rosary to Mary to become a gentlewoman who knows how to run a house and entertain folk."

"Why, for God's sake?" Monte softly asked this woman he had married for the sake of terrible loneliness, his own loneliness, for Melantha had always been content with her rosary beads, or playing the harp, or cleaning, cleaning, always mops, brooms, pails littering the hallway, and slick, wet floors he had almost slipped and broken his neck upon a hundred times now. When Melantha stood haughtily, Monte went on. "Cassandra's actions seem perfectly normal for a seventeen-year-old." Upon hearing a moan behind him, he turned to see his daughter shaking her head. "I'm sorry, Cassa, I mean *almost* eighteen, come next week. Now go and put it on," he said of the velvet dress.

With a twist of her lithe young body, Cassandra bounded up the stairs to her bedroom, the oh so soft dress piled in her slender arms, the bonnet clapped to her fair head. Long wavy blond hair flew behind her like a silken banner as she disappeared at the top landing.

"Honestly," breathed Melantha, still unaware of Dulcie's round eyes peering secretly, "I just don't know what to do with her. Cassandra is so very willful . . . Monte . . . are you listening?" Absently he told her he was, then informed his wife, "Sylvestre Diamond is coming to dine with us."

"What?!" shrieked Melantha, causing the hiding Dulcie to jump in alarm. *"Please,* Monte, not him. Anyone but Sylvestre Diamond."

"What is so bad about Sy? You used to enjoy spending Christmases with the Diamond family."

"Yes. Then I learned from the kitchen gossips there that Jean-Pierre Diamont—their true name from lineage, you know—that he, Sylvestre's deceased father, had Choctaw Indian blood. Savages!" Melantha hissed while Dulcie's eyes grew rounder, more bewildered with this conversation. "That's what runs in your Captain Sy's veins, the blood of savages! And those strange catlike-gold eyes, why, he gives me the shivers, he does."

"You never told me about your ill feelings for Sylvestre before, Melantha, or that he frightened you."

"Well, you know now. I do not want him sniffing around Cassandra's skirts. It was all right when Cassandra was younger for Sylvestre to sit with her on his knee and read to her or take her for walks. Now he is a man and he's got ideas about our Cassandra, I just know he does." She flushed as she recalled the last time he had visited and she had noticed that unmistakable swell . . . she swallowed hard . . . in his tight-fitting black breeches . . . Fortunate for Cassandra she was down with a cold that day and could not come downstairs . . . to see. "He—he's arrogant, much like those two Nigras Cassandra keeps in the house."

*Oee,* thought Dulcie, shaking her long black hair, full of inky wavelets and blue highlights.

Monte could not help but chuckle. "Very little, if any, "savage taint" runs in Sy's blood, Melantha."

"You know I have longed for Cassandra to wed into the Kirby family, Monte," purred Melantha as she drifted around the room, running her hands along the heavily polished ornate appointments.

22

"Why? Because you know that Cassa hates Harlan with a passion?"

"Now that was a cruel thing to say." Melantha pouted. "You know I have always wanted only the best for our darling Cassandra. If only she could get rid of those black slaves, then we could have a normal mother-and-daughter relationship."

"Come now, Melantha." Monte cocked an eyebrow. "If not for Dulcie, who would there be to perform all the menial tasks around here? Really," he snorted, "that sweet girl works too darn hard."

With a toss of her dark head, Melantha said, "How would you know how hard the child works or doesn't work? You are hardly ever home!"

"Melantha, let's not get into that again, or else we shall speak of how you spend my hard-earned money on all this priceless"—an arm swept about the cluttered room—"junk from Italy."

*"Junk!"*

"That is what I said, damn-blasted *junk!*"

"Oh, I despise your vulgarity, Monte St. James." Her eyes narrowed before an arm swept across her brow and she performed a good imitation of swooning.

"You do not even have to tell me, Melantha, I already know," he said with a disgusted expression. "You are going to have a headache later on."

*Oh, Lord, poor Mister S'James that woman is wily as a fox,* thought Dulcie as she popped out of her hiding place like a jack-in-the-box and disappeared into the dense greenery of the gardens, blending in with all the many useless copper nymphs which guarded the grounds like fat cherubs turning green, water spewing from their mouths and nether regions.

23

# Chapter Two

Just as Monte St. James began counting to ten, Cassandra made an appearance in the frame of the drawing-room door. She came forward until she stood uncertainly, her soft blue eyes begging Melantha's approval. Please God, just once in her life let Melantha approve of something she did, Cassandra prayed.

Monte blinked his eyes twice. Cassandra was Emmaline all over again. She was an ethereal vision in the turquoise velvet, with creamy lace foaming about her lily skin, the taut bodice displaying the curved lines of her saucy, maturing breasts. Cassandra's mouth was a soft pink rosebud, her eyebrows tawny-dark upswept arrows above her mischievously dancing eyes. A real beauty whose childlike vulnerability was fast vanishing.

Cassandra reached up a slim hand to flick the plumes of her hat. She sighed dreamily. "The feathers are like silver frost." Melantha glowered at her.

Monte chuckled softly, for in her haste Cassandra had fastened the hat on askew and it presented an impudent, saucy look. He swallowed hard at the young beauty she had become. She was like a slender, unlit candle, cool, white, waiting for the right moment to be set aflame by the right man. A sleeping beauty waiting to be awakened by a kiss.

Staring hard at the velvet bodice and low-slung neckline, the foaming lace hiding nothing to the observant and calculating eye, Melantha said imperiously, "The fabric is lovely and must be very expensive." She tossed her dark head. "But it belongs in a theater and not on a young girl. I am sorry, but I do not approve."

"Melantha!" Cassandra wailed.

"Mother!" Melantha shouted back. "How many times must I tell you to call me Mother? It is not proper that you call me by my given name."

Trembling inside, Cassandra tore her eyes away to stare out the French doors at nothing in particular. She calmed herself then with the comforting thought that Letty would approve once she feasted her kindly black eyes on the velvet dress, as would Dulcie, wherever that lovely girl could be at the moment. Most likely gone to market with Letty. Oh, she could not wait until they returned. At this moment she was sorely grieved that Melantha was her mother and not Letty!

Melantha's voice continued to drone in Cassandra's pained ears. "You should not have spent so much money, Monte. The dress is entirely unsuitable for a child of seventeen."

"Eighteen—almost," Cassandra cried in a desperate voice.

"Hold your tongue, Daughter!" She turned back to her husband to continue despite Cassandra's obvious distress. "Perhaps, ah, you can make an exchange, for something more modest?"

"Oh, M-mother!" Tears began to brim in Cassandra's cloudy eyes. "I do not wish to have any dress but this one—truly!"

Suddenly Monte appeared sheepish. "I can't exchange it, dear. I've had it made especially to fit Cassandra. You are being unnecessarily strict, Melantha," he protested. "I like it the way it is, but if you want, you can put some more lace on the bodice."

"No!"

"Cassan*dra!*" Compressing her lips, Melantha regarded husband and daughter with somber gray eyes. "Cassandra simply *cannot* wear the dress."

"Come now, Melantha, love," crooned Monte. "Don't be ridiculous. You've got to allow the girl some leeway."

Cassandra, releasing an anguished cry, whirled about, then turned back with stormy eyes. "I do not care what you say, Mother, I *will* wear the dress!" She flounced out of the drawing room and up the stairs, her back held ramrod straight.

"You see," sniffed Melantha, her dark eyes gleaming oddly.

"I don't see anything," Monte said with a tired sigh.

A long silence prevailed in which each said nothing. Then Monte rose, strode to the window and restlessly gazed out at the sunlit river. There would be a moon tonight—a lover's moon . . . He almost flinched as his wife's voice came from behind him.

"What time would you like dinner?"

"You mean we still have a cook in the house?"

"Of course."

"Eight." Monte's voice came out harshly. "I'm going

downtown—but I'll make it a point to return by then."

Coldly Melantha sniffed, "You prefer the tavern to your own home."

"At least I find some warmth there!"


When seven o'clock rolled around, Monte St. James was full of drink—but not drunk. He lit a cigar, then held an extra one out to the younger man seated across from him in the dimly lighted corner of the tavern. Politely, Sylvestre Diamond refused the cigar.

Through the smoke-filled air, Monte regarded his friend and business partner with a steady gaze. Sylvestre's hair, shoulder length, swayed like smooth tawny silk when he moved, and the pale flickers of moody lights danced in the golden strands. Lean-hipped, with wide shoulders, he was a ruggedly built individual but carried himself with an air of the French nobility. Monte often thought that Sylvestre moved like a graceful jaguar, his furtive catlike movements catching the eye of many a tavern wench and gentle maiden.

"What is your pleasure?" Monte asked, playfully eyeing the sway of the tavern wench's hips as she left their table.

"I have had plenty," Sylvestre returned casually, curling his sensual mouth as he pushed his empty mug aside. He ignored the sashaying tavern wench as if she were not even alive.

"Hmm, you never think of anything but business and profits, my young friend?" Monte eyed Sylvestre carefully, as if trying to read what his thoughts were.

"Not at this moment—*non,*" Sylvestre returned

28

coolly, his keen eyes narrowed.

"What are you thinking of then?" Monte wanted to know. "I have drunk more than my share and still you lag behind. Drinking and wenching does not interest you at all?"

"Does it you?" Sylvestre shot back, eager to leave the tavern and be on their way to the pink house on the hill.

Monte sighed dispiritedly. "Not that much. Tell me"—Monte leaned back in his chair, stretching his long legs out alongside Sylvestre's equally long limbs—"what are you planning for your own steamboat, the *Gray Eagle?*" He wondered why Sylvestre spent so much time of late aboard his own *River Minx*, but it gave him high hopes to think perhaps Sylvestre was wishing for a glimpse of Cassandra now and then.

All of a sudden Sylvestre was not of such a business mind as he leaned forward, dragging his long legs beneath him. "Tell *me*," he said in a quiet voice, "why is it that you spend so much time here at the tavern when you have a beautiful wife awaiting your comfort and pleasure at home?"

"Home?" Monte snorted, beginning to feel his cups. "Pleasure?" He snorted again, tipping back with a deep-felt sigh. "Melantha is not the love of my life, my friend."

"Ahh, time for secrets, monsieur?"

Monte called for another ale, and the voluptuous, sashaying wench approached, eyeing Sylvestre's long, stretched-out limbs, flexing with muscle and sinew. The golden Sy disregarded her sly wink with an indifferent air that surprised even Monte. Though he was inwardly pleased that Sylvestre rudely snubbed Dolly McKay's advances, he was beginning to wonder just where his young friend's interests truly *did* lie, for there was not even a flicker of curiosity as to what the shapely girl could do for him in the way of pleasuring in the room upstairs . . . later. Monte knew, but he was not all that eager this night himself.

When the affronted wench took herself elsewhere, Monte again leaned forward, his breath reeking of more than a dozen foam-topped ales.

"Apparently you are imbibing more than usual," Sylvestre said casually, then held up a golden-tanned hand, a sparkling gem upon one finger, the diamond that had caught the wench's eager eye more than once.

"Imbibing, my friend? Naw, I am drinking—really drinking for once in my life."

"Why, if it is not rude to ask?" Sylvestre questioned, feeling that something was truly amiss in Monte St. James's life. He could not stand to see his friend and business partner so out of sorts, and he only hoped it had nothing to do with Cassandra. "Your lovely daughter is not giving you trouble, I pray? I know how spirited Cassandra can be at times."

"Oh—do you?" Monte asked with a slur in his voice, downing yet another ale. "Do you really?"

Eyeing the owner of the *River Minx* curiously, Sylvestre thought the conversation was to no account. "I think it is time we left this—ah . . . humble establishment." He slapped down some coin and helped Monte to rise rather unsteadily from the table. "Come, your wife is expecting us." And Cassandra, he thought, with eagerness in his long strides.

Breathing deeply of the night air, Sylvestre stepped out to hail a carriage to take them up the hill, not wishing to gamble on the chance that Monte could

30

stumble on their climb from the waterfront. The carriage rumbled on by and Sylvestre muttered a mild curse.

"I have my horse stabled not far from here," Sylvestre mentioned, knowing he would not be questioned as to why he kept the animal in the small river town of Harper. "Tonight I will borrow a horse for you."

"Naw—" Monte waved his hand in the air as if shooing a pesky insect away. "I can walk," *hiccup,* "know I can."

"Come, friend, the walk to the stable will do you some good, and then the ride the remainder of the way should sober you up enough to properly greet your family . . ." There was a chuckle in the dark. "I pray."

Sylvestre strode briskly, making his older friend work his lungs to keep up with him and cleanse his system of inebriants.

"What new business venture comes next?" Monte shouted, becoming dizzily ventilated with the fresh air and exercise.

"I am seriously considering the purchase of another steamboat," Sylvestre said. "The *Fair Maiden.* She's larger than my other two." As he spoke Monte's eyes glittered with respect, and something else. "Her engine is more powerful, the paddle wheels larger. She has the white 'gingerbread' trim, wood curlicued and gilded, knobbed and flowered beautifully."

"Soon"—Monte found it in him to chuckle without yet another hiccup following—"our boats will look like wedding cakes afloat! So—tell me more, Capitaine Sy."

"For sure. The *Fair Maiden* has central cabins, much like your own *River Minx,* in the style of ornate hotel lobbies. Chefs will be borrowed from famous restaurants with large staffs to assist them, or, if not borrowed, I shall begin to hire—after a time of searching—for the best cuisine masters."

"My boy, you are coming up in the world, and I can say I am proud to be your business partner," Monte announced, climbing on the horse Sylvestre had fetched for him. Then Sy mounted his own—a huge black.

"Uhhm, you will also be part owner in the *Fair Maiden*, monsieur."

"What?" Monte blinked in confusion, but happily, dizzily so.

"Let us say, *our* shrewd investments have made us an impressive profit."

Swiping the sweat from his brow, Monte said, "Ones I didn't even know about." He chuckled as he reached out to slap his young partner on the back. Young? "How old are you now, Sy?"

"Hmm, approximately ten years older than your Cassandra, remember? I used to bounce her on my knee."

"So . . . that would make you about twenty-eight?"

"About that," Sylvestre said with a glint in his golden eyes as their mounts approached the pebbled carriageway that split the soft pink brick house from the old frame stables.

Monte shook his head as he followed his friend out the tall stable doors after giving the horses over to the care of a pimple-faced lad by the name of Charles. They were on the path leading to the house. He continued to be puzzled, part befuddlement from drink, part from awe of his young friend. He had no idea how Sylvestre

32

managed it! Only twenty-eight, and he owned two, no, three boats now, had the responsibilities of running the huge plantation Diamondhead—plus his abundant cotton crops. Did he own slaves? Overseers? He must.

"How do you do it, boy?" Monte finally gave in to his curiosity before entering the pink brick house.

"Drive, monsieur, an intense natural drive to keep doing, keep making things happen." Chuckling deeply, he added, "And my mother Nanette, the second most beautiful woman in the world, has an army of peons working for me."

"I see." But Monte was pondering only one question: Who was the first most beautiful woman in the world to Sylvestre Diamond?

Cassandra kept fussing with her hair until she had her maid quite exasperated. Letty stood back with her hands plopped upon generously padded hips. "Dat hairdo looks jes fine t' me, girl. If you fuss with it anymore, you ain't gonna have no hair left."

"'Ain't' is not a word, Letty," Cassandra instructed.

"Shoot!" Letty puffed her huge chest out like a mother hen. "You cain't teach this ol' gal any of your fancy language any more'n you can teach me how to bark like a dawg!" Her black eyes softened. "I'm too old besides."

Whirling from the mirror, Cassandra flew into the woman's arms, hugging her fiercely. "Don't you be talking like that, hear? You are as young as you feel." Cassandra planted a kiss on the smooth, quivering brown cheek, then drew back to gaze into mischievous black eyes.

33

"Afta watchin' you fuss with your hair all evenin', I feel like I aged a hundred and one years, chile. Now, you don't got to fuss no moah, it looks jes fine, sure do!"

"Does," Cassandra said, sticking an ivory comb into pulled-back strands that thoroughly concealed the comb, it was so fair.

"Go on with you, girl," Letty growled, waving her pudgy hand in the air. "You can teach Dulcie all yer fancy white folks's words, but I ain't up to it, no sirree. Uh-uh!"

"Teach me, teach me!" Dulcie cried, bouncing up from the book she had been trying to read. Tucking her coltish legs beneath her in kindergarten fashion, her wide liquid eyes peered out from beneath long pure-black lashes in a face the color of café au lait.

Slowly Cassandra turned from the mirror with a look of loving compassion. "You know I do not have the time just now, Dulcie. Tomorrow, first thing in the morning. How would you like that?"

"Oh, I would, I would, sure enough! I want to be edjacated just like you are, Missa Cassa!"

"You will, darling Dulcie," Cassandra fervently promised. "You *will*."

Before Cassandra could draw the breath to shoo them out of her bedroom, afraid Melantha would chide her for allowing them to stay there too long, the door whipped open and slammed against the bedroom wall. Her eyes wild, Dulcie shot up from the feather mattress like a white sheet whipped from the bed by bustling Letty on washday.

Melantha's eyes swept the room, then came to rest on willowy Dulcie standing at attention like a frightened soldier meeting a mean-tempered commanding officer.

When Melantha began to deliver her stinging tirade, Dulcie's eyes went automatically to Cassandra. In her innocent mind she was picturing the enigmatic, golden-haired Captain Sylvestre who was coming to dinner. A savage. A *wealthy* savage, for Dulcie had peeked out and seen the young man dressed so fine, his tight breeches clinging to muscled legs, not a southern dandy a'tall, but just the best-lookin' white man she'd ever seen. She could not recall the other times he had come to visit because she had been too busy to notice anything but the litter of kittens that Bunny was always having, 'specially every time that young gent'mun seemed to call. Missa Cassa always seemed to be "hidden," too, when he come.

"How many times must I tell you that these 'people' do not belong in your bedroom!" Melantha screeched in her highest pitched voice. Then it lowered to a dangerously low volume. "I warn you, Cassandra, I shall have these two sold to the farthest plantation possible if you continue to comport yourself like common trash."

Black eyes flared and fleshy jowls jiggled. "Don't you be callin' my girl dem names, Missus S'James. Cassandra be as good as gold and God in his heaven know it, too."

Melantha's neck stretched out as far as it could go. "Don't you be speaking to me about God in my own house! I'll have you tarred and feathered!"

"Ooooh, Mammy!" Dulcie wailed, afraid the dark-souled woman would do exactly as she threatened. "Best do like the lady says and keep you place."

"No one gave you permission to speak!" Melantha shot across the room to deliver a hard, stinging slap to the lovely girl's smooth cheek. She shook Dulcie until her perfect white teeth rattled in her jaw, Letty daring not to touch the white woman in fear of severe punishment not only to her and Dulcie but to Cassandra herself. "Now you get out of here and do not enter except to clean this room!" She gave the silken black hair a vicious tug. "And don't you *ever* sit your backsides on my daughter's bed again!"

"Melantha!" Cassandra cried, aghast at her mother's callous insensitivity. Then her voice lowered to a humble pitch. "Please do not say such things. Letty and Dulcie are my friends. They have always been with us and I . . . I love them."

"*Love?!* For them?" Melantha sashayed closer to Cassandra. Through the mirror, Letty could see Melantha's face rigid with anger. "Ohhh, that is disgusting, Cassandra." She whirled to Letty, who had not taken her eyes from the black-haired woman's image in the mirror for one moment. "You cannot protect Cassandra from me, her own mother, you old black voodoo witch."

*But you ain't Cassandra's true mama,* Letty wanted to shout for all the world to hear. *You just a black-haired devil who snuck into dis family and, deah Lawd, I wish you was outta it!*

With her eyes narrowed, Melantha studied the emotions crossing Letty's face. She flinched at the intense hatred she saw mirrored in the pitch-black eyes. "Now you get out of here and allow my daughter to finish her toilette by herself. I don't want her traipsing downstairs clad in some scanty dress you helped her alter to make her look like a St. Louis strumpet. She can properly ready herself for dinner"—Melantha smirked as she whirled from the black maid—"and for the *savage* who is to be our guest this night."

Letty preceded Melantha out the door, thinking to herself, *There be only one savage in the house and that be that dark flower she's named after—Melantha. And that woman keeps scowling like dat and she's gonna be downright ugly in no time a'tall, yessir!*

# Chapter Three

Cassandra froze where she was at the top of the stairs. *Sylvestre Diamond!*

The deep, masculine voice had drifted up to her and she became instantly rooted to the spot, her heart beating up in her throat. She smoothed the skirt of her simple lilac-and-gray striped dress with nervous hands.

"I enjoy the profession of piloting far better than any other business I have pursued and I take measureless pride in it, Madame St. James."

"Why do you not pilot your own steamboats, Monsieur Diamond?" Melantha was asking.

"I do, madame, I do—"

"Well then—" Melantha cut across his sentence before he could complete it. She was about to press the issue when Monte saved the evening.

"When a captain gets hold of a pilot of particularly high reputation, he takes pains to keep him, my love. To load a steamboat at St. Louis, take her to New Orleans and back, discharge cargo—that all takes about twenty days, as you know from my absences. We have needed *two* pilots for the last two runs. The wage will be increased to nine hundred dollars a trip."

"Why . . ." Melantha sniffed, "that is equivalent to about eighteen hundred dollars a month. Can we afford that, Monte?"

"Of course, love." He was still a bit tipsy. "We can affor' anything." He waved his arm in the air. "Why, just look at this room, it's—"

"Excuse me, dear," Melantha broke in. "I believe Cassandra is about to join us."

Indeed, Cassandra stood in the hall. Taking a deep breath, she mentally shed the shackles that had kept her from moving into the drawing room. One foot in front of the other . . .

But Cassandra couldn't move; she couldn't breathe.

"Cassandra, don't dawdle out there in the hall," Melantha said, rising from a deep-cushioned purple chair adorned with Italian carving of dark wood. The only bit of brightness in the drawing room was a crystal chandelier which Monte had had installed against Melantha's wishes. Its prisms answered the flames from the fireplace, casting a thousand lights upon walls and ceiling. Monte grinned secretly to himself, wondering what Melantha would think if she knew the chandelier had once graced a bawdy house in St. Louis.

*My Lord, you are sweet* were the first words that entered Sylvestre's mind when Cassandra came fully into the room and stood beneath the tiny lights of the glistening chandelier.

Gathering her courage, Cassandra walked slowly, sedately as Melantha had tutored her, and went to brush a kiss on her mother's cool cheek, which

40

Melantha had offered with a false, stiff smile. Cassandra then performed a quick, bobbing curtsy before Sylvestre Diamond.

"My darling daughter," Monte said, rising to his feet as steadily as he could. "See who has come to dine with us?"

Cassandra's eyes twinkled at her father. She realized he was trying to act the gentleman for Melantha. Then her eyes drifted slowly to Sylvestre Diamond and she tried not to sound too breathless when she spoke.

"Good evening, Monsieur Diamond. I trust your family is in good health."

Sylvestre's eyes moved across Cassandra's face, then slowly fell to her high-cut neckline. He noted, as always, the delicate bone structure of a fine beauty. His gaze captured hers and he smiled.

"The truth is, mademoiselle, I have only one family member to worry about."

"I am sorry," Cassandra almost whispered, feeling shy all of a sudden. "Your mother, umm . . . Nanette."

Melantha had rolled her eyes when her daughter had stammered like a witless schoolgirl. What did it matter for now, she reminded herself, for their company consisted only of one guest this evening, one who was not all that important. It would have been a far different matter if Harlan Kirby had been present to witness Cassandra's slip up in the etiquette of social behavior. Heaven forbid!

Just then they were called in to dinner. Melantha's lips compressed into a thin line when Cassandra graciously laid her slender hand along the dark sleeve offered to her. Walking beside her husband along the hall, preceding the younger couple into the dining room, Melantha missed the lowering of golden eyes upon Cassandra's bright blond head.

The deep, hypnotic voice was low and tender. "How have you been, *ma petite?*" They walked so close that he could feel each breath she drew, each quivering of muscle and flesh as she tried not to walk any closer to him.

"I have been very good," she answered, wondering why she was experiencing such a powerful tide of dizziness.

He smiled at her awkward words. "Have you missed me?"

Cassandra's body was suddenly covered in goose-flesh and she was having difficulty getting the next words to emerge from her constricting throat. She couldn't understand what was happening to her. Sylvestre had always seemed like her very best friend in the past; now he was almost like an enemy. There was some physical current going on between them, and she was afraid that Sylvestre was feeling it, too.

*"Oui,"* she said, recalling that he was the one who had taught her all the basic French words. Aside from that, she knew no more French, for her mother had forced Italian and Spanish on her, Melantha herself owning some of the two mixed Latin bloods.

Before helping to seat Cassandra across from him as Melantha dictated, Sylvestre brushed the slender hand with his own powerful one and his mouth hovered at her temple for a mere second in time. "I have missed you, too, Cassa."

Cassandra trembled inwardly at his words. To steady her nerves, she allowed her gaze to drift from the elegantly laid table to the clear glass window, where she stared at the horned moon that was intermittently hidden by night gray clouds and framed by delicate lace curtains drawn to the sides of the French doors.

Aside from the little bit of French influence seen in the room, the other pieces were few and all massive, like the table they sat at, enhanced with deep carvings. The simplicity of the furniture's structure and design complemented the austerity of the Spanish-style room. Cassandra longed for the dainty French pieces she remembered from the Diamondhead Plantation—the satinwood, fruitwoods, the cabriole legs, the scroll foot, bergère chairs and toilette and tea tables. She missed the accompanying colors of the gray tones, of the soft pastel greens and blues, rose, ivory, and beige. She missed the small settees called canapés, and canopied beds—all that graced the halls of Diamondhead.

Cassandra blushed furiously when she glanced up to see Sylvestre Diamond watching her closely. She had been recalling all the lovely rooms Sylvestre had escorted her through and how she had fallen in love with the house, a mere child of seven clutching the hand of the gangly seventeen-year-old who saw to her every wish and whim.

Sighing, Cassandra wondered where all the laughing, sunlit days had vanished to. Were the carefree moments kept locked up in some gilded mansion in the clouds, all those wonderful, pearly memories, to be relived and cherished over again in another life?

"Cassandra," Melantha said, leaning to hiss into the shell-like ear, "you are staring at your bowl."

"You must be very hungry," Sylvestre interjected in a kind voice.

Ignoring their "unimportant" guest, Melantha went on as if he hadn't even spoken a word to Cassandra. "Dear, Dulcie is serving the soup. Which would you like? Cookie has prepared turkey-vegetable and Creole gumbo. Which do you prefer?"

*"Creole gumbo!"* Cassandra could hardly believe that Melantha had ordered Cookie to make one of her very favorite French soups. Cookie prepared it to perfection, thick and full of seafood, but the occasions it was served at their table were few and far between.

Sylvestre chuckled softly at the lovely creature across from him. Then his deep bronze features hardened as he caught the older woman tapping Cassandra's fingers with her soup spoon. His gaze met Cassandra's and her look seemed to say, *Please don't, don't say anything to embarrass me further— Please.*

Cassandra's smile peeped out when Sylvestre nodded and picked up his spoon. Then he paused when he saw her lids fluttering closed, her lips softly moving to offer up a prayer of thanks to her Maker. He did the same, with his eyes open, his spoon pausing in midair. Melantha and Monte had already begun to eat.

"Are you regretting your choice of the Creole gumbo, Monsieur Diamond?" Melantha asked. She was a Spanish Catholic, one who said her prayers without much ado at the table. And this matter of religion was yet another reason she found disfavor with the Diamont family: They had once been a strict Catholic family but had changed their faith to a simple Protestant one. From that moment on, Melantha had not wished to visit their heathen family residence outside St. Louis!

"It is quite good, really, madame."

44

With her chin held at a lofty angle, Melantha gave him the courtesy of a "Thank you, monsieur," then elbowed her husband as hard as possible, forgetting all her social graces. "Monte, you are falling asleep in your soup! Sit up and remember your place!"

Cassandra's blue eyes twinkled across the table at their ruggedly handsome guest. He was on her side, he always had been, ever since she had felt that first sense of protectiveness he had enveloped her in. She had fallen into the mud, or perhaps she had been making mud-pies, but, whichever, Melantha had scolded her severely for ruining her pretty new dress that had not been new at all, but a hand-me-down from one of their neighbors. Whenever she thought of that particular female neighbor—Mrs. Krenke—she was reminded of clucking hens and rattling teacups and a thin, haughty nose in the air.

"What is so funny, blue eyes?" Sylvestre leaned forward, aching to take Cassandra's pale, slim hand into his own. But Melantha had trained her keen gaze on Sylvestre Diamond like a chickenhawk on its prey.

"Recalling something silly, that is all, monsieur."

"Excuse me," Melantha said crisply, rising abruptly from the table when she spied Dulcie giggling happily with the cook right before the swinging door finally closed. "I have to see why the main course is taking so long to serve."

Monte discreetly slid his gaze from the younger pair sharing a conversation about Madame Nanette Diamond—Sylvestre's mother—noting how now and again they gazed into each other's eyes. He lowered his own eyes when the two drifted out the French doors by silent mutual agreement. Monte peeked only once and then finally closed his eyes as if for the remainder of the evening. He smiled at the enchanting vision of Cassandra's small hand nestled in Sylvestre's larger, capable one.

"Oh, Mother will be fit to be tied, monsieur!" Cassandra protested when Sylvestre closed the door behind them, holding her tight with his other hand.

Slowly Sylvestre turned to face the ethereal vision bathed in softest moonglow. "Will she punish you or beat you, Cassa?" He surveyed her kindly, a vestige of sympathy in his deep voice.

"N-no."

"Are you entirely certain she will not harm you?" Even as he asked this, he pulled her gently onto the flagstone path into the deeper shadows of the lavender-scented garden.

"Yes . . ." Cassandra laughed softly. "But she will be quite angry, monsieur."

"Please, *chère mademoiselle,* call me by my given name. You know what it is, Cassa. Say it."

Softly and tenderly, the name emerged, with a giggle following: "Sylvestre . . . Diamond."

"Just Sylvestre, please."

Cassandra whirled from the loose grip of warm, exciting fingers. "Are you courting me, monsieur?"

"Would you like it if I did, Cassandra?" He used her name formally now, hoping not to embarrass her further.

"I would mons—Sylvestre. If Melantha would not object, that is."

He cleared his throat. "Would she?"

"Yes . . . I think indeed she would."

46

His sensitive mouth curled upward. "Then let us merely renew our friendship, Cassandra. She would not object to that, would she?"

"It depends on where that friendship takes us."

*To heaven and back,* he was thinking, but said aloud, "We could read books together."

Amusement flickered in the eyes that met Cassandra's. "I would like that, oh yes, most assuredly," she said, observing him with her sweet, musing look.

"What else occupies your time, Cassandra, if I may ask?"

Her eyes danced with excitement. "Sewing. I would love to be a seamstress, or run my own boutique someday."

"Well, then—" He shrugged as if that was all there was to it. "We shall go boutique shopping. I will purchase materials for your future profession. Every woman loves to shop, *n'est-ce pas?*"

Cassandra's little face plunged unhappily.

"What is wrong?"

"Melantha vehemently disapproves of clothes-making, monsieur. I realize it is bad of me, but I have had my maid Letty teach me all there is to know the making and altering of beautiful gowns and everyday dresses."

His golden eyes twinkled. "I see no mischief in that. In fact, I have been led to believe that an accomplished young lady of our day is expected to do all forms of needlework—needlepoint, petit point, crewel, cross stitch, tatting, lacework, beadwork, appliqué." He shrugged. "My mother Nanette does all these." As he spoke, he detected disappointment and hurt crossing her lovely, moonlit face. "Ah, but something surely must be troubling you about the clothesmaking, *petite?*"

"To Melantha, the social graces indeed demand that the female be able to sing or play a musical instrument such as a harp, dabble a little in painting, and keep up the voluminous social correspondence that life requires. I have no friends except my maid Letty and her daughter Dulcie, and with them I require no others. Letty has the kindest heart of anyone I know. As for playing a musical instrument, I play the harp . . ." Her look was sheepish. "A little."

He smiled. "And?"

Heaving a deep sigh, she explained. "Beneath my bed in a hidden box are pins, needles, thimbles, marking devices, cotton thread for cotton and linen, silk thread for silk and woolen. Letty has also taught me that threads may be made stronger, more slick and less likely to knot by rubbing against beeswax. I have some of that in the box, too. Also in the back of my wardrobe is a huge trunk Letty brought with her from a Georgia plantation. In it are not only gowns of the finest materials but also books her young mistress there gave to Letty while teaching her the art of haute couture. Such an establishment as I wish to have, whether it be installed in an old southern mansion or on the streets of London or Paris, or New Orleans or St. Louis, will be a first-class designing and dressmaking concern—"

"Cassandra."

She stopped talking and looked up into Sylvestre's smiling face. Her features were so animated and charming, and to him she appeared much older than

48

she actually was. "You shall one day own and run your own boutique. It is already deeply ingrained in you to become a first-class designer and dressmaker, little one," he predicted aloud. He went on. "I understand how very difficult it is for you at the moment with your mother disapproving so heartily of your secretive clothesmaking."

"Oh, yes, and in truth, Melantha does not even have knowledge of just how far it has gone, monsieur. That trunk is filled with velvets, silks, lawns, lace, cottonade, muslin, and ever so much more! The gowns from the lady of the plantation are quite old, and we have ripped out seams, altered bodices, and fashioned them in hundreds of different styles in the middle of the night until the tips of my fingers ached."

He held up his hand to silence her. *"Mon Dieu,* your face is quite flushed." He realized just how excited she was about her midnight schooling in the arts of the needle. Her mouth was a smiling pink flower, and he thought she looked more delicate and ethereal than ever. "I have never enjoyed a conversation more in my lifetime, Cassandra." Placing a warm hand on her cheek, he forced her to look at him again. "I want to know more about you, all about you—" He flushed for a moment himself. "I wish to know you inside and out, *chérie,* and I would love to see you awaken in the morning . . . when you first open your eyes to the day."

Cassandra's cheeks flamed scarlet. She could hardly find her tongue to answer him. "I . . . I do not know what you mean, Sylvestre."

"Ah, I think you do, sweet Cassa, for your cheeks flushed quite responsively."

49

He continued to gaze at her, and the moment froze in time. He had docks and warehouses heaped high with produce, boats plying as far south as New Orleans and as far north as Omaha, and a waterfront office in St. Louis where busy clerks were bent twelve hours a day over bills of lading. He had just been able to purchase his very own home, in addition to the plantation he ran for his mother. This second home was a huge, lush plantation situated on a bluff above the Mississippi River. He owned property, boats, had plenty of women if he wanted them. But here was the pulse of his passion, his very heartbeat. He believed he had always loved Cassandra St. James. He had been a gangly teenager when he had first laid eyes on the angel-haired child. He had known a surge of intense protectiveness, and the feeling remained with him still.

Cassandra was aware of Sylvestre's closeness, and never, but never had he looked more attractive and virile than he appeared to her this night. Sometimes, however, Sy's face would harden and appear as if it had never known a gentle smile and at those times she was frightened of him. Letty had shared gossip about his family one night as they had sewn by the light of a single candle. Oftentimes in the past, when she was but a child, Letty had accompanied them to the Diamond-head Plantation. In her explorations of the huge mansion, Cassa would come upon Letty gossiping with the servants in the huge, aromatic kitchen. She had eavesdropped on their conversation, but could only understand a few snatches of what they were saying to one another.

Then one night not so long ago, Letty had told her a

story about the Diamonts. Jean-Pierre Diamont, like Jean Lafitte, had mingled with the mongrel Baratarians. Some of them had been descendants of runaway slaves, others the spawn of pirates and their captured women. She had heard this latter story connected with Sy's grandfather and his earlier exploits; also that Jean-Pierre had carried the Indian blood of his grandfather down to his only son Sylvestre. His father, Jean-Pierre, had possessed ebony-dark, dead straight hair inherited from a true Indian ancestor who'd stolen a white maiden and mated with her.

Inhaling deeply, Cassandra opened her mouth to question him about his Indian ancestry when the French doors were flung wide and Melantha's voice carried out into the garden, calling for her daughter to come into the house.

"Please—wait a moment." Sylvestre caught her arm when she whirled to return to the house.

Her heart was beating in her throat. After an awkward moment had passed, in which they did nothing more alarming than hold each other's wrists— his feeling very large in hers, hers feeling fragile and dainty in his—Sylvestre leaned forward to brush a gentle kiss across her forehead. "Do not let her steal your innermost thoughts, Cassa," he said thickly.

Suddenly he stepped back and Cassandra looked at him with bewilderment in her moon-blue eyes. She knew a burning desire, a sweetly aching need for another kiss.

With inexplicable tenderness, he said, "Mark my words, *ma petite*. One day I shall bruise your lips with

51

my kisses and make you glow with fire and passion. And *love,* yes, that, too."

Cassandra ran to the house, her thrusting breasts coming to throbbing life beneath her bodice. She felt like dying, she was so embarrassed, for nothing like this had ever happened to her body before. She took a deep breath, then met her imperious mother on the flagstone path leading to the French doors.

Melantha's face was pinched and severe, causing the dark good looks of her Spanish-Italian blood to suffer, making her appear as austere as the furniture that lined the walls of her home. *Crrraaack.* Melantha spun her daughter about and, delivering a stinging slap to her already flushed countenance, she snarled, "You . . . you . . . *slut,* do not ever, but *never,* go out into the garden with a man unchaperoned!!"

And Cassandra took it. At the moment, she simply didn't care and, strangely, the slap lessened some of her embarrassment and restored some sense to her brain, where silvery bells still rang.

"Go to your room—immediately!" Melantha ordered.

Her feet moving swiftly, her skirts flying behind her, Cassandra could not run fast enough to reach her room where she could throw herself down on her bed and hide her face that flamed with the fiery heat of embarrassment and newly awakened desire.

Meantime, Melantha whirled to see Sylvestre Diamond striding along the flagstone path, his face dark and dangerous-looking. This gave Melantha St. James pause, but when she recovered from the blow of his hard look, she ordered him to leave her house at once.

With a measure of grace, Sylvestre inclined his head. His voice was soft, respectful, despite the chilly circumstances. "As you wish, madame. But I will return for a visit with your lovely daughter one day, make no mistake about that."

When Melantha was quite alone, after Monte had settled himself in the drawing room with a half-drunk glass of brandy on the table beside him, his head lolling against the high cushion of the chair, she hurriedly passed through the kitchen and out the back door, hoping she was not too late for her clandestine meeting with Jared Casey.

Like an enticing spider, Melantha waited in the dark cover of the backyard, beneath the spreading arms of a huge magnolia tree. Its blossoms smelled so sweet, but she could not enjoy its delicate fragrance, for tension lay heavy in the air, and she almost jumped from her skin as a shadow emerged from behind the stables. Then Melantha relaxed, realizing that Jared Casey had actually come as he had promised in the note she had earlier received.

The roguish lawyer, handsome and devilish beyond belief, grinned broadly as he came to stand before her. She gave a soft sigh of secret despair. The least sound from the kitchen behind made her nerves tingle in fear of being discovered in her clandestine meeting with Jared Casey. She drew a shaky breath and tried to still the frantic beating of her heart.

In the dark of the moon, Melantha's eyes darted nervously over the roguish face. "You should be more careful in your approach, Mr. Casey." She set her jaw at a haughty angle, still glancing nervously over her shoulder. "Someone might see you!"

"You mean *us,* don't you, fair lady?" he drawled lazily, looking her over and making her shiver.

*"Mister Casey,* let me remind you, this is business that brings us together—not pleasure!"

"Ahh, dear lady, if it only was pleasure and *not* business," he whispered, trying to take her hand, which she snatched away abruptly as if she might be burned by his touch.

"If I gave you the impression that I wished your advances, I am sorry, Jared. You know I am already married."

"Ah, but something is making you unhappy. Could I perhaps hope that you and your husband are not getting along all that well?"

"That is none of your concern, sir. And stop calling me 'dear lady' or I shall not do business with you anymore!"

"Whatever you say, dear lady," he replied, his lazily seductive eyes taking in her midnight hair. If only she would not dress so plainly, so severely, he was thinking, gazing at her gown of blue-green moiré, the scarf at her throat *très distingué,* truly, of the same color as her dress. She could be a great beauty, and if only she weren't so rigid she could have lovers aplenty. Himself, for one.

Melantha closed her eyes for a moment, wishing the circumstances were different. Devilish Mr. Casey had been shrewdly pursuing her ever since she had secretly made his acquaintance for the sole purpose of setting up a trust fund for Cassandra, *for our daughter,* she had instructed—in the event that she found herself the proper husband, which the girl would certainly do if Melantha had anything to say about it!

"Monte has not even thought about the importance of a trust fund for our daughter," she had informed Jared in his shabby office on the waterfront when she had gone there surreptitiously for the first time.

Jared's cobalt-blue eyes had raked over Melantha St. James as she gazed down into her lap with a look close to sadness and despair. He had almost felt sorry for her—*almost.* "We will have to do something about that, Madame St. James," he had said with mock respect.

She had sat stiffly in a shabbily cushioned chair and leaned forward, clutching her purse with white-knuckled, quivering fingers. "I have heard about your, ah . . . reputation, sir."

"So you have," he said, wolfishly eyeing her other hand, which gripped the modest front of her demure lace bodice as if the heat in the room was too much for her to bear.

"Let us . . . uhmm, get down to business, sir," she went on, dropping her fluttering hand to her lap.

"Would you care for a drink?" he had asked, already pouring himself a liberal shot of brandy.

She cleared her throat. "Y-yes, I think I shall—I mean, if you do not mind."

Jared Casey chuckled and poured Melantha St. James a like amount into a cracked cup he had first swiftly wiped with his handkerchief. While he watched,

55

she downed the stiff libation in one swallow, then clutched her bodice again. "That is most strong, monsieur," she said.

"It is meant to be, fair lady, to ease your, ah ... nervousness." His eyes turned shrewd, for he was interested in more than just Cassandra St. James's dowry. A passionate lover of women, he could not wait to meet the little minx Melantha spoke of. "Shall we get down to business now, *madame?*"

Melantha had conducted her business with him—and now he had called for this clandestine meeting to question her further as to how to proceed. "You could have waited for me to come to your office, Mr. Casey!" She was feeling the effects of the strong wine she had liberally consumed at dinner.

"This is an ugly business, madame, and you don't seem the type to be deceiving your husband, if I am not too rude in saying?"

"You are not, monsieur. You are correct, however, in stating that it is indeed *ugly*. But I cannot do otherwise."

"I know, you have already informed me that your sole wish is for Harlan Kirby to wed your, ah ... enchanting daughter Cassandra, that the man who takes over the responsibility of Cassandra's trust fund must be above reproach. Kirby is that, I take it?"

"Most certainly. And I have already told you this. Why do you question me further?"

"I have to make certain that all the facts are straight, you must realize."

She went on hurriedly. "I insist that Cassandra's mind be kept off Sylvestre Diamond, for I am afraid

56

my husband favors him as a future husband. I despise the Diamonts of St. Louis!"

"Diamonts?" Jared said, confused.

"Yes. That is their true French name; it was changed to sound more American by Sylvestre's own father, Jean-Pierre."

Jared Casey did not voice what he had gathered from her last visit, that Melantha despised the Diamonds not so much for the rumors of their Indian ancestry as for the fact that Madame Nanette Diamond had changed her faith to the Protestant religion. "There are only the two of them, madame. Sylvestre and his mother."

"Only two, indeed, sir, but a powerful force to be reckoned with—and cautiously. I do not wish to allow Cassandra too much time to become reacquainted with Sylvestre Diamond. I believe they shared some intimate moments tonight in the garden while I saw about the dinner."

Jared's dark eyebrows rose interestedly. "They were in the garden alone? For how long?"

Melantha's nostrils flared. "Too long, I am afraid."

*Why was she telling him all this?* Jared cleared his throat. "Yes, I am beginning to understand. Your plan is to send your daughter to the Kirby household for an . . . ah . . . visit before she can become further enamored of Sylvestre Diamond?"

"Correct. Soon he will exert his full influence on her, and I am afraid that what I see in his eyes now is not merely a desire for her friendship as was the case when she was a child."

"Hmm. Are you saying you wish for me to step in somehow, to prevent Sylvestre Diamond's courtship of

57

your daughter?"

"If it comes to that, yes, sir. For now, all you must do is draw up the papers saying that the trust fund will be held by Oscar Kirby, in the future event that both Monte and myself should perish, God forbid. You see, my husband and I will soon be making a trip to Memphis by steamboat and I wish to make certain that my daughter's trust fund falls into the right hands should any disaster befall us. And I also wish for you to prepare a will and become our executor if such a case arises."

"How will you manage to get your husband's signature on the papers?"

"That will be your job, Mr. Casey."

He wore a smile that Melantha could not read for what it truly was. "Forgery, hmm?" He raked his fingers over his chin thoughtfully.

"I'm sure you know all about that, sir."

Once again Jared Casey cleared his throat in mock embarrassment. "You sound very fatalistic, madame. Do you think something might happen to you and your husband on this trip to Memphis?"

"One can never tell what the fates have in store for us. I have been having bad dreams having to do with riverboat disasters, some involving my husband and myself. Yet, these nightmares cannot keep me forever from traveling. I like to get away and see the sights, for I am still a young woman."

"Yes, you are that." His blue eyes twinkled merrily. "When will you be leaving for Memphis?"

"Not for several weeks. We will be leaving Cassandra at the Kirbys and we will go on from there."

"You have thought of everything, haven't you?" Jared said, his eyes boldly assessing her.

"Yes, I have. Monte St. James and I, his wife, have battled on the subject of who our daughter will marry. I am Italian, as you may have guessed. I wish to do as my ancestors did, to pick and choose who my daughter will wed—even though I chose my own husband."

"You do not think you are being cruel to Cassandra, by picking and choosing her mate?"

"Not at all. Cassandra is a willful child, and I will not see her life or our properties fall into the wrong hands."

"And Sylvestre Diamond's hands are not capable enough to handle all of that?"

"I have already told you. I do not like him, nor do I like his mother. They are arrogant and haughty, like all others who have drifted from the South boasting the French nobility. French, bah—it has become the most widely spoken language of America, second to English."

Her eyes cold and calculating, she went on. "Sylvestre Diamond flits about like a male butterfly. He is not very good husband material, for he never stays in one place for very long, and all he has on his mind is steamboats, the plantation business—and my daughter Cassandra's skirts!"

Jared Casey grimaced. "Ooh, not so loud, your husband will hear." He almost laughed aloud then at Melantha St. James's contradictory statement. He could find no fault with Sylvestre Diamond so far, and, in fact, it seemed the man's lineage was impeccable. It sounded to him as if Diamond was in love with Cassandra St. James, and this made him want to meet the little minx all the more. "When can I meet this

59

daughter of yours, madame?"

"In the event of a marriage situation you will meet her, sir. Meanwhile, I will do all in my power to see that Cassandra does not become Sylvestre Diamond's bride. Cassandra will one day adorn the Kirby house and make Harlan Kirby the perfect wife. If she does do the willful and spiteful thing by marrying Sylvestre Diamond against my wishes, she will not get one penny of the trust fund or our properties, including the *River Minx* and the *Southern Star*." Her eyes became shrewd, narrowing at Jared Casey's easy grin. "If Monte objects and still wishes to give Cassandra something in the way of a dowry, he will have a terrible battle on his hands. Then I shall have to do something, ah . . . a little more drastic."

Jared was taken aback at the woman's viciousness. "Such as?"

"We will have to see when the time comes, won't we?"

With that, Melantha St. James whirled from Jared Casey to swiftly enter the house by the back door, leaving Jared staring after her with surprise and puzzlement, niggling questions racing in his mind.

*What in hell have I gotten myself into? Is Melantha St. James of sound mind, or is it only that she is insanely jealous and hates her daughter with a passion?* Jared slipped away through the shadows of the garden, a grin on his face as he thought how it would make Melantha St. James look like an utter fool if Cassandra decided to elope with Sylvestre Diamond taking nothing with her but the clothes on her back and giving not a hoot for any trust fund or will?

*Damn, I've got to meet Cassandra St. James—and Sylvestre Diamond!*

Walking tipsily, Jared returned late to his shabby office. It had been quite a night upstairs in the Water Street Tavern, he thought as he let himself in the dark room. A ripple of remembrance crossed his roguish countenance and he grinned, looking silly to himself in the wavy mirror as he lighted a match and leaned against the dresser. Women had always come willingly into his arms, like Dolly McKay, the sensuously plump tavern wench who had brushed against his legs two months ago, starting a fire which only she could put out.

Put it out, she did! Jared grinned at himself, then shouted, *"Ouch!"* burning himself with the match that had been intended for the lamp on the dresser. After he managed to get the lamp going, he slumped into his favorite chair, yet another glass of brandy held loosely in his large hand.

"G T T," he mumbled. "Gone to Texas." But he had never truly made it there . . .

The notice had been posted on the bulletin board at the courthouse, worded to the effect that the United States was at war and that every man was expected to do his duty. *"Honor and glory await you in Texas and Mexico, fellow citizens. Fellow patriots will honor you . . . our hearts go with you. Go!—fight your country's battles as I have done!"* hammered away the commandant of the local militia in a small town of his native Illinois.

Jared cynically smirked into his glass. He had gone with the Fourth Illinois Volunteers, Colonel Baker commanding. It was composed of the diehards who were going to the wars like himself, shouting *Come hell or high water!*

Their regiment had been moved to Jefferson Barracks. There had been no action and it all moved too slow for him. He had not become a hero overnight as he'd thought he would. He couldn't take any more and so he decided to desert, but his desertion was never officially recognized. He had hunted up the colonel to tell him he was tired of war, that he was going back home to his law books, maybe settle down in Harper, Missouri, not too far from his Illinois hometown.

"Hell, boy—we're just gettin' started," the colonel had chided mildly.

"Maybe you and the boys are," Jared said. "But not this boy. If you wanted to, sir, you'd just naturally resign—right?"

The colonel blustered, then said, "Just don't take any government property with you when you cut loose."

"I might return when the action gets going." He twisted his lips arrogantly. "If it ever does."

So Jared Casey had gone to Missouri, by steamboat. Only twenty-five, he had plunged into politics and helped to stir the political brew boiling in the state capital. Then he had finally settled down in Harper with his law books and an inexhaustible supply of brandy. Women he had aplenty, a different one every night when he made his frequent trips to St. Louis. Now he had made the acquaintance of the domineering Melantha St. James. He grinned devilishly at the bottom drawer of his scarred, secondhand desk. There, in that drawer, were a few wills he had altered—for a price. Hell, he wasn't doing anything more devious than aiding folks in getting what was coming to them, and he was no more greedy than the next person, truth be told. In a few more years, he was going to be rolling in cash and he would have his own brass nameplate above his door—in St. Louis, not here in this one-horse town. He might even take a bride for himself—like Cassandra St. James!

Sweet Holy Mary, he was on his way . . .

In fact, Jared Casey was just getting started!

*Chapter Four*

Cassandra paused in polishing the curved arms of the Venetian settee to glance bleakly out the window at the achingly familiar view. Two days had passed since Sylvestre Diamond had come to dinner, and now, despondently, she wondered if he had truly meant all that he had said. Would he really return to court her? She doubted seriously that he would, after the embarrassing scene Melantha had created the other night in the garden. Sighing, she accepted the inevitable. He might never return again, ever.

She continued in her self-imposed labors, hurrying now before Melantha caught her helping with the huge load of work that was piled on Letty and Dulcie every day. Melantha worked Cassandra's dear friends to the bone, washing floors, polishing all the woodwork and furnishings, beating rugs, washing and hanging and ironing clothes, putting all the many things in order that Melantha scattered about every night as if out of spite. Even the silverware and glassware had to be taken out from drawers and cupboards to be polished, each and every day, as if Melantha expected the president or royalty to drop in for a visit any time of day.

Alone in the study, her dust cloth slowed over a particular piece of antique furniture with apple-green motifs scattered all over it, Cassandra again paused before the window she'd opened to allow fresh air to enter and stood listening to the tranquil song of the enchanting river below. She always felt an inner excitement in the sound of its perpetual cadences. The night before, as she had stood at her bedroom window with her clothes off, the river had run in perfect timing with her pulse.

Cassandra thought of her father then—down there somewhere, working with his chief roustabout, Goliath —his deep voice undoubtedly dinning above the rest, booming with the authority of his lofty position. Goliath was an outspoken but kindly black man, huge of muscle and hard of sinew, his strange yellow eyes never missing a thing.

Monte St. James ruled his crew with flailing fists, belted his boat through the bends, cursed the snags and vicious, whipping pieces of driftwood called sawyers. He also muttered quick prayers, she knew, prayers for sunken boats that dotted the river from one end to the other. For all this, Cassandra knew that Monte loved the Missouri and Mississippi rivers as passionately as Melantha hated them. Her mother had always been afraid that one day the river would take her life, even had nightmares of sinking below the muddy waters . . . screaming, waking up in the middle of night and heaving with great gulps of air as if she had indeed

66

drowned. Even so, Melantha took a trip occasionally to St. Louis or Memphis. As she soon would once again.

"Girl, what you doin' in here, working your dainty fingers to the bone again? You supposed to be practicin' the harp and your ladylike airs like your mama says."

Turning from the window, Cassandra saw Letty standing there with mop and sloshing pail in hand, shaking her bandanna-wrapped head.

Cassandra's bright blue eyes twinkled with mischief. "I am helping you and Dulcie out with your work, Letty. There is just too much for the two of you to get done by the end of the day."

Shaking her head and chuckling deeply, Letty said, "You jes be careful with those fine pieces of Louis Keen furnishings. I don't wanna have de house fall down on dis old head if you scratches one of dem, Cassandra S'James."

Cassandra giggled. "The name is *Louis Quinze*." With her dusty rag held at a lofty angle, she sashayed about the room like a grande dame. "Mesissonier himself, creator of the Rococo, was Italian, you know, and Italian versions of Louis Quinze may be recognized by the *extreme* forms," she, too, exaggerated, stroking a woody piece, "which the bombé curve is wont to take. The extent of the protrusion often is *grotesquely* out of proportion to the size of the piece."

Playfully Cassandra went on, unaware she was being shrewdly observed from the hallway. "Some very gay furniture was fashioned in Venice, but you see none of that here, Madame Letty, only an *effect* which is at

67

times rather hectic . . . Oh, and the odd-looking settee—" She paused at the mentioned piece. "And chairs, desks, et cetera, that need placing with great care so as not to appear like a Venetian carnival . . . Of course, you may *wish* it to look like that . . . uhmm, in which case, the best of Venetian luck to you, madame—"

"Cassandra!"

"Oh!" Cassandra shot across the room to stuff the polish-rag in Letty's apron and, as the servant took her cue and scurried out of the cluttered room, Cassandra sheepishly turned to face the rigid form draped in rust-colored silk framed in the doorway. "Yes . . . Mother?" she said, her blue eyes wide, unblinking.

"You have the impish tongue of a hoyden," Melantha hissed, "and the manners of a lowly French maid!"

Cassandra had the grace to look apologetic. "I was only having a little fun, Mother. Letty works so hard all day and I had it in mind to ease her plight a bit—that is all."

"Naturally." Melantha strode about the room, her crisp Victorian skirts rustling like the crack of a whip. A long finger whipped out to test the bow-fronted corner of a side table decorated with an inlay of bone marquetry, its veneer of olive wood. "This was made in Majorca, as you should know, but apparently you do not. Some of these pieces can be seen in the palaces of the aristocracy in Palma."

"I realize that, Mother," Cassandra began, and coyly went on. "And also in some of the country houses in Spain, the names of which are prefixed by the word 'son,' and were used in hunting lodges. Indeed, the marquetry often illustrates hunting scenes, but we see none of that here."

Melantha arched a dark eyebrow. "That may not be to everyone's taste, as the hunting scenes often portray a savage quality. I despise anything depicting savagery." She was thinking of Sylvestre Diamond.

"I realize that, Melantha."

"Mother!"

"I know that, Mother."

"You are an insolent child, Cassandra, and you have ever been a trial for me."

"I am sorry, Mel—*Mother*. Believe me, I shall try to do better." She hid an impish smile beneath her slim hand.

"In what?" Melantha said, swiping her finger off a polished surface, her eyes glittering up at her daughter. "Your housecleaning? Your interest in the latest fashions and fabrics?"

Moistening suddenly dry lips with the tip of her tongue, Cassandra looked this way and that, unable to find a truthful answer.

Cassandra would have liked nothing better than to be able to confide her innermost feelings to Melantha, but there was never any indication that Melantha was interested in *her* wants and desires, nor that she was aware of any troubles or difficulties Cassa might be having.

"Well, as long as nothing seems to matter to you, Cassandra St. James, I will suggest you consider a thing or two. You have learned nothing of the social graces I have attempted to teach you. You are not able to sing or play a musical instrument. You care nothing for painting, you only dabble once in a great while. You should further your schooling in polite conversation, especially everyday platitudes—"

"Platitudes, Mother?" Cassandra blinked. *Everyday platitudes?*

"Do not interrupt me when I am speaking, Cassandra! You must learn how many subjects to broach in a conversation with a gentleman." Melantha puffed up her chest, adding, "And I mean gentlemen—not that savage rogue, Sylvestre Diamond!" She let go of the breath she had been holding, looking as if she were having a fit of the vapors. "Nor do you keep up the social correspondence that life requires and—"

"Mother, you are rambling. I have no one to correspond with, for my only true friends are Letty and Dulcie—"

"Which are no friends at all!" Melantha thundered, then flicked lint off the puffed lower sleeve of her severely cut dress. "They are merely servants. If you continue to defy me, Cassandra St. James, I will send those two Nigras to a slave-breeding farm. It will not pain me to do this, either, for I can get eighteen hundred dollars apiece for them. And you should know that a slave owner always possesses two or three male studs!"

Cassandra paled. She had heard of cruel slave owners and overseers who supervised the mating of their studs exactly as if they were breeding horses and not human beings. The slave owners rationalized that the black woman and man was a subhuman species, that there was significantly more profit in such enterprises than in horse- or cattle-breeding. Letty had told her many horror stories of what happened to runaway slaves, and Cassandra shivered now to think of her best friends with torn and bloodied backs . . . lovely Dulcie scarred for life . . .

"Oh, please, do not send them away!" Cassandra begged, wishing she could tell her father, but knowing from instances in the past that it was unwise to go against Melantha's wishes, for she would only cause everyone in the house suffering—including Monte!

With a downtrodden look, Cassandra meekly asked, "What do you wish me to do? I will do . . . anything."

"First . . ." Melantha began with an imperious shake of her dark head, "I want you to steer clear of Sylvestre Diamond and reject any advances he might make. He is not to court you, do you hear? Ah, yes, I can see by your look that Sylvestre Diamond had just that evil thought in mind. He is to be sent away if he should come here—I will personally see to that.

"In two weeks you will go to the Kirby Plantation and comport yourself like a proper little lady, and before that time you will learn the harp."

"When did you say we were to go there?"

"Two weeks."

Cassandra stifled a gasp of outrage. "If Harlan Kirby makes any advances toward courtship," Melantha went on, "you will accommodate them." She cleared her throat. "Properly, of course."

"B-but—" Cassandra stammered tearfully, thinking of Sylvestre Diamond.

"You need not be so put out, Cassandra. Sylvestre was seen, by your own father, in the company of a flighty redhead the other night at the Water Street Tavern. They have rooms upstairs, you know. Your Captain Sy did not resist her overtures, and, in fact, was seen going upstairs with her. Tipsy he was—with the gorgeous redhead on his arm."

*Oh, Sylvestre.* Cassandra cried in her heart. *I thought you liked me more than any other woman.* She could see now that she had been dreadfully mistaken. A foolish girl with even more foolish dreams. Then . . . could she believe Melantha? She would find out for herself later, when Melantha was abed.

"Now I want you to get rid of all the useless clutter in your room, and you know just which clutter I mean, Cassandra. Tomorrow you will begin your lessons and repeat them over and over. After that, I will tutor you at the harp personally. You pluck the strings as you would pluck chicken feathers from a hen and I do not wish to see my precious instrument so sorely abused! Now, can you remember all I've ordered you to do and will you carry out my wishes?"

"Yes, Mother. As you wish!"

Cassandra whirled from the room, tears of anguish burning her lids and blurring her eyes. As for that . . . that *lecherous* Sylvestre Diamond, he could go clear to blazes! She could never love— But perhaps she should go see for herself. Later. At the Water Street Tavern— if she could summon the courage . . .

Cassandra's black slippers flew up the stairs, her slender limbs a flash of white in her long silk stockings.

Perhaps there was someone else for her in the world besides either Harlan Kirby or Sylvestre Diamond. A kindly young man who would love her, and only her. "For I shall marry neither *one* of them!" Still, she was going to sneak out later and discover for herself if Melantha had been lying or not. She sighed, already feeling tired at the many tasks that loomed before her.

"Everyday platitudes, bah!" Cassandra made a sour little face. Asinine chatter, that's what!

She dug deep into the back of her cherrywood wardrobe, dragging out the old trunk, huffing and puffing until she had moved it to the center of her room. Flipping open the arched lid, she surveyed the contents, straightening her back as she stood with her hands on her hips.

A recalcitrant wave of pale hair kept falling over her forehead as she bent to her task. She brushed it off her face with her elbow while munching on a sandwich hastily constructed in the kitchen while the cook was out doing the shopping for the evening meal.

After a time, Cassandra discovered a pair of tortoiseshell combs which she set aside, for her mother could not object to her not wishing to dispose of such lovely, expensive combs. When the wave of hair continued to give Cassandra trouble, she swept her hair up high in back, on either side of her head and fastened the combs there. The heavy mass of pale blond hair cascaded down her back, almost to her tiny waist.

Cassandra was sick at heart as she rummaged through the beautiful cast-aside gowns that had at one time belonged to a southern belle. Gorgeous, she must have been, too. How could anyone give away such beautiful things? She knew that Letty would not just have taken them. No, Letty did not lie, for she had told her that the trunk of possessions had been given to her, to do with as she wished. Then, after she had grown a little older, Letty had given the trunk to her, Cassandra, saying she had no use for all the beautiful things. They had played fashion designer, taken some of them apart, altered the bodices, lowered the hems, added lace to sleeves, given waistlines a slight point in the front as well as the back. They had also taken a lavender ballgown apart to be used for making patterns.

Cassandra carefully handled the silky undergarments and separate bodices of lingerie made of alternate puffings of thin muslin and embroidery, materials she had never dared use herself. Here was a clipping dated February 10, 1840, from a fashion magazine showing Queen Victoria's dress, fashioned of lace made in the picturesque village in Devon, France.

Lifting out a bonnet of rice straw trimmed with pink ribbon, Cassandra shook her head woefully as she tried to revive it from its crushed state. She laid it over her knee to try to finger-press the wrinkles out of the large veil of white gauze which was drawn into fullness by a ribbon stitched along a hem, fastened round the crown, and intended to be then thrown back over the wearer's shoulders. But the hat was too far gone to be of any further use and Cassandra sighed, sticking it back into the trunk.

There was no use in trying to conceal some of the nicer things, for Melantha would just discover their hiding place and make her throw them out with all the other "trash."

Fashion books. Magazines from Paris, France. Ballgowns, some very old. And the doll, the gorgeous doll. Cassandra wondered how she would ever be able to part with it.

She held it lovingly in her arms, then fingered its delicate face, silken hair, perfect eyes. These fashion dolls had been especially made and dressed in Paris, sent out each month to the capitals of Europe, some reaching as far as the United States, as in this case, a Georgia plantation. She turned it over, noting the tiny buttons and perfect eye-holes. Fashion dolls continued to be made and sent out, even now in the nineteenth century. The current modes were supplemented by fashion journals, publications which gave news and illustrations of fashions which were currently being worn as well as those which were likely to soon become very fashionable.

She had sent for the *Ladies' Gazette of Fashions*, but *somehow* she had never received her first copy of that publication. Someday she would send for it again, perhaps when she was installed at the Kirby Plantation while her parents went off on their trip to Memphis. In fact, she would send for it tomorrow, and by the time she reached the Kirbys, her first copy should have arrived. She would have to think of how she was to pay for the subsequent publications when the time came for payment.

Sitting cross-legged, fingering a lovely silken ringlet, Cassandra wistfully stared at the beautiful doll, with the long pearl teardrops hanging from the little ears, the dainty parasol resting over a small porcelain wrist.

Even the doll's white dress was a magnificent creation trimmed in fine lace ruffing and dark-green velvet ribbon, and, beneath, several layers of crinolines peeped out in a froth of pink and cream.

Before she knew what she was doing, Cassandra began to fuss with the gown, adding a bit of lace here and there. She tipped her blond head, studying the doll as she murmured. "Perhaps a Palatine, a cloak made of black satin, lined with blue, rose, or apricot satin trimmed all round with black lace. Hmm, it would reach to about here—no, to the knees—in front, and the hood could be made to be drawn over at pleasure."

As time ticked away, Cassandra became deeply engrossed in the creative art of fashion designing. Coming to her feet, she went directly to her writing desk, bringing with her an old, yellowed sketchpad. Rummaging in a lower drawer, she came up with a charcoal pencil—and she began to draw, her teeth caught in her lower lip, her mind sunk into the deep wells of concentration while the ball of orange sun glanced over the windowsill in its late-afternoon descent.

Cassandra looked up and aside now and then, pausing to consider changes she could make here or there. Her pencil flew over the paper, swooping and shading and defining, then slowing over a long ostrich feather placed at one side of the velvet hat, lying perfectly flat across the bonnet, drooping to the opposite side. "This feather may be white—" She chewed thoughtfully on the end of her pencil and mumbled, "Or the color of the velvet itself."

"What feather you be talking 'bout, Missa Cassa?"

76

Cassandra whirled, staring up into black eyes flecked with the palest shade of green. "Oh, Dulcie"—Cassandra placed a hand over her palpitating chest—"I do believe you just scared the daylights out of me."

"What are you drawing, Missa Cassa?" She bent over the blonde's shoulder. "Can I see?" She blinked in the failing light. "Oooh, a pretty lady in a beau-ti-ful dress. Oh, and there's the feather you were talking 'bout. I sure'd like to own a dress like that."

"I am sure you will someday, Dulcie," Cassandra said, tearing the sheet from the pad and sticking it in her drawer, way in the back.

"Oh no, Missa Cassa. That dress is too fine for the likes of me."

Dulcie shook her head, her silky black braids brushing her homespun dress as she rocked on her heels to and fro. "Anyway, I think I likes all my old clothes jes fine thank you."

"You say that now, Dulcie. Someday, though, you will wish to dress up and look pretty. Not that you are not pretty enough now, because you are, but you could be made to look even prettier."

The whites of Dulcie's eyes enlarged. "And that would make me *beautiful?*"

"Very. The Lord has already blessed you with charm and grace"—she smiled affectionately—"and with great dark eyes flecked with green lights."

"My eyes really got green in dem?"

"Sure do."

Dulcie shuffled toward the drawer shyly, pointing to where the drawing was concealed. "I doan know how I could ever wear a dress like that, though. My skin

77

ain't so black, but folks'd know I got Nigra blood somewheres in me."

"Everyone on God's beautiful earth is special, Dulcie, some even more so than others. Some are not better, just more loving and kind-hearted—like your mammy for one. You could wear the beautiful dresses someday, Dulcie—if you become a dressmaker like I am going to become." There was a glow in Cassandra's eyes. "I will one day own and run my own shop, Dulcie. Perhaps even open a boutique in St. Louis, maybe even next year, or the year after, for I shall be twenty years of age at that time. I will be a grown woman, Dulcie, as you will be yourself." She suddenly recalled Sylvestre's prediction, which she had just echoed almost word for word.

"Could I work there with you, Missa Cassa? I could make sure there ain't no pins and needles layin' around to get stuck in those fine ladies' feet when they try on those fine gowns you'se gonna make someday."

Cassandra was not listening to Dulcie, for an idea was beginning to form. If she was going to sneak down to the Water Street Tavern, she had better shake the dust from her feet!

"What're you going to do, Missa Cassa? You got that funny light in your eyes that makes me scared what's gonna happen to you when you gets done doin' what you be thinkin' about just now. Trouble's brewin' when you look like dat, Mammy always says."

"Hurry, Dulcie. Help me put these things back in the trunk." Cassandra reached out as Dulcie did what she was told. "No, not the doll! Oh blast, where can I hide her?"

"She's not too little, is she?" Dulcie remarked, aping the sweet smile pasted on the doll's lovely face. "I seen her before; she's really pretty."

"Oh, Dulcie, I hate to have to burn all this!" Cassandra wailed softly, holding her head as if it ached while her gaze sifted among the precious items placed carefully back in the trunk.

"Oooh, it'd be a sin to burn all this fine stuff Mammy brung all the way from Gee-orgia."

"I have to, Dulcie. Melantha ordered me to have done with all these things."

"I gots an idea," Dulcie piped up.

"You *have* an idea," corrected Cassandra.

"Yes'm—I do. See, I'm gonna scoot on down to the *River Minx* and fetch Goliath. He will know where to hide all this stuff so's you won't have to get rid of it all."

"Oh, yes, Dulcie . . . I think . . . I know what we can do. Uhmm, perhaps Goliath can hide my trunk . . . with all my sewing items, the dresses, and even the doll on the *River Minx*!"

"Goliath can do anythin' a'tall, Missa Cassa."

Dulcie got down on her hands and knees, helping Cassandra drag out all the rest of the sewing stuff, which they packed carefully into the near-bulging trunk. "You so *smart,* Missa Cassa!" Dulcie exclaimed happily.

"No, Dulcie, you are the smart one. This was your idea, not mine, you know. To save all these cherished things your lovely mammy gave to me."

"Mammy will be so excited and happy to know you didn't have to d-dispose of all this fine sewing stuff she brung all the way from Gee-orgia."

Her eyes flashing bright blue, Cassandra stared at Dulcie's grinning imp face. "Dispose? Where on earth did you find that word? Under the bed somewhere?"

Still wearing the impish grin, Dulcie declared, "I remembers it, thas all. I pick up some special words and then stuffs 'em in my memory box." She shrugged her bony shoulders. "Thas all."

"You really be somethin' special, honey chile, you know that?" Cassandra said, funning with Dulcie.

"Oh, hurry! I think I hears Missus S'James comin' home! Hear? Doan that sound just like the front door openin' and closin'?"

"Don't worry, Dulcie." Cassandra shrugged. "Melantha will think we are packing all this stuff to be burned out back with all the other trash."

"Oh-oh." Dulcie shook her head as if an ominous thunderhead was in the making.

"What now?" Cassandra said in a low voice, tipped back on her slender haunches.

"De proof be in the ashes, Missa Cassa."

"Ashes? Whatever are . . ." Cassandra compressed her soft pink lips. "Oh, yes, that is most certainly a point to take into consideration, Dulcie. The ashes. What are we going to burn to make it look like a trunk full of clothes and sewing paraphernalia went up in smoke?"

A serious expression came over Dulcie's pert face. "Mebbee Goliath can fix that up for you, too, Missa Cassa. Must be some old trunks on board the *River Minx*?"

"Oh, Dulcie—I believe you will have to do all my scheming from now on. Where would I be without you today."

"Still over there drawin' like there ain't no to-morrow?"

Cassandra laughed. "I believe you are right." At times Dulcie was not as slow as others would believe of her.

"Didn't use to always be that way, Missa Cassa. You use to have a mind all yer own. What you gots on your mind this day anyhow? That fine-lookin' gent Mistah Sylvestre with de kittycat eyes? He's a real man, if'n I ever saw one!"

Feeling the heat creeping up from her throat, Cassandra said nothing. In fact, she could not find her voice all of a sudden, so shaken was she.

"I be back!" Dulcie whispered, moving out the door lickety-split.

"Wait! Where are you going, Dulcie?" Cassandra asked, shivering from the apprehension crawling along her spine.

"Tells you when I get back, Missa Cassa!"

Then she was gone, leaving Cassandra alone with her mixed feelings and a certain brand of fatigue she had never experienced. Leaning against the bed, her eyes drifted shut but before she knew it Dulcie was shaking her awake.

Rubbing her eyes, Cassandra asked in a sleepy voice, "Did you see Melantha downstairs?"

"Nope. She went out again visitin' that long-nosed neighbor who comes here all the time with her beady eyes lookin' dis way and dat."

"Oh, that describes Mrs. Krenke to perfection. How do you know Melantha is visiting her?" Cassandra wanted to know.

"Thas what Charles told me. I hope Goliath ain't too busy this time of day. I tole Charles to explain the whole situation to Goliath. Charles'll do anything I asks him 'cause I sneak sweets out of the kitchen for him!"

Letty popped her bandanna-wrapped head in the door just then, asking, "Goliath? Charles? What're you two up to?" She came fully into the room, and closing the door softly behind her, she turned about to face the innocent-appearing faces. "Now I knows somethin' be going on with you two smilin' like angels eatin' strawberry pie an' ice cream." She eyed the bulging trunk that had been dragged over beside the door. "Hmm, Goliath and Charles, huh? I think I gets the picture. Your mama done tole you to get rid of all dat stuff in there?"

"Yes, Letty."

"You gonna do as Missus S'James aks you to do?" Letty shook her head in unison with the other two. "Uh-uh, I didn't think so." She ambled closer to the pair standing shoulder to shoulder in a careless fashion of camaraderie. "Wipe dem guilty-as-sin looks from your pusses, an' you busy bees come along now—and shake de dust off from your feet!"

Cassandra and Dulcie exchanged looks of bewilderment, which Letty answered aloud with, "Well, don't be standin' there lookin' so dumb. I doan care what you be doin' with that old trunk." She chuckled deeply, her fat cheeks wobbling. "Goliath be waitin' in the back hall." Her hand came up and she thumbed in the direction they were to go. "Hurry on now!"

Together Cassandra and Dulcie raced to the trunk, as if they could not get there fast enough. Letty kept a watch at the window, shaking her head in mirth as the two charming conspirators gave the precious trunk over to the waiting hands of the giant black man, Goliath.

# *Chapter Five*

Goliath and Jake, another roustabout from the ship, carried a huge, arched trunk to the spot fenced in with chickenwire, where they prepared to set fire to the trunk and its contents—nothing but old oily rags that would ignite swiftly and be consumed along with the trunk in no time at all.

The fire was set; the five gathered there stood back.

Before Goliath and Jake could slip away, Cassandra stepped up to the huge black man and planted a quick kiss of thanks upon his lower jaw, for she could reach no higher than this. She whispered a question just below his ear and he answered her back, just as swiftly and softly, then nodded his big head. His strange yellow eyes searched Cassandra's as he spoke aloud. "I jes hope Monte St. James won't mind if he finds out what you been up to, Cassa girl."

"He will not mind, Goliath. It is Melantha whom I have to worry about if she discovers this little deception."

"Ain't so little a one, Cassa girl. You jes be careful

now, you hear?"

"You be careful, too, Goliath. And Goliath . . . thank you, I am very grateful for what you have done. Please don't let Melantha see you and Jake."

"She'll never see us in de shadows, honey chile."

"Well, well." Melantha sashayed up behind the three still figures standing at the fenced-in garbage heap, silhouetted in the orange glow. The night seemed deeper where the shadows flanked the fire. "What is this? A funeral for an old trunk of rags and useless paraphernalia?"

"I . . ." Cassandra had always detested lying, and she was having a hard time mouthing the untruth, even now. But Melantha had said rags, and so "rags" they were to her for she did not know the difference. "Yes, rags, Mother."

Melantha glared at the servants, silently giving them leave to take themselves elsewhere.

"It's about time! And have you practiced on the harp—as I told you to?"

"How could I? You told me you would stand by while I practiced."

"I was much too busy. Agatha Krenke just got her new tea service, all the way from England. I plan to send for a set exactly like it. We discussed the news of the day and talked politics. When do I ever hear you asking the neighbor girls over to do the same? You are way behind in what is going on in our world, Cassandra."

Cassandra sighed, glancing up at the silver splendor of the moon. Her eyes wandered off the hill, for they could not resist the beauty of the river with the moon sprinkling diamonds across the surface.

"See, there you are, dreaming about God knows what!" Melantha turned to go inside. "Now, go and finish your chores and then, and only then, can you have your supper."

Cassandra's shoulders drooped as she watched Melantha swing a black umbrella that hung over her arm. She carried that thing wherever she went, even when there was not even the hint of a raincloud in the sky. Cassandra sighed as she moved in the direction of the kitchen door. "How can I love her?" Cassandra asked herself. *How?*

Cassandra slipped into the darkened hallway to fetch the clothes she had earlier hidden beneath the stairway.

Melantha had gone to bed, and Monte would not be coming home, for he had sent a roustabout up with the message that he would be working late on the *River Minx.*

After she had outfitted herself in Charles's clothes, Cassandra slipped noiselessly toward the back door. There she encountered Dulcie just coming in.

"Did you get me the hat I need?" Cassandra whispered.

"Ooo-eee, Missa Cassa. You looks jes like a boy, you do." She dug into a deep pocket of her skirt, coming up with the asked-for item. "It's a little crushed 'cause I didn't want Missus S'James to catch me with it."

"It will do fine," Cassandra said, smoothing the crown out as best she could and, fitting it on her head,

87

she pulled the brim down as far as it would go. "There—how do I look, Dulcie?"

Dulcie grinned widely, then her face fell as she said, "Truth be told, Missa Cassa, you looks jes like you be asking for lots of trouble. You better take care, 'cause you could get hurt real bad where you're going. No place for a skinny lad to be hangin' around this time o' night." Dulcie chuckled.

"I can take care of myself, Dulcie."

"That's what you always be sayin'."

Cassandra dragged in a long deep breath. "Well—here I go. Wish me luck, Dulcie."

"Yes'm." Dulcie pulled her back before she could step out the door. "Tell me, Missa Cassa, why you going to that tavern? Like I says, it's dangerous—even in daytime. You never done anything like this afore. And how do you even know for sure Cap'n Sy going to be down there?"

"Do you remember when I stepped close to Goliath and gave him a kiss?"

"Yup."

"I quickly asked him if I could find Sylvestre Diamond at the Water Street Tavern this evening. He nodded quickly. Did you not see him?"

"No, he must've done it real fast." When Cassandra brushed past her, Dulcie whispered, "You take care now . . . I be waiting up for you."

Dulcie bit her lower lip, knowing that Missa Cassa had not heard her. She was in too much of a hurry to be away from the house before she was discovered sneaking out. Dulcie paled, wondering just what her beautiful friend was up to this night. "God go with you,

Missa Cassa, 'cause you're gonna need all the help you can get."

Dolly McKay wound her generous frame in and out among the customers swilling and dining in the tavern room, her greedy eyes cast upon Captain Diamond seated in the same corner booth he occupied every night before he went upstairs to his room. She had knowledge that he spent some nights on the *River Minx* and that he owned several boats of his own, that he had some fine clothes hanging in the closet, for she had snooped in his personal belongings when Betsy had been in there cleaning. She had even taken Betsy's place in doing the cleaning just that morning, for Betsy had been too busy to get to Sylvestre Diamond's room. Dolly McKay had done Betsy a favor. After touching all his personal belongings and snooping through the papers in the desk drawers, Dolly felt as if she knew the young captain. Now all she had to do was *really* get to know him. Intimately.

Sylvestre was just finishing his dinner when Dolly McKay sashayed up to stand close to his booth. She took up his empty plate, then stood there making no move to leave. "You like the meat loaf and gravy, don't you, Guv'nor? It's real good, I know, 'cause I usually has myself a helping or two on the day the cook makes it."

"Uhm?" Sylvestre finally glanced up at the pleasingly plump Dolly McKay. "Oh, yes, Dolly, and so you must be quite full of the fare yourself this day. It is indeed very delicious."

Dolly still made no indication of moving on. "I heard that you was stayin' here now, that you had a room upstairs all to yer own." She flashed him a bright smile, displaying incredibly white teeth in a heavily rouged face. Her face was quite nice, too, Sylvestre was thinking, and she had green eyes and coal-black hair that added to her striking appearance.

But Sylvestre saw none of Dolly's rough, sensual beauty, not in the way of being tempted or showing interest as so many of the other male customers were in the habit of doing. He envisioned instead a young beauty with crystal-blue eyes and head full of thick, angel-blond hair. Where Dolly McKay was padded generously and sat on her wits, the one he dreamed of night and day was slim, graceful, intelligent—and undoubtedly a virgin.

"Thank you, Dolly." Sylvestre slapped down the needed coin upon the rough-hewn tabletop and an additional one or two for the tavern wench herself. He missed seeing the greed aglow in her wide green eyes as he rose and began to make his way to the stairs.

"Thank ye, guv'nor!" Dolly exclaimed, bending over the table to sweep the extra coins up and stuff them between her jiggling bosoms. Her glance sped to the proprietor, who nodded his balding head, telling Dolly McKay she was off work for the day just as another tavern wench came in to take Dolly's place. The leering proprietor, who'd had a time or two with Dolly McKay himself, winked just before Dolly swept off her apron and headed in the wake of Captain Sylvestre Diamond.

The skinny wharf rat at the end of the counter, with dirt-smudged cheeks and nose and dressed in rough-cut clothes that had seen better days, took all this in

90

from beneath the drooping brim of his overlarge hat. The bright blue eyes were in shadow but had taken in everything that had gone on between the tavern wench and Sylvestre Diamond—even the lascivious wink the proprietor had sent in Dolly McKay's direction.

Stray wisps of pale hair sprang from the old battered hat and Cassandra hastily tucked them back inside, keeping her head down as she made her way toward the stairs. She kept her profile low as she wove among the tables and moved agilely into the shadows at the foot of the stairs. She paused there for a moment or two, to make entirely certain no one noticed what she was about, then she whirled and crept up the stairs, holding her breath as a board creaked halfway up.

Cassandra breathed easily then, for she was in the deep shadow of the overhang. Still, she cast a swift look over her shoulder before almost running the rest of the way to the second-floor hallway.

Sidling close to the door, Cassandra once again held her breath as she pressed the side of her face to the door that had been left open a crack. Yes, this was the room Sylvestre Diamond occupied. And she listened, not knowing she had missed the first part of the conversation going on inside the dimly lighted room.

"I am sorry," Sylvestre had been saying, "but I do not recall having asked you inside my room, Dolly McKay."

Dolly was toying with the top hook of her olive-green dress. "It's all right, guv'nor. I took Betsy's place this morning and cleaned yer room real good."

Sylvestre's tawny eyebrow lifted. "So?"

"Hope ye don't mind havin' me doin' up yer bed instead of that pimple-faced Betsy Lander."

The golden-haired man almost whispered the words as he bent over the full-bosomed Dolly McKay. "I like her that way," he said of Betsy. "She cleans my room just fine."

"Ye do like 'er?" Dolly asked, wondering at the sarcastic tone in his deeply modulated voice. "How do ye like Betsy, Cap'n Sy?" She winked, surprising him with the knowledge of the familiar title. "Knows ye're a cap'n, I do, and yer one of the best pilots to boot."

"I thank you, Miss Dolly. Now—"

"What was that—did ye hear that?"

"I heard nothing," Sylvestre said, becoming bored with Dolly's obvious flirting, the deep purr in her voice designed to seduce a man, and the sway of her generous bosom and hips. It was nothing new to him, but he was tired and wanted to seek some sorely needed rest. Besides, Dolly did not fit the description of the young beauty who filled his most ardent thoughts each day and fired his desire, a desire that only the blond angel could slake.

"Guess it wasn't nothin', guv'nor. Now—"

Sylvestre's eyes narrowed as she sashayed closer. "Now"—he finished where she had faltered as her gaze ran the length of him—"if you would be so kind as to make your exit, and *swift* so that I might get some badly needed rest."

"Been up all night and at it, have ye, guv'nor?"

"No," he drawled. "In fact, I have been up all day"—he had the good manners to grin—"and at it."

She waved a curvy arm in the air. "You been workin' on the paddlewheeler all day, you don't fool Dolly

McKay none!"

"Do you know what?" Sylvestre asked, and she shook her head. "You are most intelligent, Dolly McKay." A deep sigh issued from his firm mouth. "Now, if you would—"

"I jes gotta fetch my feather duster I left in here this mornin'." Sly Dolly fell on her hands and knees before the bed, peeking beneath, her plump buttocks waving in the air.

Sylvestre shook his head, his booted feet widespread, hands on his hips as he rolled his eyes heavenward. "I hope this is not going to take much longer," he muttered to himself, eyeing the plump backsides with a nasty grin while the toe of his boot itched to make a forward launch.

Out in the hallway, the one peering blue eye took everything in: Sylvestre with his long, tapering back to the door; the curvaceous tavern wench on her hands and knees before his spread-eagled legs. Cassandra shifted to her other eye, and it widened at what she observed next . . .

"Hey, guv'nor! Ye're playin' games with me, hmm? You hid me feather duster, jes so's ye could get a good peep at me neat bottom, eh?"

Before Sylvestre knew what hit him, Dolly McKay had laid a bearhold on his torso and, tackling him to the featherbed in a loud crash that must have been heard downstairs, she pinned him down like an oak tree felled upon a sapling.

Growling angrily, Sylvestre whipped Dolly onto her back, but Dolly's hefty limbs swiftly clamped about his lean waist in a viselike grip. "No, sir, ye ain't gettin' away, guv'nor. I got you where I wants ye now, and I'm

gonna hold ye here till ye give me what I came here for."
Quickly she flipped Captain Sy back to his former
position beneath her.

Sylvestre croaked out, "Honest, woman, I have no
idea where you've misplaced your feather duster." He
gritted his teeth, thinking she must have consumed a
ton of bricks and not the usual Friday night meat loaf
and gravy and mashed potatoes.

Cassandra pressed her ear to the crack, trying to hear
what they were saying, but they were speaking too low
and grunting too much for her to understand their
words. She had almost seen enough when Dolly spoke
again, this time louder, and Cassandra wondered at her
words.

"You know it ain't the feather duster I want, guv'nor.
I wants what ye're holding back!"

"If you want my money, Dolly, it is right over there,
where I placed my buff jacket. Go see for yourself."

"Ain't money, either, Cap'n Sy."

"Lord," he gasped. "You are being horribly obvious,
I must say, just like some painted hussy off the streets.
Have you no shame?"

"Don't be puttin' on any fancy airs, guv'nor," she
hissed into his ear, tickling the golden curls with her
panting breaths. "I know ye're a rough-cut diamond,"
she giggled at her pun.

"Off, damnit—before I do something drastic,"
Sylvestre ordered in angry undertones.

"I ain't lettin' ye go fer all the tea in China, guv'nor.
Once I show ye how good Dolly can fix ye up, ye ain't
gonna want no one but," she whispered close to his ear,
making her voice husky and intimate.

Cassandra, disguised in the boy-clothing, stood in

94

the hall bent to the crack in the door. She straightened once, to undo the knot that had grown in her back. Now she bent forward again, and what she took in made her shiver from head to foot. How disgusting. If that is what lovemaking consists of— Round and round they rolled, with Sylvestre Diamond on top again.

Just when Sylvestre thought he was free of the leg-lock, lifting his backsides high in the air, Dolly clamped all the tighter and yanked him back to her plump, straining body.

"My, but you are strong," Sylvestre groaned. "I don't believe you are all human, woman."

"I'm a tigress!" Dolly hissed loud enough for the lovely urchin in the hall to hear.

On and on the battle went. The result became a hilarious pumping motion, up and down, sideways, with Dolly's skirts tangled about her waist, grunts and groans issuing from both.

The little face beneath the borrowed hat assumed an envious scowl. Her heart leapt into an accelerated beat and she could watch no more of this silly play. She fled from the hallway, running down the back stairs, tears burning her eyes as she groped blindly through the darkness and turned her foot instinctively in the direction of her home. For once in her life she would be happy to be there.

By this time, Dolly had managed to greedily undo Sylvestre's front flap, and just when she was reaching inside, Sylvestre drew back his arm, his voice first issuing a warning before he let fly with a left hook.

It was a warning that Dolly McKay unfortunately chose to ignore. When she returned to the taproom to gather up her things, she wore a pretty blue-and-purple reminder of her amorous tussle with Captain Sylvestre Diamond.

A low wolf whistle preceded the question put to Dolly. "That Captain Sy must be some lover, eh, Dolly?" said the tavern wench who had earlier relieved her friend. "What was it that contacted with your jaw and eyeballs?"

"His gol'damned elbow, dummy, what d'ye think?"

"Oh and sure," Dolly's friend snickered and taunted, relieved to find that promiscuous Dolly could not always get her way.

Everyone had witnessed Dolly McKay's humiliation —everyone but the tearful little ragamuffin who had slipped out the back way, all romantic ideals of love's first dream snuffed out in a matter of fifteen minutes.

# Part II

"Her hair was long, and her foot was light.
And her eyes were wild."

—*John Keats*

# Chapter Six

The discordant note of the harp reverberated then terminated suddenly as Melantha entered the drawing room. Her features appeared harsh as her shrewd eyes swept over Cassandra seated at the musical instrument looking ironically like an angel.

Melantha went to stand beside her daughter. She looked down, and Cassandra looked up waiting for the boom to fall—

"The harp should sing *sweetly,* Cassandra, and be soothing to the ears—not harsh as you have made it sound."

Cassandra blinked up at Melantha, saying, "I had no idea anyone in the house was listening—Mother."

"How could anyone help but hear that noise! You are not plucking a banjo, Cassandra—the notes should flow from your fingers into the instrument. You should *caress* the strings tenderly."

Annoyed and impatient, Melantha picked up Cassandra's slim hand, holding it up between them. "Tsk, tsk. Your fingernails are much too short. Look at

99

mine." She dropped Cassandra's hand almost forcefully, then held up her own longer, larger hand. "Long fingernails produce a ringing, bell-like sound. You will have to allow yours to grow longer. The days of sticking your fingers into sewing thimbles must end!"

Cassandra almost sighed aloud in boredom as she was forced to stand at attention while Melantha situated herself comfortably before the harp. Knowing she must stand and listen, Cassandra steeled herself to remain patient for a time.

"Now—listen," Melantha instructed, stretching herself from the shoulders in order to lightly embrace the instrument.

Soon the heavenly notes filled the air, softly, soothingly, and Cassandra found herself responding to the dreamily romantic music as Melantha played with a passion that was never more in evidence than when the dark-haired woman sat before the harp. Cassandra caught herself floating away on the beautiful notes and stared down at Melantha's rapturous countenance, then she began to frown.

The truth came to Cassandra in a twinkling: Melantha was shallow, a lover of *things,* not *persons.* There was no gaiety in Melantha unless she was in the company of folks who rattled on about material things. And there was no passion in her save for those times she was in the company of *things*.

Smoothing her hands over the muslin folds of her simple, turquoise-green dress, Cassandra wished to be anywhere but where she was at the moment. She longed to be down on the *River Minx* working to help her father ready the paddlewheeler for the next trip along the Missouri and the Mississippi. He might even be leaving tonight if the schedule for passengers was filled by that time, she realized.

An idea formed in her mind. With genuine sweetness, she complimented Melantha when she finished with the melodious tune, then blurted out that it was "teatime!"

"I shall go and fetch the tea and frosted cakes at once."

"Cassandra!"

She did not turn about, but said, "Yes—Mother?"

"Don't run—*walk!*"

On perfect behavior, Cassandra executed a graceful curtsy. "Yes, Mother."


Cassandra leaned far out her window, breathing the damp air, the musky odor of the levee and its water-wet timbers. Melantha might have had a fit of vapors had she known that Cassandra sometimes stood in the raw before the open window, permitting the night air to steal around her body like a young man's caress. This night, however, she was fully covered, wearing her cotton nightgown, with her blond hair wild as cornsilk, long, loose.

Holding the lamp close, Cassandra scrutinized her face in the mirror. It was mysteriously enchanting to do this in the dark. She recalled now, with a delectable shiver, the way Sylvestre had gazed at her across the dinner table, his face devastatingly handsome. It was not long ago . . . and yet it seemed like ages had passed since they had strolled in the moonlit garden instead of just a week.

Restless now, and moving across the room, Cassandra set the lamp down on the washstand, paused for a moment, then drifted back to the open window.

The *River Minx* was half outlined in the dark by flames from the pineknots burning in their iron baskets. The river men called them jacks, but to Cassandra's way of thinking, they were like mammoth candles that cast silvery paths upon the water. They beckoned . . . as if one could come and dance across them.

Alone this afternoon, she had once again shed many tears over the velvet dress she wasn't allowed to wear. In the semidarkness she had fled to the edge of the bluffs where she had watched the roustabouts loading the lower deck of the *River Minx*. She had distinguished the stalwart form of Goliath, her father's chief roustabout, his voice dinning above the rest. As she stood there, she realized the spent tears were not only because of the dress, but because Sylvestre had not returned as he said he would. He had only been playing with her—as he had when she was a little girl in a soiled pinafore.

Now, alone in her room, she had been watching the darkness as it settled over the Missouri. She knew the *River Minx* was nearly loaded. She could hear the sounds of the cattle and horses on the lower deck, and ever so faintly, the strains of a waltz picking up. Lovely. Ever so romantic . . .

Cassandra sighed impatiently. She knew that in an hour or so the paddlewheeler would be pulling out

102

again, her father—and Sylvestre—with it.

"Oh, how I wish I could be down there, dancing in my beautiful turquoise velvet gown!"

Who had a better right to be on the *River Minx* than the owner's daughter? "No one," Cassandra said aloud.

The light paths on the waters danced and whispered a tantalizing call to her. *Come . . . come, Cassandra.*

For a year she had so desired to slip aboard one of Monte's boats, to make the trip with him, but she hadn't been able to summon enough courage to do so.

Perspiration glistened upon her upper lip, and her eyes were overbright little stars.

Suddenly she grimaced, reminded of the young man Melantha had always intended for her to wed. Harlan Kirby. The name alone gave her willies. She recalled that when she was a little girl Harlan had pinched her derriere. On his last visit here, he had kept his wily eyes trained on her skirts. Ugh! She would never, but *never* marry a man unless she loved him through and through—and she was positively certain she would never come to love Harlan Kirby!

It thoroughly terrified her to think of being a captive bride in the gloomy Kirby House, having him kiss her, maul her cringing body, having his babies . . . No, no, never!

All of a sudden Cassandra was galvanized into action. Her spirits soared dizzyingly.

Shucking off her nightgown, she tossed it carelessly upon the bed. Then she donned her best white satin shoes, silk stockings of the same paleness, her finest underthings, a camisole and one petticoat. She paused, then blurted to herself, "Why not!"

103

Hastily Cassandra pulled on five more frothy petticoats and snatched up the forbidden velvet dress she had laid across the bed that afternoon in order to admire its loveliness and stroke its soft folds. Now she would wear it!

"Oh, Lord, how soft the velvet is," she murmured. Soft as a week-old kitten, Cassandra thought impishly as she drew it carefully over her blond head. "So tight in the waist I can hardly breathe."

When Cassandra had completed her intense toilette in the dimness of a turned-down lamp, she peered at her reflection with satisfaction. "Oh, Letty, and Dulcie, too, I wish you both could see me now—but I am afraid I will have to go without my precious dears."

Straightening her shoulders, pulling air into her constricted lungs, Cassandra told herself, "All I have to do is walk up the stageplank as if I were a passenger who had strolled off"—she giggled—"and was merely strolling back on!" She gulped. If someone stopped her all she had to do was say, "I am going aboard to wish my father farewell . . . No. Fiddle! I am coming back on board—to join him. No, that will never do, either. I have it. I shall tell them to mind their own business!" Cassandra frowned and shrugged. After all, she was not a *child* anymore.

Beholding herself in the shadow-blurred mirror, Cassandra observed with satisfaction that she had marvelous blue eyes, black-lashed and uptilted. She pouted then. "But my mouth is entirely too wide. Worst of all, my nose is too delicate . . . it should be more arched, like Melantha's." She turned her head sideways—"My chin is rather impudent—not bad at all," then gazed downward. "But my feet are much too small—"

Cassandra started then as she heard her father's voice booming up the stairs. "Good-bye, Cassa dear!" Then more softly as she sped to the door to crack it open, "I'll be back in two weeks, Melantha." And her reply. "You do not have to remind me of your return, Monte." The rest of the conversation was lost as she shut her door and leaned back against it.

A moan emerged from her throat. "Ahh, I am counting on Father's kindness to allow me to stay on the *River Minx* when he discovers my presence." She turned and reopened the door, calling out, "Good-bye, Papa!" while fingering the hank of wavy silverfire hair she had let float loose about her velvet-clad shoulders.

Quickly now, Cassandra slipped into her quilted pardessus, blew out the lamp—and waited. Everything . . . everything depended on proper timing. Melantha always accompanied Monte as far as the front gate.

She heard voices, then the door opening . . . and closing. Cassandra listened intently, cracking the door a mere inch. No sound from the parlor. If her plan was to succeed, she must get on the *River Minx* before her father came aboard.

*Now! Now was the time for her to go!*

Taking a deep, steadying breath, Cassandra held up her skirts and scampered in unladylike fashion down the dim stairway and out the back door, into the gothic dark of the garden.

Cassandra moved like a brisk wind, brushing leaf and flower petal, her slippered feet darting and dancing over the grass.

She glanced back at the house just once in failing courage, then whirled back to her purpose, her delicate features mysterious in moonshadow. Excitement pounded in her heart.

Not following the usual path, she cut across the bluffs to a dirt slide used for play by children of the town. Awkwardly she pulled up her pardessus, hitched up her velvet skirt and six petticoats, then sat down and gave herself a great shove. It was a shortcut to the docks, but Cassandra had a feeling her best drawers would be utterly ruined!

Cassandra crouched behind the woodpile. She had made it aboard the paddlewheeler!

How lovely it is, she thought, all white and gilt, with the pilothouse perched on top like an enormous bubble. She sucked in a deep breath as she heard gay music coming from the main saloon and saw dancers flash by the windows.

Excitement such as she had never known engulfed her. There was a mingled smell of horses, cattle, muddy water, sweating men, and decaying wood from the levee. It all smelled so good.

Shifting a little, Cassandra craned her neck. On the passenger deck above, the carpets were plush and the ladies wore exotic-smelling scents that wafted in the night air. How am I to get up there? she asked herself. In daylight it would be a simple matter to walk aboard, mount the great stairway, and mingle casually with the gay crowd on the passenger deck. But, at night, all the ladies were inside and a girl alone would be quite conspicuous.

Her heart was beating a rapid tattoo and her palms were cold and clammy. Wherever she looked she saw men, most of them loudmouthed and a bit tipsy.

Anxiously she glanced at the steps leading to town. Her father would be along any minute now and he must not catch her or else she would be ordered back to the house . . . back to Melantha. At once. She decided to stay for a few minutes longer, then return to the house. She could not become a stowaway and make the trip as she had planned. It was too risky, in more ways than one. She was afraid of what Melantha might do to Letty and Dulcie in her absence. *I should have thought of that in the first place,* she recriminated herself now.

*Only a few more minutes and then I must go.* Taking a deep breath, Cassandra tossed back her blond head and stepped from the woodpile with more confidence than she felt. She was so intent on getting aboard quickly that she failed to see the two men staggering in front of her. She almost walked into their arms!

"Well, well," one chimed drunkenly. "What d' we have here?"

One of them grabbed for and caught her. "Please . . . let me go!" she cried, jerking her arm free. She was not all that frightened of the men . . . her main fear was that Monte might come along and find her in the company of the drunken louts.

"Eyy, don't be coy, darlin'," one well-dressed man crooned drunkenly and stepped up to her. "Give us a kiss, girlie."

His sour breath was on Cassandra's face, and suddenly he was drawing her to him, reaching for her velvet-covered breasts. "Enough, I say!" Cassandra half-screamed, slapping him hard across his ruddy cheek, then gasping at her loud outburst and violent gesture.

"Ahh, a wharf kitten with sharp claws! Well, missy, I like kittens with some spunk. Come here, lovey, and let me tame you." He pulled her roughly against his body and Cassandra's heart thumped with fright and rage as she began to struggle with him in earnest.

"You . . . evil-minded lout!" she cried, kicking out at his shins.

Suddenly, to her intense relief, she was released from the drunken hold. It was as if the brute had been plucked up by a Titan and set down several feet away, albeit none too gently.

A deep voice resounded. "Are you having trouble, miss?"

Cassandra looked up, shaken and trembling, seeing a tall, broad-shouldered man thrusting the remaining drunk aside as if he was but a toy.

The man stood tall and commanding. Flushing beneath his intense scrutiny, Cassandra found her voice, not knowing how she managed to do so.

"I don't know what I would have done," she told him, blushing at her vulnerability of a moment before. "I had just—" Her voice broke and she felt foolish all of a sudden—and vulnerable again.

The men who had annoyed Cassandra suddenly began to babble foolishly, inadvertently saving the day for her. "W-we didn't mean any harm," the younger one blubbered. "A thousand pardons, Mr. Casey, all in

108

fun, y-you know—" muttered the one who had tried to kiss Cassandra with his wet, sloppy lips. They both backed off and stumbled up the stageplank, looking more inebriated than ever.

"Well!" said Cassandra's rescuer with a drawl, as his blue eyes swept over her surreptitiously. "I guess there's nothing like an infamous reputation to scare off cowards, hmm, little lady?"

Shyly Cassandra smoothed her disheveled hairdo, adjusted her bodice that had gone askew, then looked up as he removed his hat and Cassandra saw his face for the first time. He was tall, rawboned, with dark, wavy hair and high cheekbones. He had a long jaw, stubborn chin, firm mouth, and tiny dimples showed faintly on either side of his mouth. His blue eyes were long-lashed, deep set, and full of gentleness at the moment.

Jared Casey grinned with devilish amusement. She was thoroughly enchanting, whoever she was, and he thought to himself that he had just found himself the elegant bride he had been seeking. She was no doubt the daughter of some wealthy merchant, dressed in rich velvet as she was, her bearing like that of a princess, just what he needed, he told himself shrewdly, to further his career. Who would dare question his integrity with such an angel at his side? No one, he again told himself.

To hell with his desire to meet Cassandra St. James; he wouldn't need her now. All he wanted and needed was right here beneath his clutches. She would soon be his for the taking if his reputation as a great lover had anything to say in his favor . . . and over a hundred

109

conquests *had,* long before this charming angel ever came along to whet his jaded appetite.

The sky was heavy with stars and with black smoke piling out of the paddlewheeler's chimneys as Sylvestre stepped out of the pilothouse for a moment. He lit a cheroot, waiting for Captain St. James to board the boat.

Earlier, in the pastel spring afternoon, he had watched from the texas as the *River Minx* was being loaded. Women with carpetbags, sundry items, and crying babies. Drays and baggage vans had clattered here and there in a wild scramble, every now and then getting blocked and jammed together. The half-naked crews had lowered freight into the hold (and one mysterious trunk with arched lid, he noticed, had been placed down there very carefully by Goliath and another roustabout!) and were inspired to sing aloud amid the chaos of turmoil and racket of the last loading day that always drove man and woman alike mad. They were running late.

Now the hurricane and boiler decks were packed with passengers, and Sylvestre heard Goliath's booming voice call out, "All dat ain't goin', please git asho'!" Sylvestre saw Monte St. James jump onto the stageplank, and a moment later it was being hauled in.

It was inspiring to hear the black roustabouts sing, especially at nightfall when the forecastle was lit up with the red glare of the torch baskets and a magical excitement filled the air. At these times his mind wandered. With the moon floating above, he thought

110

of Cassandra. Cassa, who was like a tiny topaz jewel waiting to be cut and polished and placed into its rightful setting! When he dreamed of making love to her, even thought of merely spending a whole, unfettered day with her, he moved about like a caged tiger.

His dark lashes fell over his yellow-gold eyes in passionate response to the image he created in his mind.

*Cassa in his arms. Losing himself in her feminine flesh.* In his mind he could almost feel the slim length of her young body. Desire for Cassa reared in him like a hot-blooded stallion eager to mate.

Lust, *oui,* he lusted after her. He loved Cassa . . . would never love or want another. Perhaps he should have gone to visit her. But he had realized that merely visiting Cassandra would not be sufficient any longer, for he was bursting with need and desire to hold her and fulfill his expanding love and lust for her. And this was the main reason he had not called on her—this more than Melantha St. James's protestations and dislike of him.

Endeavoring to forget the lonely emptiness of his arms and the eagerness of his desire, Sylvestre tossed his half-smoked cheroot overboard and thoughtfully watched its glowing descent into the churning water where it sizzled out. Then he did a double take as he was about to step inside the texas, freezing in midstride, a strange light in his yellow-gold cat eyes.

*Cassa?* he asked himself softly. Can this really be *she?* He blinked his eyes as a puff of smoke rolled from the towering chimneys and blew his way as the wind

111

changed direction.

She was dressed in a gorgeous velvet gown, the color of rich jade—or so it looked to be that shade in the torchlight. Her silken hair hung loose in wild waves and looked like angelfire, with creamy ivory combs hitching the glorious locks up on either side of a shell-like ear. Her dainty feet were clad in white slippers that peeked out from the turquoise hem, looking like silver satin in the firelit night. Creamy mounds of flesh were displayed over a frothy lace bodice and she pulled a pardessus together in front as the man continued to study her. The *man!* An angry oath fell from his lips—that man was none other than the unscrupulous lawyer Jared Casey!

On the lower deck, Cassandra thanked her rescuer once again, employing a charm far beyond the surface niceties her mother had taught her.

"I'll escort you to your destination, ah—" Jared Casey paused, trying to force the young minx to state her name.

"That will not be necessary, sir. I know my way," Cassandra declared.

"But I must insist—"

"Oh, the stageplank is being drawn in! Forgive me, sir, I must go!"

"To where?" Casey took hold of her arm, afraid she would vanish without a trace. He wouldn't like to lose this angel now, when he had just made her acquaintance. "You just came aboard, fair maiden."

Cassandra shook his arm off. "No, I have to go—you

112

do not understand . . ."

Casey cocked a dark eyebrow amusedly as the delightful angel ran off in a rush and a flurry of turquoise velvet. Folding his arms across his chest, he watched, wondering what mischief she was up to. She was half child, half woman, he thought, watching her weave between bales of hemp, tobacco, barrels of foodstuffs and staples, and every few seconds bumping into astonished members of the crew.

The dark-haired man chuckled. She would not get far, for the paddlewheeler was already moving away from the levee.

Swiftly Cassandra fled and, finding the stairway at last, she scampered up to the passenger deck. Her hair flew on either side of her shoulders like blond-white angel wings. Upon reaching the deck, she paused to look back at Jared Casey. She had found the man attractive and worldly in a way she had yet to fathom.

Like one who has captured an exotic butterfly, Casey stared up at her, wishing he had not released that butterfly so suddenly. He called up to her in a deep voice, "Miss Angel! If you are in further need of my assistance, just ask the steward. My name is Jared Casey."

Nipping her bottom lip, Cassandra put her back to the charming Mr. Casey, murmuring his first name to herself. "Jared . . . handsome Jared." Too handsome, too worldly. . . .

For a few moments longer, she stood there, beyond fearing, until she heard her father's voice only a few feet from where she stood.

"We'll be all right if there's no fog in the bend. Sy, are

113

you listening?"

"Yes, I heard, Monte."

*Sy . . . Sylvestre Diamond!* Cassandra clasped her shaking hands over the velvet folds of her turquoise gown, which shimmered in the glowing light of the torches set about the rails and decks. Her hair was like sunlight and fire, a pair of golden eyes noticed. She must have stolen aboard, for she was not acknowledging the presence of her father—or him!

Sylvestre's eyes, now the color of dark amber, were troubled as he thought of Cassandra spending time with the notorious rake Casey. Even a few moments were too long for one as innocent and unworldly as Cassandra St. James to spend in the company of that womanizing rogue!

"Perhaps . . . uhm . . . we should wait until morning?" Sylvestre was saying to Captain St. James. Had he imagined he'd just heard the soft intake of breath from the young minx standing only a few feet away? "Although," Sylvestre went on, "the moon is certainly bright enough, wouldn't you say, my friend?"

"You are right—we will not delay," Monte said.

Cassandra shivered with renewed excitement. The boat shuddered hard and she heard the giant pistons of the boat throbbing in time with her mad pulse. She was on the paddlewheeler to stay. The *River Minx* was well under way!

Stealthily Cassandra moved away to mingle with the crowd, to hide herself from her father's line of vision. Now that she had gotten this far, she might as well go all the way!

She could not help but smile when she heard Goliath's voice. "Look lively now and drag, you

114

niggers! Swing, to make dis ladyboat go!"

The sound of giant hawsers dragged thunderously across the wooden deck. Slap-slap-slap went the mammoth paddle wheels as the *River Minx* made her way upstream beneath the majestic moon.

This night she had long dreamed of had become a reality.

## Chapter Seven

Trying to better conceal herself, Cassandra leaned against the bulkhead, behind the curtains, and remained hidden there beside the pilothouse for a quarter of an hour. Her father and Sylvestre had moved away. She could tell that someone had stepped into the pilothouse to relieve the second man who had been at the wheel.

The motion of the paddlewheeler was like a swing . . . and Cassandra suddenly felt quite sleepy. She slid down and peeped out the curtains.

Her face drained of color, for she recognized Sylvestre at the wheel, the back of his lean male body tall and commanding. He was so close, all she had to do was turn about, push aside the green curtain, and he would see her hiding there! She had carefully gone to the trouble of concealing herself, only to place herself in close proximity to Captain Sy once again!

Her father entered the pilothouse then, and Cassandra blanched. It would not be long before she was found out!

117

*If only I could slip from my hiding place . . . but where then would I go? I know I will be discovered at some time on this trip. Today. Tomorrow . . . Oh . . . how do I always get myself into so much trouble?* Cassandra wondered. *When am I going to grow up?*

*When everyone lets me!* she answered her own question.

*I might as well step out and show myself.* Taking a deep breath to embolden her confidence, Cassandra was about to reveal herself when Sylvestre and Monte began to converse. Her heartbeat became a heavy stroking within the confines of her rib cage.

"We'll be stopping at several of the small landings to pick up and deliver produce from merchants and farmers," Monte was saying. He chuckled. "If we're lucky, some of the legislators from the Assembly might come aboard at Jefferson City to entertain us with political talk at dinner."

Cassandra's ears perked up. It was Sylvestre's turn to say something.

"At Glasgow we can always figure on a heavy cargo, since it has the best levee on the river."

"And those Brunswick merchants will be itching to get rid of their tobacco."

Sylvestre made a mental note to purchase some new hawsers for his *Fair Maiden* from the hemp man at Waverly. His senses became suddenly alert. The night winds blowing across the decks brought a softly exotic perfume wafting his way. There was only one woman he knew of who smelled so wonderfully sweet and feminine, and the scent was all her own . . .

Sylvestre was excited to learn that Cassandra was so near, but Monte would not be so inclined to joy at

118

discovering her presence aboard the *River Minx*. And it would not be long before she was discovered, he knew.

He would just wait, for he had not the heart to turn her over to Monte St. James.

Suddenly he had a change of mind, for the lovely minx must be shaking in her pretty satin slippers. It was indeed cruel to prolong her misery, so he decided the best course was to get it over with for her.

Leaning close to Monte, Sylvestre spoke in a whisper. "We have charming company on board, monsieur, although perhaps you will not be as delighted as I to learn of this. See for yourself—behind the curtain."

"Curtain?" Monte said.

"Aye—the green curtain."

"Are you serious?"

"I am."

Monte frowned. *Charming company?* "I don't understand," Monte said, just as low, turning to eye the curtain.

"You will" was all Sylvestre said.

Reaching back with a long arm, Sylvestre snatched open the curtain, then returned both hands to the wheel as Monte breathed incredulously.

"Jesus! Cassandra?"

"G-good evening, Father."

Swallowing hard, steeling her nerves, Cassandra stepped out from the dark-green shadows, and her woebegone expression was like a knife thrust in Sylvestre's heart. She looked very much like the little girl he had strolled hand in hand with in the rose gardens of Diamondhead Plantation.

119

*I pray God you do not ever find out what I have done this night.* Sylvestre turned back to the wheel he had allowed to spin aimlessly for a few moments as he had looked into the little face of his enchanting angel. He had never seen her look more beautiful. She had bloomed into a beautiful rose. Yes, Cassa was fast becoming a woman. For now, however, she appeared very lost and without a friend in the world.

"Cassandra," Monte began, this time his voice a bit gentled. "Why did you do this?"

"I do not know, Father. But—really—I did not intend to stay. I only meant to . . . ah . . . look around a little."

"I know you do not lie, Cassandra."

"It is true, Father." She would not let him know how she had changed her mind.

She hung her head dejectedly, truly feeling like a naughty child caught redhanded in some mischief. And with Sylvestre Diamond standing only a few feet away, in charge at the wheel, she felt doubly embarrassed and foolish. After the way Melantha had embarrassed her in the garden, Sylvestre already thought of her as a child. And now it was happening again. No wonder Sylvestre had never come to call on her. In his eyes she was probably still a little girl in soiled pinafore with an ugly green frog nestled in her pocket!

To Sylvestre, however, she was anything but a child. He wanted her more than ever. The deep thudding of his heart attested to that truth, as did his body, aching to possess her fully. And he could tell by the way Monte was studying her that Cassandra was no mere child to him anymore, either.

"Cassa, girl—" Monte began again, feeling utterly

helpless in this situation. "Your mother is going to be very disappointed."

"I realize how Melantha feels, Father. She just does not care how *I* feel," she continued, trying to suppress hot tears. "But you understand, Father, you have always understood." Her blurry eyes strayed to the commanding male at the wheel. Why did he not say something in her defense? He used to defend her when she was a little girl.

Cassandra blinked, and the fuzzy image of the magnetic Captain Sy wavered and swam. Why doesn't he turn around and say something? Why is he so cold and distant? Cassandra wondered, feeling heartbroken and shattered.

Then she thought she knew.

*I will always be "Little Cassa" to him.*

*This is not true,* her heart argued.

*But it is so. Look at him. He wants nothing to do with you and your silly child-games.*

*He wants to court you, Cassandra. He said as much,* her heart continued the debate.

*No! No!* Cassandra's thick lashes fluttered. *He was abed with a mere tavern wench, and God only knew how many other women he had been with before* that one!

All of a sudden Sylvestre turned. Just for an instant. But Cassandra had cast her head down shamefacedly as his golden cat eyes swept across her face to halt on her breathlessly parted, velvety-soft lips, her prettily flushed cheeks . . . and softly, softly, in that instant, his eyes caressed her face.

And Monte saw. He knew Sylvestre desired his daughter deeply.

121

Cassandra heaved a deep sigh and blinked back hot tears. She might as well go all the way and spill her heart—right in front of Sylvestre Diamond.

It did not matter much now, anyway, for she had already made a foolish spectacle of herself and Sylvestre did not care. She was nothing to him. Nothing special, anyway. Tavern wenches were more to his liking. They were worldly, knowing just how to please a man, to make a man desire them. Sylvestre would never desire her that way. But there was one man who just might. Jared Casey!

Cassandra's spirits lifted like gypsy moths into the perfumed night air. Now there was a worldly man—so handsome and daring and charming. And he had looked at her as if she was a woman. She would wager that Jared Casey never sought the company of promiscuous women. No, indeed.

It was chancy, but on this river journey, she just might be able to make Sylvestre turn his eye toward her and become jealous. Perhaps . . . if he really and truly cared the least little bit for her.

With that exhilarating idea in mind, Cassandra begged, "You *will* let me stay, Father? Please say yes! I have always longed to make the trip with you—" She looked sheepishly at the toes of her white slippers. "Without Melantha!"

In her heart she must know that Melantha was not her true mother, Monte thought, ashamed that he had never told her this. He could reveal it to her now, on this trip, without Melantha's domineering presence to make the scene all that more emotional. He would think seriously about it. For now, however, he had to make arrangements for his daughter to have her own stateroom.

The next morning Cassandra had to pinch herself to make certain she was not dreaming as she moved . . . no, *floated* about her own little stateroom. She grimaced as she thought how Melantha's presence had always made the stateroom they occupied together seem so stuffy and crowded. She was so thrilled that she did not question in her mind—as she'd done in the past—the reason her mother never shared the captain's cabin with her father.

But now she had a stateroom all to herself!

Her father had informed her the night before that he would send a rider back at the first landing to inform Melantha that Cassandra was safe aboard the *River Minx* and would remain with him the entirety of the trip.

Before she slipped into bed last night, she had removed the velvet gown and hung it carefully in the rosewood wardrobe so it would not become wrinkled, the velvet crushed. This morning, after she had washed—using the pretty lavender-flowered washbowl and pitcher—she had slipped the gown back on, feeling very grown up and elegant to be wearing the velvet gown in daytime. She had nothing else to wear unless she could get to her trunks. When she found Goliath, she would ask him what had become of the trunk of clothes and sewing paraphernalia.

Cassandra walked in just her silk stockings, and delighted in the plush feel of the thick carpet beneath

123

her feet, pushing her toes deep as she paused at the window, fingering the lace curtains there. When her breakfast of bacon and eggs, warm, buttered toast, and sugared *beignet* arrived, she lingered at the little table beside the window, sipping chicory coffee at her leisure, careful that she did not spill anything on the velvet softness of her lap.

The whimsical current of the river serenaded Cassandra with its song of glorious liberty as she gazed out the window, seeing men, women, and chattering children stroll by on the white-railed gallery. The Missouri River wound itself through the fertile land in a series of serpentine bends, and the landscape unrolled like a giant scroll to reveal the pastel scenes like exquisitely embroidered tapestries depicting spring-time.

Seeing herself in the mirror across the stateroom, Cassandra smoothed her blond hair and straightened the folds of her turquoise velvet dress. As she did this, she began to dream about the fashions she would someday create. But thoughts of Jared Casey intruded. And Sylvestre Diamond. She was not at all the sort of woman who could plan to entrap a man, she thought, taking a slow bite of a *beignet,* as she cast a critical eye over the gown she wore, down the line of her young breasts peeping over the frothy bodice, and then up again to her glowing face.

Her lips were sugary from the little roll, her expression was wistful, and the blush of anticipation was in her glowing blue eyes. She could flirt with Jared Casey . . . She caught her breath and lowered her lashes, fluttering them, practicing the best way to entice a man like Jared Casey. "Jared," she whispered softly, blinking her dark lashes, devising ways of making him fall in love with her.

"Oh, it is just no good," Cassandra said with a defeated sigh. "No, I am not the type to entice a man—" She licked the sugar from her lips. "Not your usual indelicate tavern wench, for sure. But I could give it a good try if . . . Jared Casey is willing!"

And Jared Casey was, indeed, as he frantically searched the decks of the *River Minx* for the enchanting angel he had encountered the night before. He leaned against the railing now, wondering what had become of her. He gazed out over the ever-changing river, sighting a number of pretty little islands covered with willows, cottonwoods, and luxurious under-growth, watching birds flitting through them like swift-moving shadows.

And there was another shadow. It moved from the overhang and came to stand a few feet from where Jared was relaxing at the rail, enjoying the spring morning and the delightful memory of the angelic beauty he had encountered the evening before, telling himself he would be in her presence that very day or his name wasn't Jared Casey.

"Monsieur Casey," the deep voice not far from him rumbled. "Is it the view that gives you such a wistful expression, or is it perhaps a ladylove you left behind in your native Illinois?"

Languidly, leaning against the white rail, Jared turned to face Captain Sy. "Men do not wear wistful expressions, Captain Sy."

"No? Well, you did just a moment ago, if I am not too rude in stating so again."

"You are . . ." Jared drawled. "And what is your

125

business with me, Sy Diamond. Surely you did not leave your place at the wheel to come and pass the time of day with me?"

"There are two of us. Pilots, that is. Willie Elmo likes his liquor and ladies, but most times he's quite capable of taking charge when I wish to fetch myself a cup of tea or coffee." He did not say that Willie Elmo had been imbibing heavily during the night and he must get back before Willie dipped his cup into the rum devil again. "And perhaps I even need to eat a morsel or two during the course of a day."

"Really?" Jared said with a sneer. "I thought maybe you had all your nourishment brought to you on a silver platter, friend," he ended facetiously.

"In the single day that I have come to know you, Casey, I have decided you are not the sort I would call 'friend.' I would rather say we made passing acquaintance and that is all."

"The feeling is mutual, *Captain Sy.*"

"I am not captain of this steamboat," Sylvestre said, not liking the unscrupulous lawyer he had finally come face-to-face with the day before as the *River Minx* was being loaded. "Monte St. James holds that title."

"But you are captain of your own ships, true?"

"I see you have done some investigating of your own while you have been aboard. Let me see," Sylvestre said, tapping his chin with a lean, tanned forefinger. "It must have been none other than that painted tart who has once again wiggled herself aboard. Why do you appear so surprised, Monsieur Casey. I know who Miki Rhea is. In fact, she is quite well known by a number of 'gentlemen' from here to St. Louis and on to New Orleans."

126

"So, you know her, too, do you?"

Sylvestre breathed forcibly through his handsomely shaped nose. "I must say I have not had the privilege of knowing Miki Rhea intimately, although there arises the question of whether or not it is truly a privilege, as many men seem to think."

"I am certain now that you have not come to have a casual chat with me, Sy Diamond." Casey's blue eyes narrowed in suspicion. "I don't suppose this little visit has anything to do with the enchanting angel you saw me conversing with last evening? If it does, I must inform you, Sy, that I'm going to do everything in my power to get to know her better. She appeared troubled over something, and I mean to aid the fair damsel in distress."

"You needn't trouble yourself any further, Casey. You see, her father has taken charge now that he has discovered her presence aboard. In fact, she should be coming out for a stroll any time now—and I do want to warn you that she is to be left alone. Do you comprehend?"

"Obviously you have designs on the little minx yourself or you would not go to such lengths as to be taken away from your demanding pilot's tasks, eh?"

"I realize you are feeling me out, Casey. Let me assure you that I can leave my post at any time of day to see if you are carrying out my demands."

"You say"—he began more shrewdly—"the enchanting angel has a parent on board?"

"I did" was all Sylvestre offered for the moment.

"I suppose her mama is along for the trip also?" Jared questioned coolly.

Sylvestre studied Jared Casey, knowing the unprincipled lawyer could be a dangerous man to reckon with —not where he was concerned, not at all, for he could hold his own with any man. It was Cassandra's virtue he was thinking of. Not that she would give a man like Casey more than the time of day. No, it was just that she was so vulnerable. And there was something else: Cassandra was put out with him, that he knew, for he had seen the freezing glare she sent him before Monte took her to her stateroom. He could not blame the charming blonde her feelings, for he had not gone back to visit—and court—her, as he had promised her. He could not trust himself to act the perfect gentleman and had at last admitted the truth to himself. He was in love, deeply in love, with Cassandra St. James.

Realizing now that Casey had no knowledge that the charming angel of his acquaintance the evening before was Monte St. James's daughter, he decided the best course would be to let Jared Casey squirm and wonder whose daughter she was. It would do the rogue some good to learn that not every woman was at his beck and call.

"Let me just say that 'the blonde' is off limits, Casey." Sylvestre turned to make his way back to the pilothouse. "We shall leave it at that."

Expelling his breath in a snort, Jared Casey snatched his hat up from the bench where he had placed it moments before and planted it on his dark head with a twist of his wrist.

"No one tells Jared Casey what he should or shouldn't do," he breathed to the empty promenade deck, "or who he must court or not court." His eyes turned wily and dark. *Captain Sy must have plans for the blond minx himself. I wonder what Cassandra St.*

*James would think if she knew he had turned his eyes toward another, for Melantha St. James had mentioned that Sylvestre Diamond had designs on her daughter.*

Stuffing his hands deep into his trouser pockets, Jared continued to mumble to himself as he paced the deck, unaware that the velvet-clad blonde was just rounding a corner, coming his way.

He was angry with Captain Sy for treating him like a rascally blackguard he could put off at the next landing. "I must meet Miss St. James. That will fix the arrogant Captain Sy. She has to know that he has set his attentions elsewhere—and I will report this as soon as we return to Harper."

Cassandra smiled as she passed stout matrons sitting in a semicircle with their backs to the curtained windows, crocheting and murmuring amongst themselves like busy bees. As soon as she left the ladies' cabin, Cassandra sensed a pair of eyes watching her.

The man who had been pacing the deck turned and saw her. His dark, arresting face was expressionless but for his brilliant blue eyes that caught and held hers at once.

Cassandra felt color flood her cheeks as she recognized the tall, dark-haired man of the evening before: Jared Casey.

Now she blushed to think that she had been scanning every face in the dining room and had taken numerous turns about the promenade deck the evening before—in hopes of seeing him again. She had stayed out in the evening air so long that Goliath had come up to warn her that she must be abed now. It was well past the mid of night. And so she had done as faithful Goliath had beseeched her to and gone to bed, dreaming of a tall, dark stranger.

And—here he was again.

Now that she had finally encountered Jared Casey again, she was at a loss as to what she would say to him. Suddenly it was as if a hundred hummingbirds were in her chest.

Their glances clashed briefly as they came face to face. *Easy,* Jared warned himself, *she is not a delicious tart you can pop into your mouth and consume all at one sitting. You'll have to go easy with this one. She's an untouched maiden, and a damned tempting morsel to fire your jaded blood and get it boiling again.*

Jared smiled, saying, "I've thought of nothing but you since I made your acquaintance"—he decided to employ a French word—"mademoiselle. 'The efforts which we make to escape from our destiny only serve to lead us into it.'"

"Emerson," the blue-eyed blonde said, recognizing the poet's lines at once. She laughed, and it was as if crystal drops tinkled on the soft morning breeze sweeping the decks.

The rogue laughed, a low, deep friendly laugh, before he doffed his battered brown hat and bowed, sweeping the deck with the thing as if it sported a red feather, cavalier fashion. "Jared Casey, at your service, but most folks call me Jared. Just Jared."

"Good morning—Just Jared."

"My Lord, you are a delightful young lady. Has anyone ever told this to you?" Jared almost frowned, his tongue was so twisted in the presence of the mysterious angel. He felt poetic again. "Mystery's angel. What is your name, might I be so rude as to ask.

130

You know mine. Still I don't know yours. What is it"—
he gave her his most charming male smile—"before I
fall to my knees and have to beg!"

"Mr. Casey, I will tell you. In time," Cassandra said.
"First, I wish to learn what it is you have to inform a
certain young lady of, when you return to Harper. I
heard you mention the name Miss St. James, sir. What
has she to do with your intentions? Could she possibly
be the one you mean to visit?"

"She . . . could be," he said. "But she is not
important at the moment, Miss—?"

She waggled a finger in his face. "Oh no, sir, not until
you tell me your business with Cassandra St. James."

"How did you know her first name?"

"I live in Harper myself, Mr. Casey and"—she
grinned impishly, "I know Cassandra very well. The St.
Jameses have only one daughter and we are closer than
you could ever realize, Mr. Casey."

"Well then—maybe you just can deliver my message," he said with deceptive casualness, as he had it in
mind to use any method he could to get to know this
angel better. To keep her conversing with him. To
charm her, as he had charmed hundreds of others
before her.

Cassandra was thoroughly intrigued now to learn his
message—one that was meant for herself!

As the sun warmed the decks so did it warm
Cassandra's spirits. She glanced at the folks promenad-
ing the deck, noticing the women's heads together,
whispering God only knew what. She did not care . . .
let them talk. The sunlit air washed over her. How fresh
it was! How free! How utterly grown-up to be standing
here conversing with a man of the world . . . without

Melantha exerting her haughty authority over her.

Her heart leaping into an accelerated beat, she watched the slow, roguish smile turn into a serious frown. "What is it? Can it be all that important?" she said excitedly.

"Ah, I might as well have you give this message to Miss St. James: Tell her that Sylvestre Diamond looks elsewhere than to her heart." Watching her sweet face sour a little at his words, he went on, unaware of the great damage he created with them. "He has roving eyes, miss, and she must also know that there is a woman aboard this boat who has already caught his eye this trip. I would be doing Miss St. James a great disservice, I believe, if I did not inform the young lady of his indiscretions."

Mild shock yielded quickly to mounting rage. She was so disappointed, doubly disappointed, she could hardly speak, but she finally managed to say something. "The truth of the matter is, Mr. Casey, the fact of Mr. Diamond's abominable behavior has already been brought to light—Cassandra knows."

Jared nodded. "Cassandra knows. Well"—he waved an arm in the air—"what has the young lady done about it? Don't tell me she continues to pine after the callous young man?"

"Oh no, sir—not any longer!"

He studied the glorious blue eyes. "You are a very passionate and charming creature, miss. I must have your name—now!"

"First you must tell me who the 'fortunate' one is who has caught Sylvestre Diamond's eye this time?"

"That is easy, for she has caught his eye before." He spoke for himself, employing his own behavior in place of Sy's. "She is Miki Rhea. You can find her playing—or gambling in the lounge."

She gasped. "With the *men?*"

"Of course. Miki Rhea is easy to find. She has red hair and she always wears pink."

"Pink? With r-red hair?" How awful, she thought. "Seriously?"

"Seriously. With this ah . . . lady, the effect of those two colors is spectacular."

"I—" Cassandra shook her own bright blond head. "I would have never thought—"

"Pink petticoats, too!" Jared winked slowly.

"Mr. Casey—how would you know tha—" Cassandra whirled embarrassedly from the man. Her cheeks flamed scarlet from what he had said. Discussing petticoats and such with Dulcie and Letty was one thing, but with a total stranger, far and away another!

Jared noticed that when she became excited or incensed, her glorious eyes changed hues of color. "Now, you lovely creature, may I have your name—?"

"Oh!!"

A sudden lurch of the deck threw Cassandra against the bulkhead. "What is happening—?" She gripped Jared Casey by his coat sleeves, and, up this close, Jared's roving gaze assessed the lovely face, the pink cupid-bow mouth, long, sweeping lashes, and blue, blue eyes. "There is trouble, Mr. Casey."

The man whose arms she was in breathed, "Don't I know it, Angel!"

Clang-clang-clang!! went the pilot's bell while excited voices and running feet mingled with the loud warning.

"Let's go see!" Jared cried, taking her by the arm.

133

From the deck below, Cassandra could now see her father and Sylvestre bursting into the pilothouse. "Let's get a closer look," Jared said.

"Not too close, Mr. Casey," she said, finally pulling away as he drew her to a place where they could see and hear everything. They were too close to Sylvestre and her father now and she did not wish to be seen in the company of Jared Casey. She knew her father would object very strongly.

"Don't be afraid, missy." Jared stood close to her. "I'll protect you from that lecherous Captain Sy."

Cassandra's breathing was quick as she heard Sylvestre and saw his face turn livid with anger. He was shouting at someone. "I told you it would be a mistake to be imbibing at the wheel. Look at you—you're three sheets to the wind! Damnit! You'll ground us!"

With a soft gasp, Cassandra continued to watch. She had never seen a man so angry, let alone Sylvestre Diamond. He had always seemed so easygoing and gentle, but he was not so kind and gentle now!

"Oh, yeah? Drunk or sober, I'm a better pilot'n you any time, Sylabester Dia-mine . . . er, hic!"

Swearing savagely, Sylvestre lurched forward and grabbed Willie Elmo by the shoulders. Monte stepped between the two and ordered Willie away from the wheel so that he himself could take over.

"Get 'way!" Willie yelled. "I'm doin' the pilotin' on this boat . . . I know what I'm doin'. I drove 'er into a bank to keep away from that snag. Don't try 'n tell me what to do, Cap'n Sy!"

Sylvestre again attempted to take the wheel, but Willie Elmo shoved him aside as the *River Minx* backed and slammed into the opposite bank. There was a loud "clunk" and then an even louder "bang!"

"Oh!" Cassandra was thrown off balance again as the whole cargo shifted and there was the thundering sound of rolling barrels, bawling cattle, strident chicken squawks, and shouts from passengers who had fled from their staterooms to see what the commotion was all about.

Sylvestre, regaining his balance after stumbling over an empty rum bottle, advanced upon the frenzied pilot Willie Elmo. "I mean to take the wheel now, Willie. Give it up peaceably or I shall have to lay you low, and you know I don't want to do that to a man in your inebriated condition."

"Hell no, you can't take this wheel. Now get out of my way!"

*Boom. Thud.* The *River Minx* scraped against the bank and then righted itself. "Elmo, I give you fair warning," said Sylvestre, and, when Willie only sneered in the dangerously handsome face, Sylvestre grabbed Willie by the scruff of the neck and flung him away from the wheel.

"You ain't gonna do that to Willie Elmo. I'm the best damned pilot on the Misery and Missipp!" He went for the pistol that bulged in his hip pocket.

In the same moment that Sylvestre leaped for the pistol, Cassandra screamed, afraid that someone might get shot. Sylvestre easily snatched the lethal weapon from Willie Elmo, and then shoved him into the burly arms of two roustabouts waiting to take Willie off to where he could sleep off the inebriants.

Having recognized his daughter's voice, Monte now yelled down to her. "Cassandra! Get back to your stateroom!"

135

"Cassandra?" Jared Casey, yet standing beside the delightful young blonde, looked at her and breathed again incredulously, *"Cassandra?"*

"Where . . . ? I do not see her," Cassandra said, still shaking from the rowdy scene she had just witnessed.

"Ahh," Jared breathed exultantly, feeling that he had been thoroughly duped by the charming minx at his side. "I know who you are now!"

"Do you—*really?*" she said to Jared Casey.

Giving him a saucy look, she whirled and headed straight for the dining room—not going to her stateroom as her father had ordered her.

Sylvestre narrowed his amber-darkened eyes as he went to take over the wheel. He scowled blackly, implacably. Murder, taking over every other emotion and feeling, rode him high as he maneuvered the once-again graceful *River Minx* back into the mainstream.

*Chapter Eight*

Port Gibson to Memphis to St. Louis, Natchez to New Orleans to Vicksburg . . . steamboat life in the 1840s had a swift, zestful tempo. Past the paddle-wheelers' decks swept a panorama of the South. Towns suddenly sprang up at the muddy river edges; cities aloft occasional breezeswept heights; quaint bobbing shanties. Tall houseboats. Low flatboats. Isolated huts perched on a shelf of land at the riverside. On board the paddlewheeler itself, above everything else—literally and otherwise—stood the pilot in the pilothouse. As the saying went, his post gave him the right to be arrogant to anybody on earth. Master of the fate of all on board, the pilot scanned the river, made decisions, snapped orders to the engineer and his helpers in their blazing quarters below. While the vessel moved, no one could countermand the pilot.

Sylvestre Diamond, at the moment, was a very busy man. There was not to be a second of time off, not until Willie Elmo slept off the demon rum and came fully to his senses.

For several hours following the incident in the pilothouse, Cassandra was immersed in watching the bubbling humanity pass by on the promenade deck. Some headed in a beeline in the direction of the saloon—despite the early afternoon hour.

With a riverswept breeze in her hair, Cassandra was lighthearted and gay after taking her delicious lunch of shrimp rémoulade and cherries Jubilee with her father, who strode his world like God's overseer on the river. Gay as she was, Cassandra could not keep from remembering that Sylvestre Diamond had been toying with her emotions. She was grimly determined to push the memory of the pleasurable moments in the garden from her mind. But she had to confess to herself that Sy's mesmerizing presence on the riverboat was most unnerving.

Cassandra had caught sight of Sylvestre earlier that day . . . for only a fleeting moment. He was all supple grace and strength. Tall, with the lean, muscular build of an athlete. His clothes appeared superbly tailored to fit his lean frame at all times. His trousers were snug—always—and the jacket she had seen him wearing just that morning emphasized broad shoulders and a slender waist. As usual, his black boots were highly polished. He only nodded to her and then went straightaway to his task. A myriad of emotions swept over her, but she was determined to maintain her reservoir of icy silence—just as he was determined to do the same.

Cassandra would so love to caress the strong, manly line of his jaw . . . run her fingers through his thick golden hair. But as she did not know directly of such things, she could only dream of them.

It seemed impossible that Sy could have treated her so tenderly and then simply avoided her as if she were not even alive. Sylvestre Diamond was a practiced rake, she now realized painfully, and she would never, but never allow herself to become just another silly female to add to his growing collection of conquests. She intended to put him out of her mind completely, but his abandonment of her had been driven like needles into her heart.

Cassandra now paused before a sign on a wooden door leading into a dimly lighted, smoke-filled room. She had never been to this part of the paddlewheeler, for Melantha had not allowed her access to every corner of the *River Minx*.

The sign read: "Gentlemen who play cards for money —play at their own risk!"

Monte had informed her that such warnings stopped no one, especially the men who worked with "Cappers" —bland-looking confederates who carried on elaborate performances during which one, then another lost as they baited the suckers on.

Cassandra walked on past the sign, then waved gaily as she saw her father talking with some passengers. Everyone listened to Monte St. James's advice, all, except, of course, certain "prized" customers among the river gentry who did their heavy shipping every season and neither beamed upon nor bowed before anyone on land or on the Big Muddy Rivers. Monte had lavished upon his daughter much information on the workings of the paddlewheeler and its captain. She had questioned him to the point of exhaustion and he had informed her that many vessels, including his own, would halt at nearly any point to drop off freight or pick it up, take on goods or passengers. Cassandra had seen for herself as folks, usually the slave of one who lived on a plantation nearby, would stand for hours and then, when the riverboat was sighted, signal with cloths or burning brands.

Monte St. James even performed shopping services for the wives of planters, and delivered purchases to the store—from a new gown prepared by a Royal Street shop to a set of chairs made to order in Memphis.

On board, passengers were divided into two classes: main deck and upper level. The first remained among the machinery, merchandise, flotsam and jetsam. The second class ascended the ornate branching stairway to the upper deck and private rooms that lined the sides—with their small outer walk and usually, at the end, a kind of southern porch in which they could catch a gentle breeze.

Here, Cassandra had lingered outside the night before and watched the moonlit splash of water under the paddle wheel which left a luminescent path in its wake. She hoped there would be a great midnight moon again, for she fully intended to stroll the decks once all the passengers were settled in their staterooms for the night.

For a moment Cassandra stopped to gaze upward toward the pilothouse. Jared Casey's blue eyes darkened as he watched Cassandra St. James from the end of the deck. As she gazed up, her eyes seemed large and expressive, dominating the fragile beauty of her little face. She was so dainty, perfection itself, and she reminded Jared of a French doll he had lifted from a chair in the parlor of a certain lady friend of his. He had taken the angel-haired doll into his hands to peep beneath the silk skirts while Lillian was out of the room seeing about refreshments. The legs of the doll were slender and shapely, encased in lovely, little white stockings and other ladies' unmentionables. All in all, that remarkable French creation could have been fashioned as a replica of the living, angelic doll Cassandra St. James.

Blond and shining in the afternoon of a fine Missouri day, Cassandra's hair was pulled back softly from her face with a lavender ribbon, the remainder of the glorious mass allowed to fall in a mantle of snow-blond against her back. Earlier, she had found Goliath among the roustabouts, having no idea that he had been watching her, carefully, so as not to arouse suspicion. Monte looked up at his daughter once again, then went to meet with some new customers in the lounge. He had not wished for Cassandra to learn that her own father had set the huge black to guard his daughter from any rowdies that might be aboard.

Monte waved at his daughter and she waved back.

Cassandra spun about, feeling the magical day coming to a close. She could already see hints of pink and mauve pastels in the sky where the sun was lowering. There would be a lavender sunset this evening. And then the moon . . . the mellow, languorous moon would come out to sail above the winding river to dress it in crystal robes for the night.

*       *       *

141

The moon indeed made a majestic appearance, but later than usual, to spread a delicate coating of moondust all over the river, the paddlewheeler, and its midnight strollers on deck—which were only a few in number. In fact, only two at the moment took air outside the doors of the *River Minx*.

One was Sylvestre.

The other was Cassandra.

Drawn like a moth to a bright candle, Sylvestre left the hurricane deck after he had tossed a cheroot into the water—a smoke he'd only just lighted—and made his way to the beacon that had beckoned him only moments before.

Daring much, Cassandra had donned a pink-and-mauve gown. When she walked, her skirt rustled over her petticoats. The gown was a delightful creation that had once belonged to a southern belle and, thanks to Goliath, who had earlier brought her trunk to her stateroom upon request, she was now able to wear it. Although the gown displayed a goodly amount of flesh above the plunging neckline, she felt at ease in it out here where no one could observe her reckless daring.

As soon as she heard the soft footsteps behind her, Cassandra splayed a hand over her chest, not daring to turn about to see who was there right behind her. But she had a good idea who it was, and her heart beat a rapid tattoo and prickles of apprehension played along her spine. Sylvestre's voice seemed to come with the gentle whisper of the night breeze, as if the wind had brought him to her side. She had been dreaming of him, though a bit reluctantly—and now he was here.

"It is quite late, *chère mademoiselle*. Are you not

afraid you will catch a chill?"

"I am afraid of nothing, monsieur."

"Then"—his voice deepened as he fixed his glance on the awkward positioning of her arm—"apparently you are trying to keep warm?"

Cassandra tipped her head, looking at his dark frame over her shoulder. "I am . . . not." With a deep swallow, she bravely allowed her hand to fall to her side. "It is just a little indigestion, I think." Which was true, for suddenly her stomach was tied in hundreds of little knots!

"I could have some chamomile tea sent to your stateroom. Would you like that?"

"Oh, yes!" she exclaimed too quickly. If she turned about, she would have to hide her chest again. Cassandra almost moaned aloud at her distress.

*Oh, why am I being such a ninny! Surely a man like Sylvestre has seen a bit of breast before!*

"Now?" His eyes narrowed, burning her with a gold flame.

"Oh . . ." Cassandra faltered, then went on. "I will linger for a little longer here on deck to watch the river. It is very beautiful at night, with the silver moon dappling the water—"

"The frothy path stretching out behind," Sylvestre finished for her, having read the lines somewhere himself.

Eyeing her suspiciously, Sylvestre moved to stand beside Cassandra, hitching a booted heel on a lower rung and leaning his forearms upon the railing. His gaze fell, noting that her right hand was flattened against her chest again. "It must be bad." He indicated

143

the afflicted spot with a nod of his golden head, his dark lashes sweeping low over his eyes. "Does it ache very much?"

Cassandra all but choked on her next words. "It is worse . . . than ever." *True . . . true!*

"Perhaps I should help you to your stateroom. If you lie down, that might relieve some of the pressure of that bubble in your chest. Here, give me your arm."

"Oh, no . . . not that one!" Cassandra cried when he reached for her right arm.

But it was too late—he had already taken her hand from her chest.

"My God, Cassa." His eyes flared for a moment, then lowered. "Where did you get such a gown? You are all but spilling out of it!"

Clutching the railing with a white-knuckled hand, Cassandra wished a hole could open in the deck and wash her out into the river. She was embarrassed again—no, mortified! Humiliated! Chagrined! And vexed, all in the same package!

"How dare you mention such a delicate thing . . . subject, monsieur!"

She knew she was stammering and hesitating like a stupid schoolgirl again. Oh, why did Sylvestre Diamond cause her to feel so young and vulnerable!!

*"Au contraire,* Cassandra, you are most beautiful and womanly. I did not wish to place you in such an embarrassing situation again." He laughed lightly. "Although it must seem to you I am always doing just that. I apologize. Will you accept?"

*He is so virile, so charming, he could seduce the moon from the sky and the stars would never notice!*

144

Sylvestre tried not to chuckle as he asked, "How is your stomachache now, *petit chou?*"

"What does that mean—*petit chou?* I have never heard you employ that French word in our conversations, Sy."

The man whose heart Cassandra held in her small white hands answered on a shaky note. "It means— *sweetheart.*"

"Oh. I like the sound of most French words, but those two combined are very nice indeed."

*Sy! Golden Sy! Please go away, for I do not want you to hurt me!*

"Excuse me. Did you say something?" Sylvestre asked Cassandra, feeling a velvet arrow of warmth inside.

"Why did you not return to my home, Sylvestre?" Cassandra blurted; then emboldened, went on further. "I watched for you. I prayed you would return . . ." she left off.

Moving closer, Sylvestre closed warm fingers over a dainty wrist and applied gentle pressure. "I did not know how badly you wanted me to return, Cassa. Had I known, believe me, I would have come on wings" was the whispered response.

Breath, warm as semitropical wind, fell against Cassandra's cheeks and his male scent invaded her nostrils. "I could slay a few dragons for you, Cassa, if you would allow me to."

Rigidly Cassandra stepped a foot away. "Do you say that to *all* your *petits choux,* Sylvestre Diamond?" She kept her chin pointed straight ahead so that he could not detect the sparkle of silver-hued tears in her eyes . . . the glitter of freshly awakened desire. "I have reason to believe you do. Like the buxom tavern wench on Water Street, to name only one?"

In the back of Sylvestre's mind a warning bell sounded but he paid it no heed.

"Dolly McKay?" He laughed shortly. "You surely jest, Cassandra. That calculating wench who sought to insinuate herself into my life with her willing body? Hardly, Cassa. And how do you know about *that?* You were safely tucked in your bed while—"

"Was I?"

"Cassandra." Sylvestre's eyes fell to her throat, and below, where it was creamy white and smooth. My God, she was tempting him mindless! "Cassa, how would you know about such things?"

He ached to hold her, kiss her, touch her.

"I have had women, Cassa, but it was nothing lasting, nothing you would call permanent." He gave a Gallic shrug. "I am only a man . . . the others did not matter to me, *ma petite.*"

"Did they not?" She could not believe a word he spoke. She moved away from the searing brand of his eyes. He was tempting her . . . and she was not going to be willing, as the others who had gone before her. "I think perhaps *all* females matter to you, Sylvestre Diamond."

"Cassandra, I cannot believe this is you." With a small grin, he moved to take her hand. "Why, you are trembling." Then, "Can I hope that you are jealous, just a little bit?"

She stared ahead, unblinkingly.

Sylvestre could not tell Cassandra, his darling,

innocent Cassa, of all the frustrated discontent with the empty-eyed women who had filled his life until this past year. Even as a young teenager he had been helplessly drawn to Cassa, the memory of her ever refusing to vacate his mind. Now his brain spun and he gazed to the diamond-studded waters, staring back in time . . .

"How old are you?" he had asked the little girl who had just come to his mother's plantation.

"I am five!" The girl-child popped up four fingers, then another. "How old are *you?*"

"Fifteen . . . ten years older than you."

"Is that a lot?" the childish voice asked, the girl flipping white-blond hair, done up in a fat silky braid, over her shoulder.

"Quite a few years older, Cassa." She had been "Cassa" to him from the first.

"But I am not a baby," she had said firmly, huge blue eyes daring him to contradict what must have been to her a very intelligent statement.

"No, you are not. I can see that."

"Are we going to be friends, Sir Diamond?"

"Forever, Cassa."

She had shown him a pixyish grin before she bounded off to scatter the chickens and the geese residing on the grounds of Diamondhead Plantation . . .

"Are we still friends?" he asked her now with a low murmur, smiling down at her. His eyes remained on her bent head, and the beauty of Cassandra in moonglow fired the passion in his enchained heart.

"Please do not watch me like that, monsieur."

"I am sorry, Cassa. It has become a habit." His golden eyes wandered over her soft, flushed face when she looked up at him, surprise registering in her eyes. "You did not realize that, did you?"

"How long have you been watching me, Sy? For weeks? Months?"

"Years," he answered the question burning in her mind.

It was as if time slipped into a standstill around them now, and the silence seemed to go on forever.

A low-hanging mist swirled, mesmerizing for a moment.

"J-just because I once believed you to be my knight in shining armor, do not become pleased with yourself to think I am still stupid enough to moon over you, Sylvestre Diamond."

Suddenly the golden eyes flashed, and Sylvestre felt the fire of anger throbbing within.

As she could not see the intensity of his emotion, only the peculiar expression washing over his darkened features, Cassandra was totally unprepared for what happened next.

Reaching out, he took hold of her shoulders, and when he pulled her tightly against him, Cassandra became paralyzed with fear. Strange feelings were tugging at her heart.

"I am not fashioned of stone, despite the fact that you seem to believe I am. When you were a child, I allowed you to get away with anything short of murder."

"What?" She watched as a pensive look furrowed his brow. "I do not understand what you are saying."

"I will elaborate. You are not that little girl in pinafored apron any longer. We are both thirteen years older, but do not for a moment think you are immune to me."

"How dare you!"

Cassandra struggled to be free of his imprisoning grasp, but he held on to her all that much tighter. She felt her cheeks grow hot as she realized what he was going to do.

"Don't pull away from me, Cassa."

His eyes flashing wildly, he held one of her small hands tightly in his and, bringing the closed pair of hands between their pounding chests, he tipped her chin up, merely brushing his lips against hers.

"Please, Sy, don't—"

"Why not? You like it as much as I."

When his hand dropped hers and slid around to her back, Cassandra's heartbeat accelerated as she felt the muscular tension in his legs, hips, and thighs. "You have got . . . nerve. I told you—"

"You let me hold you once. Don't you remember, Cassa?"

She shook her head because she couldn't trust her voice.

"I love your hair like this," he murmured huskily. "It is very womanly."

"Sylvestre . . . please do not—"

"And I love the gown. It is not befitting a virgin, but it makes you all the more interesting, Cassa."

The color in Cassandra's cheeks was high, and she ground her teeth together to keep from slapping him. He was so close that she could smell the manly scent of him and she wondered how it would feel to press her lips to his—of her own accord—for a thrilling kiss and give herself in wild abandon.

"Should you not return to the pilothouse?" she asked, a tremulous note in her voice.

"I would prefer to remain here—" His voice went even deeper as he bent his golden head again. "With you, Cassa."

"The engines are hungry for fuel, Sylvestre. Do you not have to wood up?"

"The main-deck passengers help with that, for they have a special service to fulfill—you must know that, Cassa. Engines are indeed hungry for fuel and usually twice every twenty-four hours the vessel stops at a point at which woodchoppers have large stores ready—"

"And men jump out, work swiftly by early-morning light or in the glare of bonfires"—she reported softly, thinking of her father—"while the captain frets over the minutes lost."

Sylvestre took up where she left off. "The second the *Minx* has had her last piece dragged on—or even before that—the boat rolls away."

"Yes, I recall it all now," Cassandra softly announced.

Cassandra realized that she was defenseless against Sy's superior strength. Overhead the stars were hundreds of sparkling diamonds and the moon was a breathless orb of yellow gold as Cassandra felt Sy come near, his lips close over hers in the first full kiss they had ever shared.

Cassandra had always wondered what this moment would be like. Allowing her tense muscles to relax little by little, she finally experienced the provocative feeling

150

of her breasts pressed against the strong, warm, vibrant wall of his chest.

Wonderful, frightening, expanding sensations began to gather in her breasts and lower region as, gloriously, with abandon, Sy's kiss sang like a fever through her veins. Her dusky lashes lowered and then closed over her creamy cheekbones.

Soft moonlight flowed over them. Sylvestre held Cassandra, willing the heat of his body to soothe her, warm her until the trembling in her untaught body ceased and he felt the treasure of her yielding.

He moved his mouth gently over hers, savoring her honey, devouring the velvet softness of her lips, and it was a penetrating sweetness that turned him inside out. He seemed to be drowning in sensations and he couldn't get enough of her sweet nectar and his mind repeated the aching words over and over in his brain:

*I love you.*

It was as if she had heard his words, and Cassandra did not hear her own low, answering moan, which revealed a need that she had not known existed.

"Do not be afraid of me. I am not going to hurt you, Cassandra." He moved to kiss the top of her head. "Trust me, *chérie.*"

Trying to calm his labored breathing, his mouth returned and slanted crushingly across hers. Cassandra felt as if she were being transported to heaven on silver-tipped wings. The moon, river, and the Milky Way of stars spun around her. She was enveloped in a downy cloud of sensation, coming alive beneath a man's kiss and gentle caress for the first time in her life.

"My God, woman," Sy whispered huskily as her slim

arm curled about his neck trustingly, drawing a deep groan from his throat. His eyes opened, dancing over her face, studying, memorizing every dainty contour of her moonlit face. There was a triumphant smile on his lips and he wanted her to feel his hard and muscular frame pressing intimately to hers. He was breathing hard, he knew, and he had no wish to frighten her with his mounting urgency.

Sylvestre's heart sang with joy, for he knew that Cassandra had never experienced this moment with another man before him.

Degree by slow degree, her lips yielded and opened beneath his tutelage until his tongue found free access to the petal-softness within her mouth. His probing flesh expertly teased, devoured, and titillated, his magic touch filling Cassandra with a euphoria she could not have believed possible. She had lost the battle of mind over body.

A deliciously slow sweep of movement brought his hand to her breast and ignited little explosions deep within her young, inexperienced body, sending vivid shock feelers to the nubs of her breasts, warming her like liquid honey gold.

"Sweet," he whispered against her mouth, nipping at her open, pleading lips. "I have to have more of you than this. Do you know what I am saying, Cassa?" He wanted to lie with her, to feel her beneath him, if only just to hold this lovely virgin who had known no man's caress before his enflamed one.

Cassandra moaned against Sy's mouth. "Oh, monsieur . . . monsieur!"

"*Sy*, darling, call me Sy, just as you did when you

were the enchanting child who captured my young heart." Gently he lifted her into his arms and spun her about while he continued to lazily stroke her sweet-nectared lips. "I love your sighs of pleasure, Cassa, and how you come alive under my caress. When will you be mine, *ma chérie*. "When?"

"I am afraid, Sylvestre!"

"Oh, my darling, what are you afraid of?" He let her down on her feet once again. "I shall never force you to do anything we both do not agree upon. You are trembling, Cassa. Please do not be afraid. I am on fire for you, and you are on fire for me."

Cassandra's breath caught as she faced Sylvestre once again, the moonspun night and Sy's presence sending spiraling pleasures through the delicate elegance of her body, causing her heart to hammer against her ribs.

In the moon's glow, there was something lazily seductive about the smile he was trying to hide as he said, "I have something for you I think you will like."

Cassandra endeavored to catch her breath as his eyes reflected glimmers of moonlight. "What is it?" she asked, not trusting her voice to quaver.

"This is for you."

From his buff vest pocket, Sylvestre pulled out an object that shone dully in the light of the moon. "Do you not remember what special occasion warrants this gift?" he asked huskily.

"I am not sure . . ." Cassandra said, her heart beating a rapid dance in her breast. "Oh," she breathed as he held up a delicate chain with a gold cross dangling from it.

"It is beautiful," she gasped, taking it from his outstretched hand. "But why—?"

"Do you not recall that today is your birthday?"

"Oh" was all she said, disappointed that her father had not remembered.

"I am sorry, Cassandra. I realize where your thoughts are." Sighing deeply, regretfully, he said, "Monte has been very busy, but I am quite certain he will remember, and when he does, I believe there will be a nice celebration on board the *Minx*."

"Oh, do you think so, Sylvestre?"

Suddenly, following the intimacy they had just shared, Cassandra was terribly shy. Realizing her discomfort, Sylvestre sought to put her at ease, snatching her against him in a hug that was both gentle and fierce. Letting her go, he took the birthday gift and, turning her about, he fastened it at the nape of her neck, then, kissing her cheek most tenderly, he said, "Good night, birthday girl." He backed away from her. "Never forget this night and that you are in my heart. Forever."

"Good night . . . Sy."

Cassandra watched him walk into the dark of the moon, feeling as if her heart was breaking in two parts.


Once inside her stateroom, Cassandra heaved a weary sigh and lay down on the bed, still dressed in the pastel gown. Rolling over onto her back, she stared at the swinging lamp and at the design the mellow light cast over the embroidered lace curtains. Holding the dangling cross above her face, she thought of the way Sylvestre's kiss had dominated and controlled her mouth. The thrilling kisses would always be imprinted in her soul as the most wonderful sensation she could ever have imagined. Her lips still felt bruised and her body still trembled with a virginal heat.

What a wonderful, sweet night . . . She closed her eyes and carried its tapestry of memories off with her into the elusive whispering shadows of her aching dreams . . . And slept, dreaming of a faceless knight in shining silver armor . . . a knight astride a cantering, moon-gold horse. The fine gold cross was clutched in her hand over her beating heart.

## Chapter Nine

The dress Cassandra wore to dinner that evening had the colors of radiant autumn leaves. She had stitched on the creation all day, until the tips of her fingers were red and ached. The *River Minx* had made numerous stops at the Missouri river towns to unload some wares, but she hardly noticed, for the gown had kept her so busy she barely had time to stop, even for lunch. All she had eaten, in fact, were some Creole macaroons and a milk punch.

Digging in her arched trunk, Cassandra had come up with a gown she and Letty had worked on for hours one night, Letty seated in the comfortable, deep-cushioned chair that occupied a corner of her bedroom, Cassandra in the middle of the bed, and the dim lanternlight between them. In the lantern's spinning shadows, Dulcie had been sound asleep on the fluffy hearth rug in front of Cassandra's . . . actually, it was *Melantha's* wide Italian marble fireplace. Cassandra felt that nothing, not even her bed, truly belonged to just her and her alone in the Harper house. *Melantha's house,* she had always thought of it.

Today she had finally finished work on the rust, scarlet, and ocher-yellow gown. It was predominately red silk, with the fall of a wide bertha collar in cream encircling her bare shoulders, the rest in narrow rust-and-yellow stripes. She had taken an old pair of shoes apart, and with the help of Bernie, the shoemaker who made the trip to St. Louis twice a year, she had covered the shoes with the red silk she had had left over from altering the gown to fit her dainty frame.

The dining room of the *River Minx* seemed to Cassandra that night, like an enchanted crystal cathedral lit up with magic lanterns. The high-pitched ring of crystal touching crystal was heard as passengers drank toasts to success in the Mexican venture and to, generally, a good time aboard the *Minx.*

The ladies were wrapped in dazzling gowns of taffeta, gold brocade, and jewel colors of velvet that cascaded in soft folds from their pinched-in, or sucked-in, tiny waists. Cassandra's own waist needed no corset and she moved about comfortably, with youthful, natural grace.

Over the immaculate white-draped tables, the crystal chandeliers trembled, gently swaying like clusters of dewdrops, rainbow prismed, and catching the soft glow from the maze of silverware and fine china settings.

Cassandra looked around the room again, wondering which of the many spinsterish women was the Erica Barrett her father had told her about. To her delight, Cassandra saw that she'd overlooked a lovely auburn-haired woman sitting alone at a table. Could this be the woman her father intended for her chaperone? She

158

would be happy if this was so, for the woman was pretty, if not a bit overdressed for dining.

As Cassandra approached the young woman, she thought how delightful it would be to have a woman just a little older than herself to spend some time with, to talk about the latest fashions and whatever else interested them.

Now that Cassandra was closer to her, she noticed that her hair was truly a sunlit red . . . and that she was wearing a bright pink velvet dress trimmed with black satin. Pink petticoats peeped from beneath her skirt. One would not think of wearing pink with red hair, but on this woman the effect was quite spectacular. *Where had she heard those very words of compliment before, having to do with a red-haired woman?*

Miki Rhea glanced up at the lovely young woman who just stepped up to her table, and she slanted long and sooty lashes, her green eyes like summer grass, knowing at once who the lovely blonde was. "Can I help you, Miss St. James?" Miki Rhea drawled.

Cassandra blinked slowly. She had never heard such a deep, throaty voice coming from a woman before, and though she was breathtakingly pretty, she was not as young as Cassandra had first thought. "Are you by any chance Erica Barrett?"

Almost choking on the red wine she was sipping, Miki Rhea said with a sharp laugh, "Hardly!" She raised her lashes and shot a resentful look at Cassandra.

"I am sorry, please excuse me, but—" Cassandra thought for a moment, and considered the woman's rough manner of speech and garishly moded clothes. "Well then, you must be an actress or perhaps an

159

entertainer of some sort?"

Cassandra heard a loud gasp and turned to see a pert, gray-haired lady who had dropped her spoon back into the shrimp Creole soup she had just ladled up to her mouth. Another woman at the next table crooked her finger at Cassandra, insisting she come and sit with them.

Wonderingly, Cassandra looked from the gaping women to the gorgeous redhead. What was wrong? Why were the women beckoning her over? For some reason, Cassandra sensed they did not wish her to talk with this woman.

The redhead turned to the women adjacent to her table, smiled with a crooked twist to her full red lips, then rose gracefully from the table. "You want to know what I do, honey?" she asked the delicate, unworldly blonde. "I'll tell you. I market a commodity which those scrawny hens over there never had," she purred and then, in a whirl of cherry-pink skirts, she walked out without a backward glance, a dull, throaty laugh falling behind her.

Cassandra pursed her rosebud mouth. Nobody had to inform her as to what that woman was—or did with her lush body. But that laugh, oh, Lord, there was a laugh any man would follow to the ends of the world.

"Come, come, dear," the woman at the next table clucked. "Sit down, Miss St. James, and please join us. We see your father has not come in yet. We'd love to have you with us for a spell."

"Lord, what a lovely gown you have on, dear!"

"Indeed, have you ever seen such a delightful creation?"

"Where in the world did you come by such a gown?

160

Could you tell us who your dressmaker is, dear?"

Cassandra asked a question of her own first. "Can someone tell me who that woman in the pink is? I believe this is the first time I have laid eyes on her."

"Oh! The nerve of her!" tsk-tsked the woman with silver hair, very few strands of it. "That Miki Rhea . . . Never mind what she says, dear. You must never, I say *never,* believe anything she tells you."

"Like what?" Cassandra asked, blinking innocently and folding her dainty hands in her lap.

"She's a strumpet!" hissed a tiny, stooped-over lady with several strands of pearls wound about her wrinkled throat.

"Did you see those fancy skirts and frizzed hair? Did it with one of those curling irons, I tell you. Ain't natural, it ain't. Not even the color, I'd wager."

"She is quite pretty, though," Cassandra said to the clucking gossipers.

"Ha! Pretty on the outside, dear—and carnal on the inside. You are very wrong to call such a one as her 'pretty,' dear."

"She's correct. You'll understand when you're older, sweetheart."

*"Uhm-humm."*

All the women agreed, nodding their gray and silver heads in unison and peering down at the soup spoons they had taken up again, dipping forward, then back a little as they daintily sucked the soup. All together they froze, too, when Cassandra spoke to them again, asking where she might find Erica Barrett.

"Oh, Erica. She *is* a dear. You'll find *Miss* Barrett in the corner, where the mirrors line the walls." The elderly woman hoisted her grand nose in the air. "Erica

161

always sits alone." She sniffed haughtily. *"Always."*

"Wait, dear!" One of the spinsters grabbed Cassandra's slim wrist. "Will you please be a love and tell us who your seamstress is?"

"Yes—oh please, *please do."*

Cassandra felt thrilled to be able to tell them. "Yes, ladies, I do all my own sewing and altering. This gown, in fact, was quite plain before I made all the changes and lowered the bodice."

"Love it! Simply divine!"

"And"—one woman giggled beneath a gnarled hand—"a little daring, too, if I say so myself!"

"Look at this . . ." the silver-haired lady announced. "I have a tear in the bodice of this fine royal velvet. I have tried so to do something to hide it. This happens to be my very favorite dining gown. Do you think you could do something, dear? Add a bit of material?" Tittering under her hand, she said, "Perhaps you can even, ah . . . drop the bodice?"

"Oh, Millicent, how could you even think of doing such a thing? You are no longer a spring chicken, you know."

"Catherine, hush your mouth. I'm not planning to make myself up like some strumpet, you must understand. Not like that tramp, Miki Rhea, with her flaming red hair. It would only be an inch, anyway, that Miss St. James would drop the bodice."

All of them spoke at once then, requesting she do this and that to alter their many day dresses and gowns. "Yes, yes, ladies." Cassandra held up her hand to halt their loud chattering that must be carrying all around the dining room. "I will take care of all you ladies, if you just give me the chance."

162

"Oh! I'm first!" Millicent jumped up and down. "I'm first. I've got a magenta gown that needs something . . . like a wide bertha? How does that sound?"

"And I've a plum velvet that needs to be taken out at the seams," Seraphina Landers said with much excitement.

"Excuse me," Cassandra said as gently as possible under the circumstances. "I will take you ladies one by one. Just come to my stateroom and I will see what can be done."

"We'll pay well, you know."

"How long do you think it would take for you to make me a new gown, Miss St. James?"

Cassandra waved over her shoulder as she departed from their noisy table. "Tomorrow" was all she said, holding a yellow lace shawl over her shoulders loosely. It draped down midway in back, a feminine bit of material that the matrons eyed covetously as the blonde made her way across the room.

"Well, well, if it isn't Miss St. James," Jared Casey said cheerfully, eyeing her up and down with a lascivious leer before she turned his way. He swaggered over to her, his deep blue eyes twinkling with mischief.

"Mr. Casey. How are you?" Cassandra said graciously, feeling womanly and beautiful when his dark eyes swept over her appreciatively as if she were the only female alive on God's earth.

"I'm fine, Angel. However, I've missed you. Where have you been hiding your beautiful self?" His eyes were drawn to the soft swell of flesh above the low cut of her scarlet bodice.

Her nostrils quivered at the strong smell of alcohol, telling her Jared Casey had been imbibing quite

163

heavily this evening. It would be rude of her to walk off and leave Mr. Casey standing there looking affronted, but Cassandra was in a hurry to find the woman her father had intended for her chaperone and make her acquaintance. Besides, Mr. Casey always made her feel nervous. He always looked as if he were about to swoop her up into his arms and kiss her most thoroughly.

"Your gown is most becoming, Cassandra. The yellow in it matches the gold threads woven into your own silver-blond hair."

Cassandra laughed, looking around the room in hopes that her father and Miss Barrett would come to her rescue. "My hair is not silver yet, Mr. Casey. Melantha calls it snow-blond."

At the mention of Melantha St. James, Jared squashed a shiver of repulsion. Melantha and Cassandra were as different as black and white. Now that he had met the woman's delightful daughter, he could see why the vain, domineering Melantha was jealous. Then again, from the little he knew of mother-daughter relationships, there was something that told him the female parent had no right being jealous of her own flesh and blood. It just wasn't what one felt for one's own beautiful and charming daughter.

"All right, Angel. Snow-blond." He shrugged. "If you say so, then it's true. I would believe anything you told me, even if you said there was snow in California."

"There is indeed at times, Mr. Casey. It has been known to snow there, in many parts of California."

"You are not only lovely, graceful, and charming. But you are also witty and intelligent."

"My mother does not share that same view, Mr.

164

Casey. She believes me to be an untalented child with no ability to converse on worldly subjects, like the Mexican War, for instance."

"I was in the war."

"Were you?"

"Yes indeed. Would you like to hear about it sometime?"

"Sometime, yes. But not now. You see, I have to make the acquaintance of a certain Miss Erica Barrett just now."

"Well then, I shall steer you in her direction. Oh, dear, I am sorry, Miss St. James, but Miss Barrett has already left her table. Shall I walk you to her stateroom?"

"I do not think that would be proper, Mr. Casey."

"Please, not so formal, my sweet. I've asked you to call me by my first name."

"Yes, I know you have. But I have thought it over, Mr. Casey, and it is not what a young woman should do—call a man by his first name when she hardly knows him and has not been formally introduced."

"Bah! I suppose Melantha filled your pretty head with such nonsense?"

Cassandra's head snapped up. "Why, Mr. Casey, you speak as if you knew my mother personally."

"What?" Jared's dark eyebrow rose in mock innocence.

"You did not say Mrs. St. James. You said Melantha."

Her eyes seemed to blaze with a blue fire then as she happened to glance across the room and see Sylvestre standing there, speaking with Miki Rhea just outside the doors. She believed he had not noticed her standing

165

there with Jared Casey just yet. Miki Rhea was tugging on Sylvestre's black sleeve. "Do they know each other that well?" Cassandra wondered out loud. She was not sure she wanted to know, but the blurted question had left her lips before she could bite it back.

"Remember I told you there was a woman on board who had caught Sylvestre's eye? Again?"

Cassandra could only nod.

"Well, that's Miki Rhea. The gossip is that he is trying to win her back after a long estrangement. They had been lovers for quite some time," Jared fabricated. Actually, he was telling her his own story, with one exception: Miki Rhea did not interest him all that much now that this charming angel had come aboard the *Minx*.

"That is not the kind of news I wish to hear, Mr. Casey."

"They make a nice couple," Jared drove the knife deeper. "Quite attractive together, wouldn't you say?"

"Good evening, Mr. Casey." Cassandra brushed past him. "I am returning to my stateroom . . ." Then it struck her. This was what she had been planning from the first, to make Sylvestre jealous. Then she moaned inwardly. She could never hope to compete with the flashy, worldly Miki Rhea, a woman who obviously knew just how to please a man in every way a man wanted to be pleased.

Before reaching the doors, Cassandra whirled about and put her back to them. Miki Rhea had spotted her coming toward them, and Cassandra had no wish to stop and chat with them at the moment. Not when her heart was breaking into pieces. Just when she had thought Sylvestre could possibly be falling in love with

166

her, Jared Casey had to come along and let her in on the ugly secret that the couple had once been in love.

Jared had followed Cassandra and, slowly now, he came to stand beside her. "What is the matter, Angel? You look a bit put off . . .or love-smitten?" He shrugged languidly. "I can't decide which."

The happiness over the enchanted evening melted in Cassandra's translucent eyes. Everything had been going smoothly. In her heart, she had forgiven Sylvestre for all the other women and had gladly accepted his gift of the gold cross. She had even meant to wear the cross, but at the last minute she had taken it off, feeling a wave of premonition at the time. Now, even the happiness she had experienced over obtaining her first customers that evening paled in significance.

Turning her misted gaze on Jared Casey, Cassandra smiled, forcing her gaiety. "I will take that walk with you now, Mr. Casey. You did tell me you knew which stateroom was Erica Barrett's?"

"Yes." He beamed, taking her arm and placing it in the crook of his. "Yes, I most certainly did."

First loves were not easily forgotten, but Cassandra was determined to put Sylvestre Diamond from her mind and from her heart. For good this time!

Sylvestre felt Cassandra's presence even before he saw her walking with Jared Casey, her arm tucked into his. Anger and jealousy stabbed him like a painful knife thrust into his chest. A bitter laugh escaped his lips as he watched Cassandra lift her blond head and smile at something Jared Casey had said to her.

"What's so amusing, Captain Sy?" Miki Rhea questioned with a deep purr to her voice.

"Hardly amusing," he snorted, clenching his hands

167

at his sides.

"You have been acting strangely since that lovely little piece came on board, Captain Sy." Miki Rhea swept her gaze over the couple walking past them as if they did not exist. Her eyes narrowed hatefully over the blond beauty and Casey—the only man she had ever cared for. "God, don't tell me you have eyes for her, too. With Casey it will only be a passing flirtation, but with you, Captain Sy, I wonder if it ain't more serious than that?"

"Excuse me, Miki Rhea. I have to return to the pilothouse and make sure Willie Elmo is doing his job and not nipping at the bottle."

Miki Rhea called after him, pausing at the railing to look down at the moonlit water and purposely making her voice loud enough to carry to the couple just down the way. "Maybe we can get together later, huh, darlin'." It was made to sound not like a question but a rendezvous they had earlier discussed.

Going in the opposite direction, Sylvestre gritted his teeth in frustration and anger. He foresaw all too clearly losing Cassandra to another man before he'd even begun to show her the extent of his love. He could not imagine a future without Cassandra at his side. So, he thought, he would need to act quickly and expertly before Cassandra lost all her maidenly inhibitions to another.

Before Sylvestre strode in the opposite direction, Cassandra had felt his gaze riveted to their backs. Jared had been telling her about New Orleans—a place she had never visited—and she had laughed gaily, slanting

168

her lashes when Jared had bent his handsome head to hers.

"Is the old French part of New Orleans anything like the American side?" she asked Jared, forcing herself to seem interested in the crescent city.

"The parts bear no resemblance to each other. The houses in the French Quarter are plain but dignified."

"Dignified?" Cassandra inquired with rippling laughter, knowing her voice carried and Sylvestre was still watching, for she could see in her side vision the dark clothing which fit the tall frame like a black glove. Feeling vastly cheered by the thought that the golden Sy was studying her closely, she pretended to be alive and inquisitive to everything Mr. Casey was telling her.

"The houses are all plastered on the outside and just about all of them have long black iron-railed verandas that run along the several stories. Their real beauty lies in the deep, warm, different-shaded stains of color. Time and weather have enriched the plaster until it harmonizes with all the surroundings."

For a moment Cassandra envisioned Old New Orleans, picturing the houses in her mind's eye. She could see a delicate cobweb pattern of baffling, intricate forms wrought in steel, and brilliant gardens alive with orange trees and blossomy shrubs. She could almost smell the pecan pralines baking, and wondered if they could compare to the ones Letty baked up the first Saturday each month. Someday she would love to go there with someone . . . someone she could love . . . someone who could love her.

". . . In the cemeteries lie the ashes of the early pirates," Jared was saying.

Cassandra nodded, smiling. But she was staring

unseeingly into the midnight blue of the enchanting river.

Jared kept talking, mesmerized by the beauty of the dainty, ethereal woman beside him, and he was so caught up in thoughts of seducing her that he did not feel her stiffen beside him. While he continued to verbally illustrate New Orleans for her, he began to dream of the pleasures that awaited him in the near future with Cassandra as his bride.

Cassandra had indeed stiffened. In his mention of pirates, Jared had painfully but unwittingly reminded her that Sylvestre bore the Indian blood of his ancestors, had a deceased grandfather who had consorted with the pirates of Barataria and mated with a white woman, mingling his blood with hers and carrying his own Choctaw blood down through the generations. With a deep suffusion of a flush staining her cheeks, Cassandra wondered how Sylvestre's children would look. She could picture a dark-haired, dark-eyed girl wih creamy olive complexion, an exotic pixie who would be called Jennifer . . . Cassandra shook herself from her perplexing and troubling mind-wanderings.

"Did you say something, Mr. Casey?" Cassandra caught a glimpse across her shoulder of Sylvestre just striding along the gallery, making his way, no doubt, to the pilothouse. "I am afraid I was not listening."

"There you are!"

Turning about at the sound of her father's voice, Cassandra's eyes met the dainty brunette walking with him. She was exceptionally pretty, no, "lovely" was the word. Her eyes were hazel, the green in them predominant, and they stared straight into Cassandra's

170

after they had looked her over with a graceful sweep of brown lashes. She held out her small, dainty hand, which was white-gloved and moved like a butterfly.

"Good evening, Miss St. James," she greeted after Monte had made the introductions.

"It is a pleasure to meet you, Miss Barrett," Cassandra said, delighted to find that Erica Barrett was nothing at all like the flashy Miki Rhea. At once, she cast aside the thought of that one meeting Sylvestre later on the moonlit deck, the two of them alone . . . clutched in a hot embrace.

"Shall we go in to dinner?" Erica said, then dipped her slightly graying head as if embarrassed. "I am sorry, Miss St. James. Have you dined yet?"

"No," Cassandra said, unaware that Jared Casey was eyeing Miss Barrett as if he would like to toss her overboard. "Suddenly I find that I am quite famished." Cassandra hoped she was not overdoing the art of social graces, for she so desired for Erica Barrett to like her. There was something about the attractive woman that pleased her and made her want to get to know her better. Erica was clearly a lady, a special kind of lady.

"They are having my favorite fare this evening," Erica announced graciously.

"What is that, Miss Barrett?" Cassandra wanted to know. Immediately she felt like a ninny, for she had not even noticed what was being served in the sumptuous dining room.

"Teal ducks in port wine sauce and chicken rochambeau. The elegant chicken dish is said to be named for Count Jean Baptiste Donatien de Vimeur de Rochambeau, who commanded the French forces that supported Washington in the American Revolution."

171

"Of course," Cassandra said, almost licking her lips at the mention of the rochambeau—chicken and ham on rusks with mushroom and béarnaise sauces. "It is one of my favorite also."

"Which?" Erica asked with a twinkle in her eye.

Cassandra laughed lightly, saying, "The rochambeau, naturally." Now she did allow her tongue to peep over the soft fold of her lips, the sensuous action not lost on Jared Casey. "Mmm, I am very hungry." Jared wanted to attack.

"Excuse us, will you, Mr. Casey?" Monte St. James said to the man who looked anything but happy at the moment. "I have promised these ladies that I would take my dinner with them."

"Go ahead," Casey drawled. "I was just about to return to my stateroom anyway to catch up on some paperwork."

"Of course," Monte said, trying to hide his distaste. He had no wish for his daughter to be alone with the roguish lawyer.

While Monte stepped away to join Erica, Cassandra lingered with Jared for a moment longer. "Thank you, Mr. Casey. Your talk of New Orleans has been very informative. I should like to visit there one day in the near future."

"I'd love to take you there, little angel," Jared said softly, his gaze trying to capture something in her eye that would give him some hope. But there was nothing, nothing but a charmingly informal smile.

"Perhaps Miss Barrett would be so kind as to accompany us there," Cassandra said, thinking that Jared was just being gentlemanly in his desire to court her further. "Someday, perhaps."

Jared touched his lips to Cassandra's hand. "Later, Cassandra," he said meaningfully, picturing a moonlit clinch.

"Yes." There was a little twinkle in her blue eyes. "Tomorrow then."

Clamping his jaw together, Jared watched the charming minx vanish into the twinkling, murmuring dining room. "Damn that prim and proper Miss Barrett," he snarled low. "She's already turning Cassandra into one of her own kind." He laughed deviously. "I'll just bet the only thrusting Erica Barrett has known is the tip of her needle slipping to and fro in her embroidery frame. If I've got anything to do about it and my name is still Jared Casey, I'm going to see to it that the little angel minx knows what it's all about before she leaves this boat!"

# *Part III*

"'Tis one thing to be tempted,
Another thing to fall."
                    —*William Shakespeare*


"The passions and desires like the two twists of a rope,
mutually mix one with the other, and twine inextricably
round the heart; producing good if moderately
indulged; but certain destruction, if suffered to become
inordinate."
                    —*Robert Burton*

# Chapter Ten

It was a blue, sunny day in late May when the *River Minx* was pulling in to dock at St. Louis. Setting her sewing aside, Cassandra left her stateroom to walk out onto the deck, lifting her face to feel the sun warm her, her eyes diamond-blue in the light of day. Sun-kissed strands twined about her shoulders and cascaded down to the middle of her back.

A week had passed since she had been introduced to Erica Barrett and now that the boat would be docking in St. Louis, she knew she would be losing a great friend. Erica had taught her so much in that short time that Cassandra felt she was now truly grown up and would know how to comport herself in any social gathering.

Cassandra perched on the railing, happy to be alive and full of glowing health. She watched the docks swarming with people, and steamboats, festive as wedding cakes, were docked so close together a person could almost step from one deck to the other if he wished. She canted her bright head, hearing the chant of the roustabouts as they rolled barrels of sorghum and shifted bales of cotton from here to there. She breathed deeply of the sharp, pungent smell of wet hemp and damp wood, her eyes drifting to the levee where huge horses pulled enormous dray wagons.

As the *River Minx* docked, moving so smoothly for her hugeness, Cassandra gave credit to Captain Sy for his expertise in handling the great floating palace. She thought him the best pilot in the whole world. Suddenly, as her features grew winsome, she began to wonder why she had not seen much of him in the past seven days. No doubt he had been dividing his time between the pilothouse and Miki Rhea!

Cassandra's face was alive with excitement. She was very aware of the city's history. Early French explorers had opened communication from Canada by way of the Great Lakes, and the Mississippi River in the latter part of the seventeenth century and Fort Orleans was built on the Missouri riverbanks. The first permanent settlement, however, came about when French-Canadian inhabitants of Kaskaskia crossed the Mississippi from Illinois country to work in the lead mines. The founding of St. Louis as a fur-trading post by Pierre Laclède came in 1764 and, before that, French Roman Catholic missionaries had set up a short-lived station with a large Indian population. Moses Austin sank the first mine shaft, built furnaces, a shot tower, and sheet lead plants in the woods, as well as a sawmill, flour mill, road, and bridges.

Cassandra loved St. Louis and its Indian history, which she had studied extensively under the tutelage of Richard Cavelier, distant relative of René Robert Cavelier, Sieur de La Salle, who had claimed formal possession of the entire Mississippi valley for France.

178

Melantha had insisted on the French tutor. At first, Cassandra had resisted, but now she was glad for having learned the history of not only Missouri but all the southern states.

Cassandra's eyes widened as here and there she saw men lying about, drunk or asleep, so many of them, like so much driftwood cast upon the levee. White men. This time she saw no Indians. When the white man came, the Osage and the Missouri were the main Indian tribes. Sauk and Fox war parties had almost destroyed the Missouri Indians in the late eighteenth century. Early explorations of the upper reaches of the Missouri were performed by Meriwether Lewis and William Clark. The governorship of Clark and his later administration of Indian affairs developed confidence among the chiefs, who often visited him in St. Louis, the administrative center. Friction with remaining tribes was lessened by giving them lands farther to the west before settlers swarmed in.

Shifting on the railing to get more comfortable and to feel the sun full on her face, Cassandra's eyes and ears missed nothing. She noted everything and she imagined how it must have been for the first wave of settlers, comprised mostly of southerners. They had taken over the fertile bottom land as farmers, unlike their French predecessors, who had gathered in communities and tilled only small cotton fields, living mainly on the fur trade.

Reminiscently Cassandra thought of the early Diamonts of St. Louis and she wished that someday in the near future she could make a visit to Madame Nanette Diamond, Sylvestre's dear mother. A long time had passed since she had visited Diamondhead, and she had a yearning to go there and walk the fields of the well-managed plantation, to ride the fine Thoroughbreds that were stabled there.

Erica Barrett suddenly walked up to Cassandra, breaking into the younger woman's reflections. "Is it not exciting?" Erica announced, gazing out over the activity on the docks of St. Louis.

"I love St. Louis," Cassandra said wistfully, breathing deeply and hugging her shoulders. "Erica?"

"Yes, my dear?"

"Are you getting off here?" Cassandra blinked, from the sun and the curious mistiness in her eyes.

"Yes, I am afraid this is the end of my journey."

"What were you doing in Harper?"

"Visiting an old friend. Here in St. Louis I will also be visiting an old friend—but this one is an aunt. Prudence Hitchcock, my deceased mother's sister. Prudence's husband's brother is Lieutenant Colonel Ethan Allan Hitchcock, the philosopher. Colonel Stephen Kearny, commander of the First Dragoons at Fort Leavenworth has asked Colonel Hitchcock to be his inspector general."

"How interesting to have friends directly involved in the Mexican War," Cassandra said.

"Hitchcock, who is supposed to be on leave in St. Louis and still being treated by Dr. Beaumont, thinks his army career is over and has buried himself in Spinoza, Swedenborg, and Strauss's *Vie de Jesus*. I believe he will recover by the end of the summer and join General Scott and make himself invaluable in the campaign for Mexico City."

"You know so much about everything, Erica. I hope that some of your wonderful intelligence and graciousness in the social arts has transmitted itself to me."

"Oh, my dear, you needn't thank me for your charm and grace. You had plenty of that before ever meeting Erica Barrett!"

They were silent for a time, enjoying the noise and the sights, each knowing their time together was short.

To lighten the mood, Erica suddenly blurted, "Is it not horrible about the buffalo?"

"Buffalo?" Cassandra shook her blond head, strands of her hair sparkling snow-white in the sunshine. "I don't know—I have not heard."

"Thousands upon thousands of the beautiful beasts have been slaughtered, their tongues shipped here to St. Louis. Don't ask me what they do with the tongues, I have no idea about that. But the American Fur Company has also brought back thousands of buffalo robes. What a pity! Cargoes of tallow from bear and buffalo, used in place of lard, were poured into hollowed-out boats and towed to market."

"Someday the buffalo may become extinct, you are saying?"

"Oh, yes, Cassandra, I believe that will happen in the not-too-distant future. And the poor little beaver! The hats! I've never owned a fur, I tell you."

"That is so sad, God's beautiful creatures having to become extinct someday. I do believe, however, that the development of the silk hat and the fashion for other furs will soon diminish the market and we will see fewer buffalo robes and beaver hats."

"You are interested in materials and fashions, I have noted. Indeed, you have always been bent at your sewing when I have come to visit your stateroom. I

181

believe you have a natural talent with the needle and fashion designing and you have already gained yourself quite a little following on this journey."

"I plan to open my own shop one day, Erica."

"I believe you, indeed I do. Will it be here, in St. Louis, that you plan to open one?"

"Yes, I do think this would be the ideal place for a shop."

"It would indeed be perfect, because the steamboat traffic is expanding rapidly. The steamboat is well on its way to dominating the economy, agriculture, commerce, and social customs of our middle area of the United States. Cotton is spreading over the South and Southwest and sugar has become the major crop of the area below New Orleans."

"As I said before, you know so much about everything," Cassandra observed with a charming grin. "I hope to know half of what you do when I reach your age, Erica."

"Give my brother the credit, dear. He was a steamboat pilot like our Captain Sy. Speaking of Sylvestre Diamond, he's so ruggedly handsome—and yet there is a certain rare elegance about the man. And to mention his physical attributes, he has eyes like liquid gold, hair like a lion's mane, and the physique of a Greek athlete. All in all, Sylvestre Diamond is quite the man. He seems to belong in many places at the same time." Erica sighed poignantly. "My brother Richard has settled down now with a family and cotton plantation. A man who can pilot a steamboat has a rare ability, Cassandra." Her hazel eyes twinkled merrily. "The safety of the passengers and crew depend on the pilot, day and night.

182

"The art of piloting a steamboat is an unbelievably complicated subject. Just ask my brother Richard or, better yet, ask our Captain Sy Diamond. Lord, I wish I could be several years younger. It would be nice to feel your age again, to experience all the freshness of blossoming womanhood all over again, to fall in love for the first time."

A vision of the golden Sy flashed into Cassandra's mind. But she could not know what Erica Barrett was thinking: *This attraction between Sylvestre Diamond and Cassandra St. James was coming faster than either of them suspected.*

"What are you saying, Erica?"

Erica replied evasively, "Oh, I would have done things differently. Much. There was a young man . . ." She waved her slim, white-gloved hand in the sunshiny air. "I shan't go into that."

"Why not, Erica?" Cassandra asked, wondering at the shininess in the older woman's splendid eyes.

"First, it would take several days in the telling, dear Cassandra." Erica's slim shoulders lifted and fell. "Secondly, I must go now. You know that, dear."

"Oh, must you?" Cassandra dragged her gaze to the golden-haired man speaking to a correspondent of the St. Louis *Reveille* just making ready to disembark.

"Is that not the young correspondent who joined us for dinner last evening?" Erica said, knowing he surely was watching Cassandra as her eyes met Captain Sy's across the short distance. When Sylvestre looked away first, Cassandra frowned unhappily. "Yes, dear, I must go. Chin up, darling. I must gather all my belongings to disembark and you, my lovely young friend"— She tapped the blonde's hand, as if she held a lacy fan—

"you must be anxious to be on about your sewing. You *desperately* need a sewing machine for all the work you are going to have in a few years, love."

"Oh, I do not know about those newfangled contraptions, Erica. I've heard terrible stories of women stitching their fingers."

"Fiddle. Elias Howe invented that 'contraption,' as you call it. A great man, I can tell you, for he will change industry for this country, I predict. You needn't fear the machine, dear. The three basic features of the sewing machine are a grooved needle with the eye at the point, a shuttle operating on the opposite side of the cloth from the needle to form a lock stitch, and"— Erica shrugged—"an automatic feed."

"Again, I must ask you how you come by all your information?"

"That one is easy, minx. I went to the National Fair with a friend last year and saw Elias Howe's exhibit of the sewing machine. I, too, was skeptical at first and then I witnessed the speed with which the needle traveled through that bit of cloth."

"You are exciting me, Erica, and I, too, wish to see this"—she laughed—"contraption operate one day."

"I know you are not getting off the steamboat this time in St. Louis, your father has said, for his schedule is behind—" She did not add her knowledge of Cassandra's mother fuming back home, awaiting the return of the daring castaway. "But next time you visit, please look me up. Your darling father is the most gentlemanly steamboat owner I've ever had the pleasurable occasion to meet. Such hospitality!"

"Erica, I must tell you . . ." Cassandra began with a look of mischief in her sky-blue eyes, "that is only when

184

Father is in a good mood!" Cassandra laughed. "You should see him thundering orders when others cross him."

"Oh? I have not witnessed Monte St. James's temper, but oh, my dear, that Sylvestre Diamond—did you see *him* when he became angry with the other pilot . . . ah, Willie Something-or-other?"

With an emotion that vacillated between curiosity and desire not to speak of Sy anymore, Cassandra hurriedly said, "Willie Elmo. In truth, Erica, that man enjoys his rum."

"I thought Captain Sy was going to deck that Elmo fellow!"

"Deck?" Cassandra laughed. "What is that?"

"You know—give him a solid blow to send him to the deck! Oh, listen to me, I'm sounding like brother Richard . . ." she remarked. "Dear Cassandra, please come and visit me at my relatives'. I shall be staying in St. Louis for quite some time, you know, either at my brother's or my rich aunt's. I will write down the addresses and leave them with your darling father."

Erica cupped Cassandra's face on both sides and rubbed noses with the blonde. "Be happy, minx, and remember, dear, someone very wonderful loves you very much. But the inevitability of conflict between newly awakened lovers is high. Just do not be weighted down by it, darling. It is a conflict you cannot avoid. But you can face it boldly. Otherwise your love might wither and turn to ashes."

Cassandra was thunderstruck.

"B-but who do you speak of?"

It was too late, for Erica waved as she breezed off down the deck, her creamy lace skirt twitching with feminine movement, her heels clicking smartly on the wood. "Write me, dear!"

"Good-bye, Erica . . . my dearest friend," Cassandra called out at the last minute before Erica disappeared around the corner. "I will miss you!"

"Me, too, dear . . ."

Then Erica Barrett was gone. The woman who had been more like a sister than a friend.

With a sense of mission, Cassandra worked on altering Lavender Peyton's gown, all morning and well into the afternoon. She had sent out for tea and lunch from the cook's galley and stayed closeted in her sunny, mote-filled stateroom, bent over her task, the table cluttered with pins, thread, and the vignette Miss Peyton had drawn for her to copy.

By five o'clock Cassandra was ready to stretch her legs and get some air. She put on the dress she had found time to alter for herself, staying up late at night with the moonlight drifting into the window, where its pale light glowed into her room.

Cassandra would have liked to have gone into St. Louis, but her father had ordered her to stay on board, for very soon they would begin the return trip home. As soon as all the wares had been unloaded and a few minor repairs were made to the steamboat, they would be on their way again.

Cassandra felt restless as she stepped outside to walk the decks. The dress she wore was a lavender-blue sprigged muslin with pale-yellow off-the-shoulder ruffles, and at the hem of the skirt there were tiers of three more ruffles. She had brushed her hair out, leaving it flowing free halfway down her back.

From his high perch, Sylvestre watched Cassandra on the promenade deck. She was like a lovely misty violet-and-yellow portrait of a freshly blossomed flower perched on the railing, as if waiting to be plucked by the first person who came along—and at the moment that person happened to be Jared Casey, who was boldly ogling her from his stance at the lower deck, a tall drink in hand.

Sy heard the screech of children playing ball and careening toward the young woman perched on the railing. They had no care as to the disaster they could create while their parents imbibed freely, enjoying the sunny air and the sights, totally oblivious to the mischief their children were creating . . .

"You silly little fool!"

Cassandra had no idea what hit her. She had been sunning herself when, all of a sudden, she was stunned by the unexpectedness of the strong arms reaching for her and the broad chest she was brought up against. So surprised was she that she had no recognition of the deep voice in her ear until she found herself embraced in Sylvestre's strong arms.

It was not a loving embrace. No, far from that. It was more like being thrust up against a tall, live oak!

Half in fear, Cassandra stared into the golden eyes of the man she had most dreaded encountering that day. Sylvestre's features were set in a grim mask.

Forgetting herself, Cassandra shrieked, "Blackguard!" pounding against the rock-hard chest. "What do you think you are doing!?"

Sylvestre stared down at Cassandra's soft coral mouth. "You were in danger! Or are you so blind that you could not see the children racing along the deck! They would have crashed into you and—"

She cut in, "I would have fallen to the deck below and broken my fool neck, you were going to say!" Her chest heaved with her excitement at finding herself in Sylvestre's arms. "Go ahead, Captain Sy, call me a silly little fool again. You are being very irrational—I was in no danger."

"None that you could see, Cassa!"

For some reason Sylvestre could not apply the cool logic that had always been a part of his makeup. Where Cassandra was concerned, his feelings were far from rational! These emotions, compounded by Cassandra's proximity, once again had led his better sensibilities to the point of frustration and unmitigated anger. Perhaps jealousy had played a large part, too. He had been compelled to seize her and, his mind made up, seeing her in possible danger, he had moved with quick, determined steps.

He took in her pale face and cursed softly. He was surprised that he could even speak. "Cassa . . . Cassa."

It was a strange moment. Sylvestre could feel the turbulent emotions in Cassandra pulling at him, tugging his heart. They both wanted something to happen.

"Cassandra," Sylvestre began silkily. "I must take you to your stateroom where you can lie down. Your near-accident has you in quite a state . . . and I believe we should have a talk, *ma petite,* a pleasant conversation to soothe your frayed nerves."

She drew a deep breath and steeled herself. "Do not speak to me as if I were still a child, Mr. Diamond. I do not wish to enter into any form of conversation, pleasant *or* unpleasant, with you!"

"This is not up to you, Cassandra. I am saying if you will not come along willingly I shall have to seek out your father to talk some sense into your head."

"No . . . please, don't do that."

"Then—what? Will you come along willingly?"

Cassandra did not answer for a moment. And then: "I do not see where—"

"Damn the consequences!" Sy hissed under his breath as he scooped her up and carried her to her stateroom.

"You will be sorry, Sylvestre!"

"Like it or not, I am taking you to your stateroom."

"You scoundrel," she hissed into his ear, embarrassed. So many people could see what he was doing, she thought bleakly.

"As I said—you will be sorry."

"I am not sorry, Cassa. Not now. Not ever."

Lavender Peyton saw them pass and called out, "They're all scoundrels and blackguards, Cassandra. Beware lest you fall into his trap!"

"Atta boy! I'd take some wind outta her sails, too!" Willie Elmo called down from his perch in the pilothouse.

Kicking open the door to Cassandra's stateroom, Sylvestre bore her inside and placed her none too gently on the bed. Grasping the crocheted bedcover, Cassandra levered herself up to a sitting position and then she was off the bed in a flash.

"How dare you!!"

She whirled about to face him like a spitting tigress, upsetting a plate of sugared beignets she had been munching on as she did her sewing that afternoon. There were three of the deep-fried confections left, and they, and the plate, were all on the floor by now.

Sylvestre slammed the door shut, growling, "I dare anything where you are concerned, Cassa!" not even noticing that as he came into the room he had stepped onto the beignets and crushed them flat as pancakes.

Cassandra paled. He had locked the door. They were alone!

He came toward her and she fell heavily against his shoulder with the impact of his movement. Sylvestre sucked in a breath, dropping her onto a nearby chair.

Using all the nerve she had in her, Cassandra stayed where she was and waited. She breathed slowly, deeply.

"Are you all right, Cassa?"

"Yes, I am fine. What are you going to do now?" She looked up under her silky lashes. "Are you going to beat me for disobeying your orders? I did not come willingly, you know."

"Yes, I know."

Sylvestre knelt beside her—unaware that some of the beignets were stuck to the soles of his black boots—and took her slim hand in his own. "I think you look lovely in lavender, and most blondes do not look good in yellow—"

"What?" Cassandra felt the levity of the moment and almost laughed out loud.

". . . but you do."

A footstep sounded outside the stateroom door.

"Miss St. James? Are you all right?"

It was Jared Casey's voice.

"Do not answer it," Sylvestre said. *God, how he wanted to lovingly and intimately touch her.*

Before Cassandra could answer, Sylvestre's mouth lowered to hers in a punishing kiss. His firm body lay half across her, pinning Cassandra down into the deep-cushioned chair.

"Oh . . ." she whimpered softly.

Cassandra could not have pushed him away even if she had fought because suddenly she felt no inclination to struggle against his greater power.

"Shh . . . he will go away if you do not answer," Sylvestre whispered close to her flushed cheek.

"I . . . I don't want—" she stammered.

"Shh."

Suddenly a deceitful languor was stealing through Cassandra's jellied limbs, leaving her limp as a rag doll and open to Sy's golden touch. He kissed her then, most thoroughly, most ravenously.

There was no help for it.

Cassandra's velvety lips parted of a natural accord under the insistent pressing of Sy's probing tongue and she readily found herself inundated by a sweep of flaming desire so great it shook her slender frame.

A deep groan and a golden sigh issued from Sylvestre's throat. A wealth of sensations coalesced into one shimmering urgency that compelled Cassandra to arch her slim body against Sy's. Mutely she was begging to prolong the contact of Sy's arm encircling her tiny waist, the hard muscles of his thigh pressing against her own trembling limbs.

*Dear Lord,* Sylvestre thought. *I love you!*

The footsteps outside the stateroom faded away, but Cassandra hardly heard them, she did not care, for now she was so wrapped up in Sy's masculine nearness, loving caresses, and tantalizing kisses.

Gently Sy lifted his tanned hand to stroke Cassandra's cheek with one finger. Cassandra could only sigh, for the tenderness of the gesture reminded her poignantly of her young years, of the first time they had met, when the slender, reedlike Sy had lifted a vagrant lock of angelic hair from her dirty face with the same tender, caring touch.

Embarrassed now, Cassandra felt tears stinging under her eyelids and lowered her lashes so that he could not see her struggling tears.

"You have been angry with me, Cassa. Why?"

He slowed his touch to a lambent glancing like the sun's rays.

"Y-you frightened me today, that is why." She told the white lie as a light giddiness continued to steal over her.

"No, *petite.* I saved you from a bad fall. And I do not speak of your anger this day. No, it began long before this one. I have felt it in you, an emotion very strong. It was not there, however, when last I visited you at your home in Harper."

"I do not wish to speak of it—Sy."

"I love it when you whisper that shortened version of my name. Sy. Sigh . . . you make it sound like a breathless *sigh.*"

This day he had revealed more of his heart than was wise, Sylvestre told himself and warned himself also to go a little slower with Cassa, for she was very maidenly, he had come to realize while they had kissed and caressed . . . himself doing the most of the caressing.

The long fingers that brushed Cassandra's face, just skimming over her flesh, left her skin achingly sensitive to even the smallest movement of air in the room.

"Cassa . . . Cassa . . . *ma petite* . . . *chère mademoiselle.*"

Oh, when he spoke those French words, rolling off his tongue so beautifully, Cassandra could almost swoon. She could feel her own breathing becoming as ragged as Sy's. "I am not angry with you, Sy," she managed, in a soft tone that hardly sounded like her own voice.

"I believe someone has set your heart against me, Cassa. I mean to find out who this person could be."

"No . . . no, there is no one." Then she thought of Jared Casey, who had told her much of Sylvestre's liaisons with other women.

"I think you speak a little white lie. No matter." He shrugged. "I will discover the person's identity, Cassandra."

In the next moment Sy's tormenting touch went down along the line of Cassandra's throat, unalteringly, and she gasped softly when Sy traced the curve of her bodice. Strong fingers rested on the yellow ruffles and then slid them lower, slowly, maddeningly slow, until the ruffled edge scooped wide to reveal tempting white swells. A deep breath was taken by Sy as he traced the upper curves of her breasts with a teasing finger while she gazed deeply into his passion-laced eyes.

All the while, his featherlight touch caressed her, his

eyes, intent and golden fire, never left hers for a moment.

Muted sunlight filtering through the embroidered lace curtains fell across the crushed beignets on the floor, and the ray lengthened to stretch and fall across Cassandra, making delicate patterns where Sy had laid back the lavender-and-yellow edge of her gown to display the delicate white skin. Cassandra found herself moaning softly, the sound coming from far away, it seemed. Each sensitive peak was tingling with unfulfilled desire.

Her lashes lowered very shyly to veil her eyes, her dilated pupils . . .

"You need never be embarrassed or shy with me, Cassa." His voice was deep. Sensual. All male animal.

When Sy laid his hand against the side of her enchanting face, Cassa felt the warm hardness of his fingers and turned her head to press the moist delicately soft kiss into his large palm.

Closing his fingers and thumb about the fine line of her jaw, Sy lifted Cassa's face to meet his gaze roaming her face for a small, wordless moment in time. Shadows in time. Golden, glorious moments in time. Precious. Stirring. Invaluable.

"Innocent," Sy breathed. "So sweet. Loveliest innocence. You are like a naughty child transformed into a golden angel to me."

"Naughty? Was I really that bad, Sy?"

"No, I am sorry. You were a child of many contrasts. Brilliant. Gifted. Affectionate. Emotional. Never typical. On the other side, you were unruly. Venturesome.

194

Melancholy. Passionate. A babbling bundle of inexhaustible energy."

Caressingly his eyes ran over her face, staring down the white length of her neck. Cassandra looked back. Up this close, in the light of day, Cassandra could see Sy's compelling eyes were an exceptional shade of yellow-gold. "Sy—" She heaved her shoulders and went on. "Sy—"

"I am here." He chuckled deeply.

"What do you think of Miki Rhea?"

There. It was out.

"Ah." Clearing his throat, wondering at this sudden odd question, Sy answered, "She's passingly pretty." He shrugged.

"What else?"

Now he chuckled harder. "She is a bit coarse and much too flashy for my tastes. Does that answer your impertinent question thoroughly, *ma petite?*"

She could tell he felt nothing for the loud-mouthed tart, could read it by the dullness in his eyes and the flatness in his voice as he spoke of the worldly bedhopper. Then what about all the other women?

The tavern wench she had caught him cavorting with? How about her?

Burned into Cassandra's memory was the picture of Sy straining with the wanton Dolly McKay on the room's sagging bed . . . Could she be certain, entirely certain, he had been really having a tête-à-tête with her?

They had been together, in full view of her curious eyes . . . Cassa, too, longed to discover those muscles which shaped his strong shoulders, to caress the smoothness of Sy's bare back, to feel the ripples of

195

strength in front that tapered down to Sy's . . .

With a gentle tug, he arched her even closer. "Why do you continue to deny the feeling between us that grows stronger each time we are together like this?" he asked, pressing her at this moment when he believed she was most vulnerable.

"I do not deny it, Sy. I am only afraid of it . . . growing stronger like you say." *I do not wish to be in love with a womanizing rogue!*

"We will make love one day soon, Cassa, and when we do you will belong to me, body, soul, and spirit."

He was thinking of marriage—

—But Cassandra could not know this. She thought he was speaking of making her his mistress, for surely this is what he must want of her.

"When we return to Harper and leave you with Melantha, I will be making the trip upstream again back to St. Louis." *Home.* "I cannot say when I will be back. But when I do return, I want you to have come to a decision concerning our future together, Cassandra."

He only called her Cassandra when he was very serious about something. She did not know what Sy was asking her and she watched him go. Then, after the passage of three long minutes, she found herself staring soulfully at the space he had occupied only moments before.

"His aura remains with me," she whispered. "Warm. Alive. Vibrantly male . . . Sy. A man who wants something from me . . . but what? I should have asked him to make himself clear."

There had been no need to ask Sy, she decided, for he had made his intentions quite clear. His body had spoken. He had articulated that they would one day

196

make love.

By whose demand? Whose orders? *His?*

Did she, Cassandra St. James, not have a say in what he planned one day to do to her own body? *I do, most assuredly!*

Sy did not actually *love* her. *He wanted her.*

Indeed. Sy Diamond wanted only one thing of her, and it was certainly not her heart!

# *Chapter Eleven*

The mist hung low over the river like a huge gray beast, sending long tentacles snaking over the lower decks of the paddlewheeler that rested at dockside. The golden sunset had faded only a quarter of an hour before and already it was dark outside.

"Forgive me, Cassandra," Monte St. James was saying to his daughter. "I woke up this afternoon following a much-needed nap and remembered it was your birthday, but apparently it is *not* today."

Cassandra smiled with forgiveness. "My birthday is the seventeenth of May, Father, not the twenty-seventh."

"I knew you would forgive your father his forgetfulness." He felt ashamed for allowing Miki Rhea to finally catch his eye; the redhead was seductive, to say the least. Monte sighed, fighting to submerge the aching guilt he felt. "I have only one regret now, Cassa."

"What is that?" Cassandra tossed her head, linking her arm in the crook of Monte's arm.

"That your dear friend, Erica Barrett, is not on board any longer . . . to join in the celebration." His eyes twinkled mysteriously.

"Yes, Father, I regret . . . *Celebration? When?*" Cassandra fingered the pearl necklace Erica had given her not long ago. The gift would always be cherished, as would Sylvestre's gold cross.

"Everything is ready for this night, dear." Monte took her hand and gave it a loving squeeze. "However, you might just wish to wait a day longer to prepare yourself for—"

"To stay the celebration another day? Oh no—" Cassandra shook her bright head, causing a long lock to bounce over her shoulder. "I am not letting you off the hook that easy, Papa. You may proceed with your earlier plans."

"But—"

"What is it?"

"Ah, well, I might tell you now, dearest. We have docked shortly below St. Louis to take on some spices and nuts we have run short of—"

"And?" Cassandra's tawny eyebrow rose in curiosity. "What else?"

"Uhmm . . . chicken. I know how you love—"

"And . . . Father?"

"And"—he sighed most regretfully—"Harlan Kirby has come on board and will be our guest tonight. I am sorry."

"Oh. Exactly the one to spoil my birthday . . ." She grinned. "Belated birthday, hmm, Papa?" She endeavored to brush off the distasteful thought of Harlan Kirby's presence on board with a lighter mood.

"I love it when you call me Papa. Makes me recall

when you were a fast-paced little minx. Always getting into some mischief, you were."

"I still am, Papa. Look, I am here on board the paddlewheeler, aren't I?"

"You certainly are. And we shall make the best of it on the return trip home so that when you face your mother—"

Frowning lightly, Monte cut off his sentence, wondering if this might be the proper time and occasion to reveal the truth about Melantha. He decided not to spoil Cassandra's birthday . . . Maybe tomorrow. Yes, tomorrow would suffice, after Harlan Kirby had taken himself from the riverboat to return to Kirby Plantation.

Cassandra forced herself to shrug lightly and smile. "I will face Mother. I am brave."

And so you are, Monte St. James kept to himself. So you are, my darling and daring and wonderful Cassa. Aloud he said, "With the strength of resilience I know you capable of, and with God's help, you will face Harlan Kirby and anyone else who comes along. You will win, Cassa, and get everything in life you deserve." *One day.*


During her birthday dinner, Cassandra was mildly surprised to find Miki Rhea glaring at her across the chandelier-lighted room. Miki Rhea's look was one of smoldering resentment, and Cassandra could not fathom the redhead's obvious hatred of herself. Dismissing Miki Rhea for the time being, Cassandra set forth to enjoy herself. There was only one other thorn in her side this night . . .

Harlan Kirby sat at their table, directly across from Cassandra, his mouth going constantly, chewing his choice from the platters of game, hams and chickens, jellied meats, wild rice cooked to perfection. And when Harlan was not stuffing himself, he was elaborating on the fine points of his very self and what he was doing in business at the time.

Harlan was extremely large and solidly built, possessing big feet and a long, aquiline nose. He also had an air of authority, plus the appearance of one who demanded instant obedience, this usually from his wretched slaves whom he tyrannized.

Avoiding Harlan's waxy eyes, Cassandra spooned her bouillabaisse into her mouth. She noticed the women in the immediate area surrounding their table. They were staring at Harlan Kirby, and she had to wonder—as Harlan smiled at her jauntily—why it was that most women found the man so appealing. To Cassandra, Harlan owned the craggy look of an incomplete sculpture, and his full black hair flowing back from his face looked somehow untidy, rakish. Yet, even in a crowd, his presence was compelling. There was a disturbing air about him that somehow reminded her of Jared, but Harlan, she knew for sure, had a mean streak in him, resting just below the surface of his amiable facade.

Speak of the devil. Jared chose that moment to walk in and head straight for their table. Cassandra hoped Jared would join them and enliven the party, for Sylvestre and Monte had excused themselves moments before to check out some trouble among the engine-room personnel. Cassandra was bored to the hilt with talk of money, plantation slaves, and politics.

Harlan leaned forward, his forkful of ham pausing in midair. "Who is this man, Cassandra?" Kirby questioned outright when Jared lifted her hand, kissed the back of it, and said, "Happy Birthday, Angel."

"Angel?" Harlan looked up at the handsome intruder with the dark-blue eyes, and a secret expression passed between the two men that was lost on Cassandra. Harlan made to rise and shake the man's hand.

"This is Harlan Kirby, Jared. Jared Casey . . . well, you have already heard the other man's name so I need not repeat it."

Cassandra realized she was being ungracious, but she could not help it—she was bored to death of mantalk. She sorely missed Erica Barrett's presence and she could not wait to see Letty and Dulcie. For once on this trip she wished she could be at home with her beloved maid and her lively daughter Dulcie. She even missed her mother—a little.

"Harlan Kirby, glad to make your acquaintance," Jared said with a suavity that was not lost on Cassandra.

"You did not tell me this was your birthday, Cassandra dear," Harlan said with much aplomb.

"But, Harlan, Monte announced it at the table when we first sat down," Cassandra said, hoping she was hiding her irritation well.

"Oh, but of course, sweeting. Forgive me for being so remiss." Harlan turned to Jared then. "Have some bouillabaisse, Mr. Casey, it's delicious."

"I know," Jared said. "I've had it on board before."

Making himself comfortable, Jared sat and filled a bowl from the tureen, and before he could get the spoon to his mouth, Harlan posed a question to him.

"Now, tell me, Casey, what is your line of business?"

Clearing his throat, Jared pulled his enamoured gaze from Cassandra, who looked truly ethereal this night, almost unreal in the twinkling chandelier lights. He could hardly keep his eyes from drifting her way. The golden-white mist of her hair surrounded blue eyes and fair skin and her dress was lovely on her. It was a gown with wide aqua and white stripes, a silky material with sleeves long and fitted, with a bodice edged with embroidered rosebuds that molded itself naturally to her blossoming curves. She had filled out nicely, no doubt from all the rich food she had been consuming. All in all, her toilette and the pastel gown lent her a tall, slender grace, and an air of cool sophistication that she had gained while in the studied company of Erica Barrett.

Cassandra sighed, for it began again, the talk of money and plantation slaves and Jared's occupational skill as a lawyer. Although she was beginning to adore Jared more and more, she was ready to yawn into her chicken pontalba in boredom when Sylvestre and Monte at last saved the night from becoming a total disaster by their timely return.

At once Sylvestre's spicy cologne touched her nostrils as he took the empty space beside her once again. Cassandra's face beamed with pleasure when Monte presented her with yet another velvet dress while grinning mysteriously at her as she looked it over. This one was white, and Cassandra lovingly caressed its soft folds, and then, to top it off, Jared gave her a gold coin that was very old.

Breathlessly she exclaimed, "I did not expect all this."

"You deserve it all, *chère mademoiselle*... and more," Sylvestre said, looking a little disappointed when he noticed she was not wearing the gold cross he had given her for her birthday. Instead she was fingering the string of pearls Erica Barrett had given her.

Cassandra read Sylvestre's thoughts at once, suddenly feeling bad for not having worn the gold cross. He looked at her through his tawny lashes and lowered his voice. "I like the pearls, and they become more than elegant against your fair bosom." His eyes dropped to the material and the aqua rosebuds that stretched across her bosom. She had gained a little weight here and there, and she carried it very nicely indeed.

"Thank you, Sylvestre. I am sorry that I did not—"

"Hush." He touched her lips with one long, tanned finger. "You need not apologize."

"But how can you know what I was about to say?" She blinked her long, silky lashes, feeling flirtatious suddenly, while Jared watched from under black eyebrows and Harlan kept his expression self-concentrated.

His face illuminated with tenderness, Sylvestre said in a voice decidedly soft, "You need not have finished your sentence, Cassa. I am finding myself able to read your mind of late." His gaze unabashedly scanned her face and ivory throat.

Cassandra was blushing; she could feel its heat. "I wish you would not look at me like that. Mr. Casey is watching."

"And do you think that I give a damn?" he said gruffly.

Cassandra sat silent as a church mouse as Sylvestre stared at the snow-blond head bent in thought. Never before had Sy seen her so wonderfully tempting and womanly beautiful. Bold as a lion, he continued to lavish his undisguised attention upon her, and his thoughts turned dangerously to scooping her into his arms and bearing her to his private stateroom. There he would make love to her all night long, until she screamed for him to cease.

"It is a beautiful night . . ." Cassandra's voice trailed off and her cheeks began to burn. Goosebumps ran up and down her arms as Sylvestre continued to stare at her profile. Jared Casey stared, too, with a somewhat bemused glower.

"So it is," Sylvestre murmured. He was bored with any conversation that did not have to do with Cassandra, he told himself, then blanched as Miki Rhea walked by their table and Cassandra caught the redhead throwing a kiss his way. Damn tart, Sylvestre was thinking. Miki Rhea was going to spoil all the magic that was starting all over again for him and Cassandra.

As the talk shifted back to Harlan's plantation slaves and various other boring topics, Cassandra smiled, realizing Sylvestre seemed to have eyes only for her, obviously listening with half an ear to the conversation that was apparently dull to him also.

Sylvestre's bronze skin pulled taut over the elegant ridges that marked his cheekbones, and with a challenge in his catlike gold eyes, he perused Harlan Kirby and skimmed over Jared Casey with dislike that the latter had intruded on their little celebration. They could do without Kirby, too, he decided.

"Ah, we have refreshing company." Sylvestre stood, gallantly kissing Millicent, Catherine and Lavender's white-gloved hands. "Ladies—do join us."

Cassandra watched breathlessly as the material of Sylvestre's tailor-made waistcoat stretched tautly across the muscled broadness of his shoulders. With the eye of a seamstress, she noticed that he did not need to pad his waistcoat like Harlan Kirby and Jared Casey!

"I am sorry, Mr. Diamond," Lavender tittered under her gloved hand. "We already have a table. But it was so gracious of you to invite us—" She nudged Millicent in the ribs. "Wasn't it, Milly?"

"Indeed it was, Captain Diamond." She blinked powdered lashes and bit her nearly nonexistent red-rouged lips. "You are very ch-chivalrous, sir, but we've already got a table."

"I already said as much," Lavender scolded Millicent.

"Where is the lovely Seraphina Landers?" Sylvestre asked, still holding the hand of the furiously blushing Catherine. "I have not noticed her among you ladies."

"Oh, she got off in St. Louis to visit an old friend." Catherine giggled softly. "Bettina Gordon is a lot older than us, and she couldn't make it back to Harper with us ladies, so Seraphina stayed on in St. Louis." Catherine shook her white head. "Bettina is getting on, you know, and she's rather sickly."

Cassandra could not believe what she was hearing. "You ladies did not leave the boat and join your friends in St. Louis?"

"Oh no, dear," Lavender said. "You've got it all

207

wrong. We did get off for a visit with Bettina, but then we got back on the *River Minx*. Now we are returning to Harper—where we live!"

Cassandra gasped softly. "You three live in Harper?" The white heads nodded simultaneously. "If I had but realized, I would have visited you long ago."

"You can't know *everybody* in a town," Millicent piped up. "But now that you have become our friend and our very favorite seamstress, we shall visit much more often, won't we, Lavender."

Lavender Peyton nodded. "Indeed. With all the fashions we go through in a year, Cassandra St. James could open a shop in Harper just to service us!" Lavender bent to pat and hold Cassandra's smooth, slim arm. "We won't have to go to St. Louis to purchase clothing any longer and won't have to make as many trips to have our dresses altered."

"But I do not think—"

Sylvestre intruded, "Excuse us, ladies, but we have a birthday to finish celebrating."

The golden eyes seemed to penetrate Cassandra's innermost thoughts and she cultivated the idea that he again had read her mind. She had been about to announce that once back in Harper she was sure her mother would not allow her to continue with her job as seamstress; it had only been temporary while on board the paddlewheeler.

"Happy Birthday, Cassandra," the ladies chirped together, then went to find their "Reserved" table, one they especially liked because it afforded them a view all around the room.

Harlan leaned forward to touch his glass to Cassandra's. "To us, then," he grinned wolfishly. "Perhaps to our wedding in the near future."

Cassandra was outraged, but she allowed his glass to clink with hers. There was nothing she could say, for Melantha had already planned for a wedding in the future. If she spoke up now, it would only end in an argument, and an unresolved one, for she had heatedly discussed the undesired event with Harlan once before. She did not wish to marry him. But he seemed to think she would break down and come willingly to him as a radiant bride.

Sylvestre gave a short laugh, muttering something nasty under his breath. Cassandra's head swiveled around at the profane words she had only heard once before, when Goliath and the roustabouts had been especially frustrated over rescuing a bundle of perishables clumsily dumped into the river by several new lads they had taken on as extras.

As Harlan continued to bluster, Sylvestre began to frown, deeply annoyed upon hearing about Kirby's ill treatment of his slaves at Kirby Plantation. Too, he had witnessed the man's cruelty to blacks only that afternoon as they had been loading.

At last Sylvestre spoke up, unable to check his temper. "We use no slave labor at my home, Diamondhead, for my mother and I believe in paying those hirelings in our employ."

Ignoring what the other man had said, Harlan went on as if Sylvestre had not spoken at all. "I got myself two big black bucks and my overseer is working the slave crew seven days a week—"

Cassandra cut in, "Why, that means they work on the Sabbath also. Those blacks are humans, not animals."

"As I was saying," Harlan again continued as if he'd not been interrupted, "they work seven days a week, from dawn till dusk, cultivating and clearing new fields."

"I cannot believe you would not give them one day a week free," Cassandra exclaimed softly. "That is inhuman treatment."

"Your slaves are going to drop in their tracks one day, Mr. Kirby," Sylvestre put in, thinking the man must be mad. "Does it not bother your conscience that you wring out every ounce of sweat from your wretched blacks?"

"Conscience!" Cassandra snapped. "You have none to speak of, Mr. Kirby!"

"Ah." Harlan wiped his greasy lips with a fine napkin. "Miss Cassandra, this never seemed to bother you overmuch when you visited our plantation before."

Blue eyes flashed, shining like precious sapphires as Cassandra clenched her hands into tight balls on her lap. "Untrue, sir, and I also remember witnessing men and women collapsing from exhaustion during the heat of a summer day while overseers swung their bull-whips."

There was not a shadow of a doubt in Sylvestre's mind that Harlan Kirby seduced the young black female slaves. Power over helpless women slaves! He had heard of plantation owners using their young females, submitting them to one indignity after another. The women were too cowed to fight their advances, trying to satisfy the plantation owner and the overseer in any way they could just to be able to eat and stay alive.

Monte noticed the faintly cynical smile on Kirby's lips and spoke up. "I have two blacks I brought with me from Georgia, a woman who is maid to Cassandra and her lovely daughter Dulcie. They gladly work for their food and their freedom."

"I know," Kirby said, licking his lips as he recalled the young female with skin like café au lait. "Your wife brought them along when you made the first trip to New Orleans with the *Minx.* Dulcie must be about the same age as Cassandra. Pretty little thing."

*And you shall never get your grimy hands on her!* Cassandra promised herself here and now. *And I shall never marry you . . . you evil bastard!* Cassandra's hands were still clenched into tight fists on her lap as she regarded the man who reminded her of a snake in the grass.

Kirby was clearly affronted by any leniency with blacks. They were to be used, and used well, as God intended them to be, he thought wickedly.

With a twitch in his jawline, his golden eyes flashing like shards of topaz, Sylvestre was recalling to mind a scene that very afternoon when he had witnessed, from the pilothouse, Kirby's ill treatment to a female slave. No doubt she was one he had just purchased and was taking her home when he noticed the *River Minx* docked just below St. Louis. Kirby had called the woman Yendelela. She was lovely, dainty, with black, liquid eyes, and Goliath had been helping her with a weighty burden when Kirby stepped up and knocked the roustabout to his knees on the dock. Goliath, being very large and strong, revived soon enough, his black eyes hiding a magnitude of hatred for the slave driver and the wishful thought to kill Kirby

211

with his bare hands.

Sylvestre glared at Kirby, just as he had done earlier that day. But there was nothing he could have done for the lovely Yendelela, Kirby's unfortunate slave. The man owned her. Many men in the South owned slaves. Even in Missouri, more and more was the talk about slavery and what might be done about it. If things turned out well, one day black men would be their own masters. The court said these Negroes could not be taken back to Africa; in Mississippi it was against the law to free them.

As Cassandra's outrage abated somewhat, she turned to see Sylvestre's eyes caressing her face tenderly. Every fiber and muscle was alive in her as she took in the manly sight of him. She glanced about the room, which was a shifting kaleidoscope of movement and color, then she peered downward, at her tight hands in her lap, her gaze finally drifting to Sy's long legs encased in a pair of dark breeches, which hugged the hard, smooth muscles of his thighs.

Almost gasping out loud, Cassandra ceased her scrutiny of that unmistakable swell and sought to conceal her anxiety by casting her gaze aside. It was not long, however, before she looked up to catch the hungry, lustful glint in the golden orbs. She was caught and held by them. Her cheeks bloomed with a scarlet hue, her mind became jumbled, and her knees grew weak.

Her breath caught in her throat at the sight of his ever-growing desire—in his eyes, in his body motions. His lips were slightly parted, his eyes dark with male hunger. How could he do this to her, embarrass her in front of everyone!

"Excuse me, Papa." She kissed his cheek. "Mr. Kirby, I will see you when Melantha brings me to visit." She suppressed a shudder of revulsion. "Mr. Casey . . . Sylvestre. I am thoroughly worn out and must return to my stateroom. Good night, everyone."

Sylvestre stood, holding her chair as she walked past him. "Would you like it if I walked you to your stateroom?" he asked close to her hair, pressing into her arms the white velvet gown she had almost forgotten to take with her. His sexual magnetism was galvanizing in its potent effect, and she almost forgot to move.

"No," she answered out loud. "I can find my own way, Mr. Diamond."

"Whatever you wish," he murmured, desiring to pull her tightly against his body.

Without further conversation, Cassandra walked out of the room and paused outside the door. The night was lovely, the sky a deep midnight-blue frosted with stars. She hurried to her stateroom.

With that, the party was over.

# Chapter Twelve

Slipping outside to the gallery, Cassandra strolled under the brilliant moon. As she moved to stand beside the rail, her gown looked like white jade, her step revealing glimpses of the ruffled white petticoats beneath, swaying gracefully in the night breezes.

Cassandra had not really intended to go for a midnight stroll, but once she had changed into the heavenly velvet gown, she felt so wonderfully alive, romantic, and vibrantly aware of herself as a woman.

The night was bathed in silver, brushed with blue-black shadows. Her gaze wandered and was caught by the foxfire luminescence on the decaying wood of the dock. Now she saw it; now she did not—substance and shadow, reality and unreality.

Feeling daring, Cassandra had applied a touch of coral lip rouge to her lips and smoothed a suggestion of violet-gray shadow on her lids. Erica Barrett had given her the cosmetics and Cassandra felt very grown up using them.

Breathing deeply of the dark fragrant smells of

nighttime on the river, she had a feeling of well-being just standing alone underneath the resplendent moon and stars. Sighing, she whispered a name.

"Sy . . . golden Sy . . . why do you keep haunting me even when you are not here beside me?"

The night gave her no answer.

She was gazing wistfully at the moon when suddenly she strained her ears. She quivered while she waited, hearing the soft fall of footsteps coming her way.

About to pull back into the shadows, Cassandra realized too late that the person, the man, by the sound of his heavy steps, had already caught sight of her. Her heart was hammering in her throat. Could it be Sylvestre?

Suddenly she was surrounded by the smell of liquor. "Mr. Kirby—it's you."

"Of course, m'dear. Who'd you think—Jack Notes or Tom Stiles?"

"You're tipsy, Mr. Kirby."

"So I am."

Cassandra licked dry lips. Where was Sylvestre?

Harlan laughed bitterly as he drew nearer, enveloping Cassandra with his horrible whiskey breath. Harlan was drawn by the fire in her moonlit eyes and the steady rise and fall of her delectable breasts. She had put on some weight, and it looked very becoming on her slender frame. Ever since he had met her, he had wanted her, even though she had been always icy and unapproachable.

"Come here, my love. My sweet little bride," he mumbled, reaching for her as she side-stepped.

Watching the moonlight play on her snow-blond hair, his self-control broke and he snatched her to him.

216

"Bride . . . my angel bride."

"I am not your bride, Mr. Kirby!"

Harlan's eyes narrowed dangerously. "What in hell is this?" he snarled. "You've known me for longer than that, sweet Cassandra. Call me Harlan . . . damnit . . . You hear?"

"Harlan!" Cassandra struggled against his great brute strength, shivering in disgust. "I am not one of your wretched female slaves you can talk to like that. Unhand me now, I say!"

He laughed down at her evilly. "Gotten awfully sassy, haven't you, missy?" Bending down, he placed a repulsively moist kiss against her heaving bosom.

Twisting free, Cassandra pushed against him with all her might. "Harlan—w-what do you think you are doing?!"

"Just what I should be doing, angel," he answered arrogantly. "Let me remind you, puss—one day you and I are going to be getting hitched"—he made a salacious gesture—"like two li'l peas in a snug li'l pod," he ended in a taunting parody of a Negro voice.

"Never. I find your touch utterly repugnant, *Mister* Kirby!"

Cassandra miraculously found the strength to disengage herself from Harlan's snaking arms and wet, seeking kisses.

"Better behave yourself, puss. You know as well as I that your mama and my papa have made plans for our upcoming wedding."

"Again I say *never!* I would rather marry a—a—" She faltered for words and finally found them—"a snake!"

His scowl deepening, Harlan reached for her again.

217

"I don't think you really mean that, sugar."

"You lets Missa Cassa go, Mistah Kirby. I means it!"

Goliath appeared upon the tail of his deep voice. He was a looming black giant, a formidable shadow of impending doom. The whites of the man's eyes glowed, his nostrils flaring angrily in remembrance of the beating he'd received earlier that same day by this same plantation man.

Goliath puffed up his already huge chest. "You kin pick on me any day you wants, mistah, but you lay one hand on Missa Cassa when she don't want you to and you gonna be nothin' but muck 'n piss in dat river when I'm done with you."

Harlan was livid with rage. "Why, you no-good bastard! You can't talk to me like that." He reeled drunkenly, like a ship floundering at sea. "I'll have your black ass whipped and chained so fast to the dock it'll make your fuzzy black curls bounce!"

"Yeah?" Goliath stepped ominously closer. "I says get away from Missa Cassa else I gonna do like I promised."

Without protection, Harlan backed off, his voice grinding out the warning. "One of these days, black boy, you're gonna get yours and I ain't just whistling Dixie!"

Goliath only grunted as Harlan Kirby hastened back to his stateroom, swallowing hard over the murderous look he had seen in the big black man's face.

All smoldering anger gone, Goliath turned to Cassandra. "You all right, Missa Cassa?"

"Yes," she murmured softly.

"You sure?"

"Yes, Goliath." Cassandra adjusted her disheveled

odice. "I am fine now, just a bit shaken."

He peered down at her and took a deep breath, pursing his lips to an even greater thickness. "I'm gonna stay outside your stateroom, Missa Cassa, make sure no one tries to come in."

Cassandra laughed shakily. "That will not be necessary, my dear friend. I believe you frightened Mr. Kirby half out of his wits."

"You shakin', honey chile."

"No, I am just a bit chilled."

Goliath shook his dark frizzy head. "That man got no wits, Missa Cassa. He don't care 'bout nobody else but Mistah Harlan Kirby."

"Well, you've heard it said, Goliath, that every bean has its spot and there's a salve for every sore." She smiled, lightening her mood.

"Yes'm. He's a man who'd make his own dawg bite him." Goliath's huge shoulders shrugged. "If you don't need me anymore, missa, I'm gonna go check on a pretty li'l black gal, make sure she's good 'n comfortable on the boiler deck where that mean gent put her."

"Ah." Cassandra smiled. "She must be breathlessly awaiting your coming, Goliath."

"She cain't go nowheres anyhow. Mr. Kirby's got her chained to a post down there." He clenched his hands into angry fists.

"How awful." Cassandra shook her head. "I wish there was something I could—"

"You cain't, Missa Cassa. It's the black man's lot these days." Again he sighed deeply. "Let me walk you to your cabin afore I go to check on Yendelela and sneak her some hot food and chicory coffee."

"Please, Goliath. I wish to remain here—just a few

219

moments more alone before turning in?"

His big head nodded. "Promise you don't be staying out here much longer. I be back a little later to make sure you done tucked youself away safe 'n sound, Missa Cassa."

"I promise, Goliath. And thank you again for being my protector. I appreciate your safeguarding."

"I be around." He began to back away. "'Night, Missa Cassa."

"Good night."

Alone, taking a deep breath, Cassandra leaned against the railing. Still unable to unwind after the events of the night, she decided to check to see if her father had gone to bed. She had a need to be close to someone, to have him wrap her in the security of his embrace, kiss her cheek, call her his "little Cassa" like he used to in her younger days.

Bathed in pale moonbeams, looking like an ethereal goddess of the night in her white velvet, Cassandra walked along the gallery, when she came to a sudden halt outside the cabin she knew was Miki Rhea's.

Her winsome smile faded.

Laughter . . . male laughter floated out to her. *Her father's laugh!*

"Oh, no . . . not Miki Rhea . . . Papa—"

Cassandra cried softly, whirling to clutch the railing, her knuckles showing whitely.

Hurt filled her.

*Papa!*

"No! It cannot be. God, tell me I am abed and only just dreaming," Cassandra whimpered, pounding the railing with balled fists of frustration.

"Cassandra . . . what is it?"

She spun about, her white velvet gown and petticoats swaying with the startled motion. Sylvestre was suddenly at her side. How he got there she could not say. One moment she was alone with her aching heart and the next moment Sylvestre was there, pulling her against the warmth and strength of his body.

She sobbed and drew away.

"What has made you act this way? It hurts me to see you like this. *Answer me.*"

"Papa . . . and Miki Rhea!"

Sylvestre let out his breath in a hiss. He was answered before the question left his lips as sensual laughter drifted underneath the door, accompanied by the deeper laugh of Monte St. James.

*"Mon Dieu,"* Sylvestre breathed against her silken head, scooping her up into his arms. "Is your room locked?"

With her face burrowed in his neck, Cassandra could only manage to shake her head in the negative, once.

Turning the knob and kicking the door the rest of the way open with his booted foot, Sylvestre bore his tearful burden into the dim interior of the stateroom and set her down on the edge of the bed.

At once Cassandra whirled about and lay down, curling herself into a tight ball of anguish. "H-how c-could he . . ." she sobbed wretchedly and gulped aloud. "H-he is my f-father."

Securing the door, Sylvestre joined Cassandra on the bed, reclining beside her as she lay on her side, rumpling the white velvet dress. With her hair disheveled she looked like a young bride left alone at the altar, her cheeks stained with tears.

"Here now, *ma chérie,* no more tears." Sy held his

handkerchief in one hand, dabbing at her flood of tears while his other hand smoothed her hair back, out of her eyes. "The world has not come to an abrupt end," he murmured. His hand switched to the other side, draping the loose hank of hair behind that ear, too.

Sy stroked her silky hair and soothed her tangled emotions with calm, gentle words, cautiously setting forth to explain a man's sexual urges. His hypnotic voice crooned into her ear while he held her tenderly, as if she was but a babe in need of gentling for bedtime.

Cassandra took a deep breath. "B-but why does he need another when he h-has Melantha?"

"I cannot answer that question for you, my darling Cassa." *Perhaps it could be Monte does not love Melantha,* he did not say out loud. He watched a tear make its way down her cheek. "Who knows the reason?" Sy shrugged against Cassandra's ribs, sore from sobbing out loud.

"Y-you mentioned a man's sexual urges. Why does a man need so many women? Can h-he not be content to lie with one?"

"Cassa," Sy began, and drew in a steadying breath. How to explain this touchy subject, dear Lord. "I only know that I could be content my whole life with only one woman at my side, in my bed, and—"

"Liar!" she cut in, with a loud hiccup following. "All you m-men must be liars—"

"Not so," he said, stroking back silken fibers that insisted on falling over her face. Sy leaned over Cassa and kissed her hair over her cheeks, her ear, the nape of her swanlike neck. "No other would share my life or my love if there was one special woman waiting for me at home being faithful always."

222

"Home?" Cassandra swallowed and looked up. "You mean a place set away from home, do you not? Men do not love and cherish their wives. Men love their mistresses—or they p-pretend to love. I do not believe men can love 'one special woman,' Sy."

"I have already told you—*I can.*"

"Fiddle!" Cassandra shoved away from Sy, taking his handkerchief to blow into it noisily.

"You must learn to trust." His hand tightened over hers.

"Oh. Trust. Indeed. All you randy men must 'know' Miki Rhea. And how about Dolly McKay? And how many others that go unnamed, Sy?"

Sy chuckled warmly. "You *are* a jealous little minx, aren't you. And where did you ever come by the crude word 'randy'?"

"Erica Barrett used the word. It means . . . well, never mind. I shall not repeat it, for you must surely know the meaning."

The twisted image of her father straining and grunting on the bed with Miki Rhea came to her, alive, with full force, the same image of Sy with Dolly also burning in her mind's eye. "I saw you!" Cassandra blurted without thinking.

"What are you saying?"

When Cassandra lay down upon her folded arms, half on her stomach, her knees drawn up, Sy reached out to touch her moist cheek. "You saw me *what,* Cassa?"

"No. I will never say it all."

*Mon Dieu,* Sylvestre began to wonder just what she could be referring to. There could not be much that she had witnessed, for he had not been abed with another woman for the entire past year . . . unless she had seen him fighting off the lusty advances of Dolly McKay . . . That must be it.

"Cassandra. Did you, ah . . . perchance happen to witness a scene in the Water Street Tavern in which, ah . . . a certain tavern wench was with—" Lord. Sy ran his fingers through his hair, raking the golden mane back from his forehead.

"Yes!" she almost shouted. She was unbearably conscious of his hard length pressed so intimately against her curled body.

"How?"

"What?" Cassandra blinked damp lashes.

A gleam of humor lit his eyes to a topaz hue. "Mmm, I am trying to consider the possibilities of a hiding place in that tiny tavern room."

"I . . . I was outside the door. Your energetic floozy no doubt forgot to close the door all the way." Cassandra sniffed and pressed her lips together. "In a hurry I would naturally presume."

Sy watched her duck her head as a scarlet blush stained her delicate cheeks. "Cassandra, do you not recall that I already have told you that that woman does not interest me in the least. She was after more than my male body, that is certain. A few more coins to slip in her bodice perhaps . . ." He shrugged one shoulder against hers. "I haven't the answer to that scene, either. One moment I was getting ready to turn in after an exhausting day on the paddlewheeler—"

"Why did you not stay aboard the *Minx*? Why did you have to seek lodgings at the Water Street Tavern?"

"The food was good, delicious in fact. And when a man is full after a satisfying meal, he wants to seek his bed soon thereafter. Besides, there was always clean linen and a bath ready in the tavern. Not," he said and repeated, "not for the reason you think, that there was a hot-blooded wench at the ready, mademoiselle!"

"You were in love with Miki Rhea at one time, were you not?"

"What? *Love?* With that painted slut! Hardly, Cassandra. That kind of woman is kept more than arm's length from my presence. I do not relish the idea of contracting a social disease, either."

"But Jared Casey said you two were very much in love and you were trying to get back together with Miki Rhea."

*"Merde!* Excuse my bad French, but that is preposterous, Cassandra." Sylvestre shook his head; then his rage quieted down. "That man wants you, Cassa. He is like a rutting stag and he will do anything short of rape. Let me rephrase that—short of *murder,* to get at you. You are still fresh, virginal, and I believe he's never tasted such a delectable morsel as yourself." He shivered hotly at his own words.

"I believe you speak for yourself, Sylvestre."

Cassandra stared up at golden Sy. The moon cast a glow into the room, on Cassandra's blond hair, and the strands seemed alive with silver and gold highlights. Her gown shimmered in the rays of filtered moonlight.

"You are correct on one accord, my love. You, young lady, are all virginal sweetness, softness—with a woman's wildfire." His voice turned gruff. "And I want you so desperately, Cassa."

Sy moaned deep in his throat. Then, moving closer, hovering above her, he lowered his face with slow deliberation. To assuage the deep thirst he had for her honeyed lips, his mouth moved to plunder hers thoroughly. At once Cassandra was lost to the pulsating fires that had been burning so long in her . . . ever since her first erotic dream of Sy Diamond.

The more Sy kissed her and the more she returned those kisses, the greater was Cassa's womanly allure. He purred deep in his throat like a big cat, and she answered with a softer mewling of her own.

Cassandra gave herself up to the yearning passion that clamored in her veins while Sy heard an inner voice warning him to leave Cassandra a maid untouched; but it was a voice that was growing fainter and weaker with each moment that passed.

"I have never experienced these intense feelings with another. I swear this to you," Sy groaned against her temple, and he did not lie.

Suddenly the frightened virgin, Cassandra rose and backed up to the oaken headboard. She could see his strained expression in the pale rays entering to bathe in silver the area surrounding the bed, and them in it breathless and staring at each other, aglow with moonlight that intensified even the shadows.

Sliding along the embroidered cover, Sy followed her to the top of the soft, springy mattress. Touching her tingling lips with a fingertip, he said, "'Lost in the moment thou art won.'" A deep sigh of disappointment escaped his throat. "I must go."

"What did you say?" Suddenly she was afraid of him leaving her alone to face the night.

"'Soft child of love—thou balmy bliss, Inform me, O delicious kiss! Why thou so suddenly art gone—'"

"'—Lost in the moment thou art won.'"

They exchanged a few more feathery light yet

passionate kisses. Hot kisses. Steamy looks. Cassandra was shaken to the core, as was Sy.

"I must—" Sy broke off, feeling as if his desire was strangling him. Should he possess her now, make her his woman? Wait for marriage? That was a laugh. Cassandra was tied to her mother's apron strings. He desired and needed Cassa more than anything he had ever wanted in his twenty-seven years. But she had to be totally willing to come to him. Of her own free will. He could walk away now. Or he could stay. Seduce her, for she was primed for loving. "I should—" Sy groaned, then, with a moan, he resumed hungrily kissing her, pulling her close, giving himself to the pounding, driving force that leaped through his body at the taste of her sweet lips against his own. A few threads of her golden hair came between their lips and, stroking seductively with his tongue, he licked the hair aside, then, suddenly, he inserted his velvet tongue into her mouth.

Coming from deep within her, Cassandra, too, moaned and pressed herself closer, filling his arms with a graceful movement that offered herself up fully to his demanding kiss. His lips left her for a moment as he said, "Lie beside me, love. Here."

When their clothed bodies came together, Cassandra could feel his swollen desire pressing into her soft cup of womanhood. Sy flexed his buttocks to get even closer while his tongue once again thrust between her moist, hot lips and raped her mouth. Cassandra ached for the fulfillment Sy's virile body promised her.

Sy's free hand lowered, lifting her skirts slowly while he continued to kiss and plunder her mouth. There were so many petticoats for him to get through, but, finally, his fingers slipped into her pantalettes, causing red-hot quivers to go through her as he found the mound he had been seeking.

Through half-closed eyes, Sylvestre gazed down at her, lifting his head in order to see her fully, to watch the emotions in her eyes laid bare to him.

Laying a hand across his lean cheek, Cassandra experienced new tenderness for Sy, aching feelings she had not dreamed possible in a lifetime.

At the first brush of his fingertips in so intimate a place, Cassandra drew taut, and then she breathed a sigh as he inched into the honeyed cradle of love.

"Just a little more," Sylvestre said in a husky voice. Dear God, he was burning up!

"Sy!!"

With featherlike softness, his fingers circled over her dewy membrane and she arched and arched until at last she cried out at the ecstasy his movements were giving her. The palm of his free hand found her buttocks and he pulled her gently closer to his swirling fingers.

"Sy . . . I-I cannot breathe!"

"I know, love . . . I know."

Suddenly her eyes flew open and she checked herself from reaching the blazing star. "No, Sy . . . no more. Please. I am afraid of what is happening!"

To calm her, he took her hand to his breast. "Feel my heart, it is beating as wild as your own. I can scarce breathe myself. You want me to stop?" He shook his head and muttered, "I cannot stop even myself, love."

One long-fingered hand closed over a swollen mound and found the pink pearl of womanhood. He could feel her tense arousal right through his fingertips.

"You must . . . you must stop." But as Cassandra said this, her head rolled from side to side, her feverish body demanding total surrender to whatever Sy wanted of her.

His hand continued to worship her, his fingers to brush the succulent bud. She was as smooth as silk. Cassandra was ripe and ready for a man to come into her, to love her. She was definitely hungry. Hungrier than he would ever have believed possible. For one wild instant he asked himself if he dared take her this night.

No, his conscience argued.

*Yes!*

No!

*Yes!*

For he would never be able to halt the inevitable. He had only one aching regret: It should have been their wedding night when Cassandra embarked upon her maiden voyage into the world of sensuality and bliss, an experience more appropriately experienced and sanctified within the framework of marriage.

"Cassa," he moaned softly, stirred by her sweetness and fire. *"Oui,* yes, Cassa . . ."

As he said this, a soft, passionate murmur came from her throat.

There would be no regrets.

It would happen now, for she had stirred him in an unbearable way. He removed his hands and began to strip away her white velvet gown, moving swiftly, efficiently, while at the same time he strung kisses upon her face, her throat, and, at last, her bare shoulders.

"All your trust, Cassandra—give it to me."

But trust for Cassandra would come haltingly . . .

# Chapter Thirteen

The white velvet gown, Cassandra's birthday gift from her father, lay in a heap on the floor. A yellow moon rode high in the sky illuminating the stateroom, and Sylvestre's golden gaze was bright with passion and hunger as he took in her perfect, ethereal body.

She had worn several layers of petticoats and, like the petals of white flowers, he had peeled them away. "I will not take you in a hurry, nor will I take you against your will," he promised with a tenderness that moved her.

"I know," she whispered mindlessly, feeling all warm and wonderfully aglow inside. "It does not matter to me how many women have shared your bed and warmed your heart in the past." She smiled secretly to herself. "Now is what matters, Sy. This night I belong to you."

His eyes hardened for a moment. "You will belong to no other man after I take you to paradise this night, Cassa. You will be mine—forever. Do you understand, chérie?"

She nodded slowly as Sylvestre touched her flaming

cheeks, smoothed her hair, all the while his eye adoring her, glazed with wondrous desire over the sigh of her naked body. He, too, had removed his own clothes and they joined hers in a puddle on the moonli floor.

He stared at her with glittering eyes as he pushed her back to the bed. "You have time to stop me yet. But I warn you, once I begin to make love to you, I wil complete the act and there will be no turning back. I will take you to paradise and back, my love."

She smiled up at him, experiencing maidenly shyness now that they were unclothed. "You will not stop if I want you to?" she asked, not really wanting him to, but afraid just the same.

"I will not force my attentions upon you. But as I said—I warn you, and you must choose, Cassa."

"Please," she said breathlessly. "Do not leave me. I need you to stay with me." She thought about her father with Miki Rhea. "I am so lonesome."

Slowly he pulled her into his waiting embrace, murmuring in her ear, *"Que je suis heureux;* How happy I am, my sweetest heart."

His lips began to slide across the flesh of her silken throat, his fingers playing over the flawless column of her arched neck. He felt her shiver. Realizing her innocence, he told himself to move slowly as he initiated her into the artful bliss of lovemaking. A man was driven by stronger emotions, a woman gentler ones. He needed to remember this, and he would make this night one she would never forget. He wanted to bind her to him forever, and he intended to make her his bride as soon as possible. All he needed was her

illingness—and be damned with what anyone else
nought!

"I want you . . . to show me, Sy."

In answer, his mouth moved down her arched neck,
is tongue warm as it gently lapped the coral crests of
er small breasts. Now there was a sweeping weakness
mat made her tremble with a gamut of beautiful new
insations.

"Ahh . . . Cassandra," he moaned as he explored the
welling mounds, swirling, moistly sweeping his hot
ongue over them, tightening her nipples.

Cassandra could feel the long and powerful legs
ressed against her own softer ones. She discovered
hat her breathing matched his, for she could feel the
ise and fall of the muscled wall of his chest. She saw
iefore her heavy-lidded eyes a shifting blur of
novement and silver rays of invading moon.

Sy's gaze dropped to the flatness of her stomach and
he tawny patch of her womanhood, leaving a glowing
rail to her loins. He slid his body lower and stopped
here. His tongue tasted the intimate spot between her
egs, circling the throbbing, most sensitive part.

Her breath was trapped in her throat as an odd
eeling of virginal shyness washed over her. She moved
anguorously under him, biting her lip as he became
oolder. Her pulse beat dizzily against her forehead as
he swelled, burgeoned, blossomed.

Cassandra abandoned herself to the new spiraling
ensations that sent ripples of warmth through her.
Suddenly she was apprehensive of what was happening
to her. "Sylvestre . . . *wait!*"

Her mouth was dry and the blood in her veins

pounded hard throughout her body as he lifted his golden head to stare at her. "What the . . . hell?" he said in a flat voice.

"Will—" She swallowed hard. "Will this mean that I shall have to marry you?"

Sylvestre watched her for a long moment, struck dumb by the question she had just put to him. "You *are* an innocent, aren't you," he stated.

"Well . . . yes, in this area." She blushed furiously. Then she went on with what was on her mind while he shook his head slowly, raking his hands through his golden mane of thick hair. He was waiting, patiently. "I . . . I do not intend to marry anyone. There is too much for a woman to . . . to lose in tying herself to a man."

"Lord, you are incredible. Or has Erica Barrett filled your head with this fluffy nonsense? Answer me, Cassandra, you owe me an explanation."

Drawing the sheet across his lap, Sylvestre lifted himself to sit on the bed. He was in a caustic mood as she answered, "Why? Do you believe I have led you on?"

His eyes narrowed dangerously. "I pray you have not, *ma petite,*" he said quietly, his eyes intent on her face as his gaze skimmed his shoulder to look down at her.

Pertly she sat up in bed, feeling brave now—now that he had ceased making her feel like a mindless jelly. She did not like what he had been doing—it made her feel out of control. Or was she only fooling herself and she was only terrified? It had felt . . . good.

"Has Erica Barrett made you into a 'liberated' woman?"

234

With bravado, Cassandra tossed her head. "There is no such thing."

"No? I believe there will be such one day. In fact, I think *Miss* Barrett is the first of their kind." He prayed Cassandra would not become one of them, and if he had anything to do with it, she would definitely not!

"Your defenses are frail, to say the least, my love." His eyes darkened to amber. "You only postpone the inevitable, Cassandra."

"What do you mean?"

"You love this play, don't you," he drawled, smoothing the sheet over his lap with the flat of his hand.

"I wish to belong to myself, Sy."

*"Non,* Cassandra. You wish to hide inside yourself while you shiver and wonder about what can happen between a man and a woman. You wonder why my lovemaking has thrown you out of control. You have pulled into that shell you sometimes hide in."

"Perhaps," she murmured, her silken lashes hiding her eyes.

"Do not hide from me, Cassandra. Love is something you feel together—not apart. You cannot look at me from afar with stars in your eyes, wishing I would not come and touch you, because I will, Cassa. When you stroll the deck under the midnight moon, it is not because you are counting the stars, Cassandra. You are dreaming of love with a certain man, and while you stand beneath that moon, you are waiting for him to come to you."

"You believe I am waiting for you to come to me."

"I do." He nodded once. "You are a romantic, Cassandra, and you dream of a perfect love with the

235

right man."

"Love? Is that what is going on between my father and Miki Rhea this night? Was that what was going on between you and Dolly McKay that night in the tavern bedroom?"

"You amaze me, Cassandra St. James. Not long ago you wished for me to stay with you because you were so wretchedly lonesome." His face contorted with something near frustration. "Is that what you are still feeling—or would you like me to leave you now?"

Haughtily she said, "You can leave, Mr. Diamond, for all I care."

"Wait a damn minute. Before I go, I would like to know how it was that you sneaked into the tavern and watched that stupid scene between Dolly McKay and myself."

Releasing her bottom lip from her teeth, Cassandra raised her face to meet his eyes. "I was dressed"—she dragged in a deep breath—"as a boy."

"What?!"

"You heard me. A boy. I borrowed some clothes from the stable boy Charles, and walked boldly into the taproom, when I saw your buxom wench making her way to your room. I followed her—" She shrugged matter-of-factly. "And you, monsieur, know the rest. More than I."

Sylvestre was thoughtful for a moment before he worded his next thoughts carefully. "Did that perhaps hurt you . . . seeing me with another woman?"

"No," she gritted out.

"Hah! You lie."

At Sylvestre's terse words, Cassandra's pulse gave a little leap of apprehension. Not wanting to, she remembered the taste of his warm, exciting mouth kissing her deeply a short time ago, warming and laving her most intimate part. She had been terrified of losing control to him, and never had she thought a touch could fire her blood so much. Even her mischievous escapades had not made her feel so thoroughly excited and drained.

Sylvestre heaved a deep sigh. "You have been teasing me, Cassandra."

"No—t-truly I have not. You just do not understand."

"Then please, *chérie,* explain yourself to me. I will wait here all night if I must. We are docked, remember, so there are no immediate tasks awaiting me. Tell me, is it passion that frightens you so much, Cassa?" He pulled himself above her again, pushing her down gently as he watched and waited. "Is it?"

She would not answer him.

The look on his face was suddenly inscrutable. He slid his long, lean fingers through her blond hair, creating a fan to spread like liquid gold and silver about them as he lowered his chiseled, bronze face.

"There is nothing for you to fear, Cassandra. You have already had my word that I will not force my attentions upon you. Now tell me that which I do not fully understand. As I told you, I will wait all night for you to speak your mind. I am not a dragon come to breathe fire on you. Instead, I wish to slay those dragons for you, m'lady."

"I . . . I—" Cassandra found her voice cracking. "I am so lost!"

"Poor child."

Sy lifted her chin so that she could see into his loving eyes. "Indeed you are lost, my sweet. Who—or what—

has made you this way? Moments ago you declared yourself as a free woman . . . in so many words."

Cassandra embarrassedly avoided meeting the stare of Sy's long-lashed golden eyes. He realized she was overwrought by what she had heard coming from beneath Miki Rhea's door, but there was more. Perhaps her domineering mother had denied all joy and security from Cassandra's young life! He hated to think so unkindly of Melantha St. James . . . but soon Cassandra would be returning home to face the woman who he was sure was one of the dragons in her untrusting little world.

"Cassa, I want for you to give me your trust, wholly and completely. I love you. I will never hurt you."

"Sy . . . oh, Sy . . ." *He loved her!*

"Please let me . . . love you."

"C-can I believe you?" Cassandra asked, swallowing hard.

"Trust me. I shall never, *never* let you down." Taking her hand to his lips, he kissed her fingers, one by one, and then he squeezed tightly while pressing her hand to his cheek.

Once again Cassandra felt a breathless anticipation slowly moving through her, and she could feel his powerful muscles beneath her fingertips as, this time, she dared to begin caressing him—as he had done her.

"There is no turning back," Sy rasped into her ear as her dainty fingers trustingly found him and touched tentatively. His warm breath fanned her cheek and throat. "This time you must swim, my love, otherwise you will drown," he said right before his lips took hers in fierce possession.

Cassandra took the turn at the crossroad that led to

rapture, and Sy was there to take her hand into his, to bind their very souls together. His hands roamed over the delicious mountains and valleys of ever-tightening flesh. She was flushed with erotic warmth.

Touching him intimately, she would have brought him to a hasty climax had he not taken her hand to his lips and pressed a kiss into her palm, shaking his head while gazing into her love-glazed orbs. "I wish to be in you all the way when that happens, *mon poulet,*" he said. Cryptic words to her untaught ears.

His mouth became firm and his kiss deepened, leaving Cassandra to do nothing but sigh and whimper with pleasure as he seemed to take her into a trembling world of passion from which there was no way back.

*Swim or drown, Cassandra.*

A bold sound of triumph broke from Sy's throat, and he moved to poise himself above her. Kneeing her thighs apart, his fingers slid into her, probing with a sensual quest, deep and deeper until he was not so gentle and he broke the skin that covered her maidenhood with a swift jab.

Cassandra's body heaved upward in protest at the pain he had unexpectedly given her.

Sylvestre ached at the sound of her pain. When she was quiet, he began to move again. "It will soon be over and there will be nothing but pleasure."

He prepared to enter her with his swollen member. "Oh, Sy . . . please," Cassandra cried, confused by her desire to be filled in her aching core, but not knowing what she was asking for.

"Yes, my love, *mon poulet,* yes."

She felt her body expand to receive his full possession. He muffled her next moan of bittersweet

239

joining as slowly his body overwhelmed hers. The tenderness of his movements made her want to cry. He was so good . . . so good . . .

The pain had already receded. In its place was the fast rhythm of his movements as he thrust into her, burying himself in an entry as deep as he could make it and a wrench that almost carried her tightness with him as he lifted himself.

It was so beautiful a moment in time that Cassandra forgot her anxiety and yielded herself to the incredible intimacy of belonging to Sy. She was swept along in a tidal wave, undulating and smoothing out, taking his manhood deeper into herself.

"Ahh, Cassa, Cassa . . . what are you doing to me?" he murmured into her ear, feeling her silken limbs clench his waist.

"We, my golden man, are slaying some dragons."

"Aye, that we are."

This was her destiny, to belong to Sy!

Her teeth bit into his hard flesh in an agony of pleasure and she began to pant, arching her back to meet each pounding thrust in mutual fire, her slender hips rising to meet him.

A low scream tore from her throat as Sy throbbed deep within her, flinging back his head with teeth bared, while she followed him, shamelessly pressing, trembling wildly in tiny explosions, abandoned to the paradise Sy had promised!

Side by side. Smoky motes of moonbeams stealing into the stateroom. Their breathing had quieted, their hearts had ceased to thunder, perspiration cooling on their skin.

# MORE PASSION AND ADVENTURE AWAIT... YOUR TRIP TO A BIG ADVENTUROUS WORLD BEGINS WHEN YOU ACCEPT YOUR FIRST
## 4 NOVELS ABSOLUTELY *FREE*
### (AN $18.00 VALUE)

Accept your Free gift and start to experience more of the passion and adventure you like in a historical romance novel. Each Zebra novel is filled with proud men, spirited women and tempetuous love that you'll remember long after you turn the last page

Zebra Historical Romances are the finest novels of their kind. They are written by authors who really know how to weave tales of romance and adventure in the historical settings you love. You'll feel like you've actually gone back in time with the thrilling stories that each Zebra novel offers.

## GET YOUR FREE GIFT WITH THE START OF YOUR HOME SUBSCRIPTION

Our readers tell us that these books sell out very fast in book stores and often they miss the newest titles. So Zebra has made arrangements for you to receive the four newest novels published each month.

You'll be guaranteed that you'll never miss a title, and home delivery is so convenient. And to show you just how easy it is to get Zebra Historical Romances, we'll send you your first 4 books absolutely FREE! Our gift to you just for trying our home subscription service.

## BIG SAVINGS AND FREE HOME DELIVERY

Each month, you'll receive the four newest titles as soon as they are published. You'll probably receive them even before the bookstores do. What's more, you may preview these exciting novels free for 10 days. If you like them as much as we think you will, just pay the low preferred subscriber's price of just $3.75 each. *You'll save $3.00 each month off the publisher's price.* AND, your savings are even greater because there are never any shipping, handling or other hidden charges—FREE Home Delivery. Of course you can return any shipment within 10 days for full credit, no questions asked. There is no minimum number of books you must buy.

# 4 FREE BOOKS

The man touched the woman's arm with the back of a brushing hand. *"Avez-vous sommeil?"*

*"Non,"* Cassandra answered. "I am not sleepy." She smiled in the dark of the moon. *"J'ai faim."*

Sylvestre's heart sang with joy and laughter as he rolled over to look down at her. "You are *hungry?*"

"Terribly!" she whispered fiercely.

"Well then—" He hopped off the bed, standing up to drag his breeches on. "I shall go to the Mess and fetch m'lady a morsel or two."

"Mmm," Cassandra murmured and rolled over, splaying her hand over the still-warm spot on the sheet where he had lain. "That sounds wonderful, m'lord . . ."

"Lady Cassandra . . ." He bowed in a low swoop, using a pert little hat he had snatched from the wall-shelf. "Lord Sylvestre's swift steed stands ready outside the door. I shall hasten to the Mess and—"

Bending over the bed, he listened to her even breathing, which told him she was fast asleep—"and get myself something. Perhaps not. Besides, I am not very . . . hungry."

Sylvestre shook his head, raking his fingers through his mussed hair. He searched the room for his boots, his shirt. Finding them, he finished getting dressed.

In the pale moonlight sifting in, Sylvestre stood very quietly by the bed, watching the love of his life sleeping. He touched his lips with his fingertips, then touched hers, and she stirred, cracking her eyes to look up at the blurred figure. A soft, tender smile touched her lips for a moment, and then she drifted back into wisps of sleep.

"Good night, fair maiden . . . ah, love. I will see you in my dreams."

Then he was gone, the door closing softly behind him.

". . . love . . . dreams," Cassandra murmured, and then only the sound of the water caressing the *River Minx* lingered on through the rest of the night.

# Chapter Fourteen

"C'mon, Cap'n Sy!"

The sun, obscure and hazy, was just rising as Goliath clutched the reins of the eagerly prancing horse near the dock, waiting for Sylvestre to take the spirited beast out of his hands. The black man had always been a little afraid of horses, ever since his younger brother had been kicked in the liver and killed by one with a spirit to equal this beast's.

"I cain't hold 'em much longer, Cap'n Sy. I don't like dis black beast." The horse rolled huge liquid eyes at the black man. "Yeah, you jest mind your manners, you black debil."

"All right, Goliath. I will take him now."

Suddenly the sky darkened and the sun was obscured by a stormy gray sky. The wind picked up, tossing the stacks of the *River Minx* and flattening the tall grass on the riverbank.

"You got everythin' you be needin', Cap'n Sy?"

"Yes, Goliath." As Sylvestre mounted, took the reins, and patted the bags he had just fastened to the saddle, he conferred a grim smile on the man. "Thank you again for finding the horse for me. I know how difficult it was for you to do this, since horses are not to your liking, Goliath."

Puffing his large lips, Goliath rolled his eyes at the sideways-dancing horse, giving the beast back some of his own eyeballing. Because of the whistling wind and the clanking of the chain links on the docks, Goliath had to yell. "I jest hope you ain't too late and your mama ain't gonna die, Cap'n. That'd be terrible, suh."

Goliath had come to like and trust the golden-haired, golden-eyed man, and ever since he had been so nice to Yendelela, Kirby's unfortunate black slave, Goliath was sure this Captain Sy was just the man for Mistah St. James's daughter, Missa Cassa. He knew, too, that Captain Sy had spent an awful long time in Cassa's room the night before. Actually, he'd known Captain Sy a long time, but he had never realized just how nice the tall, handsome man was until he got to know him better this trip.

Sylvestre flipped a few more coins into the black man's hands. "Give this to the lad who delivered the message to the *River Minx*, Goliath. In my haste to ready for my ride back to St. Louis, I forgot to pay him. I know the *River Minx* will be pulling out today—" Sylvestre held on to his battered hat in the wind while the spirited black stallion pranced sideways from the puffs of dust swirling in the zephyr breeze sweeping down on them. "Goliath!"

Goliath leaned into the wind as he made his way back to the paddlewheeler. "What's you got to say, Mistah Sylvestre?"

The black beast reared and danced on his hind legs

244

until, finally, Sylvestre gained control, jerking on the reins and kneeing him to make him obey his every command. He had to get to Diamondhead, for his mother was very ill, the note had stated. His mother or her doctor must have heard that the *River Minx* was docked just below St. Louis and sent the lad with the message for him to come quickly, it was urgent, his mother could pass away any time.

"Tell Cassandra what happened, that I had to . . . !"

"What's dat, Cap'n Sy?" Goliath tried yelling above the din of the wind and oncoming rain. "I cain't hear you . . ."

But Sylvestre and the black horse blended into the swirls of dust and the slant of slashing wet wind as they dashed off at a mad pace, finally vanishing into the gray, somber woodlands.

Cassandra hugged to her stateroom, curled up in the deep-cushioned chintz chair, the embroidered coverlet tucked around her as she sipped the delicious hot tea. She did, however, forgo the sugared delicacies Cook had sent to her room on the tray with her ham, eggs, toast, and jam—the beignets she devoured every day as if she couldn't get enough of them.

Cassandra picked up her fork to push the creamed eggs Chartres around on the plate some more and then finally gave up, shoving the half-finished food to the middle of the table. Looking up at the rattling window with rivulets of rain smearing it, she shivered, wondering how the folks who walked by her window with umbrellas and raincoats could venture out into the damp weather. It was unusually cold for the end of

May, and being on the river made the day seem even colder.

Gloomy.

Cassandra felt as gray as the weather outside, her spirits just as damp. She wondered how she could feel so bored and lonely when just the night before she had experienced the most thrilling event, making her life up to now seem terribly dull. Then she had awakened to find herself alone. How shaken she had been to find that her lover had deserted her, left her to face the morning alone.

He was gone . . . gone . . . not even on board the *River Minx*!

"He could have come to see me before going off like that," she murmured miserably, recalling her hurt when the steward had answered her by saying Sylvestre Diamond had left the boat in a hurry early just that morning.

Taking a sip of her tea, Cassandra realized they were pulling out when the boat began to back out into the mainstream making her tea slosh a drop onto her lap.

She felt numb when she took another sip of the lukewarm tea, then put the cup aside, hearing the mournful sound of the paddlewheels slapping the wild gray river.

After she had bathed, she pulled her hair back from her face and braided it into a gleaming coronet atop her head, interweaving it with pink ribbon that trailed down to her shoulders. All of a sudden tears brimmed in her sad blue eyes, then made streaks down her unhappy face.

"Men!" Cassandra cast aside the coverlet and, uncurling her long, slender limbs, she pulled out her sewing basket, sat in the stiff-backed chair, Millicent's gown waiting to be altered lying across her lap. "Bah! They are all wandering cads ... every last one of them," she said with a loud sniff. "Not a decent one among their lot."

She dried her eyes and then set to her task, her needle flashing in and out of the purple material with a vengeance as she pretended it was Sylvestre's heart she was stabbing. "I am just another one of the countless females who fell prey to Captain Sy's fatal attraction—"

But Sylvestre shouldn't be blamed if women fell in love with him, her conscience argued.

Cassandra argued back: He has neither the desire nor the intent to live with me as his wife.

Cassandra twisted the fabric of the gown until her knuckles turned white. "I am gullible—and blind—to love such a rogue!"

*He won't come back. He won't come back. He's had you now and deserted you for good, he won't be back, you silly ninny.* She plied her needle to the chugging rhythm of the paddlewheeler, the circling, confused wind, and the lonesome song of the rain-splashed river.


While the huge pistons and the paddle wheels worked all through the night, bringing her slowly closer to home, Cassandra slept. She was dreaming. It was night. The trees were ashimmer with delicate purple leaves.

In her dream she was back home. She was dressed in a gown she'd fashioned for herself, a pale-green polished pin-striped silk with white ruffled silk trim and yellow-silk rose ornamentation. She was lonelier than ever, watching the empty river and pining for her lost love. She spotted a smaller craft plying the moonlit waters, and she knew it was the *Raggedy Dreamer*, Sylvestre's cabin cruiser.

Like a child playing in the magical, moonspun night, Cassandra raced down the hill, sliding part of the way on her derriere. She could see the golden Sy waving to her from the river craft and, like a mermaid, she swam through the water, smiling happily as he pulled her on board, her sodden silk gown clinging to every inch of her wet body.

His hands were powerful, lean, as strong as steel, yet when he touched her, it was with a gentle, golden caress. After her love stripped her of the dress and dried her off and took her to his bunk, she succumbed easily to the mastery of his experienced hands and feverish kisses that touched her all over. Her body was suddenly on fire beneath his hands and mouth and tongue. His skin was like rough velvet when she touched him, feeling his muscles jump reflexively.

"Kiss me," he whispered, his breath sending liquid-gold warmth coursing through her veins. "Kiss me, Cassa."

Sylvestre's touch became wonderfully deeper and Cassandra yielded to his manly charms, his deep, hypnotic voice. Cassandra's white thighs parted with sweet invitation. When the inevitable was about to happen, she looked up into her lover's face . . . and found herself in bed with Jared Casey!

Her long eyelashes fluttering open, Cassandra awoke with a low scream and up she sat immediately, shivering in her bed.

Casting her frightened gaze about the stateroom, her eyes fell to the crumpled pillow on the floor.

The pillow . . . she must have thrown it onto the floor. Reaching down, she retrieved the fluffy white object and lay back down to hug it to her breast. The dream was already fading. In it she had seen both Sylvestre and Jared.

Chug, chug, chug went the *River Minx*, taking her closer and closer . . . to home and Dulcie, Letty . . . and Melantha.

Family, that is what she wanted most. A real family to love and care for her; for her to care for them—

—But first . . . first she wanted to become a famous dressmaker. Her mouth twisted wryly. Well, if not *very* famous, then a *little* famous. Love could come later and she need not worry herself about that now, anyway. She was young and healthy and she had many years in front of her . . .

"Oh Sy . . . golden Sy . . ." He had deserted her in her time of need again!

Cassandra finally slept, and this time it was a peaceful rest she found in the heart of the faithful paddlewheeler taking her home.

Her adventure would soon be over. And then—

—Home at last.

# Part IV

"Cassandra doth foresee . . ."
—*William Shakespeare,*
Troilus and Cressida

## Chapter Fifteen

Diamondhead sat atop a small rise situated in the Mississippi Valley, several miles north of St. Louis. Even at this early hour, with the sun just beginning to touch the higher reaches, servants bustled about the mansion, polishing furniture and floors, cleaning every nook and cranny.

Sylvestre stood at the open French doors—tall hand-framed light-oak doors set with small glass panes. The bedroom doors opened out onto the gallery and were draped at either side with rose velvet and white lace, pink velvet chairs nearby flanked by vases of trailing ferns and deep-hued violets. The walls were papered in pinks and greens, white predominant in the dainty French furnishings and canopied bed.

All in all, it was a woman's bedroom—feminine, lacy, airy.

The morning was already hot and steamy as Sylvestre turned to look at the small, gold-framed likeness of his *grand-père*. His grandfather had been no coward. The first thing he had done, when he had purchased the plantation, was to tear down the whipping-shed near the slave quarters. No slaves he had ever owned had felt the whip. He had worn Indian moccasins and smoked a clay pipe made in Minnesota, a pipe he carried with him everywhere in a sealskin pouch with a flint, suspended from his belt with a Toledo steel knife and a small Indian hatchet.

As Sylvestre returned to gazing out the window, memories came flooding back. Years ago, before he had even become a teenager, his life had changed dramatically while he had been visiting his uncle Louis, on his mother's side. Louis had replaced his aged French maid with a younger one, a beautiful dark-haired Creek with black-jeweled eyes and long, gleaming hair; he had remembered her well.

How could he ever forget the young, sensual maid? She had been called River Rose, and she was the woman who'd introduced him to sex—not love, just sex—very simply and very generously. She took him to bed one night when they had been alone in his uncle's house. The Creek woman had possessed such pent-up energy that it had fascinated him how an "older" woman could keep up with him.

Sylvestre's golden gaze shifted to the slave quarters just warming in the rising sun. What ever happened to River Rose, he wondered. Was she still alive? Most unlikely, he thought, since her whereabouts had gone unknown for years, and, in fact, Rose had disappeared when his uncle Louis had passed on. The old plantation had been left to him, since his beloved uncle had been childless, unmarried, Nanette's family being his only living relatives. Sylvestre's own father, Jean-Pierre, had died not long after.

Grand-Chemin was a huge, lush old plantation situated on a bluff above the Mississippi river. Its name meant "high road." Sylvestre had retained the name in honor of his beloved uncle who had been a lonely man, forever pining away from a first love who had jilted him.

"What are you dreaming about, *mon fils?*" came the feminine voice, weak from illness, across the room.

Sylvestre turned and, as he stepped closer, his eyes full of love and concern, he said softly, *"Maman,* did I wake you?" He bent down to fluff her pillow as she lifted her shoulders for his assistance.

*"Non,* my son." She sighed, breathing deeply of the fresh air he had let in. "If I sleep any more I will become like an invalid." Nanette looked up into her handsome son's face. "You are looking fit as ever. Perhaps better, eh? Was it the woman of your dreams who held you so enraptured at the window?"

"Ah, but you are the first love of my heart, Mother." He smiled and looked at his mother through lowered lashes as she reached up to brush back a wave of golden hair.

Nanette studied her son who was dressed smartly this day, so different from the other day when he had rushed to her bedside, unshaven and dressed in rough travel clothes. Today he was dressed in a jacket of chocolate-brown superfine which fitted smartly to his long torso, stretching taut across broad shoulders, his long legs encased in a pair of second-skinlike buff breeches disappearing into highly polished black knee boots.

Nanette beheld her son's features, seeing in them the same rakish handsomeness as her dead husband. The only thing that was different between father and son was the eye and hair coloring, which was her own. His skin was dark, while hers was fair. The golden-bronze of his skin came from the Choctaw Indian blood of his grandfather, as did his lean but strong features and the slant of his cat-shaped eyes.

Sylvestre leaned closer, brushing a kiss across his mother's forehead. "You are still lovely as ever, even with your yellow hair tousled from sleep," he complimented, his golden eyes dancing with merriment before a cloud appeared suddenly within their depths. His gaze fell to the bedside table, to escape her wise detection more than anything else. "I see you are still reading your Bible, Mother."

"Of course, and I shall study the Word until my last breath." Then, all of a sudden, she asked, "What is it that troubles you so? There are disturbing clouds in your eyes, *mon fils.*"

"There is a knowing gleam in your eyes," he told her. "I have seen it often in the past and you are about to make me admit something I shall greatly regret afterward."

"Pull up a chair and sit here, where I can look upon your handsome face without straining my neck."

Bringing the sturdier of the two pink chairs over to the bed, Sylvestre sat, bending one long leg up over his stationary leg, across his knee. Nanette smiled at his slow, precise movements.

"I can tell it is something very important . . ." she laughed lightly. "Go ahead, son, take your time—I have all of it in the world." She held up her hand. "Uh-uh, and don't you tell me you will tire me out. I suddenly feel more energetic than I have in weeks."

His shoulders lifting in a deep shrug, Sylvestre began, his eyes glancing off the ceiling where they had rested momentarily. "This will take all the courage I have ever had to muster. To tell you . . . I believe I have committed the unpardonable sin, Mother."

Something deep within told Nanette that nothing her son had done could be that bad. He had for the most part been a good boy in his growing years and had never once groaned over the fact that she insisted he attend church services with her. He had turned many a feminine head his way, and she had no doubt he was not above a mild flirtation or two—and perhaps even more. In her mother's heart of hearts, he was the perfect son and she had always had reason to be proud of him. He had never once let her down.

Sylvestre did groan now. "I, ah . . . I have seduced a young woman."

"Oh?" Nanette's silvery-blond eyebrow shot up. "Was she so inexperienced then?"

"Oh, yes." His laughter was warm though troubled, and his handsome face had a twist of wryness about the lips.

"I suppose I have not had the honor of meeting this young female who has twisted your leg into doing the unpardonable?"

"Indeed you have." He cleared his throat once, twice. "She is Cassandra St. James."

Now Nanette's eyes lit up merrily, surprising her son. "Ah. The young maiden with the wiles of an imp, the face of a delightful pixie, and the heart of an angel? That Cassandra St. James?"

"Mother, please, be serious. You know there is only one female who goes by that name."

"Oh, I don't know, *mon cher*. There could be another with that name somewhere else in the world—but not with such a winsome face." Nanette patted her cheeks. "Ooh la, but that child had such angelic beauty as none other I've seen. So white and fair and dainty. Has she grown up much?"

"'She walks in beauty, like the night . . . of cloudless climes and starry skies . . .'"

"From Lord Byron," Nanette said, clapping her hands together softly. "Go on . . . go on."

"'Oh, thou art fairer than the evening air . . . clad in the beauty of a thousand stars.'"

"Marlowe," his mother said, beaming from ear to ear.

Lifting a hand from the covers, Nanette rested her palm against his cheek. "You love Cassandra so much, my son?"

Sylvestre looked deeply into his mother's eyes and wound her frail, slim fingers in his strong ones. "I believe I have loved Cassandra forever, Mother."

"You are a loving, dutiful son." She smiled with pride. "And a man of deep sensitivity, capable of loving a woman with all your heart. To some you might appear arrogant." She smiled with a touch of sadness. "I believe you have a bit of the scoundrel in you just like your father did before I married him. But I see none of that in you now, Sylvestre, my most wonderful son."

Sylvestre's shoulders moved in a great sigh. "I believe Cassandra is afraid of love. She is so . . ." He could only shrug helplessly.

"Afraid of love?" Nanette cried. *"Que c'est beau!,* it is beautiful!"

"Cassandra is still a child in many ways. I believe I

258

should have allowed her to grow up a little more before I—"

"Seduced her with your loving heart? This cannot be bad, not when two love such as this." Nanette was thoughtful for a moment when her son retained his silence. "Ah. Does Cassandra return your love? She must, for you to have been able to do the lovemaking with her, *non?*"

"I . . ." Sylvestre cleared his throat. "I believe that I overpowered her in my *gentle* seduction."

"Ah." Nanette stared at the embroidered roseleaf-threaded coverlet before looking into the golden eyes so like her own. "Hmm, I recall the way Cassandra's eyes used to follow you wherever you went—let alone her dainty feet traipsing after you all over the grounds. I believe she heard your heart even then, young as she was, *mon fils.*"

"I do hope you are right, dearest heart."

"So. When are you going to ask Cassandra to become your bride, eh? The sooner the better, for she could be with child at this moment."

"Ch-child?" It was the first time Sylvestre had ever stuttered in his life. He blinked and lowered his leg to the floor, right in the middle of a huge pink rose stamped into the plush carpet. "You mean . . . a baby?"

"Of course—*enfant!*"

Sylvestre raked nervous fingers through his hair. "No. It is too soon." He stood, scraping back the chair he had almost knocked over. "Much too soon."

Nanette made to rise and Sylvestre rushed to her bedside. "What are you doing? You have been most ill!"

259

"Bah!" She shoved his hand aside. "My fondest wish is to leave this bed, and my wishes are always granted. Call Colleen and Laverne to assist me. Well? Don't just stand there looking dumbstruck, call my maids in to me!"

"This is indeed crazy." Sylvestre ran both hands through his hair this time. "I should have never opened my mouth. *Damn!*"

"Tsk-tsk, do not cuss in my presence. You know better than that. Your papa never swore after I came down on him the first time."

"Mother—you are delirious." Sylvestre rushed to her side once again, only to be brushed aside for the second time by a hand that gained strength by the minute. "Get back into bed and we will discuss this sensibly."

"What? There is no such a word as sensible when two people are in love, my son . . . Ah, Colleen is here. Please, fetch me my stationery and a pen—with lots of ink."

"What are you planning to do?" Sylvestre questioned the woman he couldn't believe was his sick mother.

"Why, I am going to invite the St. Jameses here, what do you think?"

"For what occasion, might I ask?" Sylvestre jammed his hands deep into his pockets, staring at his mother as if she'd gone insane.

"Well, for a start, after they arrive, you might take Cassandra for a stroll in the garden and put the question to her. Or, perhaps you might ask her father for her hand beforehand?"

"Do you realize how ridiculous you sound?" He

waved his arm about the French-influenced bedroom. "This is supposed to be a sickroom."

"Not anymore. It's a *well* room now," she said with a giggle. With determination riding her brows, she turned to Laverne as she entered the room, blinking twice when she saw her mistress out of bed. "Laverne, get out my afternoon dress—the brown silk with the chiffon overskirt."

*"Oui, madame."*

"Are you going visiting?" Sylvestre asked, pacing the room from wall to wall.

"No. I am going down for dinner, I think. First I am going to pen that invitation to the Jameses."

"She will not come."

Nanette turned to face her son, her pen poised in midair. *"Who* will not come?"

"Melantha St. James."

"Oh . . . well, that's too bad." She turned back to her French secretary and pulled out a drawer for an envelope. "I shall just invite Monsieur and Mademoiselle. Hmm"—she tapped her pen on her chin— "that would not be the proper thing to do. I must invite them all, despite what that haughty Melantha St. James thinks of us."

"You already know of her dislike of our family name?"

"Ohh, of course. It was written all over the woman the first time they visited. Why did they come, you are going to ask." Nanette shrugged with a feminine motion. "She came along to check us out, I suppose. It is what Americans call *nosy.*"

Sylvestre removed his hands from his breeches' pockets and strode to the mahogany doors. "I am going out. First I must see my factor who is in St. Louis on some business. Then I am going to ride about the grounds and visit the overseer."

"And the bookkeeper?"

*"Oui,* and the bookkeeper, as much as I dislike the idea that you have taken on a bespectacled female after the last one messed up the books— I know I must see her."

"Good." Nanette sighed as if that was all there was to it. "Send that off, Colleen. Laverne, have you seen that my afternoon dress is not wrinkled?"

*"Oui, madame."*

Nanette smiled. "Oh, yes, and, Laverne dear, have Webby check in the garden for some baby lettuce. I would like some of that leftover Louisiana chicken made into big sandwiches, lots of baby lettuce between—and Creole vinaigrette sauce over leeks, heavy on the hot red pepper. Oh, don't forget to tell Cook I want the leeks arranged attractively in a serving dish and to pour the vinaigrette over them and chill it all thoroughly before serving."

"Who is going to devour all this?" Sylvestre wanted to know, for he would be taking his lunch in St. Louis.

Nanette said simply, "I am."

"But, madame," Laverne began. "The doctor forbids—"

Nanette broke in, "Never mind the doctor, Laverne. I am famished after fasting for nearly two weeks. Ah— life is exciting once again."

"Sandwiches? Tsk, tsk, such a food for a lady," Laverne muttered to herself as she shook her head, then wet her finger and steamed Madame's dress in a corner of the room—as the madame allowed. "Next thing you know, she will want her favorite sherry-baked bananas. Though I do not know where she will get bananas or apricot preserves at this time," Laverne clucked to herself. "Madame will just have to wait for the banana boat to come in."

Overhearing Laverne, Sylvestre chuckled softly. He watched his mother flit about like a new butterfly, happy to see her acting like her old self once again.

"Well?" Nanette said to her son as he lingered in the doorway, his shoulder against the jamb. "Do you not have some work to do?"

"Indeed I do, madame." He bowed and backed out of the room, scraping his fingertips on the floor in a humble fashion. "I hear and I obey."

Madame Nanette's merriment followed him all the way to the front door. Sylvestre shook his head and slammed the door behind as he went out whistling a merry tune.

# Chapter Sixteen

Outside, the sky was heavy with stars. A single lamp illuminated a bedroom window of the St. James house on the hill. Inside, a very troubled Cassandra sat on her bed with her knees drawn up, her chin resting on her folded arms. Her dress was wrinkled, she was in stocking feet . . . but she had no care as to how she looked and had no idea that she looked as gloomy as she felt. But the lovely Dulcie knew; she felt the same way.

Unblinkingly, Dulcie watched her best friend and knew instinctively what she was feeling. Never had two people grown so close as the two young women had in the past week, each lending to the other their own special kind of support.

Dulcie Tanner. Cassandra had never given a thought to the fact that Dulcie had a last name. Letty Tanner—deceased.

The sad words still rang in Cassandra's ears as Monte had spoken them softly on the dark day of Letty's funeral: "Who breathes must suffer—and who thinks must mourn."

The evening was very warm and Melantha had retired early; she had been in the habit of doing this ever since Cassandra returned from the river journey. Her mother was different—frighteningly subdued, and would not speak of Letty's accident.

Upon questioning Dulcie, as carefully as she knew how, Cassandra had discovered that it was a fall down the back stairs that had ended beloved Letty's life. Cassandra had known a strong premonition of disaster as she stepped off the riverboat a week ago. Her worst trepidations had been justified, for when she entered the house she realized that something horrible had taken place.

Melantha's voice had been shrill and she had been unable to control her highly emotional state when facing Cassandra's father: "Oh, Monte . . . something terrible has happened—!" A pause while Cassandra had lifted her staring gaze to Dulcie standing at the top of the stairs in a near-trance. Heart pounding in her throat, Cassandra had heard the rest. "Letty is . . . dead. She . . . she, oh, Jaysus, she fell down the back stairs Monte—!" Melantha wailed, her strident voice lifting like the cry of a banshee.

"All right, dear. I'm home now." A telling pause. "I'll take care of everything. Come now—you must rest, otherwise you will be no good to your daughter or anyone else."

"Believe me, please, I . . . I did not have anything to do with it. I . . . I know what you and everyone else is thinking. T-truly, it was an accident. Oh, Jaysus . . . I would not do anything to hurt the black woman or her d-daughter! It . . . it just happened."

"I believe you, dear. Come, you are overwrought. I insist that you go to bed now."

Cassandra had not seen much of her mother for several days, since Melantha took all her meals in her room and hardly ever ventured out of the house. For the entire week she had not gone visiting nor did she receive folks who came to pay their respects. The house had become like a tomb—almost ghostlike in its eerie atmosphere.

Sipping very black chicory coffee, Monte St. James sat in the drawing room, brooding and alone with his disquieting thoughts. What was going to become of Melantha? Her unhealthy mental state was beginning to take its toll on him, and he had not been able to work since he'd returned to face the tragedy of Letty Tanner's death. Ol' George Tanner's wife . . . Letty. He had never known their last name before and, even sadder, he had not thought to ask it, ever. Too late he had taken the black folks' presence for granted . . . There was still Dulcie. Lovely, kindhearted Dulcie . . . Cassandra had tucked her further under her wing and had become like a twin sister to her, even to the point of Dulcie sleeping on a daybed in Cassandra's room.

The roles had seemed to be put in reverse, for now Cassandra saw to Melantha's every need, even dressing her for the day as if her mother were but an invalid.

Monte ran his fingers through his already mussed hair. "I've lost a wife," he said, feeling sorry for himself. But only for a moment. Could he honestly say that Melantha had ever been a loving wife to him? Or a loving mother to his daughter?

267

He had realized by now it had only been an accident, Letty falling down those stairs. The dear woman had been carrying a heavy basket of ironing that Melantha had wanted her to finish by the day's end. Melantha still blamed herself, crying over and over that she had been too harsh on the black woman and set tasks to her that only an army of servants could have accomplished in one day, even with the help of Dulcie.

Neighbors from far and near had come to pay their respects, but Melantha had not received one of them. Cassandra had taken over with the strength and patience of Job, a strength Monte had never seen in her. She seemed to have transformed into a mature woman overnight, seeing to the running of the house, greeting callers, and even running errands and planning their menus each day.

When did Cassandra sleep, Monte had begun to wonder. She was a tower of strength. Melantha still behaved as if she were in a trance, shutting out the truth that Letty was really dead, refusing to accept that she was not at fault.

Monte read love and concern in his daughter's delft-blue eyes as she painstakingly cared for Melantha day in and day out. Now he lowered his face into his shaking hands. Tears choked him. If it weren't for Cassandra he wouldn't know which way to turn just now.

He lifted his head slowly. "Cassa," he whispered to the quiet room. "My angel . . . now I can never tell you. Not today. Not tomorrow—" His sigh was deep and aching as he whispered, *"Not ever."*

\*     \*     \*

Another week had passed and Monte's spirits had worsened. He closeted himself in his study and had only gone to check things on the riverboat once, putting his best roustabout Goliath in charge. Now he drank every day, trying to lose his grief in a bottle and putting himself in a mindless stupor.

Then the invitations came, almost one on top of the other. The first was from the Diamonds; the other from the Kirbys.

Cassandra was feeding her mother a bowl of nourishing vegetable soup when Dulcie entered the room, holding out the letter addressed to The St. James Family.

"Thank you, Dulcie," Cassandra said with a tired smile, wiping her hands on her apron before breaking the seal. She frowned as the name Sylvestre Diamond jumped out at her . . .

"What is it? Read it to me, Daughter," Melantha said weakly, turning her eyes from Dulcie to gaze out the window, since she didn't like having the black girl staring at her with those great, mournful eyes.

Cassandra tried not to let her hands shake as she read the invitation. All of a sudden her heart was pounding. "Madame Nanette Diamond and her son Sylvestre . . . request the pleasure of your company at 'Diamondhead Plantation.' Please Do come as Soon as you are able." Cassandra's eyes fell to the signature. "Madame Nanette." Down further. "R.S.V.P."

Feeling angry all of a sudden, Cassandra held the fine vellum stationery out to Dulcie. "You may drop this into the nearest basket, Dulcie."

Dulcie's nostrils twitched. She held the perfumed stationery up to her face, breathing deeply. "Sure smells good, jes like a fine lady. Missa Cassa? What's R.S.V.P. mean?" She concealed an impish grin from Cassandra as she hid the note behind her back.

Picking up the spoon again, Cassandra looked down to see that her mother was sound asleep. She whispered to Dulcie as she rose from the bedside. "It shouldn't concern you, Dulcie. Besides, it is unimportant." Taking up the tray and soiled napkins, Cassandra left the room, Dulcie closing the door softly behind.

"Missa Cassa . . . wait!"

Cassandra came to a halt at the top of the stairs. "What is it now?" She turned to quickly look at the girl who appeared thunderstruck. "I am sorry, Dulcie. I am tired . . . I have not been sleeping well at all."

"I know," Dulcie said sheepishly. "I hears you at the window pacing back and forth all night. Lawsy, Missa Cassa, you gots dark circles under your eyes. Pretty soon your face is going to be the same color as mine all over."

At that, Cassandra finally cracked a smile, the first in a long while. "You are right. I looked into the mirror this morning and what I saw there was startling."

"You're prettier than ever, Missa Cassa." She showed a row of pearly white teeth in a lovely tan face. "You jes have to quit working yourself to the bone. Pacing and fretting ain't gonna get you nowhere and your mama ain't . . . isn't going to waste away if you don't feed her. Let your mama get up out of that bed and do for herself, it'll be good for her. You needs to get back to your sewing, 'cause I cain't hold back that passel of womenfolk who stops here every day asking when Missa Cassa going to be well enough to stitch up their hems and fix this and that."

Cassandra heaved a deep sigh, hunching a shoulder to brush back a straying strand of unkempt hair. Dulcie took a step forward. "Here, honey, let Dulcie take that tray for you. Then you go lay down for a while, and when you gets up I'll have a nice pot of Creole gumbo waiting for you downstairs."

"Oh, I cannot lie down," she said, letting Dulcie take the tray from her. "I have many tasks I must see to . . . letters from creditors I must answer and the bookkeeping I must insist Father look at again—"

"Hmm, you're right, Missa Cassa." Balancing the tray on her slim hip, she fished the invitation from her apron pocket. "Maybe you can sleep later. But I think you better answer this here R.S.V.P. first."

When Dulcie began walking saucily down the stairs, Cassandra pursed her lips as she waved the perfumed stationery in the air. "Dulcie. What does R.S.V.P. stand for?" she asked, narrowing her eyes.

"Uhmm—I think it means, *Reply, if you please.* I know it does!"

Dulcie left Cassandra standing with her mouth open and before the lithe maid could round the staircase leading to the kitchen, Cassandra leaned over the banister to call down, "You amaze me, honey chile, you know that?"

"Yup, I sho enough do!"

With a finger bent to her lips, Cassandra stood at the top of the stairs, her own words ringing poignantly in her ears. *You amaze me, Cassa.*

Sylvestre had spoken the very same words. How she longed to see him, to gaze into his tigerish eyes, to feel him standing close to her, his breath against her cheeks, his long fingers entwined in her own . . . Cassandra

271

pressed her back to the wall, her head flung back, neck arched to receive her lover's kiss . . . the only kiss she would ever feel upon her lips . . . It was right . . . not bad. *No shame?*

Cassandra's slim fingers clutched her throat. Have you no shame, Cassandra St. James? You allowed a man to make love to you!

"A man who does not care if I live and breathe!" Cassandra hissed.

If he does not care, then why the invitation?

*It is from Madame Nanette, not him.*

Perhaps he put his mother up to it. Did you ever think of that?

*I do not care. I simply will not go to Diamondhead while that cad is in residence!*

Yes, you will. Hundreds of wild horses could not hold you back!

*I shall tear up this invitation and toss it into the basket!*

No. You won't.

"All right—I will do them the courtesy of answering." Cassandra gritted her teeth, almost running to the small desk in her bedroom. Whipping out her yellowed stationery, she plunked it down and then pulled out the chair, nibbling on the top of her ink pen.

"Dear Madame," she wrote, "I simply cannot come, for you see, as long as your son is in residence . . . *Ohhh!*"

She crumpled the paper and tossed it into her basket. Again she set her pen to paper. "Miss Cassandra St. James presents her compliments to Yourself, Madame Nanette Diamond, and your son, Sylvestre Diamond, and regrets that a previous engagement prevents the acceptance of your kind invitation to Diamondhead Plantation." There. That is all there is to it. "Cassandra St. James and Family." Oh. "P.S. Melantha is ill and is up to seeing no one. She, too, sends her regrets."

The very next morning, with the letter still in her possession, not having had time to send it off yet, Cassandra paused halfway down the stairs. She was startled to hear the voices of her mother and father in the dining room drifting up to where she stood.

"Cassandra, dear," Melantha greeted softly as the blond vision of loveliness entered the sun-drenched room. "Please don't look so surprised. See, I am better now. Aren't you happy?"

"Of course, Mother. I am happy to see that you are much better."

Melantha smiled as her daughter stepped closer and Monte held out a chair for her to be seated. "Your mother has some wonderful news for you." He beamed across the table to his wife, who was looking her old self, her black hair pulled sleekly into a French roll at the back of her head, clad in a tight black bombazine dress with gray embroidery at the throat and cuffs.

Hesitantly, Cassandra lifted the cup of steaming tea that her father had poured for her into a dainty vessel of pink-flowered china. The herbed brew burned her lips as she sipped from it, then slowly she set the cup down into its saucer—and waited for the good news to be broken to her. But a feeling of unease was settling over her.

"We have received an invitation from the Kirby

273

House in St. Louis."

Cassandra looked at her mother's smiling face, then looked back to her father, saying, "Yes, I am aware that the Kirbys reside in St. Louis, or, rather, just out of the town proper."

"Do you not realize what your father is saying, Cassandra?" Melantha questioned, but did not give her daughter time to answer. "Now that my health has been restored, thanks to your dutiful care, daughter, we are going to go on that trip to Memphis we'd planned months ago. First we are going to visit with the Kirbys for a day and then we will be on our way."

Monte sighed. "At last."

"You mean, first you are going to deposit your daughter with the Kirbys," Cassandra said sweet-tartly, disliking the fact that her life was still going to be laid out for her. "If you wish."

For a long moment there was silence in the dining room, then Cassandra pushed back her chair and rose from the table. Monte stood at once, taking his daughter's waspishness in stride. "But you have not taken your breakfast yet, Cassa." He held her chair while she stepped away from it.

"Really, I was not very hungry to begin with," she lied, her mouth watering as Dulcie set a platter of scrambled eggs and crisp bacon strips in the middle of the table. "Besides, there is a letter I must send off to Diamondhead."

"Oh—the invitation from Madame and her son," Melantha said, surprising her daughter with her knowledge of the letter when Cassandra had thought her to be asleep while she read it. "Well, we simply cannot make the visit this time because there won't be time to visit them and the Kirbys, too. I do hope you wrote them and gave our regrets, Cassandra."

Sweetly Cassandra said, "I most certainly did, Mother." Then, feeling as if she had behaved most ungraciously, she stepped around the table and kissed Melantha on the cheek. "I will do anything you wish, Mother, because I am very happy to see you well again."

Melantha patted Cassandra's cheek. "That's a good girl."

As Monte watched Cassandra display her usual lovingkindness, he was proud to have sired this daughter. His first wife must be smiling from her grave and, with that thought, he decided to put the whole idea of telling her the truth behind him. She might even decide it was best if she obeyed her mother's wishes and married Harlan Kirby. He would think on it no more. He and his wife were going to Memphis, and Cassandra would be installed safely at Kirby House.

# Chapter Seventeen

"I believe we understand one another at last." Melantha smiled prettily as they stepped off the paddlewheeler that had gone nonstop this time to St. Louis. Again she patted Cassandra's cheek—as she had so often in the last ten days while sharing a stateroom. "I simply adore the afternoon dress you fashioned for me, daughter, and am so happy you were able to finish my dress and your own for the Kirbys' ball. I am sorry I won't be attending the ball, but I am sure you will have a great time, since Harlan is remarkably attentive and flattering."

Cassandra said nothing to her mother's last words. She smelled eau de toilette on the late-spring wind as Melantha turned in a full circle, modeling the dress that, along with her own ball gown, had taken her a full week to stitch. Melantha's was fashioned of green-and-black checked taffeta, with long, tight sleeves and a square neckline. The skirt flared out over half a dozen full petticoats.

Melantha patted the youthful fullness of the skirts,

looking worried for a moment. "I do not look too fat, do I?" she whispered to Cassandra as Monte came down the stageplank loaded with valises and carpetbags, Dulcie bringing up the rear with her arms full, too.

Turning to her mother, Cassandra reached out to straighten the wide black belt that emphasized Melantha's narrow waist. "You are just as slender as ever, Mother, and just as pretty."

Above dark, glittering eyes Melantha's winglike brows lifted. "However, not as young as I used to be. Is that what you were going to say?" She did a double take and her mouth dropped in surprise. "Cassandra, do you see that man? Is that not Mr. Casey, the lawyer from Harper?"

"I think it—" Cassandra broke off what she was about to answer. "How do you know Mr. Casey? Is he our lawyer?"

"Why, of course he is—" Then she became silent as Monte came up beside them, Melantha giving Cassandra another pat on the cheek. "Oh, dear, do you have my hat, Cassandra? I am afraid I've left it behind."

Dulcie came up between Monte and Melantha. "It's right here, Missus S'James."

*"Saint,* Dulcie. Try to say it properly, will you, my dear?"

"Yes'm."

Bobbing a polite curtsy, Dulcie handed the hat to Melantha. The hat, a wide-brimmed black velvet creation, sported frothy green and white plumes that spilled over one side when Cassandra pinned it on and adjusted the tilt of the cocky brim over Melantha's elaborate coiffure, also styled by Cassandra.

The total effect was spectacular with Melantha's strikingly handsome Latin looks. "Thank you, Cassandra. I am most appreciative. I did not realize how good you were. You may make all my clothes and decorate my hats from now on—personally."

"Yes, I would love to do that for you, Mother."

"You look like an angel, dear," Melantha complimented. Her eyes roved the dress Cassandra had fashioned for herself from material they had purchased before leaving Harper. It was a creamy batiste smock adorned with small mist-green dots and narrow ribands flowed from the waistline, also green. She had secured her ethereal blond hair in a neat chignon, shorter tendrils left to curl about her face to frame it becomingly. "My, we are as fine as the wealthy, stylishly dressed French aristocrats who crowd the boardwalks of St. Louis." She was quiet for a moment, then, "Cassandra?"

"Yes?" She continued to walk with her mother while Monte nodded to acquaintances and Dulcie walked regally behind like a tall African queen. "What is it, Mother?"

"How *did* you come by that trunk of sewing materials I saw you digging in?"

Cassandra did not look her mother's way as she answered. "In the stateroom on the *River Minx?*"

"Yes—our private storeroom. I did not tell you, but I saw you go there often and . . . I was curious so I took a look. The gown you created for the Kirbys' ball was satin material, sequins and lace gotten from that trunk, was it not?"

"Mother, I have something to tell—"

"Oh, look, already there is the Kirbys' carriage

waiting for us! I am so excited, since I have not seen Jeannette in ages. I cannot wait to get to their house." She pressed Cassandra's arm. "I just love the food they serve at dinnertime. I cannot wait to devour heaps of that roast beef, mashed potatoes smothered in rich dark gravy, and baby peas cooked to perfection. And they always have three different kinds of cakes and pies." Melantha licked her lips. "I am famished just thinking about it. Dear, do I look all right?"

"Excellent. Like a *petit maître.*"

"Fashion plate?" Melantha laughed tinklingly. "Of course. We do, don't we."

As they climbed into the carriage that would take them to Kirby House—as the Kirbys were in town-residence and not at their plantation this time of year—Dulcie wrinkled her tan nose. *I smells a rat,* she thought, piling their packages into the carriage; then, after everyone was situated comfortably, she took a seat near the window.

As Jared Casey watched the Kirby carriage pull away from the docks, he could see Cassandra's lovely, pale face at the window. But she did not see the lawyer, because she was staring through her lacy lashes at the sky arching above St. Louis, an endless expanse of blue that was pale and pure, her thoughts turned within.

Riding smoothly along the streets of St. Louis in the well-sprung carriage, everyone but Monte watched in silence for a time. But Melantha could not contain her excitement over the visit to Kirby House. Her husband dozed in his corner, across from Dulcie, his lap piled high with boxes and smaller packages and carpetbags. The larger pieces of luggage had been strapped to the back.

"Did you see our *Southern Star* at the docks, dear?" she asked Cassandra.

"No. I did not realize she was docked here," Cassandra said, feeling sleepy all of a sudden and a bit queasy in the stomach. But she thought it was only the excitement, nothing more she should concern herself with.

"Willie Elmo is piloting the *Southern Star* this trip and Monte is going to put on two new pilots on the *River Minx* to take us to Memphis. We are not taking on a full schedule of passengers because we wish to have more time to ourselves—" She almost blushed here. "Something like a second honeymoon."

For a moment in time a lurid image of Miki Rhea's hair wrapped about her father's hand drifted in her mind's eye and then vanished. "Truly, I am happy for you both," she said, touching Melantha's arm in a light caress. "I . . . I almost wish I were going with you and Father."

"This visit is for the best, dear. You will enjoy yourself immensely at Kirby House."

"Mother . . ." Cassandra began wistfully. "It will be autumn before I see you and Papa again." Her stomach lurched for a moment and then settled back down. She swallowed hard, hoping the queasiness would abate. "Will you miss me—a little?"

"Miss you? Of course!" But Melantha did not even glance Cassandra's way as she said this. "Tsk-tsk, isn't it a shame—the outrageous prices shopowners in St. Louis are asking of their consumers. I wonder how the poorer folks afford clothes for their backs and food for their tables."

Cassandra's face brightened as she looked out onto

the streets of St. Louis with new interest. Excitement flared in her blood. *She* would compete with the boutique owners. She could cater to the expensive tastes as well as the simpler ones. The only elements stopping her were the necessary funds to begin and the practical details of business to set the wheels into motion.

Yes, Cassandra thought, I will think on this—seriously.


Kirby House was a two-story dwelling, impressively built, with pillars running across the front. It was a combination of baronial splendor and Kirby stinginess. Cassandra glanced at her mother, but she seemed preoccupied as they stepped from the carriage to mount the steps to a front door so small and dark that the facade appeared to her like a giant with undersize features.

"Come this way," the squat maid ordered at once as they entered the dim hallway.

Dulcie and Cassandra exchanged looks as, without further ado, they were escorted up the long, drab stairway and to their rooms. The maid, with a rustle of black bombazine skirts, showed her mother and father to their rooms first, then returned to Cassandra and Dulcie standing before the door they had been ordered to wait at.

"Your personal maid?" the crisply starched woman questioned as her beady eyes whisked over the lovely, willowy Dulcie.

"Yes, that's right," Cassandra said, just as crisply. "Dulcie stays with me—"

"Do you mean—?"

"That is exactly what I mean. We share a room—always."

"Humph!" was said low. Stepping back, the maid motioned them inside.

Cassandra at once dismissed the unattractive woman who had made a gesture to help them unpack. She went away in a huff, pursing her thin lips.

"Lawsy." Dulcie shivered as the tall, mahogany door closed behind them. "This must be where they keep the spiders." She almost expected to see the many-legged creatures suspended from the corners of the dusty room or come crawling across the ancient Turkish carpets.

Smoothing her hair up in back with a languid hand, Cassandra smiled as she watched Dulcie stare around with big liquid eyes at the dark mahogany furnishings and the equally dark Italian marble-top tables. Dusty draperies and old lace curtains completely shut out the light just begging to spill into the crowded, shadowy room.

Dulcie shrugged slim shoulders and thinned her dusky lips. "Leastways there ain't no plaster dropping from the ceilin'." She pulled the drapes aside and coughed, then blinked painfully as the canary-yellow sun burst into the room. "Yeah, come in, Ol Sol, you sho is welcome in here! We're gonna need all the light we can get to see around this room."

"Sho 'nough," Cassandra aped, coming to stand beside her impudently cheeky maid who always caused the sun to shine brighter for her, even on the gloomiest days. Together, hugging around each other's waists, they watched the green-spreading leafage tapping delightedly against the side of the house in a summer breeze dancing across the grounds.

When Dulcie began to hum an old Negro gospel melody, her voice deep and rich, Cassandra leaned on the girl's strong shoulder and closed her eyes for a moment. The haunting religious song filled her, reaching deep inside her innermost spirit to lift Cassandra from the cares of the world. Sylvestre stepped before her closed eyes, a handsome figure of man silhouetted against a pearl-gray sky softly stained with banners of sunset gold. His voice was a low, hypnotic whisper in her ear and she imagined herself standing beside him with Diamondhead Plantation in the background. A diamond in the sun. A place for the heart to come home to and find sanctuary and rest.

All of a sudden Cassandra's soul was alive with longing. In her dreams she couldn't stop herself from seeking out the virile Sy. But what about reality? How could she trust such a man? No. She would never again surrender her love, for she would save herself for her husband and not succumb to sinful lust as she had once yielded. Perhaps she was destined to have loved only once. So be it then.

Dulcie stopped her humming, for the dust in the room had clogged her throat and she coughed. "This room is disgustin'!"

Opening her bright blue eyes, Cassandra sighed and said, "At times appearances can be a little deceiving, Dulcie. Do not always believe what you see." She frowned lightly at her own words.

"Humph, I believe what I see—" Dulcie turned back to the gloomy, gargantuan furnishings that overpowered the small room. She shook her dark head, giggling with a hand over her dusky mouth. "But not today!"

Cassandra sneezed loud.

With that, they threw open the sash and set to work, shaking the dust from tapestries and every bit of material that was movable. Dulcie sneaked downstairs to the kitchen and the broom closet, fetching hastily slapped-together sandwiches, a jug of lemonade, and all the needed tools of labor. She almost fell into the room, her slim arms burdened with all the stuff she had filched.

When the dusting and sweeping had been accomplished, they sat in the middle of the bed stuffing themselves on the sandwiches and drank thirstily of the lemonade, giggling like schoolgirls, passing the jug back and forth until, at last, they fell into an exhausted sleep with their slender hands loosely clasped together, one dusky, one fair.

Dinner in the Kirby House was an ostentatious affair. Jeannette chirped continually in her high soprano voice. Harlan boasted and postured, as usual. And Oscar Kirby looked like a plump frog stuffing his cheeks, belching rudely every so often. Cassandra could not help thinking that Oscar Kirby's eye was bigger than his belly. Her gaze dropped to his immense girth. Well, perhaps *not,* she thought, her eyes lifting to catch him eyeing all the rich pies and cakes on the sideboard.

Cassandra observed that her mother, at the far end of the table beside her father, appeared somewhat distracted and spoke very little. It was as if she was waiting for something to happen—or someone to say something important.

Later, as they retired to the drawing room, Cassandra found herself staring at Oscar Kirby, stuffed in his great orange armchair, and back again to Jeannette Kirby. It was quiet in the nondescript room—too quiet. Cassandra thought the Kirbys acted like people who hardly knew each other, who seemed concerned only with the candy, fruit, and all manner of tempting morsels that surrounded them. Still, she couldn't help liking Jeannette Kirby and feeling a bit sorry for her lot in life.

Monte was restrained, observing over the rim of his brandy snifter, not his usual outgoing self. He appeared to be suffering from indigestion, and Cassandra could commiserate with him, since she was feeling none too well herself.

Cassandra sighed in painful boredom. Was there never laughter or music in this house? she wondered. Hopefully there would be music of some kind on the night of the ball!

Suddenly Harlan Kirby burst into conversation, almost startling Cassandra out of her stiff-backed chair. He spoke authoritatively on shipping, the Whig Party, and the war. He had brought the cakes and pies into the drawing room himself with something close to reverence, set elaborately now upon a round table with candles and fine silverware and—Cassandra blinked at the irony—chipped china plates.

"Have some cake, Cassandra girl," Oscar Kirby insisted in his booming baritone. "It'll put some meat on your bones. Damn, if you ain't a skinny gal. Pretty as a sugary confection, though." He eyed the rich fare

286

as he waited for a double portion of each item to be served him.

"Yes, darling," echoed Jeannette. "Do have some delicious cake. There is pie, too, you know."

Dulcie grinned from the sideboard as she helped a black-skinned girl—quiet as a church mouse—slice the huge cakes and mountainous pies into generous portions. She caught Cassandra's eye and billowed out her tan cheeks, but Cassandra swiftly dropped her gaze in order not to burst out laughing.

"Cassandra?" Jeannette said with a twinkle in her amused eyes. "Pie? Cake?"

"Thank you kindly," Cassandra said. "But really, madame, I am quite full from the delicious supper. You are very gracious to ask." Just then Cassandra's stomach gave another lurch as the sweets passed beneath her nose.

Dulcie bobbed beside Cassandra's chair as she hefted a double portion of cake to Mr. Kirby. "You doin' jes fine, Missa Cassa."

"Get that cake over here, li'l nigra!!" Oscar thundered, then eyed the girl's slim ankles as she began to cross the room. Cassandra caught where the lascivious glance fell. She stiffened in her chair and met Harlan's knowing gaze defiantly.

Father like son, she thought, desiring to escape the Kirby House first chance possible and take some rejuvenating air outside.

Memories of Diamondhead came unbidden to her. The drive leading up to the mansion sparkling like a diamond in the sun. The wind racing before the carriage stirring puffs of dust off the winding road leading to the house. The stately columns soaring skyward, peach-colored in the sunsets. Fanlight windows catching the sun and pouring back a golden beam into her face . . . Cassandra stirred from her reverie and blinked. The light from the candles caught Oscar's fork and reflected into her eyes stealing her dreams.

"This is very good, Mother," Oscar was complimenting his wife, though she had not been the one to bake the confections—that duty went to the cooks installed in the kitchen day and night.

Cassandra thought of what it would be like being married to Harlan Kirby. Though she liked Jeannette, she could not see herself living in a house where the sacredness of joy and love seemed to be sorely absent. Not that there was not any love between the endearing Jeannette and her obese husband Oscar, but there was something wicked she could not put her finger on. Lust for material things and lust for flesh . . .

Golden Sy . . . golden sigh. A slim teenage boy in smoke-hued trousers and checked shirt, lazily spread out beneath the arms of a magnolia tree, his slim fingers laced behind his golden head.

Diamondhead. She remembered it all. From the splendor of the immense cut-glass chandeliers, which tinkled like millions of crystal bells moving in a sensuous summer breeze, to the jewel-toned carpets one could sink bare toes into. Furniture, polished by loving hands. Tall, graceful blossoms lining the garden walks, roots penetrating the depths of the warm-smelling earth. She sat there in the Kirby House, imagining herself walking the grounds of Diamondhead with a golden-haired man beside her, and all her blood went singing through her veins with slow and slumberous measure.

"Cassandra dear . . ." Melantha was saying. "Harlan Kirby has put the question to you."

"Which question?" Cassandra asked, held by a dream of a golden man.

"You know which. Is it not romantic? Well . . . what do you say?" Melantha asked Cassandra—and waited.

Harlan Kirby sat silent. Cassandra was so exquisite, like an angel or a piece of fine Dresden porcelain a man could sit back and admire, he thought agonizingly. He felt a surge of jealousy toward Sylvestre Diamond, for he had caught the way their eyes devoured each other at the dinner party on the *Minx*.

Harlan's ardent gaze lingered on the curves of her mouth, and the long lashes that veiled her sky-blue eyes. He ogled the proud—

"Cassandra?" her mother was saying again.

—thrust of Cassandra's breasts, and all at once he was seeing Yendelela's breasts, with nipples so obviously erect; long tapering legs and the haughty carriage of an African queen. Yendelela and Dulcie; he didn't know which one excited him more. Cassandra he would wed and save, put on a pedestal while he introduced the tan beauty Dulcie to the carnal acts of insatiable lovemaking. He licked his already moist lips . . . waiting . . .

"Yes," Cassandra spoke low. "If you wish, Mother." She was unaware of Dulcie's eyes going as round as saucers.

Tears choked Monte St. James so that his eyes blurred, and when Cassandra glanced his way, she did not realize what the mistiness stood for.

\*      \*      \*

The next day Cassandra's parents left for Memphis and she regretted the fact that she had not resisted more strongly Melantha's singular decision to leave her with the Kirbys for the summer. "Good-bye, my darling Cassa," her father mumbled against her throat. "I will miss you. Take care of yourself and try to stay out of trouble."

Cassandra hugged her mother tightly next, and Melantha stood back to hold her at arm's length. "Yes, do be a good girl, Cassandra. I realize I have not been a very good mother to you at times, but I love you, dear, and shall always want the best for you."

"I know, Mother. I love you, too. Please have a good time. I . . . I will see you in the autumn."

Her mother waved as she moved to the paddlewheeler with an achingly silent Monte St. James. "I will bring you something from Memphis—" were her mother's last words.

Cassandra watched with aching heart as the *River Minx* churned its huge paddle wheels out into the mainstream, heading not for the Missouri this time but south on the Mississippi River. She could still smell the lingering scent of eau de cologne her mother wore. Tears made wet paths down Cassandra's cheeks. She watched until even the dark banner of woodsmoke was gone from sight. She shivered with a forboding of disaster, trying to shake the feeling that she would never see her parents alive again.

"Time to go, honey," Dulcie said from her side. "Carriage is waiting."

Once back at Kirby House Cassandra rushed to the privacy of her room while Dulcie joined the maids in the kitchen for a bite. All through the gossip, Dulcie's

290

concerned gaze kept drifting away. She, too, could not rid herself of the feeling that something was going to happen.

The busybody maid had come in to draw the curtains, and it was dark inside the room, but Cassandra saw none of the gloominess as she flung herself down on her bed where she wept with aching loneliness. As she drifted into her dreams, she heard a voice, an anguished voice repeat itself in her slumbering mind: *Sy . . . oh, golden Sy . . . I need you in my life.* It was her own.

Preparations for the ball began exactly a week after Monte and Melantha's departure. Kirby House underwent a startling transformation, since it was usually gloomy and silent, and undecorated with so much as a touch of bright color.

Cassandra and Dulcie raptly watched the maids, tottering precariously on chairs piled high with pillows in order to reach the heights, dusting the chandelier's teardrops. Dulcie grinned as the great prisms danced and clinked beneath the energetic dusting and polishing.

Later they watched as another group of black servants brought huge silver platters and tall, narrow candlesticks from their hiding places in the attic. "What a funny place to be keepin' those pretty things," Dulcie remarked in a whisper to Cassandra.

"Every household has their own methods of doing things, Dulcie."

"Yup. Guess you're right. Shh . . . here comes the ole man."

"All this will be Harlan's someday," boasted Oscar

Kirby around the cigar sticking from his mouth. "I only hope his bride will appreciate all she is getting, along with an intelligent and handsome husband."

Cassandra smiled, watching the busy servants bustle about. "Oh, I hope so, to, Mr. Kirby."

Oscar gave Cassandra's profile an odd perusal before he went back to the kitchen to make sure the cooks did not put onions in the stuffing. He hated onions with a passion.



Cassandra was all dressed for the ball by seven-thirty. She stood at the window breathing deeply of the wonderful night air. The moon was held captive in the trees, silvering the sky and grounds—and the guests arriving below.

She was admiring a rose-pink evening gown that looked like a frosted confection, with glistening silk leaves decorating the skirts and making a mental note to recall the style at a later date, when Dulcie piped up from behind.

"Lawsy, ain't you a sight stepped right out of the pearly clouds, jes like the angels themselves sprinkled you with stardust!"

Her ballgown looked indeed as if it had been created from moonspun threads, with its white silk-embroidered chiffon overskirt spilling over a cream satin underskirt. A white lace, form-fitting bodice swooped over mounds of creamy flesh and angel-puff sleeves drooped from bare shoulders. The skirt belled out enchantingly with opalescent sequins and white pearls in a design depicting butterflies, teardrops, and starlike flowers. A narrow satin sash went around her slim waist and tiny pearl teardrops dangled from her shell-like ears. A long braid of her tresses encircled her head, creating a shining crown of white-blond hair with more sequins and pearls decorating a single flower held securely at the back of her head.

Cassandra stared at her image in the huge square mirror and noted her larger breasts with acute fascination. She blinked, wondering how it passed her notice that she had gained an inch of feminine flesh, which made her look rounder and fuller.

"Time to go down now, honey chile, and pop some eyeballs out of them gents' heads. You gonna knock 'em dead, Cassa!"

Shakily Cassandra said, "If I do that, Dulcie, I won't have anyone to party with, now will I?"

Dulcie laughed behind her hand. "Guess not."

"Wish you were joining me, sweet Dulcie."

Dulcie sighed wistfully. "Someday maybe. But not this time."

Cassandra's satin skirt rustled softly as she walked to the door, but Dulcie's voice stopped her right there. Slowly, Cassandra turned to see that Dulcie's face had turned paler, making her look almost white.

"Lawsy, Missa Cassa." She sucked in a deep, steadying breath. "I forgot to tell you somethin' real important."

"It could not be all that bad to make you look as if you have seen a ghost, Dulcie."

"Well, you is goin' to be the one thinking that if I don't tell you what I should've told you this mornin' right after hearin' it." Dulcie lapsed into her pure southern drawl when she was nervous over something.

"Dulcie, settle down and start at the beginning."

Cassandra felt her palms begin to sweat. It could not be something bad about her mother and father, she knew, for that Dulcie would have reported to her immediately.

"There's really not much to tell, Missa Cassa. It's jes that . . . well, that Missus Nanny Diamond and her gorgeous son Cap'n Sy, well, they got an invite from these Kirbys and they says they's comin'." Dulcie shrugged. "Anyway, that's what the kitchen gossips was saying that Missus Kirby was all in a flutter because the Diamonds was coming." Dulcie began to settle down when she saw that Cassandra looked calm as a wintry December morning—

—and just as frozen.

# Chapter Eighteen

Cassandra's heart was a wild thing in her chest as she paused, at the top of the stairs, then descended to the looks of admiration from the guests gathered below. Her nerves had not thawed yet, and her palms were moist.

She couldn't believe she was attending her first ball at last, and she shook her head to clear it.

*Sylvestre was coming!* Was he *already* here? How was she to face that handsome countenance after the intimate hours they had shared aboard the *River Minx?* She felt stiff and slightly dazed, as if removed to another world apart from the one she lived and breathed in. And the strange queasiness in her stomach had returned.

The musicians were already tuning up their instruments, and the dining room was dazzling; in the center of the long oak table was a platter of confections that looked like magically spun sugar. The delicious smell of roasting meats and other festive foodstuffs cooking filled the house.

Cassandra floated about the room in her white gown, smiling and greeting people she didn't know. She had stopped to admire a yellow sugar rose with glistening leaves dyed with green food coloring when Oscar Kirby's voice sounded behind her. She almost jumped out of her white-and-cream silk dress.

"Cassandra, my word! Aren't you a sweet picture!" he boomed for everyone to hear. "Take care that you do not find yourself gobbled up by some young buck thinking you're a sugary confection." He chuckled loudly at his own humor.

Cassandra stood before Mr. Kirby, who was decked out in brown superfine dinner jacket, rust-colored trousers, and a vest of yellow brocade, an enormous red ruby glittering on his starched shirtfront. Hardly the attire for a ball, Cassandra thought, but meant to be gracious and compliment him just the same.

"You are very fine yourself, Mr. Kirby."

"Please, darlin', dispense with the formalities. Call me Oscar—you know our family well enough now to go by first names." He smiled pleasantly and perused her for a long moment, as if he expected to find someone shadowing her.

"What is it, Mr.—Oscar?"

"Where's your li'l darkie?" Oscar asked politely, wondering, too, why Dulcie was not working in the kitchen with the other servants.

"She has gone out back to visit a black family whose daughter is very ill."

"She has, huh? Does she know some special black magic to cure the Nigra girl?"

"I am not sure—" Cassandra was not allowed to finish.

"Ah, here is Harlan's distant cousin! Come here, Valerie. I would like you to meet someone. How lovely you look, m'dear." He was eyeing the table of goodies behind Cassandra and wanted to break away to sneak some before Jeannette caught him. "Cassandra St. James, I would like you to meet Valerie Beaumont. There. You know each other's names, so get acquainted, you two lovelies, while I mingle with the other guests just coming in."

Before Oscar walked away, he ruthlessly plucked one of the yellow roses off a cake and plunked it into his mouth.

The two young women were left to stare at each other, wondering who would speak first. Valerie had already decided not to pay much attention to the blonde, and she would walk away before they could get acquainted, she told herself. But curiosity kept her from moving away too quickly.

Valerie Beaumont wore an emerald, pin-striped silver lamé evening dress with emerald lamé puffed yoke and tiny pearl-trimmed sash bodice. Decorating the pin-striped skirts were huge green lamé leaves clustered all the way to the ruffled hemline. Her skin was flawless white, her eyes lavender-blue with long, thick lashes darkened with cosmetics to a spiky look. Her lips were rouged, too, and her long red curls were caught up in a net sprinkled with pearl drops, just like the ones dangling from her ears. All in all she was a veritable *petit maître*—a fashion plate.

The delicate pearl earrings swung from her ears as she spoke, at first stiffly, feeling Cassandra out. "I hardly know where to begin"—Valerie's jealousy gave added color to her fashionably pale face—"now that

297

we finally meet, Cassandra St. James."

Cassandra was taken aback for a moment before she recovered. "I remember Jeannette speaking of Harlan's cousin—vaguely." She was at a loss, because for some undefinable reason the striking redhead seemed to dislike her.

"Distant cousin," Valerie corrected. "I'm not sure how, exactly, something to do with aunts and uncles, not blood relations really. Now that I have met you, I find that you are very pretty, lovely, in fact, though I find it hard to compliment you, Miss St. James."

Cassandra felt as if she had been slapped in the face. She tried to interpret the woman's coldness toward her. She looked up then, having heard a man's voice saying, "Ahh . . . two visions! Valerie and Cassandra, excuse me, but I see someone at the door that I must greet." Then Harlan moved away and Cassandra looked back into Valerie's uptilted eyes—

—Then she knew. Valerie's gaze had clamped possessively on Harlan Kirby, like a cat with a bird, Cassandra thought, watching. Valerie's lavender-blue eyes whisked back to Cassandra's face, to see her reaction to Harlan's commanding presence. *She* might think Harlan attractive, but not so Cassandra. Valerie had no knowledge of this, however.

"We are not kissing cousins exactly," Valerie went on, with tart-sweetness. "But *more.*" Her eyes glittering strangely, she muttered, "I believe we shall cross swords one day, Cassandra St. James." She looked about the crowded room. "I suppose this is all because of you. I find it horribly disrepectful of the Kirby's to hold this ball not even two weeks following your parents' departure. They should have been included, too."

"I think so, too." She decided to be agreeable. This once.

Valerie tossed her red head. "Well then, why didn't you object, insist that it should take place when your parents returned?"

"I did—to the Kirbys. But Oscar said the invitations had been sent out far in advance, and foodstuffs from as far as Minnesota were coming in, like wild rice and venison."

"Oh?" Valerie hoisted an auburn eyebrow. "Who told *you* all this? Harlan, perhaps?" She purred the question with a taunt.

"It was not Harlan, Miss Beaumont, but Jeannette Kirby. If you must know, and I think you should, to set things straight, Harlan and I hardly ever speak at all."

"Oh, of course, tell me another lie, Cassandra St.—"

Cassandra held up her hand, halting Valerie's words. "That will be about enough, Miss Beaumont. I will tell you the *real* facts if you will only hold your waspish tongue for a moment!"

"What? *Me,* hold *my* tongue! Why you little sl—"

"Hush. You are making a scene and behaving most ungraciously, Miss Beaumont." Cassandra's blue eyes flashed a gentle but firm warning. "I do not care for your wild presumptions, either."

"P-presumptions?" Valerie looked at Cassandra queerly for another long moment. "Will you join me in a glass of fruit punch, Miss St. James?" she asked in a crisp tone. "Over here."

Inclining her head, Cassandra followed Valerie until

they stood at the long table near a huge, crystal punch bowl. Rose-pink liquid was filled almost to the jaggedly decorative brim, all manner of fruit floating atop.

"You may call me simply Cassandra," the blonde said with grace. "Otherwise you risk making yourself sound shrewish with your bitter use of my full name."

Valerie Beaumont pursed her bow-shaped, coral mouth and placed one hand upon her slim hip. "Clarify your earlier statement, Miss—Cassandra."

The blonde stepped closer to the redhead, until they were all but nose to nose. "You are so worried that I will take Harlan Kirby from you. I realize that, but I must ask you to consider what I am about to say: Harlan has never interested me in the least, Miss Beaumont . . . Valerie. In fact, I find him most repulsive at times."

Cassandra did not think it wise at this point to reveal what had taken place one moonlit night aboard the *River Minx*. Valerie was about to speak again, but Cassandra beat her to it.

"Wait, allow me to go on before you put any more of your questions to me. I am only here visiting the Kirbys because my mother wished it. Believe me, Miss Beaumont, I would not consider Harlan for marriage even if he were the last man on earth."

Valerie told herself she must consider what the blonde had just confessed. In truth, she had witnessed no flash of desire in Cassandra's face when Harlan came their way. "I don't know why I should believe you," Valerie said, "but I do. I detect a note of sincerity in your voice and think you have been honest—up to a point."

300

A curious look flitted like the shadow of a bird across Cassandra's face. "Why would you say that?" she asked.

"Well . . ." Valerie shrugged. "Oscar Kirby seems to think you and his son will one day wed. He even mentioned that you have already given your assent to be Harlan's bride."

"I have never—" Cassandra stopped herself, thinking back to the night she had said "As you wish" to her mother while Harlan sat like a cat licking his whiskers. *Oh, no.*

A red glow spread over Cassandra's features as she lowered her glass from her lips without taking a sip of the pink liquid.

"I believe I have blundered. The Kirbys must have gotten the wrong impression . . . Oh, what is the use of trying to explain everything to you? It is a long story . . . a *family* story. My mother has wanted me to marry into the Kirby family ever since I can remember. I hate the idea, but everyone seems to take it for granted that we will become man and wife."

Valerie couldn't believe her ears. "You don't want to marry Harlan? Any woman would wish to be married to him."

"Not this woman." Cassandra held an image of Sylvestre just then, and the maelstrom of emotions created within almost made her weak with longing. Where was he? Why couldn't she see him and Madame Nanette among the guests? She sighed and hung her head.

"You are looking for someone," Valerie stated. "Who?" Her almost purple eyes narrowed.

Cassandra gave a short laugh. "Not who you think—

that is for sure."

"Someone else . . . hmmm." Valerie sounded hopeful.

"Yes, Valerie," Cassandra said confessedly. "Someone else." A man with golden hair and golden eyes. A man who could make her his radiant bride if he but asked for her hand.

"Ah . . ." Valerie purred. "Now I detect a certain light in your lovely blue eyes. Who is it for, Cassandra?"

Cassandra's lacy lashes slanted low over her troubled eyes. "He is someone who has deserted me. I do not believe you know him."

Taking a dainty sip of her punch, Valerie said, "If he resides in St. Louis or surrounding area, I do know him, or *of* him."

"He is a man I believe will never give his heart fully to any woman, though he confesses to love the one he's with."

"Who is this charming rogue?" Valerie wanted to know. *Certainly not Jared Casey,* she hoped.

"Sylvestre is . . ." Cassandra's shoulders lifted in a small shrug, at a loss for words. "I am not sure what he is or what his intentions are."

"Sylvestre, hmm?" Valerie pursed her coral lips and rolled her eyes thoughtfully. "Ah. The Golden Sy." Valerie studied Cassandra's winsome face for a moment. "Ahh . . . yes. I've hit on it, haven't I? It is Sylvestre Diamond." Then she tried it in French: *"Diamont."*

Cassandra blinked. Did everyone envision Sylvestre the same way she did? All golden. Hair. Eyes. Skin . . . Well, actually it was a golden-bronze shade. Beautiful. Vibrant.

302

"Is he coming?" Valerie asked, happy to learn that Cassandra posed no threat to her. The competition would have been hard to handle considering the blonde's beauty and charm.

"Sylvestre and his mother Nanette have been invited."

Valerie looked around at the guests eating, drinking, laughing, mingling. "I don't see them. Maybe they'll arrive late." Sipping her punch, Valerie said with a nod, "I love your dress—it's quite creative. Do tell me who your dressmaker is. I believe if she—or he—has a shop in St. Louis, I'm in for some stiff competition. I've never seen anything so pure and angelic . . ."

"Competition?" Cassandra's eyes went wide and her brow was puzzled. "What sort of competition do you mean? For your dressmaker?"

With a delightful laugh breaking Cassandra's sentence, Valerie exclaimed, "Oh, no. For *me,* Cassandra. I own and run a boutique in St. Louis." She gave a graceful shrug of emerald pin-striped lamé shoulders. "A *struggling* shop, I'm afraid."

"Oh!" Cassandra leaped back before she could spill her punch on her skirts—or Valerie's. Putting a hand over her heart, she blurted, "I was afraid I might have spilled some punch on you—"

"—or *your*self," Valerie said, then looked up into Cassandra's bemused eyes. "Was it something I said?"

"Of course. You . . . you took me by surprise." Cassandra smiled happily. A dressmaker friend! "A very pleasant surprise, in fact. I wonder why the Kirbys never mentioned you were a dressmaker."

"Well, I don't do *all* the sewing in my shop. A little French woman—in fact, she's highly acclaimed—she

303

helped me with this gown. I do designing best, but I am afraid Camille is getting on in age and she will soon be leaving me. She tires easily and, though when she's working she's industrious as a bee, she cannot work as often as I would like her to. Now, tell me, Cassandra—who did your gown? I'm dying to know!"

*"Cassandra."*

"You?!" Valerie said, a hand going to her slim midsection. When the blonde nodded, Valerie shook her head, stepped forward to give Cassandra an impulsive hug. "You amaze me, Cassandra."

The blonde smiled. "Many have told me just that."

"How old are you, anyway? Why, you must be five years younger than I. How . . . ? Where is your shop? Is it here in St. Louis? It couldn't be," Valerie answered herself. "I would have known about it long before this. Are you new? Sheesh—am I in for the competition!"

"I do not own a shop and, in fact, I have run out of sewing materials to even pretend I am a dressmaker any longer. I have altered some dresses for some new friends of mine—four very endearing little old ladies."

"Ah." Valerie pouted prettily. *"My* little old ladies, I'll bet. Don't tell me: Seraphina, Lavender, Catherine, and Millicent."

"Yes! Are they not wonderful!"

"I thought so." Valerie tapped her slipper.

"Oh, please, Valerie, do not be vexed with me." She saw that Valerie was not, but was only making light humor over it.

For a moment, the blonde and the redhead looked at the respectable ladies who made a great pretense that the Kirby Ball was the high point of this season's activities. Their most elegant gowns—and some not so elegant—were decorated stuffily with lace, velvet, overbright beads, and braid trimmings. They had been fashioned shorter at the front hem, with cumbersome material trailing behind. They wore flowered, feathered, and beribboned hair decorations, carefully matching their costumes. Painted fans, flashy rings of diamond, gold, pearl, ruby were also on display this evening.

Valerie amost shocked Cassandra into insensibility when she took Cassandra's fingers in a strong grasp. "Cassandra—you can come to work at my shop!"

Cassandra pulled her hand away as her face fell. "I am afraid not. You see, I have neither the funds nor the—"

"Funds!" Valerie tossed her head, setting flaming red curls to bounce over her shoulders. "You really know nothing about business, I can see. All you have to do is bring your lovely self. I shall hire you as a . . ." Valerie skimmed the white gown with great appreciation. "You created *this* yourself?"

"Yes." Cassandra felt suddenly shy and embarrassed.

"You *are* good, Cassandra." The redhead looked Cassandra straight in the eye. "Will you work for me? As designer *and* seamstress?"

"I . . ." Cassandra's heart was beating so fast she thought she might faint. *Work in a real shop?*

Cassandra stood so quietly for a moment, surrounded by Valerie's perfume, which had a light, petal soft fragrance reminiscent of crushed lavender and roses. "Give me some time to think about this, Valerie. This is all happening so fast, I . . . I am quite dizzy."

"The name of my shop is LeBeau-tique, but I'll

change it to Valandra's Boutique if you like."

"You would change the name of your shop for my sake?"

"Of course, Cassandra. You are going to be absolutely famous one day and I want to be included. I'd like to say I gave you a little boost along the way."

Cassandra felt as if Valerie had already given her a great *shove*. But was it the right direction? Was this not what she had always wanted? To be a dressmaker, famous or not? Just to be able to design and create wonderful gowns for wonderful ladies? What could be more fulfilling than realizing a lifelong dream? Why, suddenly, did she feel something was being left out of the wonderful dream? Where was the magic she was supposed to feel?

Swaying, Cassandra muttered, "Excuse me, but I . . . I feel a little queasiness suddenly . . . and I am dizzy—"

"Oh, no." Valerie put an arm about Cassandra's back to support her. "I hope I have not overexcited you. Are you . . . in a delicate condition perhaps?" *Not pregnant, I hope!*

"Like what?" Cassandra found an armchair in the shadowed corner while Valerie stood over her helplessly, her hands over slim hips.

"Ah . . . perhaps you have not eaten anything today?" Valerie suggested.

"You are right, Valerie. In all the excitement over the party, I just plumb forgot to come down for lunch."

*"Plumb?"* Valerie laughed. "You got a little black gal in you somewheres, honey chile?"

"No." Cassandra smiled weakly and shook her head. "But I do have a black maid who is my best friend. We

306

have been through much together and we are insepar-
able. Actually Dulcie is an octoroon. We are the same
age . . ." Cassandra sucked in a deep, reviving breath.

"I'm glad you believe as you do, Cassandra. I am not
totally for slavery, either."

Valerie skittered away briefly and returned with a
plate for Cassandra heaped high with braised quail,
baked pike, and luscious Minnesota wild rice, continu-
ing her explanations. "I would pay all my Negro help
if possible, but I can't afford to have anyone cleaning
my house; I do it all myself. White *slave* owners are as
much captive as the souls they own. They are keepers
of people sentenced to a lifetime of hard labor—guilty
of nothing but having been born with black skin."

Cassandra said nothing for a space as she ate heartily
of the flaky fish and scoops of scrumptious wild rice.
She had to commend the Kirbys' cook. Or cooks. They
had more than one.

Valerie was waiting for her to comment, and
Cassandra began. "Left alone, slavery will probably
vanish in a few generations, I pray. The southern white
man will want to take credit, but a number of northern
zealots want a cause to fret the southerners who own
slaves. They have it, in slavery. I believe some day the
North and South might come to battle over it."

"You are neither for it or against it, I see. Neutral as I
am. But there are the cruel owners of slaves—"

"—and the kind ones, Valerie. Some Negroes who
work on plantations have a good life with a kind master
to look over them." She had Diamondhead Plantation
in mind as she stared fixedly at the crystal chandelier.
"There are the good and bad in every lot in life."

Valerie sighed deeply. "I believe the Kirbys are the

worst of slave owners. I would like to remedy all that should I become Harlan's bride. We would live on the Kirby Plantation and I would gain the upper hand to make certain Harlan's wandering eye was healed too, believe me."

*Healed* or *put out,* Cassandra thought, considering the feisty redhead's jealous temper. Valerie said nothing of what would become of her shop if she became Mrs. Harlan Kirby, and Cassandra wondered if the concept had ever entered Valerie's mind.

"I wish you luck, Valerie. Indeed,you will be needing it," she said as an afterthought.

Valerie's white silk slippers began to shuffle beneath her skirts as the musicians began tuning the song of a waltz. Naturally graceful and light on her feet, Valerie would soon be whirled from one young man to the other.

"Come on!" Valerie called, pulling Cassandra up and setting their plates aside. "The men are looking for partners. Let's be the first."

"Oh, I don't know—"

"You'll be fine!" Valerie said with a laugh.

Although Cassandra declared that she knew little of the dance steps, this proved to be an advantage, for every young blade fought for the privilege of showing the enchanting blonde how to waltz.

Around and around she whirled beneath the sparkling chandelier until she was quite breathless and giddy—but thankfully not sick to her stomach again!

A handsome young man with striking features offered to fetch Cassandra a strawberry ice, and she accepted. Then, to her chagrin, the room was suddenly too full of rich, cloying odors mingled with food and perfume. It was too stuffy to draw a full breath, she thought.

Cassandra slipped into the hall for some fresh air, two young blades fresh from their teens trailing behind. "Look at that tiny waist, will you?" one said. "God, a man could span it with two hands. What magnificent blue eyes. Did you get a look at the incredibly long and curly lashes," the other remarked while gaping at her profile. "What a stunner!"

Cassandra turned just as her two admirers ducked into the crowd going in and out of the dining room, too shy to get up the nerve to talk to her and ask for a dance.

She looked about at the guests all happily eating of the saddle of venison. With a great, shining knife, Oscar Kirby was carving the succulent meat into paper-thin slices, and every time one fell onto the platter, a murmur went up at the precision of his carving technique. But Valerie was nowhere to be seen and Cassandra began to look around, curious over her sudden disappearance.

Now Cassandra realized that Harlan Kirby was absent, too. Even Jeannette was missing.

Then Cassandra saw Oscar being called away from his carving of the meat. Where were they all going?

More curious, Cassandra worked her way through the crowd and along the wide hallway to the study where all the excited voices were coming from.

She wondered what all the disturbance was about and if there had been an accident. Cassandra felt her heart skip a beat.

Another voice, this one much deeper and smoother, came from the study. Cassandra's head spun around at the deep, male sound.

"Sylvestre," she unconsciously murmured while her two admirers observed her actions. Now her heart was pounding madly and she did not know whether to keep walking toward the study doors or return to the dining room. For some reason she was afraid to discover why the Kirbys had gathered there with Sylvestre. Then Cassandra heard Sylvestre ask, "Where is she? I must go to her at once."

Cassandra's heart stopped.

The music even stopped.

Everyone seemed to have their eyes trained on her as she stepped to the study entrance. Cassandra took one look inside and her steps faltered.

Sylvestre was bowed over a table as if in pain, and he looked like a much older man, not at all like the handsome, roguish, and sometimes elegant Sylvestre she knew. He wore rough riding attire and there was a dark stubble on his jaw.

"Sylvestre!"

Cassandra flung herself into the room, under the stares of the people gathered there. Why was everyone looking at her with such sorrow. "Sy . . . oh, what has happened?"

Jeannette's voice was weepy. "Sit down, Cassandra dear."

Oscar's voice was harsh and broken. "Just stay calm now," he said.

Cassandra's entire body trembled like a leaf in a storm, but her brain sat numbly in her head as if awaiting the shock that would surely come.

Harlan's gaze was shifty while Valerie's heart was turning over for her new friend and the bad news she must hear.

As Sylvestre was approaching her, there started up a great roaring in Cassandra's ears. "Sylvestre?" Her eyes met his and she met pain in their golden depths.

Then she knew.

*Oh, God. Oh, God.*

"No!" She heard herself scream, but it was Sylvestre's hands that covered her ears to break the sound of her own grief. "Not M-mother and F-father!"

She did not need to be told that there had been an accident, for she could read the truth in Sylvestre's eyes. He leaned down and firmly grasped Cassandra's nerveless hands in his own strong ones. "They were trapped in their stateroom . . ." He swallowed and looked up to plead strength from the Almighty. "Goliath went back after them . . ." His voice sounded hollow as he went on. "He found them—but it was too late, Cassa. The explosion was a powerful one."

"Wh-where is Goliath?" Cassandra asked dumbly, staring down at Sylvestre's gripping hands, one of her own raking through her beautiful coiffure, making it come partway undone.

"He is safe. He floated on a log to shore—"

Harlan Kirby had come to stand beside Cassandra, staring down, shaking his head. He was ready, should she need him.

Cassandra calmly nodded, and her hair on one side came loose to fall down her back in long ringlets. Then, like a lost child swaying beneath a strong windstorm, she turned and collapsed in the other man's direction while Sylvestre shoved Harlan Kirby aside and sprang forward to break her fall from the chair.

Harlan watched Sylvestre scoop her into his arms

and carry her into the hall, heading for the stairs. He stood outside the room, watching Sylvestre Diamond carry his intended up to her room. Valerie came up to place her hand upon Harlan's sleeve.

"Let them be," she whispered close to his ear. "She loves him." Valerie felt Harlan stiffen at the words. "I love you. That is all that matters after all, isn't it? You told me this yourself. Suddenly I want you, Harlan, I want you as I had you in my arms just last night when you came to my house in the middle of the night. You will always come to me. No other woman can ever make you feel like I make you feel, not even those Nigra girls you have a liking for."

Harlan nodded and followed Valerie out the door, into the garden. He could still have Valerie, even after wedding Cassandra, he told himself, not feeling in the least guilty for heartening in that fact.

# Part V

"O heart, heavy heart,
Why sigh'st thou without breaking?"
—*William Shakespeare*

# Chapter Nineteen

Sylvestre was at a complete loss when Cassandra burst into a fresh torrent of tears.

In the darkened bedroom, with only a pale shaft of the rising moon coming in, he went down on his knees before the bed and embraced her, drawing her to the edge of the mattress, where she was now huddled like a sad little girl. Her knees were drawn up to her chest. The grief she was experiencing tore at this man's heart.

"Cassa, Cassa, please do not weep so!" Sylvestre kissed her tenderly, unhurriedly, on her wet cheeks and neck. "Oh, God, that I could take all your grief inside my own body, *ma coeur,* sweetheart, I would do this." He moaned deep in his throat. "I would hold it from you forever and ever."

"Sy . . . Sy . . ." She swallowed her tears along with the aching lump in her sore throat. "What will happen n-now? How will I live w-without them?" She cried achingly. "Papa was so good to me and Mother loved me . . . *truly* she d-did."

"I know, Cassa, I know. They both loved you

dearly." *But that love was not nurtured on trust, Cassa.*

Just recently his mother had revealed to him a secret: Nanette said Melantha had not been Cassandra's mother, not of her flesh and blood. How his mother came by this information was unknown, but he had not questioned Nanette further. The news had disturbed him almost as much as Cassandra's negative reply to Nanette's invitation to come to Diamondhead.

Cassandra had been in his heart night and day, and her lovely face had haunted him as he went about his usual day's work. Even when he had been at his favorite leisure in his small rivercraft *Raggedy Dreamer* upon the waters of the Mississippi, he could never forget her image. He had wanted to return to the *River Minx* to explain to Cassandra why he had left in such haste, but he knew that the paddlewheeler would have already been making her way upstream.

Now Sylvestre struggled against the moisture behind his eyes and the constriction in his throat. He wished he could absorb all Cassandra's grief into his own body.

Sylvestre's golden eyes bore witness to the fact that his heart was heavy for Cassandra's loss. But she saw nothing; only felt Sylvestre move beside her onto the bed and, as his arms went around her, she struggled weakly trying to push him away. Though she stirred restively, Sylvestre held her all the tighter.

"No, Cassa, do not push me away. You need all the strength I can give to you now." At once he discarded the idea of making love to her; but his hard body spoke eloquently of its urgency.

Sylvestre began to kiss her tenderly on her damp cheeks, and her fears about what the night would bring calmed beneath his magical touch. Her sobs quieted.

316

"Why did you desert me the morning after we had . . ." She swallowed hard. "After we . . . we made love, Sy?"

"My mother was ill, Cassandra . . ." Sylvestre smiled tenderly. "But she is better now. Much."

"I am happy to hear that she has recovered. I like your mother . . . Nanette."

"Let us not speak any more of illnesses nor sorrow, Cassa."

The subject was dropped. Achingly tender, his mouth descended on hers, slowly, lovingly. His lean fingers spread her blond hair, holding her, cradling her head as he deepened his hungry kiss. His hands caressed her breasts, her waist, hips, then savored the satin texture of her skin beneath her full skirts.

"Oh Sy . . . Sy . . . you are so good for me."

Cassandra began to feel some of the thrilling sensations she had experienced aboard the *River Minx*. Soon she was kissing him back passionately, full on the lips and with a rare brand of wildness in her heart.

Before Sylvestre realized what was happening to his body, he was responding to her aching need. His emotions rushed forth with all the love he felt for Cassandra, the woman in whom his sun rose and set.

The soothing hands that had been around her waist now moved upward to her silk-covered breasts, and Cassandra found his tender caresses rendering succor and relief in her moment of grief.

But she needed more . . . much more.

"Sy," she cried softly, between unquenchable kisses. "Love me. I need more of you . . . Oh, Sy, make love to me—now."

He drew back as their lips finally parted. "Cassa," he

began, breathing hard. "You have no idea what you are asking. You are overwrought." He ran his fingers through his hair. This was so reminiscent of the night they had first made love, when she had needed him desperately and was so upset and lonesome after discovering that her father had been coupling with the redhead Miki Rhea.

"We cannot, Cassa, not this night," he murmured against her hair, hating himself for what he just said. But he was going to stand firm on this, otherwise risk having her hate him in the morning as she almost had last time. Stand firm . . . stand firm . . . *Oh, Lord!* She felt so good to him . . .

She ran her fingers through his thick, tawny mane. "B-but I need you, Sy." She arched her throat, dropping her head back on her shoulders in a provocative gesture.

"You *need* me, *ma petite*—but do you love me?"

"Yes . . . I love you, Sy!"

"I wonder if you realize just what you are saying. There's a wildness in you tonight, Cassandra, you are not yourself. Will you look at me in the morning and despise me . . . ? God knows, I want you so badly, but I promise you I would never hurt you in the taking."

Taking the tiger by the tail, Cassandra came upon her knees and put both unshaking hands to the bodice of her gown. In one swift motion, she yanked it open to the waist.

Sylvestre blinked as the opalescent sequins and white pearls scattered on the bed. The beautiful gown was rent clear to the waist. "Cassa . . . what have you done?"

Moonlight, unfading and sifting, came into the room and Cassandra sat bare to the waist in the middle of the

318

bed, her eyes inviting him to join her. With him, with *only Sy* would she ever do this. Indeed, she found it impossible to imagine herself being intimate with any man but Sylvestre Diamond.

Sylvestre sucked in a breath at the tantalizing sight of Cassandra's fuller breasts, her unbound hair falling gloriously about their curves. *Mon Dieu,* he thought, she is like a snow-white tigress. Desirable, womanly, seductive—everything a man could ever want in one single woman.

Drawing her to him with a deep groan coming from the tunnel of his throat, Sylvestre kissed her tear-damp lashes, her flushed cheeks, and ran his fingers with aching gentleness over the pale coral peaks of her swelling breasts, and the darting sensations shot clear to the seat of Cassandra's femininity.

When Sylvestre kissed her again, his swishing tongue probed her lips, then darted between the satiny folds. Folds that were like the most secret part of her womanhood.

Cassandra felt the tiny thrusts in an imitation of his body penetrating hers and she fumbled wildly with his shirt to splay it open. Slipping her hands beneath, she felt his smooth, naked flesh, over his thundering heart that matched rhythm with her heartbeats. Sylvestre moaned and gripped her arms, and Cassandra experienced her first taste of power over man.

"Are you sure, Cassa, very sure you want this? It is so like the last time we made love."

"Is it not what love is all about, Sy? To be close to someone when hurting?" She felt a shudder rack his muscular frame in answer to her question. "Make all the pain go away, Sy. Please, oh, please."

319

The bed was relieved of his weight momentarily as Sylvestre stood and began to tear his clothes off, scattering them around him on the floor with careless abandon.

Cassandra pulled herself upright and fumbled with the pearl buttons that held her petticoat waistbands. He came to her aid, deftly removing the last tiny bit of a lace-edged pink thing. Now there was only his affectionate, long-fingered hands. They caressed and they aroused her to a feverish pitch while desire flamed and flowed and poured in her feminine depths.

"Tell me there is no shame in this, Sy . . . I want to make love with you . . . It is right between us, is it not?"

He went very still. "Why would you even mention the word 'shame,' Cassa? *Mais oui,* it is right, for ours is not a forbidden love. We are going to be married very soon."

Cassandra's hands roved the hard, muscular body. "Are you asking me to be your wife, Sy?" she asked, with a slight tremor in her voice.

"I thought you realized that the first night we came together on the *River Minx.* If you did not then, you must learn now that I want you now and forever as my bride."

"Yes, Sy—your bride."

He stroked her hair, silvered by moonbeams. "You are my bride even now, Cassa—my glorious bride."

*"Oui,"* she answered in French.

"I will hold you to your commitment, Cassandra. Tomorrow you will come with me to Diamondhead where we will begin preparations for our wedding. My mother will act as your chaperone while you are under our roof. Say yes, Cassandra, say yes—forever."

"Yes!"

His golden head bent to her, and the shivering warmth in her blood leapt with a resurgence of desire. Unhampered by clothing, their bodies met full-length in what was only a prelude to the hours of lovemaking.

When he finally moved over her, she unfolded like a flower needing sunlight. She arched her back to accommodate his heavy desire. "Oh, Sy . . ." All she knew for several minutes was that he was inside her, and it was as though time were suspended. Then, deeper and deeper with each stroke. Firm and hot. Cassandra clasped him even closer and arched her body to fuse the two into one golden sunburst. Peak after peak of shooting stars.

Much later, after Sylvestre had unsheathed himself, they lay side by side, limbs yet entwined. He leaned over her to kiss her moist forehead, allowing his lips to rest there while he gathered her hands and cupped them to his chest in tender reverence.

"Just so you will not have second thoughts out of fear, *ma chérie,* we shall take care of everything first thing tomorrow."

"What about the Kirbys?" she whispered, as if they listened at the door.

"The Kirbys be damned. Everything will be ready for the ceremony before we even tell them. We will begin tomorrow, as I said."

"Tomorrow?" Cassandra said in alarm, raising her head to peer at his face through the lavender darkness. Something did not seem right. "So soon?" Her stomach suddenly turned queasy.

"That soon," he said, unrelentingly. "Today . . . or yesterday was Saturday. Four days for banns and we

321

can be married next weekend. You will become my glorious bride, Cassa."

There was a cold silence during which Cassandra shivered in the lace-shadowed moonlight. What was it? Something was amiss, she thought, staring around at the blurred bulks of furniture.

With a groan, Sylvestre raked his fingers through his golden hair and sat up on the edge of the bed, stiffening one arm on the mattress. "I have completely forgotten a thing of great importance." His muscles moved in a long shrug. "How could I have been so unaware of it. This changes everything."

"What is it?" Now she was even more alarmed. He did not want her, not now, not after he had disgraced her for the second time. She had been too loose, Cassandra told herself. *Sy loves no one—least of all a woman of easy virtue.*

He twisted around to look down at her, and his heart seemed to be locked in his gaze. "The mourning period. It will be too soon to post the banns in our parish." He reached down to smooth the snow-blond strands from her temples. "We will have to wait, my love. There is no help for it."

The color drained from her face as Cassandra asked in a tiny voice, "How long must the mourning period last, Sy?"

"The mourning for parents ranks next to that of widows, I am afraid. It lasts twelve months, Cassandra."

"There cannot be a wedding for us?"

"It would not be proper."

"Oh." With quiet dignity, Cassandra drew herself up amongst the tangled bedcovers, bringing the sheet with her and tucking it about her breasts. "I shall have to think of . . . mourning clothes."

"Yes, of course." Sylvestre sat thoughtfully brooding, staring at the pale slopes of her breasts. "That you will." He was happy to see her mind was already busy with plans for what was proper to wear. A muscle twitched in his jaw as he said, "I am sorry, Cassa."

"Do not be." There was a tentative knock on the door just then, along with the whisper: "Missa Cassa— is it all right for me to come in? I jest heard about Melantha and your papa—"

"Dulcie," Cassandra said, hopping from the bed, grateful for the intrusion to break the stifling tension that had descended in the bedroom. She went to find her clothes while Sylvestre lit a lamp in a corner of the room after he had hastily pulled on his riding breeches.

His disheveled shirt was open to the waist as he turned to her. "Here, let me help you with that." He crossed the room to give her assistance in buttoning up the front of a light-blue frock. His fingers shook a little and he gazed into her pale, sad eyes as she tied her hair with a blue moiré tafetta ribbon.

"Missa Cassa? I know you're in there with some-o-o—." Dulcie gulped when the vision of golden maleness whisked open the door.

"Come in, Dulcie," Sylvestre said. "I was just leaving."

"I . . . I . . . I—" Dulcie stammered. Her eyes skittered to Cassandra standing in the middle of the room looking weary and somehow more mature. "Are you all right, Missa Cassa?"

"Of course, Dulcie. Sylvestre and I were just having a midnight talk." Cassandra's gaze went to the silver moon framed by the window, seeming to rest on Sy's left shoulder.

Dulcie's eyes went saucer-round and unblinking. "Is it already midnight?" she inquired.

"After midnight," Sylvestre said, glancing over his shoulder at the huge silver moon in the window, having noticed Cassandra staring out at it as if moonstruck.

Suddenly Cassandra's hand went to her stomach, the other to her forehead. "I . . . I think I do not feel so . . . so well." She began to walk unsteadily toward the chair.

Dulcie saw Cassandra swallow hard, and she intercepted the blonde in the middle of the room, taking her by the arm. "You do look mighty pale. Here, Cassa, you come over here and sit down. I heard what happened—"

It is just the grief taking over once again, Sylvestre told himself, walking over to the washbowl. He returned with a damp cloth which he pressed to Cassandra's forehead. Exchanging a look with Dulcie, he began to wonder about certain things. Cassandra looked different somehow. Her body seemed to carry a new womanly softness, especially her fuller breasts.

Sylvestre warmed inwardly. If Cassandra was with child, there would be no mourning period of twelve months! he told himself. He frowned as he turned away. Guilt feelings plagued him. Had it been his intention all along to get her with child, he asked himself. Indeed. The idea must have started immediately after the nasty scene in the garden with Melantha St. James. His courting Cassandra had seemed utterly hopeless at the time, and, even more so was the fact that Melantha had wished . . . no, demanded, that Cassandra marry into the Kirby family. There had also been the fear that Jared Casey would somehow get through to Cassandra with his charm and expertise as a lover. It had been his intention to intercept Casey on his way; and so he had. Indeed, he wanted to be first to love her—and he wanted to be last. And, by damn, he would be!

"See to your mistress, Dulcie," Sylvestre ordered, going out the door. "She is the only one you have now."

Dulcie wrinkled her nose after he had gone. "What's he mean by *that?* I never been a slave to Melantha—Ooops, I'm sorry for mentioning her, Missa Cassa."

"That is all right, Dulcie. I am over the worst of it . . . now . . . *Ohh*—I thought I w-was—"

Before she took another breath, she had flung herself into Dulcie's arms, weeping uncontrollably as the pale octoroon maid rocked her back and forth, back and forth, humming snatches of a comforting spiritual tune deep in her throat.

"Everything's going to be just fine, Missa Cassa. Hmmm-hmmm. Just fine. You'll see. Dulcie ain't never goin' to leave her beautiful angel. No sirree, not my Cassandra."

It was the first time Dulcie had ever called her by her full name. Cassandra burst out in renewed sobs and she continued to pour out her grief for several more minutes.

Cassandra quieted after a time. She laid her blond head on Dulcie's shoulder and closed her eyes. "Dulcie?"

"Uhhm-hmm. I'm here."

"Dulcie . . . I have been bad . . . a loose woman. I have sinned with . . . with Sylvestre."

325

"Hush, honey. Shoot, there ain't a dagblasted bad bone in your body and you ain't no loose woman. You've always been an angel, Cassa."

"I . . . I think I am going to have a b-baby," she gulped.

"What?" Dulcie held Cassandra away from her. She beamed from ear to ear, her dusky-pink lips spread flat. "Why, that's the best thing I heard all day. That's just grand, Missa Cassa." She frowned then. "Guess you're right about one thing, though."

"What do you mean?" she asked Dulcie.

"Well . . ." Dulcie shrugged her slim arms. "If you thinks you've been sinning and you're gonna be having a babe, then you better make it right and get yourself hitched up with that gorgeous hunk of man. Does he want you?" Dulcie shook her dark head, its kinky wavelets undulating down her slim back. "Shoot, 'course he does, I should'na asked. I saw the way he looks at you, honey. That man's got his heart in his eyes, for sure."

Cassandra tilted her head and looked aside as she rose to her feet. "I do not wish to talk about that now," she said quietly.

Narrowly, Dulcie watched Cassandra pull out a soft nightgown with eyelet bodice. "Why? What you got to be afraid of, Missa Cassa? Don't you have no trust in him?" Her eyes rolled deliciously. "*I* sure would trust Sy Diamond. Uhmm-hmm."

"Oh." Cassandra frowned lightly and pursed her lips. "He has no idea that I might be carrying his babe."

Dulcie shook her head confidently. "There's always tomorrow, honey. You can tell him then. Right now, you has to get your little rump into that bed and I have

326

to pull out my trundle bed for sleeping, too." She yawned wide and poked her arms into the air before she bent to gather Cassandra's clothes and put them away carefully.

It wasn't long before Dulcie halted her labors to notice Cassandra standing before the window where the round moon illuminated the brooding thoughtfulness on her profile.

Over her shoulder, Cassandra asked, "What am I going to wear tomorrow, Dulcie?"

Cassandra was thinking of black and gave a shudder.

"What? Oh. Guess you has to be six months in crepe trimmings, three in plain black, and three more in half-mournin'."

Cassandra dragged her hair over her shoulder and began making a long French braid. "Are the dresses full-skirted?"

A little smile played about Dulcie's lips. "Oh, I wouldn't know about that. You'd have to ask Missus Jeannette. What've you got in mind?" As Sylvestre had noted, Dulcie, too, thought it was a good sign that Cassa was thinking about what to wear—just like a woman, too.

"I will wear either parametta cloth or barathea, or any of the black corded stuff."

"Ugh" came across the room.

"I will fashion my own dresses for mourning. Such dresses could be trimmed with two deep tucks of crepe, either albert or rainproof—"

Dulcie snuffled. "Ugh again."

"Made plainly, of course, and the body trimmed with crepe and—"

"Why, excuse me, honey, but you're gonna look just

327

like a walking tent!"

Cassandra was removing the blue muslin frock. "I know," she said, whipping the fat braid over her shoulder.

Dulcie turned to see the mischievous look on Cassandra's face—but this one was a *serious* mischievous look. "Oh-oh," Dulcie said. "I think Cap'n Sy ain't gonna know what's going on for a time. You're gonna be hidin' that baby from him, ain't you."

Drawing the pale-lavender nightgown over her head, Cassandra mumbled through the soft cloth, "For a time."

"For a time. Huh. Guess you just don't trust that man yet. Love sure ain't blind in your case, honey. You got your eyes open too wide and you see everythin' you shouldn't be seeing 'cause it just ain't there, and remember you said yourself that everythin' ain't like it seems all the time. You just have to take a harder look and—"

"Hush, Dulcie."

Dulcie grunted softly, turned down the lamp, then sought her trundle bed for the night.

Cassandra lay awake for another hour before finally drifting into a restless slumber where a tall, angel-haired doll with delft-blue staring eyes danced with a dressmaker's dummy—one that had diamonds for eyes and wore the attire of a groom.

*You're dreaming, Cassandra. Neither of them are real . . . Neither of them . . . can ever be.*

She was dreaming again; another scene. A woman walking toward her. A woman she had never seen before in her life. Melantha rose from her watery grave to walk toward the other woman. The two joined hands

328

and walked back into the water until they disappeared into the murky depths. Cassandra turned toward the sinking *River Minx* and saw her father standing at the rail with two women, one jet-haired, the other blonde. Cassandra screamed and bolted upright in bed.

*"Mother! Where are you?"*

Another scream rippled from her throat when she found her hand gripped in another woman's.

"Cassa, Cassa, honey, you're havin' a bad dream. There now, there now . . . the nightmare's goin', ain't it. That's right, honey-chile, you just go back to sleep now. It's all right now. Hush. Dulcie's not gonna be far away."

There was the soft sound of a quieting sob . . . and then the even breathing.

Now Dulcie lay awake, wondering what tomorrow would bring.

## Chapter Twenty

"Harlan, Son, are you blind?" Oscar Kirby asked, wiping his mouth on a napkin. "Can't you see Cassandra is in love with Sylvestre Diamont?"

Harlan set down his coffee cup, saying, "*Diamond,* Father—that has been their altered name for years. And no—I don't recognize that at all."

"Hell, it's not *you* put that twinkle in our girl's blue eyes!" His laugh broke off; his eyes smoldered. "You better change it and make our girl turn her baby-blues on *you,* boy."

"She'll come around," Harlan boasted, forking a piece of succulent pink ham into his mouth. "Just you wait and see."

"Not with Valerie Beaumont around she won't. That adventuress will terrorize our girl away from you more than anybody. She go home yet?"

"Yes. I saw Valerie out the door just this morning. She was, uh . . . happy when she left for LeBeau-tique . . . her shop in St. Louis."

Oscar straightened his green frock coat over his dun-yellow vest. "You've got to stop sleeping around with that redheaded couturière. Cassandra's going to find out. You have to make Cassandra your bride—especially now she's got no one. I think you get my meaning."

"Our *girl,* as you call her, has not stuck her blond head out her bedroom door or Jeannette's sewing room in two days—not since the bad news. She's worn the carpet between those two rooms."

Oscar's belly shook with a deep belch. "Did she see Val?"

Harlan dipped his dark head. "Fortunately not even Val. Jeannette has gotten Cassandra some material for her widow's weeds and she's busy as a professional seamstress stitching on Mama's new contraption, the sewing machine. Hell, what'll women be thinking up next!"

"Elias Howe, it's inventor, is a *man,* boy—not some pea-brained female," he said unfeelingly.

A pretty black girl appeared in the frame of the door just then, bobbing a curtsy. "A Mistah Jared Cazey is here to see you, suh. He says you been expectin' him."

"Yes, Mandy, send him in."

Following another deep curtsy, the Negro girl spun around on the uncarpeted floor to make her way back to the front door.

With raised eyebrows, Harlan studied his father. "That two-bit lawyer from Illinois?" He often sulked like a little boy when around his father—and he did so now. "We get rid of Mr. Diamond and Mr. Casey makes an appearance. Hell, I saw the way Casey was eyeing Cassandra aboard the *River Minx.*"

"Too much competition for you, eh, boy? Still, I've never known you to disregard a challenge. Well, Casey's visit will be brief and to the point. Stay and listen—this concerns you, too, boy."

Oscar stood then as the lawyer stepped into the dining room. "Ah. Mr. Casey—just the man I've been waiting for. Let's get down to business right away then."

Cassandra wore black.

Numbly she had donned the mourning dress she had fashioned for herself. She gave a minute inspection of the blond-and-black vision of herself in the cheval glass. Touching the dreary folds of material and thinking how Monte would have hated to see her dressed in all black.

Tears welled in her eyes and it was all she could do to force them back. "Oh, Papa . . . I should have forgiven you your liaison with Miki Rhea while you were still alive . . . I do forgive you, Papa . . . I do understand. You were only human."

Cassandra blinked away her tears, then looked up as someone entered the room. "Oh, Dulcie. I . . . I feel so homely in black."

"I hate to say this, honey, it ain't right, but you look like a vision of sun bursting into the darkest night. Like that poem you read to me once: 'She walks in beauty like the night . . . all that's best of dark and bright.' Uh-huh, that's it, just like that little books says."

Cassandra was about to lower herself into the window seat when Dulcie intercepted her with, "Missa

Cassa, don't sit down now—I almost plumb forgot. The ole man wants you down in his study. Lickety-split."

"Now? Downstairs? But . . ."

Dulcie imitated Oscar Kirby's voice when he was ordering one of his girls around, going deep. *"You get your skinny ass down here right now, girl!"*

"Well then," Cassandra sighed. "If I must."

"You must."

Entering Oscar Kirby's study moments later, Cassandra found him seated behind a mammoth cherry-wood desk. He held a sheaf of papers in his meaty hand as if they had been glued there for hours.

"Sit down, my girl." Oscar motioned her to a leather chair, red-cushioned and stiff-backed. "How are you today? Better?" No answer. "Ah, that's good. We want you feeling strong for the memorial service later when Reverend Mutterperl arrives." He waited until she was perched on the edge of the chair, hands folded lightly in her lap. With distaste, he noted the black dress and her white-gold hair drawn back into a severe topknot. "Always did hate black on a woman," he casually remarked.

Looking slowly around the cluttered study, Cassandra discovered to her surprise they were not alone. Jared Casey smiled and held out his hand as he detached himself from the shadowy corner. "You have my greatest sympathy, my . . . dear." He had had it in mind to call her "Angel," but that would never do under the present circumstances, he decided.

334

Clearing his throat, Oscar brought Cassandra's attention back to himself. He tapped the sheaf of papers while Jared moved back just out of Cassandra's forward line of vision. "I realize most women know nothing about business—" Oscar stopped in midsentence. "Now, to get back to our business: Cassandra girl, you should realize what you're worth, so I will proceed. You inherit the *Southern Star*, in addition to thirty thousand when the St. James property is sold." A throat-clearing pause, then, "I shall run the *Southern Star* with the Kirby Line, if that meets with your approval." He puffed out his chest and blustered, "You should know that I never run up against an unprofitable enterprise. Your best interests are safe with us."

"Yes, that sounds just fine to me, Oscar," she agreed, though an odd warning sounded in her brain.

"Ah. She's finally calling me Oscar." He shifted his bulk and reached for a chocolate bonbon. "I hope your interest in Sylvestre Diamont . . . I mean Diamond, is only on a basis of friendship, my girl." His eyes looked hard and glittery as he watched her toy with the dainty gold cross she wore around her neck. When she said nothing, he went on. "Uhm, there is one more 'item' in the will. All these 'things' will come to you *only* within the framework of marriage. To the right person, that is."

Cassandra's gaze shifted to Jared Casey, then back to Oscar Kirby. "I see. *Only* if I happen to marry into the Kirby family—is that it?"

Jared stepped forward now, but Cassandra held up her hand before he could speak. "Let me finish. Am I also to understand that you are *our* family lawyer,

335

Mr. Casey?"

"Yes, Miss St. James, you are correct," Jared said uneasily, then repeated, "I am your, ah . . . family lawyer."

"Why did my father never mention this to me?" She kept to herself that Melantha had indeed revealed the fact to her upon landing in St. Louis.

Jared's eyes went from Oscar to Cassandra. "Miss St. James, ah . . . Cassandra, if I may." She nodded and he went on. "Monte St. James entrusted his wife with the disposition of their property on the event of death. Your mother and I spoke at length on the matter of legal documents and, whether or not you were aware, Melantha had a premonition of disaster. I'm sorry . . . I hope I haven't distressed you further in your time of bereavement."

Cassandra frowned. "Mr. Casey, you never told me before that you knew my mother." Her blue eyes took his measure. "Why am I hearing all this now?"

In a low, composed voice, he explained, "It was my intent aboard the *River Minx* to entertain you—not bore you."

"I see." Cassandra took a steadying breath. "Go on, please."

"On the will we made up, Cassandra, 'Lastly' states that your parents 'nominated and appointed' the Kirbys, H.K. and O.K., to be 'the executors' of this their 'last will and testament.' Look here." He bent to show her the signatures of both her parents, on three separate sheets of paper. "It is all there."

"So I am to understand," Cassandra began, standing to pace the room as she spoke, "that the remainder of

336

their personal estate, goods, and chattels, shall bequeath to me, Cassandra St. James, only in the event of marriage between myself and Harlan Kirby?"

"Let me say, girl, you are very perceptive," Oscar said admirably.

Cassandra shot Oscar a brief perusal as he reached for another bonbon. In many ways Oscar Kirby reminded her of a rooting hog. Her eyes drifted to Jared Casey, and she felt an undercurrent she could not put her finger on. She only knew Jared was keeping something to himself and was looking quite uncomfortable at the moment.

"No, Mr. Kirby. It is just that I am not stupid." She had no wish to slander Valerie's name, but she must have her say. "I also have knowledge that a certain lovely redhead has been sharing a bedroom with H.K., in this very house."

"I won't have it!" Oscar bristled with mock-anger. "Not under my own roof, I will not!"

He did not deny the fact. He was caught in his own embarrassing outburst, and Casey was there to acknowledge it along with Cassandra. Jared was beginning to experience guilt over the whole matter, wishing now that he had not forged Monte St. James's signature.

Oscar shifted uncomfortably in his chair. "Harlan will change for the better, my girl. You shall see what wonders marriage can do for a healthy man such as my son and he will be different—"

"A leopard is not able to change his spots or his color, Mr. Kirby," Cassandra said, breaking across his sentence.

337

"But a chameleon can—to blend in with his surroundings, that is," Oscar said with a chuckle at his own comeback.

"Not where I am concerned, sir," Cassandra contradicted. "The man I marry will have no reason to find his pleasures elsewhere than in our own home, where he will 'blend in' very nicely."

*Hooray for you!* Jared Casey thought as he gazed at Cassandra appreciatively. Here was a woman after his own heart. But Jared was afraid it was too late for him, for he had caught the vital flame burning in her eyes when Sylvestre Diamond's name came up. He sighed inwardly, wishing he could right the sins he had committed against this lady angel whose wings had brushed softly, gently, against him and kindled a deep, sincere compassion for fellow man—an emotion he'd never known before meeting her. Perhaps he could . . .

"I am afraid your displeasure over your son's behavior comes too late, Mr. Kirby," Cassandra went on. "The plum is already in the pudding. I also have knowledge that Harlan—and perhaps even you yourself—lusts after my maid Dulcie. But most important, Mr. Kirby, I do not love your son."

"Love? Bah!"

Flustered, Oscar Kirby reached for some more bonbons and stuffed all three into his mouth at once. "I forbid you to slander my son under this roof," he belted out of the side of his mouth. "You aren't all that righteous, girl—I know what you and Mr. Diamond were doing the very night you should have been weeping and grieving—you were lifting your skirts for that snobbish aristocrat!"

"I am sorry, Mr. Kirby, but I cannot marry your son." Although an angry sparkle of resentment shone in her blue eyes, she managed to keep her voice controlled. "It is not my wish to cross you or make you bitter, but nothing on earth shall make me wish to become Harlan's bride."

Anger streaked through Oscar as he came up out of his chair. "How dare you defy me!" His voice reverberated with his fury. He looked to Jared Casey for help, but the dark-haired lawyer only shrugged and actually looked a little pleased with the present circumstances.

"Mr. Casey," Cassandra said, avoiding the red-faced man across from her, "would you be so kind as to accompany me into town?" Now she gave Oscar a peremptory glance. "I am going to my room to pack—immediately."

Jared shrugged again, not meeting Oscar's murderous expression. "If that is your wish, Cassandra."

"It is."

"You have been living under our neighborly charity, girl," Oscar began slowly. "Where is your own charity toward my family?"

Almost sorry for him, Cassandra said, "I am not feeling very charitable toward you at the moment, Mr. Kirby."

"You say nothing of the generosity Jeannette has bestowed upon you!"

"I have thanked Jeannette most kindly, sir. Now, I cannot stand here and argue, because I have much to do."

"You have nowhere to go, girl!" Oscar shouted as she

exited the study in a swirl of black skirts and flash of blond hair. "What about the memorial service? Reverend Mutterperl has been notified! And mostly— what about the goddamned will?!"

Cassandra said nothing as she marched upstairs and began to pack her bags. "Where we goin', Missa Cassa?" Dulcie asked with a helpless shrug, her hazel-brown eyes wide and worried.

"To Valerie Beaumont's shop."

# Chapter Twenty-One

At precisely two o'clock in the afternoon, the Kirby stable boy brought a trim little cutter drawn by two chestnut-coated horses around to the front of the house. Cassandra stepped outside and paused for a moment before getting into the carriage, taking what seemed her first breath of fresh air since the death of her parents.

Suddenly Cassandra was thankful for the golden sun, the painted earth, and the clouds of white that were sailing in a clear July sky. She was aware of a measure of contentment and peace of mind, feeling that although her parents were gone from this earth, their spirits were close by.

"Ah, here we are," Jared said, joining Cassandra and Dulcie. "You may get in now, ladies."

Cassandra had said a polite good-bye to Jeannette as the woman stood tearfully watching her and Dulcie gather all their belongings, including Cassandra's ponderous, arched trunk. Impulsively Cassandra had hugged the rawboned woman, asking Jeannette to look her up in St. Louis.

Unremorseful over her departure from Kirby House, Cassandra sat back against the cracked leather seat and looked out at the locust trees with their thorny branches and white flowers. Trees with leafy arms spread wide, giving restful shade . . . She was suddenly and painfully reminded of Diamondhead on a glorious day like this wishing she could be there with Sy.

Feeling stimulated by her freedom, Cassandra smiled across the carriage to Jared from beneath her short black veil. He was thinking she had just the right amount of sweetness and cynicism to enable her to survive. If only it was going to be he who could give her all she deserved, but alas, he'd done some serious thinking and decided that settling down to home and children was just not in him. Someday . . . maybe.

"Cassandra, I'm not sure where to begin," he started out slowly. "About the will—"

"Please, Jared, I would rather not speak of it now. Perhaps at a later date."

"As you wish."

Jared wanted to get it out in the open, but the time was not right, he saw, and, for now, he decided to cater to her wishes.

Cassandra had applied a touch of pink rouge to her pale cheekbones and smoothed a suggestion of lavender-gray shadow on her lids. Her silk bonnet, borrowed from Jeannette, was small, exquisitely modish, and fit close to her blond head. A long crepe veil hung at the back, a shorter version for her face. She had fashioned her black silk dress with its lawn collar and cuffs from yards of satin merveilleux Jeannette had given her. She had also sewn several mourning

342

dresses, for day wear and evening. She wore a pair of black hose made of spun silk, and Dulcie had remarked how beautiful and slender Cassandra's legs looked encased in the "silk things."

Silence reigned upon entering the city, and Cassandra stared out the window at men in shirtsleeves sweeping dust from stoops and trimming vines trailing over unpainted fences. Cassandra forgot her sadness for a moment when she saw a little black girl outside a storefront feeding songbirds tidbits of crusty bread.

Dulcie's eyes were inquisitively wide as they passed an apothecary shop with its windows filled with shining bottles. Down the street was a millinery, its peaked roof baking in the afternoon sun.

Jared wished he had the words to comfort Cassandra. Doing the next best thing, he leaned forward to pat Cassandra's hand. "I'm happy to see some color in your face, Angel," not realizing the pale blush was due to the light application of cosmetics. "I . . ." He cleared his throat. "I wanted to call on you and take you for an outing before this, but you know how the gossips would have talked."

Cassandra smiled through her veil. "They will now, more than ever, Mr. Casey."

Jared sighed deeply. "We've been over this before, Cassandra. Please call me by my first name."

She noticed that he was wearing dark attire. "Why are you dressed all in black, Mr. . . . Jared?" She laughed softly.

"It is considered good taste to wear mourning in making a call to a grieving young lady."

"You are very proper, Jared."

"It is not a decided rule, Cassandra. However, I believe it is only a graceful method of sharing sympathy with those who are grieving loved ones."

This was a new Jared, Cassandra thought. "Thank you, Jared, you are very kind to offer such graceful sympathy, and you are a true gentleman in addition."

"I have a business acquaintance whom I have to meet shortly." He turned his eyes on Dulcie and saw that she was pouting about something. Jared's blue eyes twinkled with a little bit of his old self. "Now, may I set you up in a boarding house? I have a friend—a woman who has been thinking of boarding out rooms and will be very—"

Cassandra broke across his sentence. "I am afraid not, Jared." She noticed that they were approaching an older part of the city, where the houses had mullioned windows and low galleries, many of them surrounded by high white fences. "Where are we?" she asked, suddenly aware she had not told him where to let her off.

"You'll see" was all Jared said.

Presently Jared ordered the driver to stop before a stone-and-timber house. Cassandra noted that it was a quaint place, with a huge stone chimney. A winding flagstone path led to the door and greenery was everywhere.

Mild alarm streaked through Cassandra as she looked at Jared, seeing his furtive glance at her tight hands. "Jared, whose house is this? Oh. If you think that I will allow you to set me—"

Cassandra had no chance to finish her sentence, for at that moment a stunning red-haired woman stepped out of the house. The violet-blue eyes widened as the woman looked up. "Cassandra!" She hurried toward the carriage, holding up the full skirts of a pale-green afternoon dress. "You poor darling! Come into the house at once. I'm sure you must be stifling in that carriage. I was just leaving for the shop, but now that you are here I will delay going there. It is just a short walk downtown anyway."

"Valerie . . ." Cassandra's face registered her surprise as she turned to Jared. "You are an acquaintance of Valerie Beaumont's?"

"Actually, we are very old friends. She and I have known each other for a long time, since our childhood in Illinois, in fact."

"How wonderful. I am so happy." Cassandra beamed back into Jared's likewise beaming countenance. "I can never begin to thank you enough, Jared, for bringing me here."

"Oh . . ." he said, gazing down at her hand resting along his arm. "I'll think of something, Angel."

Cassandra kissed Jared lightly on his clean-shaven cheek. "This day you have proven to be my dearest friend." She looked at Dulcie, then Valerie waiting happily outside the carriage. "Actually, I should say my 'third' dearest friend."

Jared took a deep breath and his blue eyes misted. "Cassandra, there is something I must tell you. I am ashamed to say that I have done you an injustice—"

He would have elaborated, but just then the driver swung the carriage door wide and Valerie caught Cassandra's hand. The burly driver brought the trunk down from the back and, with Valerie's permission, took it into the house. "Upstairs, in the second bedroom," she called to the driver.

From the window of the carriage Jared looked out at

the blond vision standing beneath the hot July sun. "When will I see you again?" He grinned impishly. "Tonight perhaps . . . dinner?"

"Oh, Jared," Valerie groaned. "Cassandra just arrived, so please give us time to visit before you come calling." Valerie looked at Cassandra and bit her lip. "Oh, dear, what about you-know-who?"

"Please, Valerie, not now," Cassandra begged, realizing that the redhead was wondering about Sylvestre Diamond. "Can we go inside? I am feeling a bit lightheaded."

"Of course, and you probably forgot to eat again." Valerie winked at Jared and waved. "See you later, darling." Then she turned to lead Cassandra and Dulcie into the cool interior of the spacious house. "I hope you will be staying for a time, Cassandra, because this big old house sure gets lonesome, let me tell you."

Cassandra lifted her veil and looked around the beautifully quaint home. "This is all yours—alone?" she asked.

"Yes. My parents have been gone for years." Valerie lifted her shoulders in a light shrug, taking a carpetbag from Dulcie to carry it herself. "I have no one but myself, my plants, and this empty house." Her violet-blue eyes twinkled then. "Although Harlan comes by to visit every weekend to break the monotony."

Valerie removed a feathered hat and set it on a tall French table in the hall. Cassandra brushed up against a huge jade tree and could feel its rubbery leaves.

"That's Samantha," Valerie said lovingly as she began to introduce all her exotic plants as if they were real persons. "And over there is Bettina, and farther down the hall you can see Rosalee—she's shipped all

346

the way from England; Stargazer is from the North, very delicate, but he loves his spot at the turn of the stairs where his piney limbs reach to the window."

Dulcie did not question the "he" or "she" nomenclature, but she did stare around at all of Valerie's beautiful plants. Green . . . there was varied, well-kept green everywhere. "It's like the outdoors in here," Dulcie shyly remarked.

"I know. I love it."

"Valerie . . ." Cassandra began. "I shall not be intruding on your hospitality all that many days. I mean to find a place for Dulcie and myself. But first I must seek employment."

"You have the job at my shop, I've already told you that, Cassandra. As for finding a place to stay . . ." She reached out and impulsively pulled Dulcie and Cassandra in a tight hug, one woman on either side of her. "I'm not letting you two dears get away for quite some time. You're welcome to stay here a year or more if you like. Whatever it takes."

Cassandra stepped back. "Oh, we couldn't!"

Dulcie's wide eyes lowered to Cassandra's still-flat stomach, knowing that the baby would begin to show before too long. "Uh-uh, don't think it'll be that long we be stayin'." She was thinking of Sylvestre Diamond, who was going to come searching for Cassandra any day now. And when he found out she was in the family way, there would be a wedding mighty quicklike, no doubt about it.

"Hush, Dulcie," Cassandra ordered, meeting the dark eyes over Valerie's shoulders.

"All right." Valerie clamped her long-fingered hands on her slimly curved hips. "Tell me what's going on."

347

Cassandra licked her dry lips. "It is a long story."

"I like long stories. Come on—let's raid the kitchen so I can fix us some lunch, then we'll go to my shop."

Dulcie caught up with the redhead on their jungle-trek into the kitchen. "Miss Valerie, you have any servants?" Dulcie wanted to know.

Valerie laughed shortly. "I'm afraid that is a luxury I can ill afford."

"Well, if you don't mind, I'd like to fix us that lunch. I like to keeps my hands busy. My mammy used to say they can turn into the tools of Lucifer hisself if we don't keep them doin'."

"A very wise woman."

Valerie stood in the kitchen, bright and cheerful with its yellow walls, potted ferns, the sun pouring in at just the right angle from the huge ceiling-to-floor windows. Dulcie stood gaping at the sparkling-white cupboards and floors; cleanliness was in evidence all throughout the huge room. No mistake about it, this was a far cry from the cluttered, greasy Kirby kitchen.

Valerie tossed her arms wide. "It's all yours, Dulcie—see what you can whip up while I show Cassandra the rest of the house. Oh, there's a loaf of Boston brown bread in the pantry—fresh baked. Have a piece to munch on while you work. And there's lemonade in the cooler. Will you pour a glass for Cassandra and myself?"

Beaming from ear to ear, Dulcie said, "Yes'm. It'll my pleasure." She leaned to sniff a plant that tickled her nose, then straightened and set about her task.

The pretty, bow shape of Valerie's mouth spread in a bright smile as she took her new friend by the arm and ushered her through the rooms, while in the streets bonfires burned and churchbells clanged.

Cassandra turned from the tall vase of flowers she had been smelling. "What is that? I had no idea today was a holiday."

Valerie explained. "Steamers from New Orleans are bringing discharged soldiers home. The city of St. Louis will be a place of celebration tonight and I doubt if we'll get much sleep."

Cassandra bit down hard on her lip to keep from crying. Why did she suddenly feel so weepy? Perhaps it was not a baby. Maybe she had a fatal illness. She decided to make an appointment with a doctor as soon as she and Valerie went into town . . . But if she asked Valerie for the name of her doctor, then she would also have to reveal her condition . . . if pregnant she truly was. Perhaps she would wait another week . . .

"This means, dear friend, that my store is going to be flooded with customers. Which also means a heavy workload for us. I am going to keep you very busy, Cassandra, and I can assure you it will be fun."

Cassandra walked to the mullioned window and stared out at the garden filled with summer flowers. Her eyes lifted heavenward. *I just lost my parents and am stepping into a new life. I might even be carrying a baby!* Was this some dream that she would awaken from? Even though her life had taken an unexpected turn, the situation was not one of hopelessness. *Lord, give me strength, because I am going to need all the help I can get.*

"Cassandra?"

"Yes." The blonde turned to face the curious eyes of the redhead.

"I am in the mood to hear a 'long story.'" Valerie had

349

already seated herself on a pink-cushioned sofa with tall, luxuriant plants flanking the arms on either side. "Do you feel like telling me one?"

Cassandra's eyes grew expressive, soft, and she tipped her head slightly to one side and nodded. She joined Valerie on the sofa and started her story—leaving nothing out.

# Chapter Twenty-Two

It was a clear, bright afternoon when Sylvestre sat down in a St. Louis restaurant to a meal of apple-beef brisket smothered in dark gravy, fork-tender. He drank no wine, for he wanted to remain clearheaded. His only drink was chicory coffee, strong and hot.

He shoved the plate aside shortly, the meal half-eaten, finding his appetite was not so good after all.

Paying his bill, he left the establishment and stepped out into the waning sunlight. He had met with his factor from New Orleans, taken care of other pressing business earlier in the day, and was about to make a call on the Kirby residence when his gaze riveted to a slender blonde across the street.

She was dressed in widow's weeds, a summer parasol of silk, deeply trimmed with crepe but minus any lace or fringe, held at a slight angle above her head. She wore also a bonnet with long veil trailing behind, a shorter one covering her face. She moved gracefully, with a certain air of wistfulness about her. Although the blonde's features were blurred, he would know this angel in black anywhere.

He was about to cross the street when a woman from out of his very distant past stepped up to him and threw her scarlet-clad arms about his neck.

*"Mon cher,"* she all but shouted, a decided glow in her eyes. "Where have you been hiding? I have not seen you for ages." She spoke in a voice accented in broken French.

"Sherri, please," he said, becoming annoyed when she linked her arm in his and pressed close to his hip and thigh. "If you do not mind, Sherri. I am pressed for time just now." He tried not to settle his gaze into the valley of her huge, firm breasts. Had she always been this endowed, he briefly wondered.

"Later, eh?" She winked, sliding her scantily clad silk bosom up his chest and kissing him smack full on the lips.

"Sherri—*damn!*"


Her eyes flicking wide beneath lowered veil, Cassandra stopped dead in her tracks and whirled about. A questioning amber brow rose as her curiosity was piqued. She had thought there was something familiar about the man . . . And now she stood stock-still and stared at the man and woman across the street.

Valerie, coming to a halt beside Cassandra, moaned, "Oh, no, isn't that—?"

Cassandra wrenched her stare from the couple unabashedly embracing in the street, in full light of day. "Yes, it is, Valerie," she said dispassionately, adding nothing more.

Though tempted, Cassandra did not allow herself to glance back at the amorous couple. Turning abruptly, she continued to walk, Valerie trying to keep up with her faster pace.

"Ah! Men! Are there none honorable?" Valerie exclaimed softly. "We cannot live with or without the rascally beasts."

Cassandra reached beneath her veil with a black, lace-edged handkerchief. "Please, Valerie, I do not wish to be reminded what unfaithful cads they can be."

She moaned inwardly. How could she have been so stupid as to believe that Sylvestre wanted to marry her. Then she thought, *Perhaps he truly does, but wants to eat his cake, too.* Oh, he was no different than Harlan Kirby, with his wandering eyes and straying heart. Could one woman ever be enough for these men? Must they always go from the arms of one woman to another? Even Monte, her father, had strayed . . . No, no more. I have this child, and that is all that matters in the world. But . . . an unwed mother? Tears dampening her blue eyes, Cassandra felt she might die of the humiliation after the baby was born. *Listen to me, I have not even seen a doctor and already I am having a baby!*

In spite of willing herself not to recall the way the woman's well-formed breasts had pushed against Sylvestre's cool white shirtfront, Cassandra added the last painful sight of their kiss to memory and promised herself to turn Sylvestre Diamond out of her heart. However, the memory of the two pressed together in a sultry kiss could never be removed from her mind. He would never again make her believe he was not a

353

womanizer. She would listen to none of his counterfeit tales of women trying to seduce *him*. *Never again, damnit!*

Cassandra's long nails dug deeply into her palm as she took hold of the dainty chain that held the gold cross. She yanked it hard from around her neck and the tiny gold links broke away, the whole thing left to fall into the street.

Her eyes dead ahead, Cassandra kept walking and seemed not to notice Valerie or anything else. The swell of pain and anguish was beyond tears and, besides, she would not allow herself the weak, feminine notion of crying in broad daylight, widow's weeds or not.

Moments later, Sylvestre stepped blindly on the gold trinket and, unawares, crushed it underfoot. It lay there and shone dully in the sun until a skinny little boy snatched it up against his thin breastbone. He didn't ponder long whether to keep it or not. He was too hungry. Clutching it in a grimy fist, he exclaimed, *"Wow!* Wait'll paw sees this! We're gonna sell it to the jewelers and eat tonight! *Wow!"*

The bell above the frame tinkled as the door opened and closed, announcing that a customer had just entered the LeBeau-tique.

Camille La Tourette entered the showroom from a curtained room in the back. The highly acclaimed dressmaker, French by nationality, smiled through the seamed wrinkles on her little face.

"Can I be of assistance to M'sieur?" Her scratchy voice was hardly above a whisper, but this did not belie her strength of character in any way.

"Perhaps," Sylvestre said. "This is the shop of one Valerie Beaumont?" His eyes passed over a rack of gowns in every color and description, coming back to rest on the woman.

*"Oui, m'sieur."* Camille nodded slowly.

"Is she in?"

"She was, but I am not sure if she still is, m'sieur." Again the slow nod.

Sylvestre had the strongest feeling that the old woman was stalling. "Well then . . . might I have a word with her? If she is in, that is."

"Is it about a gown m'sieur is perhaps considering for his wife?"

"I am not a married man, madame."

*"Oh non,* I am not married either, m'sieur. I am *Mademoiselle* Camille, m'sieur."

"I *am* sorry." Sylvestre's gaze went to the emerald curtain separating showroom from work area. "Now, *mademoiselle,* if you would be so kind to fetch Valerie Beaumont, I would be most appreciative of your haste."

Camille laughed. "Haste, m'sieur? Camille does not move as fast as she used to when she was younger." She coughed behind her veined hand.

Sylvestre pressed his mouth into a thin line before he tried again. "Perhaps she can allow me to take a look for myself then? I do believe I could move a bit faster than *petite mademoiselle.*"

The seamed face took on a rosy glow. "Oooh, m'sieur, I cannot allow you in the back room unless you bring your lady along for fittings—or perhaps her measurements first, before we can make a gown for her."

*My lady is hiding in this shop somewhere and I mean to find her!*

"I see." He moved then, warning, "I shall be gentle, Camille La Tourette."

"G-gentle? What do you have in mind, m'sieur?"

Sylvestre stepped to the little Frenchwoman and, smiling kindly into her alarmed face, he clamped his hands upon her shoulders, then lifted her bodily from the floor and set her away from the curtained area she had been so valiantly guarding. Her eyes had never left his.

"I shall just have a look for myself, my love."

Camille's frail lashes battered away at her cheeks as she watched the tall, heartbreakingly handsome man sweep the curtain aside. Her hand was over her heart as she tried to convince herself she was not falling in love with this stranger. But was he a stranger . . . ? Where had she seen those golden eyes before, that thick hair waving away from his face. Ah! Could this be the son of Nanette Diamond? Certainly he has grown since last he accompanied his *maman* into this shop.

Sylvestre entered the small workroom. He had a thorough look around, then swept the curtain aside and paused, staring down at the floor, missing the slight movement of a purple dress swaying inside a rack of dresses. Returning to the front room, Sylvestre ran a finger along Camille's loose chin. She stared up into his eyes, unblinkingly, certain she was in love again as she had been when very young.

"There is no one there, *ma petite*. I think perhaps someone has pulled a nasty trick on me?"

The lovely old dressmaker blushed as Sylvestre's hand fell back to his side. Long, tan fingers, Camille noticed. *Oh-la,* if only she were younger, she would have a field day with this one. She had been a looker in her days. Even at that, Camille knew she could not have competed with the beautiful young woman in the plain black dress who had entered the shop just moments before this one had come in looking for her. Valerie had peeked between the gold brocade curtains at the window . . .

"Cassandra—he's coming!"

Camille's head had rotated back and forth as she watched the two busy themselves searching for a hiding place. The blonde had stiffened her shoulders. "I shall see him, Valerie, I have to face him sometime." Then she had taken hold of her lower lip with pearly white teeth. "But I am not up to it today!" They rushed to the back room, Valerie peeping her red head out and ordered Camille to, "Stall him!" Camille had followed Valerie to the curtain and then had the compulsion to hide, too, as the blurred figure stepped up to the hazy glass door . . . And now, here she was, foolishly in love with this golden-haired Apollo.

Truthfully Camille revealed, "They were . . . I mean Mademoiselle Beaumont was in back only a moment ago." She shrugged. "Oh! Valerie comes and Valerie goes. She is quite fond of those tiny French doughnuts —perhaps you can find her at the bakery?"

Sylvestre swiftly came to the conclusion that he had been subjected to a bit of female dupery. "Tell *them* that Sylvestre Diamond called while *they* were out." He smiled warmly and bid the little dressmaker a good afternoon.

When he was gone, Camille rushed into the workroom and looked about. "Perhaps they did step out for some dinner." She wagged her white head when Valerie's impish face appeared from within the colorful folds of a rack holding street dresses, some with dressmaker's pins still stuck in the hems.

The grin swiftly vanished from the redhead's mouth. "Ouch!" she exclaimed as she stepped out, reaching back to pull the lovely blonde into full view of Camille's disapproving regard.

"Tsk-tsk," Camille clucked her tongue. "It was not nice of you and your charming friend to trick that handsome gentleman so. For shame. He was very sorry to go away without the little blonde there."

Camille peered at the young woman in widow's weeds beside a grinning Valerie. *"Oh-la!* You are mourning, are you not?"

"Yes, I am," Cassandra softly answered, feeling embarrassed in front of this elderly woman. "My parents."

"Ah. It is sad to hear. Now you must count your garden by the flowers, never by the leaves that fall."

"Camille has a bit of the poet in her, Cassandra," Valerie said, warmly smiling at her friend and companion, who had been with her through the long days and sometimes nights, too, both women working to finish gowns in time for the many balls and parties of the season. A warm bond of friendship and respect had formed between the women.

Camille went on. "Remember, my beauty, one love is the treasure that counts."

"This is Cassandra St. James, Camille." Valerie shook her head and laughed at her belated introductions. "Camille La Tourette, Cassandra."

"My maiden name," Camille said. "I never married,

358

ou see."

Cassandra had never met a woman before with so
many wrinkles, ones which spoke of her happy smiles.
She dared not question the lady's age. But Camille was
sweet and kind, that was all that really mattered. "I am
happy to make your acquaintance. Truly"—Cassandra
went on—"I am sorry for causing all the trouble."

"Bah! Think nothing of it. Do not be embarrassed,
Cassandra. I was young and mischievous once myself.
Yet I must tell you one thing and heed my words well,
sweet: There are many fish in the sea, but you would be
making a bad mistake to let *that* one get away."

In her mind Cassandra was thinking of a rejoinder to
Camille's warning: *Many fish indeed, but how many
honorable and incorrupt ones, I wonder.*

"I used to stitch gowns for Sylvestre's mother
Nanette," Camille suddenly informed the blonde. "I
believe the male parent passed away, did he not?"

"Yes, he did," Cassandra said, not offering any
further conversation having to do with the Diamonds.
It was too painful just now.

But Camille relentlessly pursued the matter as she
perched on a stool and took some sewing into her lap.
"As I recall, Sylvestre Diamond has been in control of
everything on Diamondhead Plantation since his
father passed away. He organized everything, and
everyone." She chuckled low. "Mmm, perhaps not his
sweet *maman,* not entirely. He took on responsibilities
of running the plantation at an early age, perhaps too
young. He is a full-grown man now, and I hear a man
who cannot be caught by just *any* husband-seeking
female. You have accomplished the impossible, Cassandra St. James and, indeed, I salute you."

359

"I do not think that I should leave you with that impression—"

"Ah!" Camille held up a hand with needle and thread between her bony fingers. "You needn't explain any thing to me, mademoiselle. Just do not let him get away. Chase you a little? Surely. But do not let him tire of the activity."

"But I must tell you that Sylvestre does not—"

"Tut-tut. You will tire me out with useless explana tions. Now . . . I have work to do."

With that, Cassandra was dismissed by a careless wave of Camille's hand. The elderly dressmaker rose only once from her labor to brew a pot of jasmine tea on a little hot plate at the back of the workroom. Then she settled upon her stool and set to work again, a cup of the steaming brew at her elbow.

"After Camille gets to know you better, she will not talk as much," Valerie explained while Cassandra moved about, awed by the huge bolts of material in every imaginable color and texture. "This is the most I've heard her say in years. She likes you, Cassandra, I can tell. Her sharp eyes see all, and don't think for a moment she is ignoring you. It is just her way. She loves her work and puts everything into it, even considering her frail health. Soon you'll really see her in action."

Watching Camille's needle flash to and fro, Cassandra was amazed, and found much to respect in the talented dressmaker. Now she went from her stool to the sewing machine and, lifting the square wooden cover, she sat down on a little bench. Placing both feet on the ornate black treadle, giving the steel flywheel a spin, she soon had the material sliding smoothly beneath the needle while the machine hummed rhythmically. Her hands guided the material and her feet pumped and her eyes never strayed to the left or the right as she bent over the well-oiled machine to work like the professional she was.

Camille traversed from the sewing machine to the huge work table, to the dressmaker's form, moving slowly but efficiently as the mechanism of a fine old clock. Tight, perfect stitches appeared like magic as a beautiful gown was brought into creation at a pace that made Cassandra dizzy and awestruck.

Valerie paused in her instructions to Cassandra, interrupting Camille for a moment. "Cassandra is going to work here, Camille. With us."

Camille nodded. "Can she sew?"

"Of course." Valerie laughed, tossing red curls.

"Is she *good?*"

"She made the widow's weeds she's wearing."

Camille flashed a perusal at the plain black dress. "Mademoiselle would make a sack look beautiful on her person." She nodded her approval then. "It is good." A shrug. "Different . . . but good, I admit." She glanced at the black dress again, then back to the jonquil-yellow dress with meadowsweet sprinkled over the full skirt. "Too hot. Satin's too hot. We've some black muslin and lawn. Not proper for widow's weeds? Eh, so what, who would wish to suffocate in silk and satin. See . . ." Camille tossed a hand in Cassandra's direction. "She is perspiring like she is overheated."

Valerie walked over to where Cassandra was sipping a glass of water and running a finger beneath her high collar. "Are you feeling all right, Cassandra? Camille says you look overheated."

"I am fine, Valerie. True, a little hot, but certainly

not ill."

"Nonsense. You look green about the gills. Why don't you change into something cooler?" Valerie crossed the work area to flip through a rack of afternoon dresses.

Valerie nodded. "This one looks small enough for you. Come, go into the dressing room and try this on."

"Plum?" Cassandra's eyes widened as she set her empty glass aside. "I would be erring against the accepted ideas of decency and respect, I'm afraid."

"'Tis the mourning of the heart, love, not mere outward woe.' Black is so depressing," Valerie said.

"I'm afraid I must decline, Valerie. I must show my respect for the dead by wearing the usual black."

Valerie's mouth curled up in a lopsided smile. "You could wear a band of black crepe around your arm and still wear the plum."

Camille came down off her stool just then. "Might I be of some help in this?" With her hands upon her hips, she perused the black dress again. "I like it. Too hot, however. There is one from last year at the back of the room that I'm sure will fit Cassandra, Val. I think you'll like this dress, *chérie.*"

Camille walked away and then returned with a cool-black made of Victoria lawn with four tiny tucks in deference to the widow's weeds with the wide, deep hem. The slightly lower bodice was cut *en princesse* and lawn-tucked in the scooped edge.

What proved most interesting to Cassandra was the tiny white sprigs, along the hem—and the *hat!*

"How do you like this *chapeau?*" Camille held up the matching hat with jet clasp and saucy feather, the nun's veil longer in back, shorter in front, as was the current style. White sprigs decorated the veil, matching the skirt's hem.

Always the entrepreneuse, Valerie tapped her chin in deep consideration of the style; and other styles. "We need plainer sleeves, short for summer, fitting and long for winter. Elbow-length for evening. The hemline must reach the floor . . . Hmm—"

"With the feet disappearing from view," Cassandra put in. "And no trains trailing behind!"

"Especially *no* trains."

"And look at these latest fashion books from Paris," Cassandra pointed out. "Colors are becoming stronger, darker—"

Valerie grinned. "Like plum."

"If you like." But Cassandra wrinkled her nose at plum. "White and pastel shades must still prevail for evening wear, *non?*" She passed a glance over Camille, who merely shrugged with twinkling eyes. "There is a wide selection of fabrics to be varied according to season and occasion."

"What do you think, Camille?" Valerie asked.

Again the rolling shrug. *"Comme ci, comme ça, so-so."*

"I thought all blondes were supposed to be empty-headed." Valerie tipped her head as Camille helped Cassandra into the black "Victoria." "Honestly, my friend, there's absolutely nothing silly or harebrained about you."

*"Au contraire,"* Camille contradicted. "Cassandra will indeed prove herself harebrained should she pass up that *bon ami* Sylvestre Diamond."

When Camille returned to her stool, Cassandra whispered to Valerie. "What does that French word mean? I cannot recall hearing it before."

"Probably not," Valerie said, and elaborated. *"Bon ami* means lover."

A red glow crept up from Cassandra's throat and settled in her paler cheekbones, making her appear healthier than she was feeling at the moment.

Camille muttered to herself, "I would have snatched that one as my *intime* and locked him in my boudoir—ah!—in my heart."

Cassandra lifted an eyebrow at the old woman's boldness. "And I thought perhaps she might be old-fashioned!" she told Valerie.

"Not Camille," Valerie said, adjusting the tilt of Cassandra's new hat. "Uhmm, you look famished."

Cassandra laughed. "How did you know?"

"You've that hungry look to you. Come on, let's go get some dinner. Want to come, Camille?"

The older woman waved her arm negligently. "No-no, I am much too busy and happy with how the 'yellow' is coming along. You two go ahead and see"—she grinned—"how much mischief you can find for yourselves." She was hoping they would encounter the golden-haired man and everything would turn out all right between him and the delicate *mademoiselle*. Perhaps, she thought with a grin, not *so* delicate as one would be led to believe.

"I know just the place where we can sup, Cassandra. Do you like shrimp-stuffed artichokes and crabmeat crepes?"

"That sounds very delicious, Valerie. I love seafood."

"Bring me back some *chocolat,"* Camille shouted from the back room before the bell could tinkle.

"Now do you see where I garner my modern ideas?"

Valerie asked her blond friend.

Cassandra smiled, saying, *"Certainemente."*

"You know," Valerie said, closing the door behind them, "sometimes I believe Camille is not all that ill."

Cassandra laughed as they stepped into the streets of St. Louis, which were bathed in the neutral shades of twilight. Already a myriad of brilliant stars could be seen on this deepening summer's eve.

# Chapter Twenty-Three

Restless as a caged lion, Sylvestre had paced the confines of his wood-paneled office in the darkest hours after midnight. He had slept little. The next morning he located the house of Valerie Beaumont but found no one at home, at least to him. The curtains at the front window had moved aside to reveal a slim figure momentarily paused there, aproned and dark-haired, but the person had not answered the door.

Now, on his way back to his waterfront office, he dismissed it from his mind as he noted one of the steamboats putting in from New Orleans. A loud cry lifted from the crowd on the levee and was answered by gaunt, ragged men on the decks of the steamer. He watched the emaciated soldiers with flowing beards emerge from the lower deck, some leading horses from the boat to form a line on the dock as a brass band started up.

The honorary fire companies formed a line to keep the friends and relations of the soldiers back. A parade was planned, and already the politicians waited at

Planter House to make speeches. The St. Louis Grays rode about on high-stepping horses and the Dragoons formed an escort while sweethearts and wives tried to reach the bedraggled soldiers but were swept back by the official guard.

"Look!" a woman beside Sylvestre shouted and pointed excitedly. "There are women on the steamer, too!"

Cassandra's gaze was drawn to the shouting woman . . . then she caught sight of the golden head burnished by sun. She could see pale mauve shadows under his eyes, as if he had spent a sleepless night, and around his mouth lines of fatigue were in evidence. Slowly she came to suspect that Sylvestre was indifferent to his surroundings, and she wondered what dark thoughts occupied his mind. Valerie stood beside her, but Cassandra said nothing about seeing Sylvestre among the crowd gathered there.

Just that morning Cassandra had gone to see a doctor, and he confirmed her suspicions that she was carrying a child. To save herself from embarrassment, she had given the name Emmaline James. It was a name she had picked from thin air, but somehow it bore a familiar ring and made her stomach flutter when saying it to the doctor for the first time, and it had been as if the infant inside her had just quickened. Though she knew no woman by that name, she liked the sound of "Emmaline."

At the sight of Sylvestre in buff faille trousers tucked into high black boots and snowy linen shirt sharply contrasting with his deeply tanned skin, Cassandra experienced an aching feeling of pride and love. How could this man be so dear to her when he flaunted his male virility to every woman who came along? Dear God, if only she was wrong about him. She stared at him, her blue eyes misted with pain and heartbreak. How was she going to raise this child without its father?

Cassandra tore her eyes away from Sylvestre's face long enough to see a mixture of humanity still straggling from the steamer. Women in threadbare finery of once-bright colors were followed by a theatrical troupe and, as they stepped onto the docks, several bedraggled young men began beating on drums. The women stepped ashore, lifting their tattered skirts to display the tops of their boots. They were greeted by a welcoming roar from sailors and deckhands alike.

"Valerie . . ." Cassandra almost whispered as she looked around to see if anyone was in hearing distance. "Who are these women?"

"Don't tell me you've never heard of camp followers," Valerie said, smiling. "I was so wrong in my assessment of you the first time we met. You really are an innocent, aren't you?"

Her blue eyes were wide with amazement. "Do you mean to tell me that those . . . those strumpets went to war with the men?"

"It has always been this way in times of war. Camp followers are nothing new, Cassandra."

"I do not think I want to stay for the parade." Cassandra cast anxious eyes in Sylvestre's direction, praying he would not see her. "I have changed my mind and wish to go."

"In a minute. Look . . ." Valerie pointed out. "A group of the camp women are walking right past the soldiers. Huh! See how the men keep their eyes straight ahead, not daring to show interest in front of their sweethearts and wives. *Men!*"

One of the camp women stopped and turned when she spotted Sylvestre. "Valerie . . . I wish to leave now." But still she could not force her legs to move. She drew in her breath sharply when a brunette began speaking to Sylvestre. And he was smiling. *Oh! This was too much to bear!*

They talked a few more minutes, and then the generously endowed brunette moved on, taking grinning peeks at Sylvestre over her shoulder.

"Cassandra . . ." Valerie's voice came out soft. "Think nothing of it. Such women are always bold in their intentions."

"Are they." It was not a question.

The Liberty Fire Company band struck up "Yankee Doodle" just then. The parade was on.

"There's no sense leaving now," Valerie noted. "We're in the thick of it."

Cassandra had to discard the idea of leaving then for, if anything, it would just draw more attention to themselves if they were to break from the crowd and walk away.

Tall, gaunt Missourians—turned nearly savage from dragging heavy artillery and wagons across mountains, bitter from lack of pay, with no medicine for wounds and witnessing the nightly burial of friends—marched and rode proudly, a humorous slant to their bearded lips at the irony of the gala reception.

Finally the parade began to make its noisy, ponderous way to Planter House, and Valerie, with Cassandra in tow, decided to break away, hailing a carriage that would bring them back to the Beaumont residence where Dulcie would be waiting with a lunch of vegetables and fish laid out.

The afternoon was well advanced when a steamy day in August found Cassandra in the garden seated in a deep, white wickerwork chair made comfortable with pink-and-green cushions, flowered and puffy. Two weeks had passed since she had stood at the levee with Valerie and had felt the pain stab her heart while watching Sylvestre speak to that woman, that camp follower. Every day since, her mind teemed with questions. Had he visited her after she had cleaned herself up? She closed her eyes, unwilling to search out the answers to her questions.

Cassandra took refuge in the sewing of baby clothes as she picked up the tiny nightgown and squinted into the sun. Moving her chair to the left, she now faced the back wall where late-summer vines curled and crept over to the other side.

She was alone. Valerie had stepped out to do some shopping. Dulcie had gone for a long walk with the handsome young milkman who was also an octoroon. They had been seeing each other ever since they had arrived at the Beaumont house. In fact, Dulcie had revealed with a dusky blush, Cicero Jones had kissed her the very first morning he had delivered milk and ice to the back door.

The locust and elm trees almost hid her from view of the house and side gate. Cassandra looked up as a robin flew close to investigate, then flew away. The summer afternoon was a slender golden thread on a bobbin, and now it had almost spun away as she

371

brushed the loose strands back from her moist temple.

Cassandra's eyes dropped to her lap. All her dresses would prove useless in another month, or less. By the end of February, she would become a mother—an unwed mother.

In the days that followed her visit to the doctor, Cassandra had moved through the preparations for her baby in a trance. Several times Jared had taken her out to dinner at Planter House, but she was too depressed to realize what she was eating. Sometimes Jared invited other people to dine with them, but as they usually talked politics, Cassandra found herself not listening but thinking ahead to the delivery date of her child.

As usual, when she had time alone, she began to dream of Sylvestre. As she did now. She wanted to trust him, to believe in him, but she was afraid. He had tried to see her many times in the past two weeks, but she had always begged Dulcie or Valerie to turn him away. Watching his tall, hunched frame from the front window as he walked to his carriage, she had felt torn between feelings of love, and bitterness toward him.

*I will not think of him now,* Cassandra told herself. *Think of something else, Cassa.* She could almost hear a feminine voice in her mind. A wistful smile curved her mouth. It was only her fairy godmother. Or God. Or perhaps only her inner voice. Nevertheless, she would dwell on something humorous.

Just the day before at the LeBeau-tique, Camille had been exasperated, as Candice Thurston had been taking her fittings for the sixth time that week. Cassandra reflected back, a little smile at the corners of her pink mouth . . .

"If you do not stand still, mademoiselle, we shall all

go mad." Relentlessly she had pulled on Candice Thurston's corset strings. "Ah! How can I possibly make the waist eighteen inches when you have been overindulging in chocolates again!"

Heather Thurston wrinkled her pug nose. "How would you know that? I never told you," the six-year-old lied.

Her blond sisters, Marsh and Wanda, had giggled and postured haughtily before Cassandra when she carefully measured out delicate white lace trim under the keen eye of Madam Thurston. "Who is *she?*" They had nudged each other in the ribs.

Candice, the bride-to-be, protested that her waist was *really* eighteen inches, but sucked herself in tightly while Valerie measured and *tsk-tsked*.

Cassandra had spoken up. "Perhaps a wide satin sash would help, and it could flow into the wide train."

"She's wearing black, Mama— Ugh!"

Heather, the smallest Thurston, had snickered in Cassandra's face and the mother had followed suit. "Little snot!" Valerie had hissed behind Cassandra's shoulder of the pretty little Heather who could make herself look as disgruntled and homely as her mother. "Don't let them intimidate you, Cassandra. Think about my situation: I'll be lucky if they even *pay* me for the wedding dress. They owe us so much now, I'm ready to say no to the whole thing. I can't believe these Thurstons get away with never paying their creditors; they must owe the whole city of St. Louis!"

"Perhaps soldier-boy Davie Parker will pay," Cassandra had told Valerie, trying to calm the redhead's temper.

"God, I hope so!"

Now, back in the garden, Cassandra became slowly aware of a sensation of being watched. She felt it at the back of her neck, an odd, tickling sensation which gradually spread through her whole body.

She felt rather than saw the presence beside her in the garden, the tall shadow that suddenly fell over the sewing in her lap. A red flush mounted to her cheeks while an odd sensation curled in her middle.

A slight breeze stirred the flower-scented air and set the tallest trees whispering for a moment. Then all was silent.

Lacy lashes touched her eyelids as she looked up into the golden eyes.

Neither of them seemed inclined to speak, but just stared into each other's eyes with acute fascination, each feeling the music of their own hearts.

"Cassandra." His voice was soft and warm. "How have you been." No question, just a caress of his voice as his gaze fell to the loose-fitting dress she wore, the tiny nightgown in her lap she hadn't been able to put aside before he came up to her.

"I . . . I have been busy," she said, looking away from the golden eyes that had dropped to her lap.

He looked down at her blond head, the moistness dotting her temples where the finest strands of hair grew. "Too busy to see me?" Two fingers reached out to brush the fine blond strands back. "I have tried to see you, Cassandra, but have been turned away more times than I can begin to count."

Her voice was barely above a whisper. "Have you?" She kept her lashes slanted downward as she stared at the last bit of sun painting the flagstones a hot orange.

The color rose along his high cheekbones. "You

ow this, Cassandra. It is you who had me turned
vay—of course." His voice went even deeper as he
id, "Why? Why have you turned me away all this
ne?"

She came to her feet suddenly, dropping the small
rment to the ground. "I do not wish to see you
ymore, sir. You are trespassing."

"Am I?" He stopped to pick up the little nightgown
hich was dwarfed even more by the largeness of his
nd. "Making doll's clothes, Cassandra?" His eyes
re into hers like hot embers.

Her eyes flew to his, then aside. "Doll's clothes—yes,
course."

"Or baby clothes." It was more like a statement.

Taking the nightgown from his loose grip, she began
make her way to the house. "I am weary now, sir, and
ish to lie down. If you would be so kind as to—"

"Call again?"

"No."

He caught up to her and whirled her to face his taut
ountenance. "Cassandra, you cannot keep me from
our door. I will break it down if I have to. You will see
ie and you will speak to me."

Cassandra's face went white and pinched. "You, sir,
annot come here and order me around! Leave—and
ever return!"

"Cassandra!" Sylvestre took her shoulders and
ghtly shook her. "Listen to yourself! You sound like
n old shrew . . . Cassandra . . . Cassa . . . what is it?"
iis face twisted as if pained. "What in the name of God
ave I done?" Lifting her hand to his lips, he stared into
er eyes with a direct gaze. "Tell me, dearest heart."

Wrenching her hand from his gentle hold, she cried,

375

"You know ... more than anyone else ... *You know*

"Cassandra!" he called when she ran to the Fren doors and disappeared inside. With one knee bent the stoop, Sylvestre hung his head and gritted his teet "Damnit to hell—what have I done to you!"

His anguish fell on his ears alone.


Pressing his palms against his forehead, Sylvest closed his eyes. He sat behind his small desk in the ba of his office. It faced the street, and from his chair could watch the waterfront and those who passed outside.

He was working with some papers when he looke up to see Jared Casey pause out front and then walk the door. Sylvestre rose from his desk to let the man i

"Monsieur Casey, what can I do for you?" he aske indicating a chair beside his desk.

"I will stand, Mr. Diamond," Casey said. "What have to tell you will not take that long."

Sylvestre was puzzled as he closed the door, and the with a thoughtful look, he turned to face the slight nervous man. "Is this visit about Cassandra S James?" he asked, reading the undercurrent.

"Yes, it is." Jared did take that seat now. "How d you know?"

Sylvestre came away from the door. "I had a feelin that's all."

Jared cleared his throat. "I'll begin with my firs meeting with Melantha St. James and proceed to th day Cassandra left Kirby House. I wish to, ah .. change my intentions to honorable ones."

"Good." Sylvestre sat in his chair and swiveled t

face Jared Casey. "I am listening."

That night, back at Diamondhead, Sylvestre was dreaming. He heard Cassandra's soul crying out for him, heard the very words which his own heart had been repeating over and over to itself, alone and in the darkness. They walked upon a moonlit path. In a radiant, fragrant garden. He bent to kiss her brow and her silver-blond hair, with a sort of reverence. His twilight angel lifted her lips for a tender kiss. In the first transport of their quivering joy they were silent, each almost fearing to break the spell which seemed laid upon them . . .

—The moon had come up, transforming the twilight scene to one of Gothic beauty. But to them, love's radiance had suddenly made the world inexpressibly fair and golden. The very flowers breathed perfume like incense in their path, and the moonspun trees whispered benedictions upon them.

He was not dreaming . . . he tried convincing himself, but the night spun out—

—Cassandra was no longer his dream-love but a splendid, living reality, only more beautiful than his dreams or imagination had portrayed her. He stretched out his arms toward her with one word. *"Cassa!"*

A great, unspeakable joy illuminated Cassandra's face as she came into his arms, her blue eyes shining with the love called forth by his primitive cry. In an instant his arms were clasped about her, and, holding her close to his breast, his golden eyes told her more eloquently than words of his heart's hunger for her, while in her eyes and in the blushes running riot in her cheeks he read welcoming desire—

—He looked down at her, for tears were trembling on the golden lashes; and tears of passion, too. She wanted him. She wanted him in her. Then they became singleminded in their desire for each other. Her soft thighs yielded when he mounted to penetrate that first tiny morsel of quivering flesh. Her skin was pale cream with the texture of rose petals—

"You are in my power, Cassa, and you are totally mine."

"Yes . . . all yours."

—He throbbed deep within her . . . and then he awoke. It was like snapping a beautiful golden thread . . . and he was spent and consumed by his own dream.

"A letter come for you, Missa Cassa," Dulcie said, her affectionate scrutiny passing over Cassandra as she stepped into the house after a full day's work at LeBeau-tique.

Cassandra took the letter into her hands, noting the manly scrawl of its letters. "Thank you, Dulcie. I will take this into the kitchen while I have my supper."

"I'm going for a walk," she began shyly, "with Cicero Jones. Your supper is hot. You sure you don't want me to stay and have some with you?"

It was the same every night when Cassandra returned from work before Valerie. "Go ahead, Dulcie. I know how you cherish your walks with Cicero Jones. Besides, I have some drawing that I have to do on some new dresses—especially on the ball and evening gowns that are so popular now that the soldiers have returned." She trained her eyes on the letter she held in her hand.

"I be seein' you later then."

When Dulcie was gone, Cassandra made her way into the kitchen to find a meal set for a king. With letter in hand, she sat down at the table with the succulent aroma of broiled crawfish and cous-cous assailing her nostrils. Lifting the domed lids, she began to nibble as she read:

"Cassandra, my darling. What I had really come to tell you, is that come what may, I shall never be false to my love for you. I realize that you carry my child. No matter what the future may bring to you or to me—my heart will be yours. Hold it in trust until such time as I have the right to bestow it upon you. But let me tell you this: That child which you carry within your slightly rounded belly is mine. Oh yes, I saw it, I felt it as you brushed against me in the garden. I have hired agents to follow you and am delightedly aware that you have not received any other man, not even Jared Casey or Harlan Kirby, so the child is mine."

*Ohhh—ohhh.*

It was signed "your loving servant, Sylvestre."

Cassandra opened her mouth to scream, but no sound would emerge from her constricted throat.

# Part VI

"Not perfect, nay, but full of tender wants
No angel, but a dearer being, all dipt
In angel instincts, breathing Paradise."
                    —*Alfred Lord Tennyson*

# Chapter Twenty-Four

The rising sun had colored the eastern sky in a blaze of yellow, and now its brilliance probed the gloomy study of Oscar Kirby, finding him nibbling from a tray of food. He had consumed a large hunk of cheese, a bunch of grapes, and was just starting on a small roasted chicken when the Negro girl bobbed in to announce a caller.

"It's a Mistuh Di'mon, suh."

Kirby leaned sideways and stuffed the remainder of his "lunch" in a drawer.

"Send him in, girl . . ." Kirby twiddled his pudgy fingers. "Send him in."

When Sylvestre entered, Kirby followed the golden gaze and looked down at himself. He blanched. The tall blond gentleman smiled a little and arched his eyebrows when Kirby whisked the soiled white napkin from around his neck.

"It is good to see you again," Kirby said, not offering a drink, or anything else. After shaking hands, Kirby waved Sylvestre Diamond to a seat before the massive desk.

"Now . . . what may I do for you, monsieur." Oscar Kirby tried being elegant.

With some difficulty, Oscar Kirby collected his scattered wits, afraid to think what this visit could mean. Already beads of perspiration were forming above his lip and on his forehead, for he was anxious to have this "business" over and see the tall Frenchman out the door.

"I shall come right to the point, sir," Sylvestre said. "I am not sure you are aware that Monte St. James and I were partners, and that I have part interest in the *River Minx*, as he also had part interest in my newest riverboat *Fair Maiden*."

Oscar's eyes grew shrewd now. "But the *River Minx* is gone, monsieur." He gave a languid shrug. "I'm sure you were aware of that, so why this—?"

"This visit?" Sylvestre had the grace to pause while Kirby nodded. "You must turn over all of Cassandra St. James's property into my care. The trust of being made executor now falls to me, sir."

Oscar blinked and blustered, "I don't think I understand."

The light entered and wavered over the uncarpeted study in sunny patches across the floor, and Oscar had the thought that Sylvestre was like a sleek, tawny cat stretching and licking his paws as if very satisfied with himself.

"I shall elaborate then. Just yesterday I received a visit from Cassandra's lawyer—Jared Casey. He has informed me of the conditions of the will: 'In the event of marriage, the St. James property will come to

Cassandra St. James and her husband.'"

"True . . ." Oscar drawled, wishing he had Casey's neck between his pudgy hands. "But she has not married yet, monsieur."

"She will, I can assure you." Sylvestre looked up from a hooded gaze. "You see, Cassandra carries my child at this very moment."

*"What?!"* Oscar almost choked on the one word. He was keenly aware of the other man's scrutiny as he went on. "Show me the proof. Where's Cassandra? Why hasn't she come with you to tell me this herself?"

"I think that is none of your business at this point, sir. I have come for the papers, so if you will be so kind as to hand them over—"

"I will do nothing of the sort!"

"No?"

"No!!"

"Monsieur Kirby," Sylvestre began calmly. "I am an honorable man, but you force me to do something I have no liking for and, as long as you will not hand those papers over, I see no other course of action to enter upon but the one—"

"We have nothing further to discuss." Oscar waved his hand over his cluttered desk. "You may leave now. I'm a very busy man and have a lucrative business to perform."

Sylvestre leaned back in his chair, as if he was not leaving for quite a while yet. "Very well." He went on slowly, measuring his words. "You once owned a boat—*Missouri's Fancy*—did you not?"

"Yes, yes. So what?"

"Unfortunately it burned on the Mississippi River several years back."

"So it did. But I don't see how . . ." Oscar's eyes suddenly became still, watchful, his pudgy fingers unmoving, too.

Sylvestre stood up to slowly walk about the room. "There was a steward whose name must remain anonymous—a man who served aboard your boat. He also served on the *River Minx*. This man, the steward, was fond of gossip and rum—"

Sylvestre paused.

Oscar shifted irritably. "Yes . . . go on."

The tawny-haired man looked Oscar square in the eye, asking, "Are you sure you would like to hear the rest?"

Oscar's eyes were like hard marbles. "Damnit—go on!"

"You lost your favorite nephew Sydney in that fire." Sylvestre paused as Oscar's face began to drain of color. "The steward informed me that your nephew's door was locked and barred when the boat burned."

Oscar's voice was husky as he spoke. "Well . . . what is so unusual? People on steamboats sometimes lock their doors."

"True." Sylvestre agreed, his eyes never leaving Oscar's. "But Sydney's door was barred from the *outside,* sir. After questioning the steward, I learned that Harlan and Sydney had been arguing all day. There were shouts, angry threats, and bitter exchanges. Later, when the *Missouri's Fancy* was burning, the steward heard Sydney begging Harlan 'in the name of God' to unbolt the door—"

Sylvestre hesitated.

"The steward related he saw Harlan outside Syd-

386

ney's door. Your son was laughing, sir. The steward fought to open the door after Harlan made himself scarce. But the flames had gone too high. I am sorry, Monsieur Kirby"— Sylvestre ended in a low voice— "but I give you the chance of the kind consideration to release Cassandra's property to me—the man she will soon wed."

"K-kind?" Oscar remained motionless in the chair, his eyes blank and staring. Defeatedly he asked, "What is the total price of your silence, Frenchman?"

"I demand you turn over all Cassandra's property, including the *Southern Star*, any chattel, to *me*."

Oscar was even paler. "Even the *Southern Star*?"

"That is correct."

Oscar stirred, as if awakening from deep sleep. "How?" he asked dully.

"How?" Sylvestre echoed. "By relinquishing all documents to Sylvestre Diamond, I've already told you. Now. Today."

Slowly Oscar reached into his pea-green coat hanging on a coat tree beside the window. He removed a sheaf of neatly bound papers and shoved them across the desk to Sylvestre.

"I see you have little trust for anyone, sir."

Oscar shrugged. "I always carry important papers."

"Especially these, I see." Sylvestre looked them over fully.

"I trust everything is here?"

"Everything."

"If you will just sign here, *Oscar Kirby,* everything wil be in order and Jared Casey will do the rest."

Oscar watched Sylvestre Diamond get up to leave his

office. "You may tell Cassandra St. James that she is no longer welcome at Kirby House or the plantation."

"No reason to be vindictive, monsieur."

"Damnation!" Oscar slammed his meaty fist on the desk, then swiveled to face the window.

Without another word, Sylvestre left Kirby House. He now possessed everything Cassandra owned in the world; all he needed to complete the picture was her rebellious heart.

# Chapter Twenty-Five

Rays of wavering September sunlight stole through the carriage window and Cassandra, seated against the plush cushions, stared outside at the moving countryside.

After so long, she was finally returning to Diamondhead. She looked down, smoothing the folds of her simple black frock, hoping the child did not show too much in the loose-fitting dress she had made just the week before with Camille's help, and Valerie's. She smiled, thinking of her dear friends who were always there when she needed them. But for now, she was doing this alone.

Dulcie and Valerie must have been exasperated with her, she thought, although they had given no outward display of it. For weeks on end she had begged and pleaded with them to send Sylvestre away. And she had had no wish to see the beautiful flowers he sent every day, like clockwork, and the love letters he sent by the dozens.

"How long can you stay away from the father of your

child?" Valerie asked one evening as she carried the wedding-veil crown she had been adding seed pearls to.

In the LeBeau-tique window the sun had just dropped out of sight, leaving behind a blaze of gold-and-magenta banners that slowly faded against a darkening blue sky. Camille had gone home early, too weary to finish the voluminous hem she had been stitching for the wedding dress. The Thurstons had paid nothing toward it yet, and Valerie had been fit to be tied. There were rumors that the couple had been arguing and there might not be a wedding after all, but still Madame Thurston called every day to check on the progress of the gown.

Cassandra had felt a flicker of anxiety as she always did when thinking of her child's future, growing up fatherless and with an unwed woman for a mother. Belatedly she had answered, "I think indefinitely, Valerie. He is a skirt-chaser and a man I would not like my child growing up around."

Valerie had sighed. "Men do these things, Cassandra."

"Not *my* man," Cassandra had said with no foot to stand on.

"You are becoming hard, darling. You know you love Sylvestre. Give the man another chance and let him prove his faithfulness."

"No. I have seen him with too many women—that is the only proof I need."

Valerie shook her head of loose red curls. "I have never seen a man bombard a woman with so many flowers, love letters, and gifts. You didn't even open the last package that arrived. I think it's perfume. It sure smells wonderfully exotic."

"He should give it to one of his whores then—not me."

"Cassandra!" Valerie had looked thoughtful for a moment. "Tell me—do you think Sylvestre Diamond would couple with a woman he found distasteful?"

"N-No."

"I must tell you, dear Cassandra, the woman you saw with Sylvestre on the street that day is about as undesirable as a woman comes. She has put on a lot of weight. Also, Sherri Newell's personality is plaguedly distasteful, especially since she left her husband a year ago. I believe Sherri is a woman from Sylvestre's distant past." Valerie ended with a laugh.

And then the invitations to Diamondhead had arrived, not from Sylvestre but from Nanette herself. Valerie was radiant.

Cassandra did not find the humor in this, and her mouth had been thin and determined. They all knew—Dulcie, Camille, Valerie—that she could not be coerced into doing something she had not set her mind to; they would have to make her *want* to visit Diamondhead. Dulcie kept at Cassandra night and day on the subject of going to Diamondhead.

"Well," Valerie had said, still holding the wedding veil; toward which Cassandra cast a wistful eye, "at least go and see Nanette Diamond. Her letters all but beg you to come and are scattered all over the house. If you don't, Cassandra, that lovely little Frenchwoman is going to come get you herself and carry you bodily to Diamondhead!"

"How do you know she is a 'lovely little Frenchwoman,'" Cassandra had questioned stiffly.

Valerie had shrugged. "Camille . . . She knows just about everybody who is somebody in and about St. Louis. Please go, Cassandra, and I promise you we have not been conspiring behind your back to get you to Diamondhead so that big, bad wolf Sylvestre can lock you in his dark, moldy den!"

Cassandra had laughed at that. "All right. I cannot stand this anymore. I give in."

"You surprise me, dear Cassandra. I fully expected another thumbs-down."

"Hush, Valerie," Cassandra said lovingly.

Now, here she was, on her way to Diamondhead. Her trunk, bulging with black shoes, black gowns, black accessories, was strapped to the back of the elegant Diamond carriage.

It was a lemon-yellow day. The grass rustled and soughed, while, above, the sky was arching in an endless expanse of September-blue that was pale and pure.

Cassandra adjusted the black folds of her skirts while the toes of her dusty, jade-green slippers peeped out at the hem. In her hair she wore green moiré tafetta ribbons with narrow black stripes running throughout. Everyone she knew said she was beautiful in black, but she felt depressed wearing it . . . remembering the death of her loved ones.

She wore the essence of lavender, a gay touch to her somber attire. Suddenly she was happy, and that happiness made her huge, crystal-blue eyes dance.

\*       \*       \*

On this beautiful September day Cassandra never realized that her own destiny was being played out for her. Sylvestre sat in a brown leather chair in his office situated in the east wing of the Diamondhead mansion. He knew Cassandra was to arrive this afternoon sometime, his mother had informed him of such.

Weakening shafts of light filtered through the trees, coming in through the blue drapes in Sylvestre's office. He awaited the day and hour when Cassandra would be forced to ask him to release her chattels, for she would be in dire need of funds once the baby arrived. But he did not intend to wait that long for her to come to her senses. He had only to be rid of the final obstacle of her resistance—her lack of trust in him.

Anticipatory pleasure made his golden eyes glow. He stood, for he had heard the carriage pull up to the front of the house a few minutes ago.

With excitement heightening, Cassandra stared out the window of the carriage. This was Diamondhead Plantation, the place of her childhood joy, where she had romped and played throughout the glorious summer days with the willowy boy who had held her hand.

The tree-lined approach ran for miles before the magnificent old mansion finally became visible. As in her dreams of remembrance, the wind ran before the conveyance, stirring dust and memories of brighter days.

Cassandra filled her lungs with the autumnal air and squinted up at the sun to determine the time. She estimated it to be an hour before suppertime, not only by the slant of sun but by the growling in her empty stomach. It was frustrating to be hungry all the time, but she knew her child must have its nourishment. She smiled at the thought, more so when she felt the infant moving about inside her.

"Yes, my darling, you shall eat soon," she said, patting the smooth folds of her skirt.

The movements of the child had become noticeable just in the last two weeks, and Cassandra felt joy every time a small kick in her abdomen lifted her slightly rounded belly. Valerie said she was already "showing" and her face was more radiant, "lightly flushed with petal pink," like the softest, silkiest gown in the shop. Cassandra had blushed to a crimson shade.

Now Cassandra watched Diamondhead grow bigger before her eyes. The Doric columns were four times the width of a grown man's body. The columns soared up to the gallery roof they supported and seemed to pierce the sky itself. The fanlight window above the doors caught the sun, pouring back a golden beam of late afternoon in her face.

The carriage drew up before the house and Cassandra felt a moment of anxiety spurt through her. "We are here, baby, at Grandmama's house," she murmured.

A warm September breeze brushed against her cheeks and flirted with her loose-fitting frock as she alighted from the carriage with the help of the driver. She glanced at the imposing facade of the great house, and then she was facing Madame Nanette who stood with welcoming arms at the top of the stairs. Behind her stood a man in elegantly cut black trousers and jade-green silk vest. A fine pair of black leather boots encased the long, muscular legs.

Sylvestre. Somehow he represented a nobility that passed beyond the rank of plantation owner and river pilot. Sy Diamond. A lord born to the manor.

# Chapter Twenty-Six

Cassandra was aware that Sylvestre watched her. Pink roses bloomed in her cheeks as she walked the two wide steps into Madame Nanette's arms as the woman rushed forward to embrace her. The driver had released Cassandra's arm and went to see to the baggage. Cassandra was left to stand in the circle of the warm, perfumed embrace while there was the sound of a deep male voice greeting her beside them.

"Good afternoon, mademoiselle."

She saw Sylvestre in the periphery of her vision. Cassandra's traveling dress was cut severely and was very plain but did more to accentuate her ethereal loveliness than a more fancy dress might have. His sweeping regard was as sharp as the eyes of a lynx studying its prey—dispassionately friendly.

He nodded, and then he was gone.

"Come in, *ma chérie*," Nanette said, linking her arm in Cassandra's. "We have a hot meal being readied for you." She stood at arms length. "Let me look at you. *Mais oui,* you have grown into a beautiful young woman."

Madame was thrilled at the bulge of tummy she felt as she had hugged the lovely blonde. She swallowed past the knot of emotion in her throat. "Ah, Cassandra, you were always a delight to have around even as a child."

A soft smile lifted the corners of Cassandra's mouth. "Thank you, madame."

"I want you to feel as if you belong here, Cassandra, and you are welcome to stay as long as you wish." Nanette scanned the area behind the blonde. "But where is your maid? Has she not accompanied you?"

"No. She has a touch of the grippe, madame. My friend Valerie is looking after my maid, and when she is at work Dulcie's friend Mr. Jones will look in on her."

"Ah. I detect a romance blooming between your maid and this Mr. Jones, do I not?"

Cassandra smiled. "I believe there most certainly is, madame."

"Oh please, Cassandra, you must call me Nanette. We are going to get to know each other all over again. This is a most happy day for us, Cassandra." Her eyes scanned the hall for her son, but his tall frame was nowhere in evidence. "You are very precious to us all," she declared passionately. "Now . . . you must freshen up before you join us in the dining room, *oui?*"

"*Oui*. . . Nanette."

Several new servants were introduced to her, and then she was whisked to her beautiful room. After the chattering maid had put her things away and brought fresh water, linens, and French-milled soap, she stepped out, leaving Cassandra to herself to freshen up.

Placing her reticule on the mattress of the lace-canopied bed, Cassandra walked to the window seat, her shoes sinking into the pastel-colored carpet. She stared out at the cool blue-gray treetops, her gaze dropping to the winding Mississippi River.

In the deepening twilight a soft blue haze thickened the air. Night was pressing in on the splendid white mansion. A fire had been lighted in the fireplace, and Cassandra felt the lambent warmth caress her back, up and down.

Cassandra felt a sense of belonging here, as she always had in the past. Nothing had changed . . . and her heart still melted at the sight of Sylvestre, lean and strong in his elegant attire. She loved it here—and she loved Sylvestre.

Suddenly Cassandra knew she was not alone.

She turned slowly to see Sylvestre leaning against the closed door, his arms folded across his wide chest. How . . . ?

Her eyes flew to the door she had entered by, then back to where he stood. She was in a room that adjoined another . . . *his!*

His voice was deep, hypnotic. "Again, good afternoon, Cassandra . . ." His gaze went to the window. "I should say good evening, Cassandra, for night is falling fast as it usually does here in the country."

Cassandra's lips were tight. "Why have I been placed in a room next to yours, Mr. Diamond?"

*"Mister?"*

Sylvestre moved closer to her while he studied her closely, his gaze dropping to the small bulge in her abdomen and then back to her flushed face. "Come," he said. "I will show you."

Cassandra almost gasped aloud. *"Show* me your

room? Whatever for?" Her mouth was pressed into a thin pink line of disapproval. "No, sir, I have not come here to service the lord of the manor, and if you think—"

His eyes were piercing and hard as he broke across her sentence rudely. "Be still!" Then, in a softer voice, "I only wish for you to see what is in the next room and, do not worry, it is not my intent to attack you, Cassandra."

"What is so interesting in the next room?" Cassandra demanded to know, her eyes blue crystals.

"You will see, I told you. And perhaps we can discuss the matter rationally then," he answered calmly.

Cassandra could hear the birds trilling softly outside in the twilight as she eyed Sylvestre distrustfully.

He grinned as he saw her expression. "Trust me, my dear."

She was wary of an invitation into his bedchamber, but he did not appear as if about to attack her person— at least not with his mother and servants under the same roof. She decided she could trust him in this. Still, she made her way cautiously to the door he was just pushing open.

He stepped back to allow her entry first.

Cassandra sucked in her breath. The room was smaller than the one she would occupy, and here it was as if brilliant sunlight spilled through and through, as the predominant color was yellow. Touches of pink, blue, and pastel-green were in evidence, too: in the soft carpet, the curtains, the tiny blankets folded neatly at the foot of the bassinet. It was a room any mother could be proud of.

Sylvestre watched Cassandra walk slowly around

the room, now and then running her hand over the white furnishings, pausing here and there to admire the soft baby things. Her head brushed the delightful mobile and set the little animal cut outs into motion. Her soft blue eyes met the golden ones—

"This used to be the dressing room," he softly explained.

With dazzling clarity Cassandra realized the truth of what he had pointed out to her, not only in this lovely nursery but the impact the baby's arrival would have on not only her life, but on others', too. As she thought this, she felt the stirrings of life inside her, like butterfly wings.

His soft, deep voice broke into her musings. "It will break Nanette's heart if you do not marry me and give the child its proper name and place in life, Cassandra. That child is as much ours as yours."

"What?" Cassandra paled as her will struggled for its independence. She had been brought here under the pretense of a neighborly visit . . . only to be black-mailed. "This baby is mine, monsieur. You'll not take it away from me."

"My wish is not to take it from you, Cassandra." Sylvestre shook his head back and forth. "And there were two involved in the making of that child. You—and I."

She left the nursery to return to her own room. "You did not want it," she said tersely.

Sylvestre followed close behind. "I did not want it? Are you daft, Cassandra?" A muscle worked in his cheek. "I was not even informed that I was to sire a child, *Miss* St. James. If the child is a boy, he will be heir to everything I own." *Everything she owned, too!*

"Oh, why did I come here," Cassandra moaned to herself softly, pushing back the fine strands of spun-sugar hair from her temples.

The golden head was inclined slightly. "I will see you at dinner, Cassandra."

After he had gone, Cassandra sat down at the edge of the bed. The gathering tears began to flow and she swallowed, feeling sick to her stomach. It was true—so true. He sent for me not because of myself—but the child!

Sylvestre's jaw hardened. "I am indeed forcing Cassandra into marriage, Mother, because I want her."

Nanette rose from the silver-brocade couch. "You have always wanted Cassandra, my son—but you know that."

Sylvestre's taut muscles began to relax. There was no one to blame for everything but himself; he was the one who had seduced Cassandra. He wanted her pregnant, wanted her for his bride. He had done everything in his power to bring her to him.

He ran his fingers through his hair. "I realize she will never come to me in any other way."

"You may be right, Son," Nanette conceded, but not wholeheartedly.

"To put it plainly, Mother, either Cassandra agrees to marry me, or I will hold her chattel until the day she does agree."

"That is blackmail!" Nanette clutched the back of the couch. "So, have you told Cassandra this?"

"Ah . . . no."

"What have you told her then?"

Sylvestre looked sheepish for a moment, then said, "I informed her it would break your heart were we not to wed and give that child its proper name in life."

Nanette smiled. "This is so true, my son. I believe my health would indeed suffer again had I not the privilege of my grandchild's presence in this house." A sigh escaped her trembling mouth. "Girl or boy, that child would grow up surrounded by love in its own beautiful home—not in a house where only single women reside, with a mother dividing her time between being a seamstress and an unwed mother. I love Cassandra, too, my son. I have always believed you and she would someday wed and give me grandchildren."

If Sylvestre was surprised by his mother's words, he gave no indication of this. He only paced the room, wondering what it was that truly ailed Cassandra and why she had not seemed pleased with the nursery. Why in hell didn't she wish to marry him? Ah! The truth must be that she did not love him . . . But then why had she given herself to him so freely? *Damn!* What was holding her back?

Nanette watched her troubled son. It was her opinion that Cassandra loved her son with an intensity that would astound her should the girl but recognize it. However, at this point, she decided to guard her opinion and leave it up to the lovers to resolve. Something was amiss, but Nanette was not certain of the cause of the problem.

"I will await the time when Cassandra will be forced to ask me to release her chattels, Mother."

Nanette waved her hand in the air. "Is this what it must come to—a man who would buy her love?"

"Indeed." Sylvestre dipped his golden head. "At any

price. Even blackmail . . . of a gentle sort."

A miniature fear nudged Madame. "But time grows short, *mon cher*. The babe is already showing."

Dark amber was the color of Sylvestre's eyes just then. "I realize that!" he replied coolly, snatching up a half-full brandy decanter from the sideboard as he was leaving the room.

His mother called after him, "Sylvestre . . . you do not drink!"

"I realize that, too.!"

# Chapter Twenty-Seven

Sylvestre was feeling very good by the time Cassandra entered the warm, cheery dining room. His eyes were as brightly lit and as twinkly as the chandelier above the sumptuously laid table.

Six feet two inches of slightly wobbly man stood as soon as she approached. "Here, my love, let me pull out a chair for you so you can be seated."

Cassandra's nose twitched at the smell of strong inebriants, but she said nothing as she swept the skirt of her gown aside to gracefully seat herself. She looked neither to the left nor to the right, unaware that Sylvestre's gaze fell to the creamy expanse of her neck.

Madame Nanette pronounced in a cheerful tone, "My son states the obvious, *ma petite*. Forgive him, but he is slightly in his cups." She darted a warning to Sylvestre to behave himself.

But the golden-haired man took no heed of his mother's wise advice. "Is she not extraordinary, *maman?*" Sylvestre leaned over Cassandra to breathe deeply of the scent of lavender while his gaze caressed her ethereal beauty, his conduct violating good taste as his gaze dipped into the scooped bodice of her black lawn gown for the second time in the last three minutes since she had entered the dining room.

Nanette inclined her head. "I have made that observation often, my son."

Servants had been bustling in and out the last few minutes. In the center of the table a platter was heaped high with golden-brown croquignoles, still hot and steaming.

"Uhmm, they look very delicious" came a voice on the other side of Sylvestre.

Cassandra's lashes flew upward and her eyes darted to the chubby little man with sandy-gray hair and red cheeks seated at the table. When had he arrived? she wondered. Why was she not being introduced to him? She blinked. Was he a special servant . . . or what?

"Ah . . . I *am* sorry," Sylvestre suddenly blurted, turning to the man. "We have a guest. How remiss of me." His eyes twinkled across to his mother's gentle glare. "This is our esteemed parish minister, Andrew Shelton, also our dear friend. Cassandra St. James, this is . . ." He stopped, realizing he was to repeat himself. "Pastor Andrew comes to us in sickness and"— he chuckled—"in health."

The pastor's eyes shone merrily as he stood to greet Cassandra.

"It is my pleasure, mademoiselle. Let me say, you are a picture of loveliness and several lines not only from Shakespeare but also from the Bible also come to mind." He chuckled. "Someday I will tell you them, but right now I must say I am famished, for I've eaten

406

hardly a morsel the entire day."

When he sat back down, he lifted his napkin to spread it on the wide girth of his person. "Ah, the wine," murmured Andrew appreciatively as the servant placed a cut-glass decanter of sparkling Chablis on the table.

Cassandra's happy gaze met Nanette's across the table, her smile broadening in approval of their honorable dinner guest. Cassandra felt a warm glow flow through her, and it wasn't because of the wine, for, she had not yet sipped any. In fact, she could very well not take any, since she was feeling quite dizzy from happiness. For some reason, the pastor's presence seemed to mark the beginning of something new. With a slow, secret smile, Madame understood.

Glasses were set at each plate, and Sylvestre poured a little wine into each. When the glasses were raised for a toast, Nanette looked at the pastor.

"To Diamondhead," he said happily. When he would have taken a sip, Sylvestre touched the man's dark sleeve. "And now—to Cassandra!" he followed, a handsome, lopsided grin curving his lips.

The crawfish bisque was brought in just then, and they all spooned the gumbo in golden silence until the next course of speckled trout amandine and duck jambalaya was set before them. Another servant followed with shrimp-stuffed artichokes, green rice, and eggplant soufflé.

Cassandra was surprised at her hearty appetite, considering the close proximity of her attentive dinner companion. Pastor Andrew's tongue was loosened, and he sat back with shining rotund face, holding up his hand when Sylvestre would have poured more wine.

The pastor looked into the bloodshot golden eyes. "I've had plenty, Sylvestre—as you yourself have," he concluded.

"He is right, *mon Sy*." Nanette inclined her head when her son would have poured himself yet another.

Pastor Andrew addressed Cassandra. "How long have you been in mourning, Miss St. James?"

"Almost three months, sir."

*And how long have you been with child?* Sylvestre wanted to interject, with a touch of humor. But he held his comment.

Nanette leaned forward, the paler threads of her hair catching the myriad lights. "We have been thoughtless not to explain: Cassandra sustained a terrible loss. Her mother and father, Captain Monte and Melantha St. James, were lost in the Missouri—"

"The Mississippi, Mother," Sylvestre interjected. "Aboard the *River Minx*."

The pastor nodded. "A terrible loss, my dear child," he sympathized. His eyes dropped to her abdomen, then lifted quickly to her radiantly lovely face. "Yes, well, I should be going now. I need my rest. I trust I shall see you in church tomorrow, Sylvestre?"

The tall man shifted in his chair, beginning, "I—"

"Of course!" Nanette put in for her son. "We will all be there . . . Cassandra?"

"Oh, yes—I would love to attend."

"You, of course, are Protestant?" asked Pastor Andrew.

"Yes, I am," Cassandra announced, laying down

her fork.

Pastor Andrew beamed at this news. "Wonderful!" The man suddenly turned wise old eyes on Sylvestre. "Now, young man, if you would fetch my coat and see me to the door."

When they were alone, Nanette looked up from her half-eaten dessert crepes. "Come with me, dear. I have a surprise for you in the kitchen."

"Oh, I could not eat another bite, Nanette," Cassandra announced, patting her full stomach while Madame was already rising to her feet.

"The surprise is not food, Cassandra."

No? Then what could it be? Cassandra wondered as she trailed Nanette, aware of whispering as they neared the kitchen. The door opened under Madame's turning, and Cassandra found herself facing a huge black man.

"Goliath!" Cassandra cried while Nanette stepped back to shoo the maids from the kitchen. "How . . . ?"

The black man shrugged, tears standing in his big eyes. "I gots no place to winter now, Missa Cassa. Mistah Sy he let me stay in the house out back so I can help with the fires."

"Oh, Goliath," she murmured, tears in her own eyes. "They told me it was you who found Mother and Father."

"Yes'm, I found dem, but they was already . . . gone." He lowered his face prayerfully.

Cassandra stared into the kindly eyes with the yellow glints in them. "Are you happy here, Goliath?"

"Yes—and no," he said truthfully, twisting the battered hat he held respectfully in his hand.

Cassandra's eyes dropped to the hat, noting the nervous movements. "Is there something I can do to help?" She looked at him closely. "Is it perhaps something about Yendelela?"

Miserably he nodded. "I'se afraid, Cassa girl, you gonna be mad at me. We—Yendelela and me . . . we got ourselves hitched."

"Oh no. Does Mr. Kirby know about this?" Cassandra looked at the gentle Goliath in alarm. "You cannot marry without the master's consent."

"I know it, Missa Cassa. But we done it already. We's hitched up."

Chewing her bottom lip for a moment, Cassandra then asked, "Where is Yendelela now?"

"Mistah Sy—he's gonna buy her and bring her here. But he don't know can he get her for sure. He's gonna do everythin' in his power, he says."

Cassandra felt herself flush. Sylvestre had taken the chance of bringing Goliath here . . . How kind of him, but how dangerous for everyone involved.

"How did Sylvestre get *you* away from Kirby House?" she asked Goliath.

"Rumor has it Mistah Cap'n Sy owns everythin' that belonged to Monte St. James, even me now. I was given my freedom from your daddy, but Mistah Kirby says it ain't so. Mistah Kirby was gonna get Dulcie, too, but Cap'n Sy took care of that. Dulcie's papers still say she's a slave, I don't know how, but your daddy forgot to change somethin' when he come over from Georgia. Dulcie belongs to Cap'n Sy now, too."

Goliath ended with a wide grin.

Cassandra's lashes had flown upward at the start of

410

Goliath's explanation and had remained in that position.

"Sylvestre owns *everything*—?"

"That's right. I has to go now, Missa Cassa."

After Goliath had slipped out the back door, Cassandra stood alone in the middle of the spacious kitchen, the smell of food making her feel ill.

A sharp pang of betrayal stabbed her.

*No, not betrayal. It was more like blackmail.*

Everything she owned, everyone she loved most in life was Sylvestre's to command. How he had accomplished the feat she couldn't begin to guess at this moment with her head spinning so dizzily.

Walking to the door to press it open, Cassandra could feel the cool rush of night air on her hot, pinched face. She stared up at the twinkling stars, the round moon, and the petal softness of her mouth trembled. Everything she owned, everyone she loved . . . herself, too . . . his to command . . . at his mercy.

Returning to her room, Cassandra went directly to the window seat and, cuddled amidst all the pastel-colored pillows, she gazed out at the star-filled night. The moon lazed upon a fluffy silver cloud and sent ghosts of its pale radiance shimmering through the treetops.

She struggled drowsily to stay awake in order to enjoy the magical, moonspun night for a little while longer.

But her eyes were soon drifting closed and her body was sinking, sinking into the downy pillows surrounding her.

Cassandra was dreaming that she was walking along

411

the banks of the Mississippi. The day held a golden radiance, and everything around her sparkled. She could see a carriage halting before a stand of willows. Questioningly she glanced at the tall man just alighting from the carriage, and then he was speaking to the driver who turned the carriage around to return the way they had come.

Her mind was moving at blinding speed then. It was suddenly darker. In the valley the placid river murmured softly, and the hills in the distance seemed but a darker, lower sky lost in the obscurity of coming night. The fresh, sweet wind whipped through her swirling blond hair. Then she saw him again.

The man. The golden hair. The golden eyes. The decided way in which he walked with a slow swagger toward her. She would know her love anywhere . . .

"Sylvestre," Cassandra moaned out loud in her sleep.

Then the man was standing before her, gazing down at Cassandra as she slept restlessly in the window seat, her fingers clutching a pillow in front of her.

"I am here," Sylvestre said, having heard her speak his name in her sleep. "I will always be here, my love."

Cassandra rolled her head on the pillows, her eyes opening to mere slits to see the man of her dreams standing before her silvered by the moonlight streaming in . . . Or was she still dreaming? she wondered. She felt so warm and wonderful as she gazed up into the magnificent golden eyes, the flames of desire alive in their depths. Her chest rose and fell with its rapid beat as her eyes traced the chiseled outline of his face, a face that was so powerful and strong even by

412

soft moonlight.

Her voice was heavily veiled by the vestiges of sleep. "Am I dreaming, Sy, or are you really here?" she murmured with a sigh, remembering the first night he had embraced her with his loving caress.

The voice cut into her dreamlike state. "I am here, Cassa."

His lips touched her forehead lightly and her face raised in glowing wonderment to his. "I am so . . . sleepy," she said, resting her head against his shoulder as he lifted her over to the bed in his powerful embrace. "I think I drank too much wine this night . . . almost a whole glass."

He chuckled softly at her naïveté, her wonderful innocence. Almost a whole glass of wine, she had said.

Languidly reaching up, she threaded her fingers through his golden hair. "Oh, Cassa," he murmured. "How can one woman be so beautiful and wonderfully innocent?" He wanted to press her closer to his achingly swollen manhood, but he knew this was not the time. He smiled. She was too sleepy, and, besides, he wanted to make her his bride before they made love again. For now, all he wanted was to hold her while she was in this dreamy state, knowing that come morning she would once more put up her guard.

A lazy smile curved his lips as he helped her out of the black dress. Lord, the wine had really gone to her head, he thought, for she usually drank no inebriants. He himself was totally sober by now and in control . . . well, almost.

When he had found a nightgown for her to wear, he tugged it over her head while she lifted her arms and

413

swayed gently against him.

It was his undoing. He knew he had to leave her now or else the ardent flames of love would possess him and he would do her a naughty mischief by taking her when she was not herself.

And the guilt, he knew he could not handle that. Besides, he loved her too much. He slipped from the room, hearing the sounds of her even breathing telling him she was already asleep.

# Part VII

He's a fool, who thinks by force, or skill,
To turn the current of a woman's will.
                              —*Sir Samuel Tuke*


Every man is a volume, if you know how
to read him.
                              —*William Channing*

## *Chapter Twenty-Eight*

Cassandra cuddled against the fluffy pillows in the window seat, under a colorful pink-and-white quilt. The day was cool, the wind crisp, but the sun was shining.

She had been at Diamondhead for a week now, and already the leaves were changing their colors of green for autumnal ones. The Mississippi wound through the bend like a shining silver-blue ribbon. Cassandra's mood was melancholy.

Nanette's doctor had stopped in to see how Madame was doing, and Cassandra had allowed the kindly old man to check her at the woman's request. She and Nanette took peaceful long walks together along the banks of the Mississippi, enjoying the crisp morning air. The two shared many happy hours together just talking and having tea. Cassandra knew she was fortunate to have found yet another friend. Nanette had been terribly lonely before she came along. She loved the older woman and the feeling was mutual.

With Sylvestre accompanying her, Cassandra had

even been allowed to take a slow ride about the plantation on a very docile pony. Sylvestre had been quiet and brooding as they rode along the river and picked their way through the woods on bridle paths.

She knew what Sylvestre wanted . . . and she needn't ask what was bothering him. He wanted them married as soon as possible.

One night she had dreamed that he had been with her, had carried her from the window seat to her bed. She knew now it had only been a dream. The only question remaining was how she had gotten from the window seat into her bed, in the morning dressed in her nightgown . . . One glass of wine was clearly too much for her!

"Ah, here you are," Nanette chirped as she swept into the room with a rustle of amber-gold taffeta. She looked at the younger woman and smiled. Madame's hair was sleeked back and worn in a French roll, just like the one Laverne had fashioned that morning at the back of Cassandra's exquisite head. "I hope I am not disturbing your peaceful moments," Madame asked.

Cassandra smiled at Nanette. "I am glad you came in just now, Nan, for I was becoming a little bored with looking out the window." She grinned. "Not a *little* bored, but very much bored."

Nanette's eyes moved to the sheets of paper strewn in Cassandra's lap. "Bored?" She laughed; her voice rose delightfully. "With all those letters you receive from your many admirers almost every day? *La!*"

"Oh, it does not take long to read a letter, Nan."

"How *are* your lovely little friends doing? And Dulcie? Is the little maid well by now, I pray?"

Cassandra lifted from the colorful pillows and sat

418

straight, with one knee bent for comfort. "Very much has been happening!" She smoothed her hands lovingly over the letters from Valerie, Camille, and there was even one from Jared Casey. "Delightful news, too. My friend Valerie has stopped seeing Harlan Kirby and a romance between her and Jared Casey is blossoming."

"Praise God," Nanette said, having no liking for the Kirbys ever since they had purchased a Thoroughbred from a neighbor of hers and, on good faith, had allowed Harlan to take the horse before the first of several installments could be made. There had been no payments, not once, and the Kirbys had lied boldfaced, stating Nanette's neighbor had never sold them a horse. The Kirbys had sold the horse long before the issue came to the stark light of truth.

Nanette blinked as Cassandra went on. "I am so happy for Valerie and Jared. They knew each other as children growing up in a small town in Illinois somewhere. It says here"— Cassandra lifted a page of the letter—"that Harlan Kirby has taken up with Miki Rhea . . . I didn't know she was from St. Louis." When Nanette grimaced, Cassandra said, "Oh, well, it is none of my concern and I am only happy to hear about Valerie and Jared finally getting romantically involved."

Nanette smiled as she settled into a pink velvet chair. "You seem very cheerful and full of chatter, Cassandra."

"I am, now that you have come in to visit with me, Nan."

"Have you, ah . . . come to a decision about something perhaps?" Nanette ended hopefully; then, "Ah!

Not going back to St. Louis out of lonesomeness, I pray!"

"No, no, nothing like that." Cassandra looked down with a wistful air about her, smoothing her hand across her belly. "It is just that I . . . I am growing *larger* by the day, it seems—"

Nanette leaned forward a little. "And?"

Blinking misty eyes, Cassandra began with a sigh. "I am defeated, Nan, and must beard the lion in his den . . . if he still wants me for his bride."

With tears pooling in her eyes, Madame rose slowly and went to put her arms about Cassandra's shoulders. Her hand rested alongside the blonde's moist cheek. "Why don't you ask him that question yourself?" she said.

Cassandra pulled back. "Oh, no—I could never ask Sy such a thing!" Suddenly she was like a scared rabbit.

The deep voice gave them both a start. "Why do you not let the man do the asking then." More a statement then a question. "Mother dear—could you leave us alone for a few moments?" A question this time.

When they were alone, Cassandra could not bring her eyes around to meet Sylvestre's. He had gone to such lengths to get her to Diamondhead . . . he must truly love her and wish to protect her . . . Loved her, maybe just a little.

"Well, Cassa—will you marry me?" Sylvestre asked, hovering over her like a blond giant.

Her thoughts were too chaotic and jumbled with him standing there looking so powerfully attractive in tight breeches and white lawn shirt. "I . . . I will, Sylvestre." She was almost feeling shy now; she turned her face a little in his direction. "If you will meet one condition."

"Only one, Cassa?" His voice was deep and fraught with emotion.

His heady nearness shook her senses as she answered, "Yes. O-only one."

"Look at me, Cassa." Sylvestre moved her black skirt aside to make room on the window seat beside her. "What is it, my darling Cassa: I will do anything you wish"—he smiled tenderly—"if it is within reason."

Cassandra took a deep steadying breath. "That you will not wish to c-consumate our marriage on our wedding night."

His face hardened. "That, my love is *not* within reason." He stood briskly then. "However, I will do anything you wish in order to give that child—our child—my name."

"Thank you . . . Sy."

He stood then with his back held stiffly to her gaze.

"Did I hurt you so much the last time we were together, Cassandra?" he asked.

"Hurt me? Oh, no, it is not that. I found no pain in our lovemaking . . . o-only joy, Sylvestre."

He whirled upon her, but it was not his intention to make her jump. "Then why, why in God's name would you keep me from your bed on our wedding night?" He shrugged his helplessness.

*The other women!* she almost blurted. Avoiding his eyes, she said aloud, "I am not sure you will not hurt the child, but I do not know about such things, Sy."

*"Mon Dieu,* Cassa." He went to pull her up against him. "I would never hurt you or the child."

Molding her body against his, Sylvestre's lips pressed hers, demanding a response. Willingly she gave

421

it, and all the long, lonely months and hours vanished.

With gentle movements he pushed her back against the frame of the window seat, following with the press of his long, lean body. He could feel the soft pulsing beat of her throat beneath his fingertips as his lips never left hers for a moment.

He smelled of leather, animal musk, and the outdoors. A volatile and heady combination of virile male, making her feel wantonly bold. Automatically her hands went around his neck, and she clung to him, moving her softness against him, swaying slim hips in a seductive circle, her high, round breasts flattened against his hard chest, burning, branding him.

Cassandra's head was flung back. She wanted to taste him, to succumb with rapturous delight to his every touch.

"*Mon Dieu,* woman, what are you doing to me," Sylvestre groaned against her throat, wondering where she had learned such brazenness.

His hard, masculine body was already erect, hard, throbbing, and completely prepared to love her, to bring himself fully into her.

In an almost inaudible voice he whispered against her mouth, "I want you, Cassa, and it has to be soon."

As he continued his kisses and caresses, he groaned deeply in his throat. He wanted to fully possess her, to enter her and slide deeper and deeper behind the curls of white-gold hair until his body filled her up and she cried out with the sheer ecstasy of their fiery coupling.

The pleasant shock of his iron-hard length nuzzling against her mound of womanhood made Cassandra inhale sharply. She could feel him with her every feminine pore and nerve-ending.

"I *want* this child, Cassa." His hand brushed aside the loose-fitting folds of her black skirt and his palm began a rhythmic rub slowly over her belly.

His hand stilled on her abdomen as if he had felt the babe stirring, moving.

Their eyes held.

"I believe I will be a good father, Cassandra." His fingers threaded through her hair, releasing silky strands of the coiled French braid.

Through moist lips, she murmured, "I know you will, Sy." But did she in her innermost heart believe this? What about all his other loves?

Coming down once again, his mouth was hard, hungry, urgent. The force of his kisses and probing tongue should have hurt her, but she felt nothing except fierce, tender passion. Since her head was thrown back, her white-gold hair cascading in wild strands to her waist, Sylvestre was given access to the arch of her white throat. She received the drugging, devouring kisses that made her dizzy with longing.

Reality was gone. There was only the two of them making tender, beautiful love in the gray morning light surrounding them . . . kissing . . . caressing . . . the damp fire of their tongues twisting and mating for a very long time until both of them were moist and hot and shivering.

He was about to reach for the hem of her skirt to bring her to trembling release, when he stopped himself and forced his body under control.

Sylvestre couldn't stand much more of the agony of

423

wanting to complete this act, so he lifted his lips and gazed into her soft blue eyes. "Why did you not tell me at once that you were carrying my child?" he asked, with a lump in his throat.

Resting her hot flushed cheek against the whiteness of his full-sleeved shirt, Cassandra softly explained, "I had no idea I had conceived until I was already in my third month of pregnancy. Not until then did I go to see a doctor in St. Louis. It was right before that—I saw you with that woman." *That tart who pressed every inch of her brazen person against him in the full light of day!* "You know very well which woman I speak of, Sylvestre," she ended softly.

"Sherri?" He laughed, tilting her chin so he could see her face. "No one can compare to you, Cassandra, and I mean that from the bottom of my heart."

"What does that mean? That I am preferable to others in bed?" She shoved away from him. "When I am not available, then any other woman will do, correct?"

"Cassandra! You are so far from the truth that you cannot see it for what it really is. You must know that there is no other woman as wonderful as you." *I love you, Cassa, you, you,* his heart cried out for her to hear him. He would not pour his love outright to her again, not until she came to her senses and quit this blinding jealousy of hers. Her heart needed to trust and learn the truth first. "Trust me, Cassa" was all he said.

"I cannot do that, Sylvestre. I have witnessed scenes, or perhaps clandestine meetings, of you speaking to strange women, too many of them to believe that I am the only woman you desire."

424

Sylvestre's eyes darkened like nightfall. "Ah, yes—and I suppose I should believe you have been true as the blue sky? When I had wind of you dining at Planter House with none other than Jared Casey, that dashing young lawyer you have been ogling for the last several months?"

Cassandra blinked. *"What?"*

"Yes, Cassandra, you must think very hard about this conversation we are having. Do not delude yourself, things are not always what they seem." His amber-tan eyebrow rose. "Or are they?"

"How do you happen to come by all your information?" she asked with a brittle snap to her voice.

Staring at her flawless profile, his lips curled up on one side, and when she turned to him, he nodded mockingly.

"There are ways for a man who knows the city and its inhabitants thoroughly to find things out, Cassandra, my dear bride-to-be. Are you very sure this child is mine, Cassandra?" As soon as the damaging words were out, he could have kicked himself.

Her voice was low. "How dare you even imply such a preposterous thing?"

How cruel this man she had known most of her life had become. He must really despise her, she thought then. But why? If only she did not love him so much, he could not make her suffer time and again.

Realizing his disastrous mistake, the frown left his face and he reached out to her. She trembled from the contact, and he mistook it for revulsion at his renewed familiarity. She was hurting, and he had done that to her.

425

"Forgive me, Cassandra. I know the child is mine, for I am aware you have not intimately received another man."

"How—?"

He would not let her finish as he interjected, "You must ready yourself for our wedding, which will take place one week from now. On a Saturday. As you are so talented with needle and thread, you should be able to stitch something up in no time at all." He shot her a look before he left her alone. "Just make sure you do not appear in black!" he commanded. Then he turned away.

"Perish the thought," she said airily, before he slammed out of the bedchamber.

Tears of anguish streaming down her face, Cassandra lay down on the bed for a good long cry. *If only I could return hate for hate . . . but how can I* she thought.

*Oh Sy . . . I love you so much. Why does it have to be this way?*

Perhaps she had been coming to her own conclusions and she *had* been wrong. Perhaps he had been trying to avoid the woman's flirtations. Sherri? Dolly? Miki Rhea? The camp follower? Could there really be so many forward women in the world?

How was it going to be . . . married to a man who was desirable to so many beautiful women? But were they really beautiful, on the inside? Wasn't that what truly counted?

"Oh . . . I am so miserable, Father," she sobbed, wishing Monte could be here with her to answer her questions. But could he even have done so? She did not even consider her mother as confidante in this moment of her misery, though she loved her more in death now.

Smoothing a hand over her rounded belly, Cassandra murmured, "I guess I am going to discover the answer to all my questions soon, baby. As long as you are with me, I believe I can weather any storm."

But the worries which assailed her throughout the day clung to her mind like shadowed wisps of gray lonely clouds.

# Chapter Twenty-Nine

The more the merrier, the fewer the better cheer.

Cassandra's joy at seeing Dulcie again momentarily banished her trepidations over the coming wedding. She greeted her octoroon friend with genuine delight and allowed Nanette to lead them to the dining room where Dulcie would be expected to take lunch with them this time.

At first Cassandra ate the chicken and rice with relish, but as she listened to Dulcie's excited, animated accounts of all the events which had taken place in the last two weeks at the shop and at Valerie's home, her appetite fled. Everyone seemed happy but herself. She could only pick at the crepe suzettes Nanette had heaped upon her plate.

"Why, *ma petite,* what is it?" Nanette asked with concern in her kindly eyes.

Cassandra's sense of restlessness grew with every minute that passed. "Oh, Nan, how will I be able to finish the wedding dress in time? I am all thumbs when I even try to begin on a gown. I have nothing whatsoever accomplished."

Before Nanette could form a reply, Dulcie gasped and clutched Cassandra's arm. "Oh, Missa Cassa!" The octoroon girl groaned. "I plumb forgot! That trunk my friend Cicero Jones carried to your room has got a dress in it for you! Yessir!" She beamed from ear to ear. "Its a pretty white dress!"

Cassandra searched Dulcie's face, hardly able to believe what her ears had heard. "A wedding dress?" she asked. "But how—?"

They were upstairs in no time, and Madame flung open the trunk to reveal a gorgeous wedding dress that had been packed carefully in tissue paper. On top of it all was an envelope addressed to *Cassandra.*

Bemused, Cassandra sat on the edge of the bed, too excited to open the envelope herself. With her permission, Madame read the note aloud.

It was from Valerie. The redhead explained that the Thurstons had not made one single payment toward the stitching of the gown, and as long as they owed her so much on accounts of other alterations, et cetera, they would not get *this* precious wedding gown they had all labored so hard to complete. Besides, Valerie went on, rumors had been circulated that the couple were not getting along, they had been having serious arguments which probably would forestall the wedding to a later date—if at all.

Reading to Cassandra, Madame went on. "Valerie ends the letter with the promise that she and Camille will attend the private little ceremony you wrote her about." Nanette looked up from the letter "Now, I realize that my son has named a date, Cassandra, but while it is the gentleman's province to press for the

430

earliest possible opportunity, it is the lady's privilege to name the happy day."

Cassandra blushed. "It must take place as soon as possible, madame." She patted her stomach while Dulcie beamed, then bobbed a curtsy to excuse herself.

"I've got to go make sure Cicero Jones is gettin' something to eat for all his trouble, Missa Cassa."

"Oh yes, please do," Nanette said, then added, "And he may stay as long as you both wish him to, Dulcie."

"Thank you, ma'am." Then she was gone in a hurry to see to her man.

Nanette smiled. "I believe you might be losing a maid, Cassandra. But I understand he is a milkman in St. Louis?"

"That is correct."

"If you want, they can both work here on the plantation, for we have a shortage of faithful black folks lately with the uprisings happening all over the South."

"I think that would be possible, Nan, and I would be so happy to see them both in your employ. You are so kind to the black folks who work for you." She was thinking of Goliath and Sylvestre's kindness toward the black man.

"I am happy you think so, Cassandra. We treat them all fairly and none of them want for anything under Sylvestre's supervision of the overseers." She did not mention the Kirbys and their unfair treatment of slaves, for they had other matters of importance to see to at the moment. "Now, at this advance state of affairs, let us get on to the preparations of the *private little ceremony,*" she said with a tinkling laugh. "How many people do you wish to attend?"

431

"Only a special few, Nan."

"Good. I was hoping you would say that."

Later that evening, Pastor Andrew came to speak to the bride and bridegroom. They were in the drawing room, and Cassandra was seated beside Sylvestre. Both looked very cool and composed . . . so far, so good.

"The bride's costume should be white"— Pastor Andrew cleared his throat—"or some hue as close as possible to it."

"White," Cassandra spoke up. "I shall wear white."

"Do you agree?" the pastor asked the bridegroom. When Sylvestre remained silent on this matter, the man of the cloth went on. "Your look suggests you are agreeable." He smiled

"If Cassandra has settled on white, then white it shall be, sir," Sylvestre said, taking Cassandra's cool hand in his warmer one. They both felt a familiar shiver of awareness, and Cassandra was amazed at the thrill he gave her just sitting beside her.

"We shall go on to discuss the actual marriage ceremony," Pastor Andrew directed. "The bridegroom will stand at the right hand of the bride." He watched the couple as they stared solemnly at their entwined hands. "Now," he went on, "who will give her hand at the proper moment to the bridegroom?"

"I will," Nanette said with intense pleasure.

"Good. The principal bridesmaid will stand on the left of the bride—?"

"Valerie," Cassandra offered. "And the only bridesmaid—"

"—ready to take off the bride's glove, which she will keep as a perquisite and prize of her office," Pastor

432

Andrew went on. "The words 'I will' are to be pronounced distinctly and audibly by both parties, the all-important part of the cermony."

Sylvestre's golden eyes wandered slowly and possessively over Cassandra's face, down to her lips, and hardened visibly when he looked back into her soft blue eyes. She stared up at him, searching his face quietly, and she shifted uncomfortably. For the moment, there was no sound but the beating of her wild heart dancing an erratic rhythm of its own.

With supreme effort, Sylvestre dragged his gaze away from Cassandra's to look back at the minister. Swallowing nervously, Cassandra smiled at the man before them and pretended that this was all a game, with rules they must comply to. Indeed it was all very serious, Nanette's gaze seemed to remind her with expressive golden eyes very much like her son's.

"And," the minister went on, "the 'I will' being the declaration of the bride and bridegroom that they are voluntary parties to their holy union in marriage will be executed. Now—the words 'to Love, Honor and Obey' must be distinctly spoken by the bride. They constitute an essential part of the obligation and contract of matrimony on her part." His gaze settled on Cassandra as if seeing into her very soul. He looked to Sylvestre then, and the golden-haired man had the grace to look uncomfortable.

She must trust him, that was part of the marriage contract, too. Sylvestre tilted his head, looking at her uncertainly. He felt the greatest urge to tangle his fingers roughly in her hair and wind the white-gold tresses about his wrist to bind them together forever and ever . . .

"My advice to the husband will be brief: Let him have no concealments from his wife, but remember that your interests are mutual: that, as she must suffer the pains of every loss, as well as share the advantages of every success, in his business life and otherwise, that she has a right to know the risks she may be made to undergo."

*Business,* Cassandra was thinking. Sylvestre had made her business *his.* Suddenly she had a sinking feeling in the pit of her stomach. He had bought her love. She was only to be a possession then, one he could cast aside when weary of toying with it, and go on to another and yet another clandestine meeting with his worldly, painted women. Was she to stay home with her child and become an old jealous woman pining away for the day when her husband would cease his straying? God, how would she ever be able to live like that? How could she bear to see him flirting with yet another woman? She would have to do something else to occupy her many lonely hours, like continue with her sewing . . . But why did a career as seamstress seem less important to her now? The coming babe seemed to be taking up her every thought . . . that and the time she would become the new Madame Diamond.

Cassandra heard the minister's voice droning in her ears, and she looked up to see him staring into her face, gently demanding that she listen to his sound advice carefully, though at the moment he seemed to be speaking directly to Sylvestre.

She was being undone by Sylvestre's nearness. He had lifted her hand to turn it over, and now he was rubbing the smooth area delicately between his fingers, while he looked straight ahead with an amused smile.

434

He certainly blew hot and cold! Cassandra was thinking. He was polite one moment and cold the next; then warm and full of caresses. He completely baffled her!

Pastor Andrew was still talking. "Many a kind husband almost breaks his young wife's fond heart by an alteration in his manner, which she cannot but detect. From ignorance of the cause she very probably attributes it to a wrong motive while the man, all the while out of pure tenderness, is endeavoring to conceal some problem." Andrew paused as he detected the growing frown on both their faces; he plunged on wisely. "Had she but known the danger beforehand, she would have alleviated his fears on her account, and, by cheerful resignation, taken out half the sting of his disappointment."

Cassandra and Sylvestre exchanged looks, then looked back to the minister.

"Let no man think lightly of the opinion of his wife in times of difficulty." He cleared his throat noisily. "Women have generally more acuteness of perception than men. In moments of peril, or in circumstances that involve a crises or turning point in life, they have usually more resolution and greater instinctive judgment—"

Sylvestre shifted a little and tossed a negligent arm over the back of the couch. Madame was looking ready to yawn, and Cassandra looked curious as a pretty white mouse.

"A wife having married the man she loves above all others must be expected in her turn to pay some court to *him*—"

Now Sylvestre sat up, leaning forward with one arm

435

braced against his bended knee. His golden eyes said, "Go on, man, go on!"

"Before marriage she has doubtless been made his idol. Every moment he could spare, and perhaps many more than he could properly do so appropriately, have been devoted to her—"

Here Cassandra pursed her lips a little.

"How anxiously has he not revolved in his mind his worldly chances of making her happy! How often has he not had to reflect, before he made the proposal of marriage, whether he should be acting dishonorably toward her by incurring the risk—for the selfish motive of his own gratification—of placing her in a worse position than the one she occupied at home!"

Sylvestre's eyebrows rose inquiringly, then slanted into a frown. Madame blinked, straightening her skirts with a soft rustle of nervous movement. Cassandra's eyes were huge crystal blue orbs of curiosity.

"After the wedding and honeymoon are over, the husband must return to his usual occupations which will, in all probability, engage the greater part of his thoughts. For he will now be desirous to have it in his power to procure various little indulgences for his wife's sake which he never would have dreamed of for his own.

Now Sylvestre reclined, with his hands clasped behind his head. *He would have the right to hold her and to make love to her.*

"He comes to his home weary and fatigued. His young wife has had her quiet routine of domestic duties to attend to and perhaps a child or two . . . while he has been toiling through the day, and at the close of it he should be made welcome by the endearments of his

436

loving spouse"—he smiled gently when the intended man sat up again—"and let her now take her turn in paying those many little love-begotten attentions which married men look for to soothe them. Let her reciprocate that devotion which, from the early hours of their love, he cherished for her, by her ever-ready endeavors to make him happy with a pleasant face to greet at the end of every day."

Pastor Andrew paused to look seriously at the couple. "Love asks trust, and trust asks courage. Constancy. Now . . ." Pastor Andrew bowed his head. "Let us pray for this couple who are about to enter into holy matrimony."

Sylvestre raised himself from the back of the couch, smiled lazily at Cassandra as a vital spark suddenly came into her eyes when he took her hand to squeeze it. Cassandra and Sylvestre's heads met . . . and the Pastor and Madame paused in their prayerful attitude to smile at each other.


When Sylvestre gazed upon Cassandra floating toward him through the candlelit church, in all her breathtaking bridal glory, he whispered in his heart, *On, my God, Cassa.*

The fifty or so gathered there thought Cassandra was loveliness personified. The woman every girl wanted to be. Valerie sighed, as did Camille. Her eyes were a romantic blue and a hint of a bride's blush was in her cheeks. "Breathtaking" was the only word for her wedding gown, creamy satin with floral white embroidered-net overskirt, ruche lace and net flounces, accented with miniature roses and dainty seed pearls sewn into the snug, uplifting bodice. Her veil of fine tulle cascaded gracefully to the floor, trailing behind like a white floating wraith. She carried a bouquet of precious white roses and delicate baby's breath. Her bridesmaid stood beside her, complementing the bride with a soft lavender gown in elegantly slim, flowing lines.

Cassandra's spirits soared when she felt the presence of Sylvestre standing beside her. She felt so much love filling her heart as she repeated her vows, and she knew, without a doubt, that the man beside her, resplendent in his fine dark attire, loved her with all his heart, for when she turned to him there shone a sweet mist of happy tears in his golden eyes. Such loving tears, Cassandra cried happily in her heart.

*My love, my love,* Sylvestre whispered in his heart. *Later I will tell you just how very much you mean to me when you arch sweetly upward to meet my thrusts.*

"You may kiss the bride now."

*Oh, yes, Sylvestre, my love, kiss me, kiss me forever . . .*

When he turned to her for the nuptial kiss, Sylvestre murmured before his lips claimed hers, "You look exceptionally beautiful today, Cassa, my bride, my heart."

He lingered over her lips, then kissed her cheek, the corner of her eye, where a happy tear had gathered. After smiling tenderly into each other's eyes, Sylvestre turned his flushed bride to be presented to their guests as the new Madame Diamond.

After the ceremony, Pastor Andrew shook hands with the bride and bridegroom, and then a general congratulation ensued. Valerie, Nanette, and Camille felt tears spring to their eyes as they kissed and hugged the beautiful couple. The bridegroom led the radiant bride out of the church, and the happy pair settled in to drive homeward in the first carriage waving to the little gathering of well-wishers crowding at the window. Madame and their small party of guests followed in the next.

Amidst a shower of old slippers and missiles of good luck sent flying after the happy pair, Sylvestre gave the word and they were off, starting on their journey toward a long and blissful marriage . . .

Turning to his bride, Sylvestre took her in his arms as soon as the carriage was rolling, leaving the second one far behind to catch up. "It is going to be a long ride home," he said into her ear.

"Why is that?"

"I told the driver to take the long way home. We are going for a long ride along the river, my love, and we shall return long after the guests have been assembled at Diamondhead."

Cassandra felt the heat of desire sear through her blood. "Does your mother know about this?" she asked, seeing the mischievous light in his eyes. "Is this proper?" she added before he could answer.

He gave her a smile that sent her pulses racing madly.

"Anything is proper, Cassandra. Lest you forget— we are now man and wife."

For the first time in her life Cassandra was discovering the true meaning of happiness.

Feeling confident now, Cassandra fastened her slim, silk-clad arms about his neck and kissed his cheek. The pleasant shock ran through his body as his eyes caressed her face in fond possession.

"You are making advances, my love?" he said, his left eyebrow raising a fraction of an inch.

Before she could voice her answer, he crushed her to him, smothering her moist lips with demanding mastery. She pressed her open lips to his, caressing the nape of his neck, then the length of his back.

Murmuring deep in his throat, he seized one of her hands gently, encouraging her to freely explore. She excited him beyond anything he had ever known.

His expression was tight with the strain of checking his urge to make love to her right in the carriage, when the driver James brought the team of horses to a sudden halt.

He smiled softly into her eyes. "We have reached our destination."

Cassandra straightened her bodice and forced a demure smile to her lips when the driver held the door open for her to alight from the carriage. "Madame—"

"Oh . . ." Cassandra exclaimed. She drew in her breath softly when she saw the quaint old cottage with its trailing vines running up the sides, the great overhanging trees, and the overgrown path winding to the back door. But the flat stones leading to the front drew her attention, for they had been recently swept clean and there was evidence that a gardener had been there lately to trim the ancient bushes that had an Oriental twist to their heavy branches.

"How lovely and quaint." Cassandra said the words in a breathy voice. Then, "Where are we? Some friends of yours live here, Sy?"

"It is our honeymoon cottage," Sylvestre deeply announced, standing right behind her as the driver carried their baggage into the little house. "We are on my property, Cassandra."

Cassandra turned to face her smiling husband. "Your property?" she wondered.

"Yes, this is Grand-Chemin Plantation. My uncle Louis left it to me. This is only one of several buildings which occupy space on the plantation. But this is the loveliest, the reason I chose it for our honeymoon retreat."

She gazed up into his face. "But everyone is waiting for our return to Diamondhead, did you not say that?"

"I lied." He lifted a corner of his mouth crookedly. "They are not expecting us until late tomorrow afternoon."

He picked her up then and carried her over the threshold, pausing to kiss her tenderly, his lips warm, urgent, exploratory. His mouth grazed her earlobe then as out of the corners of their eyes they saw the driver pause to ask if that would be all for now.

"Yes, James, you may return to the house where you and the others will be served up a fine feast."

James beamed. "Thank you, M'sieur Diamond. Might I say, sir, you have a very lovely wife and I wish you two all the happiness in the world."

"And I thank you, James, for your continued faithful service in my employ."

"Yes," Cassandra echoed shyly, for Sylvestre was still holding her in a close embrace high off the floor and crushed to his breast.

When James had closed the door behind him, Sylvestre placed his bride on her feet so that she could explore the five-room house. He watched her move gracefully across the floor, the satin gown brushing the polished wood floors, her veil still trailing behind her like a vaporous wraith of loveliness. Just like Cassandra herself, he thought. His heart was warmed as he followed her about like her beloved servant.

"The rooms are small"—his eyes glowed in the twinkling firelight—"but you shall find the house pleasantly cosy. Everything we need for our meals is in the kitchen. The cupboards have been stocked with provisions that will last for a week, but"—he took in her wide-eyed glance—"we won't be staying that long. At least, not at first."

Cassandra turned from gazing into the golden flames crackling in the fireplace. "You mean we will return here after visiting with our guests at Diamondhead?"

"That is right, love."

The wood snapped cosily and sent sparks shooting up the chimney. Here and there she saw braided rugs, but it was the huge bear rug spread comfortably before the hearth that captured her gaze . . . a beckoning call for lovers.

He bowed gallantly from the waist. "I am your willing slave, my lady. Would you like strong American coffee, tea—or would you perhaps prefer some champagne?"

Cassandra laughed over her shoulder as she went to change her dress for something more comfortable to wear. "No wine. Just some tea, please."

With a deep chuckle, Sylvestre strode into the huge kitchen, where slanting sunlight was filling the space with a warm orange glow. He was just in the process of setting the tea to brew when the muffled cry shattered the peaceful domestic scene.

"Helllp!"

He rushed into the bedroom only to find Cassandra buried in a flurry of white satin, petticoats, and wedding-veil tulle. Her head was nowhere to be seen. She looked so very helpless . . . a beautiful damsel in distress.

"Sy . . . where *are* you?" came the muffled cry again.

Sylvestre's mouth turned up at the humor of her predicament. "I was just about to ask you this myself." He moved to bend down to where she sat in the middle of the braided rug, the dress and all its undergarments thrown up over her head, her arms imprisoned within the satin bodice.

He crouched beside her and began to help her out of the mess. "No wonder," he said. "You failed to undo all the tiny pearl buttons, my love, and that is why— But, *mon Dieu*—how did you end up on the floor?"

When her flushed face appeared from the veil of tulle, she wrinkled up her nose sarcastically. "You would have, too, if you could not have seen where you were going and found your legs tangled in all these skirts."

He bussed her forehead with his lips. "I would not have found myself in such a fine predicament, *ma petite.*"

She sniffed. "No?"

"Men do not wear this many clothes to get themselves into so much trouble, my love."

Pouting, she arose from the pile of clothes like a pretty white chick stepping from the sparkling shards of an eggshell. "You would prefer women to go naked, I suppose," she said, feeling miffed and slightly humiliated.

All of a sudden Sylvestre looked concerned. "You

were not hurt in your entanglement, I hope?"

His frown dropped at once to her delicate bulge of tummy beneath what remained of her underpinnings.

"No . . ." She cracked a grin at last. "I did not fall *that* hard . . . I floated down in a heap."

"Indeed," he finished for her. "I would think with all that padding surrounding you, it would be somewhat difficult to hurt yourself."

A light blush stained her cheeks. "Did you brew the tea, sir?" she asked in a voice chilly as the north wind.

When she had pulled on a lavender dressing gown, a light chemise still covering her body beneath, she turned to him, the silken bulge of tummy more noticeable now.

"It is almost ready." The muscles beneath his coat flexed as he reached out a bronze hand to her. "Come, my glorious little bride, and join me before the fire. I put on more logs to burn." He squeezed her hand. "Are you hungry?"

She smiled at last. "I will be shortly. Rather, I should say this babe has an appetite that far surpasses my own."

Just then a rapid-fire knock sounded at the door. Cassandra jumped and exchanged glances of wonder with her husband. Then all was quiet but for the crackling and turning of a log in the hearth.

Sylvestre moved slowly, stealthily toward the door. Cassandra gasped softly when she saw him remove a long-nosed pistol from beneath a pile of garments near the door.

"Sy—be careful."

He wrenched the door wide, the pistol held at the ready, his legs braced wide apart. "Who is there?" His deep voice sounded like thunder in the heavens.

Cassandra moved behind him with a hand over her mouth. A soft giggle emerged as she stared through his spread-eagled legs.

She was about to breeze past him when he grasped her by the arm "Wait—"

"Darling mine," she laughed. "Look down. Do you not see the picnic hamper with the checkered napkin spread over it? Its bright colors scream to be noticed."

"What?" He blinked, then leaned forward while his nose twitched at the delicious odors coming from the hamper. "Food?" He joined her on the dark little porch with its climbing ivy shining in the new moon. "Be careful; it might be a ploy to get us out of here." He waited. Nothing happened.

Cassandra laughed. "Really, it is only a picnic hamper filled with food that smells quite delicious. Suddenly I am very famished indeed."

"So it is."

"We must thank the person who delivered the wedding present to our door." She shook her head, spilling her long hair over one shoulder. "Or per*sons.*"

"There is no one to thank, Cassandra." He scoured the moonlit area before securing the door and stashing his pistol.

"The chicken is yet warm," Cassandra blurted happily. "And the buns, too. Mmm, there is extra butter, creamed." She licked a dollop off her finger as he watched with lazy eyes. "Jelly. Honey. Oh, and one of my favorites—strawberry tarts."

"You sound hungry, my love." Sylvestre lifted up a huge green bottle of very old vintage wine and dusted it off on his dark sleeve.

"I am!"

Cassandra licked her lips, turning to her husband. "Why did you not see the hamper of food, Sylvestre? It was right there in front of you."

His breath was warm and wild as it fanned her cheeks. "Sometimes we stand too close to a thing to see it clearly."

Eyes of golden mysterious lights narrowed and stared for a long moment into her upturned face.

He became quiet.

Was he trying to tell her something? Sometimes we stand too close . . . Things are not always what they seem . . .

"Well then," he said. "Let us have our wedding feast."

Carrying the hamper inside, Sylvestre led her across the room to the deep-cushioned loveseat and Cassandra followed, sitting down beside him.

They rummaged through the hamper in companionable silence, finding even more goodies to partake of. There were even butter knives which Sylvestre used to butter the honey-gold buns, then handed one to her. They sat munching the buns and the delicious chicken in silence for several minutes.

Cassandra crossed one leg beneath her buttocks and he grinned at her lack of social graces. However, he had done the same, with his black jacket cast aside, his white silk shirt open to the waist. As she ate, her eyes were drawn to the golden mat of curls and the muscled mounds of strong flesh. A tingling of pleasure began deep within her.

"Wine?" Sylvestre poured some into a fancy goblet, then set it aside to pour another.

Cassandra grimaced. "No, please, no wine. I find that I detest liquor of any kind, Sylvestre."

Unwinding his long legs, Sylvestre stood, saying, "I like that." He was thinking of later; he never had cared much for women who freely imbibed before love-making. "I shall do your bidding, m'lady, and fetch you your tea."

Cassandra giggled; she certainly needed no wine. "Thank you, m'lord, you are most attentive."

"For you indeed"—he performed a half-bow from the waist—"I will be anything."

When Sylvestre returned with two delicate teacups, they clinked them together and stared over the brim of the steaming brew which evoked a romantic notion of distant lands shrouded in Highland mists. They sipped slowly, Sylvestre's wine already forgoten where it sat on the floor losing its enticing bubble.

Taking her teacup, Sylvestre placed it aside on a low table with his own. With a sly grin, he leaned to press his finger into the cherry jelly, then spread some of the red stuff over her lips. Cassandra's eyes were wide and curious as he sucked and licked. When he had eaten that off, she looked at him with a mischievous smile while reaching into the butter dish. While he watched her now, she put a dollop on her finger, pressed his shirt wide, and rubbed it on the muscled swell of his right breast.

"Ahhh . . ." he murmured deep in his throat when she had licked it off the nub. "I like your game much much better, my love."

Pushing aside the folds of her loose-fitting bodice, he followed suit, this time with the honey, sliding the liquid gold over the crests of taut-swelling buds, making her slippery and delicious. He sucked all he could get, until she was clean and shining and erect.

"Mmm, let's get more comfortable, shall we."

Gently he lifted Cassandra and carried her to the bear rug where he buried her in the furry pallet, in the warmth of long, tickling hairs. With leisure, she helped him undress, and then he removed her dressing gown and light chemise. He placed these all aside.

The embers spread a glowing warmth over their bodies as they tumbled like happy youngsters on the rug, Sylvestre careful not to hurt his bride in her delicate condition. They shifted, came together, parted, kissed each other in places only married couples should dare to go.

He taught her what he liked, and when her small hand closed over him with a tight-moving fist, he groaned in an agony of exquisite pleasure.

Sylvestre gathered his willing bride close for a sweet, erotic kiss, his questing hand discovering that she was ready for his loving, to mate with him fully as man and wife, with no restrictions but for the safety of the baby placed on their bold, consuming actions.

Moving over her, he parted her legs and thrust himself smoothly inside, a bold flame spearing within the velvet sheath of his beautiful beloved. She gasped in sweetest agony and they moved in a rhythm as ancient as the ages.

Sylvestre bent his head to brush her nipples into pebble hardness and she lay beneath him, her chest heaving as he strove to bring them to fulfillment. His expert movements brought her to even higher levels of expanding delight. Their love was singing, passionately tender, deliriously sweet, a rapture triumphant, swinging and soaring in a very ecstasy of love. His harsh breathing was like a wild wind in her ear as they came together in a shattering burst of a million stars.

After the last waves of ecstasy overtook them, they lay together in golden silence, spent and consumed like the embers on the hearth. Moving slowly, Sylvestre reached beneath the loveseat and brought out what looked like a book of some sort.

Breathlessly she asked, "What is that, Sy?" Her heart gave a leap.

A charred log from the fire broke suddenly, flared alive for a moment and then lay spent, still, and she saw his face turn toward her with something of wistfulness in it during the moment of golden radiance.

"You remember once, long ago when we were much younger, we stood by the apple tree and vowed to have no secrets from each other—ever—so long as we both lived?"

Cassandra nodded. "I think I . . . yes, I remember now. But I was a little girl then."

"I must say this, my love. You still are, in many ways—a woman-child."

Cassandra did not move for several moments.

"You are speaking of trust, Sy. I know this now, for what you feel, I also feel."

"Yes. We are that close to each other."

Her eyes dropped down curiously. "What is the book you hold in your hand. Oh, I did not get you a wedding gift, Sy, if that is what you are giving to me."

"This is for the both of us, Cassandra. Remember Pastor Andrew's advice to the husband was to 'Let him have no concealments from his wife'?"

Curiously she watched him as he rose to replenish the fire and turn up a nearby lamp.

"I remember, Sy."

Lowering himself beside her once again, he pressed the green leather book into her hands and she stared down curiously at the gold-embossed letters. Softly she said, "The name is Emmaline." She swallowed hard, experiencing a gamut of perplexing emotions. "That is the name I chose were our child to be born a girl. I do not fully understand, Sy. This book looks as if it has been written in."

A golden lock of hair brushed his forehead as he nodded. "It is not new, but there are many spaces left for new entries. I thought you might like to fill the book up."

She shrugged to hide her confusion. "But . . . who is Emmaline?" she asked.

Sylvestre cupped her chin so that she was forced to gaze into his eyes. "You see, Cassandra, your real mother's name was Emmaline."

Her pulses were sent into a mad spin and she could only stare at him, baffled.

"My real mother?"

"That is correct. When I was taking care of securing your parents' home in Harper to make certain there will be no vandalism, I took it upon myself to gather some of your things together. I was curious about the rumor that Melantha was not of your flesh and blood. I searched among her things and found this journal at the bottom of a trunk."

"A trunk . . . ?" Cassandra's voice died away.

"Yes. It was stashed at the back of Melantha's wardrobe, with this book . . . *Emmaline's Journal*."

Cassandra's eyes burned and misted over the disturbing revelation.

"You mean my father knew all the while this was in Melantha's wardrobe . . . and he never gave it to m-me." It was not a question.

A momentary look of discomfort crossed his face as he said, "I cannot tell you why he held it from you, Cassandra, if indeed he knew it was there."

"You mean he . . . might not have known she was keeping it?"

"*Oui*, exactly," he said with deceptive calm.

She shook her head with sadness. "He never cared enough to bring himself to tell me that Melantha was not my real mother." Tears fell to her chest, and she flung the book aside to pull her dressing gown against her quivering form. "Get it away from me! I do not wish to have it for my own, Sylvestre, and I do not care that it belonged to my mother!"

"You do not care?" His eyebrow slanted upward. "Just like others who did not especially care? Why would you wish to follow in their footsteps and make the same mistakes to hurt yourself?"

Cassandra's gaze settled on her husband accusingly. "How long have you had knowledge of this matter. Why did you just happen to reveal this to me now?" She leaned forward to pound on his chest. "Why . . . *why?*"

"Hush, Cassandra." He pulled her against him for a good cry. "It was my wish to love you first, to make you mine forever, to seal our binds as we most surely did this night."

451

She pushed away with a violent shove. "To consummate our marriage before you let me in on that—that dark family secret!"

Sylvestre's voice was like well-tempered steel. "You expect over much from yourself and everyone else, Cassandra."

Brusquely he shot to his feet, taking the wine bottle with him. She looked at it and then up at him. "What are you going to do with that?"

"I am going to have a drink—*one* drink."

Her expression was tight with strain. "I see. Go ahead, drink the entire bottle, Sy, I do not care what you do."

He looked down at her blond head, her uncombed hair. "I am going to replenish the logs in the bedroom fireplace. You can join me in bed—whenever you are ready. And by the way, love—I did make your business mine. I indeed bought you, but not your love. I have given you all that I own, even of myself. Now it is in your hands to give to me the most precious possession you have—your love. Give me back something, Cassandra, for I have shared everything with you—"

"Even what is mine!"

"I love you. Give me your heart, Cassandra. I am aching for it."

Cassandra said nothing, but she had picked up the journal to trace the gold letters with a shaking fingertip.

"I want your complete trust, Cassa. I have not strayed from our love to seek out other pleasures. I excessively dislike the idea that you seem to think otherwise. There are no other women in my life save

452

you and—"

Her voice emerged stifled and unnatural. "And?"

"And my dear mother Nanette." He tossed his hand in her direction. "And perhaps that female child you carry whom you will name Emmaline . . ." His voice faded, losing its steely edge.

*"Never!"*

With a deep sigh, Sylvestre shook his head. "As you wish. I am going to bed now. Good night, Cassa." He carried the wine bottle loosely by its green neck, unaware now as he had been when he had uncapped it that the bottle had been unsealed.

Cassandra sat up long after he had gone to bed, sipping tea, poring over the beautiful, loving lines in her mother's journal. Emmaline mentioned her beautiful daughter often, and knew that she would not live long enough to see her grow into the fine woman she one day would become.

*Know this, Cassandra Anne, that I love you dearly.*

Before Cassandra blew out the lamp, she held the book close to her breast, tears streaming down her cheeks. "I love you, too, Emmaline. Mother. You were a beautiful person, and we would have been great friends if you had but lived to see me grow up."

Cassandra sought her husband's warmth in bed, snuggling close to the man who had brought so much to light in her life. Asleep, he took her hand in his and took it to his chest where he kissed her knuckles, then took it to rest upon his heart—where it belonged.

Gazing at the moonlight glancing across her husband's shoulder, Cassandra was reminded of her father and his weakness for the wrong kind of woman.

453

Emmaline must have been so perfect that he was blinded to any other love.

She knew in her heart that Sylvestre would never keep anything from her. They were too much a part of each other, she had happily discovered on this their bittersweet wedding night.

Cassandra squeezed her eyes tight when she thought of all that the woman Melantha had kept from her. Especially the beautiful book she intended to always keep close to her heart. First thing come morning she would write her first words in it, and with that thought in mind she couldn't wait for tomorrow to come. But for now . . . she was very tired.

Little did the sleeping couple know that outside the cottage there was one who had waited for them to put out the lights.

## Chapter Thirty

When the moon slipped beneath a dark, ominous cloud, Cassandra was awakened by a feeling of dread penetrating her brain. It was totally dark in the house, but she managed to rise and put on her robe and slippers. She looked down at Sylvestre, but he was only a blurred bulk in the bed and his even breathing told her he was sound asleep.

She moved cautiously from bedroom to living room, wondering why the hair on her nape prickled. She was puzzled and more than a little apprehensive.

Pale moonlight was suddenly filling the room and she could see outside the window where the waving trees were silhouetted and the river was silver-dappled by moon.

She was about to return to the bedroom when a floorboard creaked over in the corner. Cassandra gasped, panting in terror. "Wh-who is there?" she managed to get out.

Cassandra felt as if her breath were suddenly cut off when she received no answer.

A chill black silence surrounded her now and a warning voice whispered in her head: *You are not alone.* There was someone in the room with her and it was not Sylvestre!

Her breath seemed to have solidified in her throat and she could not call out for help.

The board creaked ominously again. Cassandra clenched her hand into a fist until her nails pierced her palm. Then she screamed!

Panicked, whirling about, Cassandra made a lunge for the bedroom. She was breathing in shallow, quick gasps right before the shadow stepped before her, barring her way.

Another scream tried to rise from her throat but was hurtfully cut off by a large gloved hand that clamped over her mouth. A scuffle ensued, but she was easily overpowered by the brute strength of her attacker. Then a rag was tied over her mouth and wrapped around to the back of her head, bound so tightly it cut into the skin of her cheeks.

The tall shadow turned with her and she was half carried toward the front door. Cassandra wondered frantically why Sylvestre had not been awakened by the noise and come to her rescue.

Dear God—where was this maniac taking her?

Outside, Cassandra tried to suck in a few deep, reviving breaths through the cloth, but she was rudely pulled about and shoved roughly against a horse that shied and danced in place. Then she saw the bulk of the buggy in front of her. She was shoved again, this time toward the opening of the buggy, her unyielding body pressed close to her attacker for a moment.

No, no, this cannot be happening, her mind screamed.

She tried to fight him again.

The man was definitely strong. He shoved her into the buggy, then worked swiftly to tie her up, winding the rope securely about both wrists and her ankles. Her binds bit into her soft flesh and she had a moment of fear as to how her baby would fare through all this. She prayed she would not lose the child.

*Sy! Sy! Why are you still sleeping?* her mind screamed.

The color drained from Cassandra's face next. The crazed man had walked to the little house, poured out some dark liquid, and began to torch the weathered boards at the foundation.

*My God, what is he doing! Sylvestre is in there! No! No! No!*

When Cassandra felt herself swooning, she grasped the seat and fought to steady herself. As she watched the rising flames through the window, her chest felt as if it would suddenly burst.

Horror, stark and vivid, shone in her eyes. The flames were climbing up the sides of the old, dark cottage. Whooshing sounds of consuming fire gushed from the windows and glass exploded, battering her mind and her senses.

Cassandra tried to take a deep breath, but it was no use . . . she was already fainting . . .

The last thing she knew the buggy gave a lurch and then it was rolling through the gothic-dark night.


Goliath saw the buggy pull away at the same time the fire danced in the windows of the house, roaring, kicking out windows like a primeval beast gone mad.

The flames flickered and consumed, and Goliath jumped from the ornery mule, running quicker than the beast had transported him from Diamondhead to the cottage.

Seeing that he could not get in the front door, Goliath rushed to the back of the cottage, banging at the door as he frantically tried to open it. Finding it would not budge an inch, he battered it with a huge shoulder turned sideways, smashing the wood to splinters that showered about his dark head.

The smoke pushed against him heavily as he ran through the rooms, trying to find someone still alive. Then he saw Sylvestre motionless in the bed. Casting a scouring look about the room, he found that there was no one else inside. *Missa Cassa must've been in that buggy that pulled away,* he thought with fear gnawing his insides.

Grabbing Sylvestre, Goliath heaved the large man like a sack of grain over his massive shoulders. "We gots to get you out, Mistah Sy—" he coughed.

Spinning and running for the door as the flames lapped behind him, Goliath made it outside into the cool night air. He was suddenly knocked to the ground with his burden as the cottage exploded, sprawling himself and Sylvestre in two different directions.

Quickly coming to his feet, Goliath went to Sylvestre who was squatting on his haunches, dazed and bewildered.

"You all right, Mistah Sy?"

Sylvestre shook his head to clear it. His eyes settled on the cottage in horror, for a steady flame was burning from the rubble. He struggled to his feet, weaving unsteadily. Then his eyes grew wider and he turned to the black man, reaching out to shake him, but his arms fell to his sides in his weakened condition. He felt like retching, for he had never been this dizzy in his entire life.

"Cassandra! Where is she?"

He tried to run toward the house, but strong arms restrained him. "She ain't in there, Cap'n. Somebody took Missa Cassa away!"

"Who?" Crazed by a sudden, blinding rage, he shook Goliath. "Who took her away? Damnit, man, answer me!"

"I think it was the younger Kirby, Mistah Sy, I think he done took Missa Cassa away. He started that fire, too—"

Sylvestre's face was the color of ashes as he broke across Goliath's sentence. "Harlan Kirby? How do you know this for sure?"

Before Goliath could answer and tell Sylvestre the reason he had hastened to the cottage, two riders reined their mounts to a quivering, foam-flecked halt, then slithered down their backs to dismount. Clouds of thick black smoke from the gunpowder charge still billowed in the sky, hanging there like a funeral pall, even making the Mississippi River look black and glassy in the twilight, the sky look charcoal.

Jared Casey rushed over to Sylvestre, his eyes fearful as he scrutinized the Frenchman. Then his gaze scanned the darkened, still-smoking rubble. He was almost afraid to ask of Cassandra's whereabouts.

James was right behind Jared and his voice cracked. "Oh no, not the little lady—"

"She ain't here," Goliath tried to make them all understand, for Sylvestre was still looking dazed over

459

the tragic happenings. "I saw Mistah Kirby at Diamondhead and he was up to some mischief 'cause he came out of the barn ridin' like the debils from hell was chasin' him. I jumped on ol Rondo 'cause he was the nearest mount. I followed him here, but I was too late 'cause the house was already afire."

"You mean Cassandra is with Harlan Kirby?" Jared questioned fiercely, balling his hands into fierce knots of fury.

Sylvestre strode over to the spirited mount James was holding. "I will have to borrow him for a time, James."

"I know, sir, and I wish you luck in finding her. Godspeed."

Before giving his mount a light kick to set him running, Sylvestre looked down at the two men. "What brings you two here at this time of night?" He looked up as the first twinklings of daylight were beginning to seep through the sky like water, to quench the redness of the sinking flames. "Almost morning, I mean." He shook his head, swaying dizzily for a moment.

"You all right, Mistah Sy?" He took the reins of the other horse from Jared. "I'm goin' with him. He still don't look so good."

Jared answered Sylvestre's question hurriedly. "The barn was on fire at Diamondhead and—"

Sylvestre's brows crashed together. *"The house—my mother?"*

"The house is all right, but I fear that the barn is gone. Your mother is fine, but James and I left the women feeling quite shaken. We lit out after the black man when we saw him chasing someone else, and that one, Harlan Kirby, must have started not only this fire, but the one back at Diamondhead, too."

"He must have an accomplice who delivered the hamper with the wine bottle in it." Sylvestre clamped his teeth to steel himself from the pounding in his skull. "Sleeping powder . . . that's what was in the wine otherwise I never would have slept through everything."

"You're lucky that you and Cassandra were not poisoned from the food you ate," Jared said, feeling a sickening lurch.

Smoke was mixed oddly with the fading night light when Sylvestre's mount reared up on its haunches, hooves pawing the smoke-saturated air. "Put out the rest of the fire so it does not spread!" he called before he lit out on the spirited, white-stockinged bay.

"Precious time is wasting," Sylvestre yelled. "Go . . . Go!" Goliath was right behind him, whipping the poor beast furiously in order to catch up to the horse flying ahead of him.

"Come on, James!" Jared yelled above the thundering hooves. "Let's find some pails and get down to the river. If this fire spreads, it will take the woods with it and even the old plantation house!"

Sylvestre and Goliath tracked the buggy easily on the tortuous, grass-grown road that meandered away from the river. Sylvestre's face was contorted by fury when he thought of Cassandra being jounced over the ruts and thrown against the walls with the furious pace Harlan Kirby must have put the buggy to.

The mind of the golden-eyed man was also working at an accelerated pace. So far, the only motive for Harlan's reprehensible act he could think of was simply that he had taken the man's bride away. But there must be

461

more! Not only had he whisked Cassandra from Harlan's greedy clutches, but he had also uncloaked some skeletons in the closet—the murder of his cousin Sydney! In addition, Sylvestre had claimed all of Cassandra's estate and effects, the *Southern Star*, a beauty of a steamboat, to name just one. Harlan had gone entirely too far this time by endangering not only Cassandra's life but that of his unborn child. He would see the man dead before the day was out!

They were entering Kirby Plantation by the back roads, Sylvestre realized. Sneaky bastard Harlan, he'd thought of everything—almost but not quite. Firstly, Harlan had not counted on being spotted in the dark nor, secondly, he didn't figure he would have been trailed from Diamondhead to Grand-Chemin as he went about his dirty work. One mystery yet remained: Who was the one who had delivered the basket of foodstuff to the cottage—with the viperous bottle of wine that had almost sent him to an early demise.

Now they were burning up the overgrown road with branches of twilight shadings along either side seeming to reach out gray fingers to them as they sped by. Flying on the wings of the wind, Goliath shouted a booming "Yessuh!" to the crannying wind, steering his horse around a fallen log. "Yessss! hoss. Go now! *Ahhhhh!*"

Suddenly Goliath was vaulting through the air over his foundering mount's head, landing on his right arm as the huge bay horse sprung to its feet and came to a shivering halt.

Sylvestre noticed that Goliath was not beside him any longer. He whirled his mount about and sped to the black man's side, seeing the horse with its trailing reins.

462

Goliath was sitting on the ground, grimacing and holding his arm. Sylvestre was about to come down off his horse when Goliath shouted up to him.

"Go on, Cap'n! You gots to find Missa Cassa! Please, sir, I'm gonna be all right."

"Are you sure?" Sylvestre looked up as the sky lightened even more, telling him that soon it would be daylight.

*"Go on!"*

Sylvestre was off again, unmercifully whipping his mount to greather speed. He reached Kirby Plantation just as the first blinding rays of sun lifted over the earth and shot through the overhanging trees. Catching sight of the buggy that had pulled up before the house, he spurred his horse toward it. He shook his head, trying to clear it, and came down off his lathered mount and ran dizzily toward the front door, bursting inside the mansion that seemed to be deserted.

Master of his emotions, fueled by a fresh spurt of adrenaline, he searched the house from top to bottom. Indeed it seemed to be deserted . . . No doubt most of the family was still in residence at Kirby House in St. Louis. If there were servants, they must be hiding out back, he thought.

He ran through the halls as quietly as possible. And then he saw it . . . Cassandra's lavender robe lying outside a closed door.

Lunging like a maddened bull, Sylvestre rammed into the door. He smashed the wood with the steely bluntness of one shoulder . . . and came face-to-face with Cassandra!

463

# Chapter Thirty-One

Eyes sparkling with tears, Cassandra saw her beloved husband crash through the tall door that yawned wide now, groaning on its one remaining hinge. *Oh, Sylvestre—please have a weapon! Harlan Kirby is like a madman!*

It had seemed like hours that she had been captive in this deserted plantation house. Where Harlan was at the moment, she could not say. But she had heard the footsteps in the hall and held her breath, praying that Sylvestre had come to rescue her. She had almost fainted with relief when the door crashed open and Sylvestre stood there.

Now he was rushing to lift her into his arms, and she flung her own about his neck, crushed in his wonderful embrace. "You are alive!" he whispered fiercely along her neck. "I thought I would never look into your beautiful eyes or hear your voice again."

Cassandra's eyes grew wide. "My God. *You* are alive . . . Oh, Sy . . . I thought you might have perished in that blaze. But I still had hope, for I could not see you dead and gone from me. All along, I clung to the one thought that you would come to my rescue, that you would be unharmed." She caressed his cheek with a trembling hand. *"Are you all right, Sy?"*

"Yes." He began to pick her up, for she seemed too weak to walk. Gazing into eyes that had turned indigo in her frightened state, he asked her the one burning question in his mind. "Did Harlan do . . . *anything* to hurt you? Did he—?"

"No, Sy. He has left me alone, so far. I have no idea where he has gone, but I believe he will be back, and, Sylvestre—he has a gun." She waited for him to reveal that he had also brought his own along.

"Damnation!" Sylvestre hissed through clenched teeth. "There was no way I could get to my weapon, love. As it was, I almost lost my life, but Goliath came along and saved me. Cassandra—that wine had a sleeping potion in it. I would not be alive and here to save you if not for Goliath. He saved both our lives . . . we owe him a monumental debt of gratitude."

"Indeed, my love. I . . . I think I can walk, Sy. But I am afraid Harlan might try to kill you, the reason he brought me here."

A chill raced up Sylvestre's spine in a premonition just before he heard the click of the revolver's hammer. Sylvestre turned slowly, putting himself between Harlan and Cassandra.

Harlan laughed, a demented sound.

"Cassandra, stay right behind me—do not move," Sylvestre warned.

Harlan was drunk. He moved in a lumbering walk, waving the revolver in the air, until he stood right in front of the crashed-in door. "So, Monsieur Diamond, how did you like my wedding gift?" He didn't wait for an answer. "Don't know how you got out of it, you must have had some help, eh? Well . . ." he chuckled evilly. "Where's your help *now,* monsieur?"

Cassandra found her voice, enough to get out shakily, "Harlan, think what you are doing. You are throwing your life away if you fire that pistol."

"Hell, do you think I care? Your lover—or I should say *husband* now—he has everything my father strove for. Do you know he even blackmailed my father to get your inheritance? Didn't know that, did you. Well, he told a lie about me murdering my cousin. I'd have never murdered Sydney—he perished aboard one of our riverboats that burned." He sneered at Sylvestre, with a demented look in his eyes.

Sylvestre began calmly, "You did murder your cousin aboard that riverboat, Harlan, murdered your own flesh and blood. But I shall not allow you to do the same to my bride," he ended in a deadly voice.

"You've gotten everything my family has ever strove for, Sylvestre Diamond. You even got first bid on the riverboat *Fair Maiden.* Well, you will not live happily ever after with the only living fair maiden I've ever wanted in life—Cassandra."

"Harlan, please, quit this nonsense. I will do anything you wish, only let Sylvestre go, and then we can start all over."

"You and me, Cassandra?" Harlan laughed harshly. "I know you lie, Cassandra. All you've ever wanted was him, so don't try to make me believe otherwise. I'm not that stupid"— he laughed—"maybe a little drunk at times—but not stupid."

467

Sylvestre's eyes moved almost imperceptibly to the left of Harlan.

"You two have betrayed me," Harlan was saying. "This is the last time, because now I'm going to end it for both of you. Everything in the will is going to revert back to the Kirbys when you are both gone ... *What?!*"

Goliath stepped forward and, with the same casualness with which he had entered, he wrapped his arms about Harlan's neck. As if the thing had burned his hand, Harlan dropped the pistol instantly to the floor. His arms windmilled for balance as Goliath continued to choke the life out of the struggling man.

Cassandra's eyes went wide just as she heard the sickening cracking sound of Harlan's neck snap, then Harlan went limp as a rag doll and slid to the floor, dead.

The black man looked up, shaking his head over and over. "I didn't mean to do it, Cap'n. I only wanted to keep him from hurting you or Missa Cassa."

With his head flung back, a sigh of relief escaping him, Sylvestre moved to place his arm around his wife's back. He pulled her close to his side, then he looked at the black man. "You did what you had to do, Goliath." He pressed a hand to his wife's forehead. "You have given Cassandra and I our life and we owe you a debt of gratitude. Name it. Goliath, and it is yours."

Reaching a hand toward the hall, Goliath waited until the tall, lovely black woman came into the curve of his massive arm. "This is all I want, Mistah Sy." His eyes spoke of his beautiful love for the woman beside him. "This here is Yendelela. I love her—"

"—and I love you with all that is in me, Goliath,"

468

Yendelela spoke in a soft, whispery voice, tinged with its exotic accent. Her yellow-black eyes spoke a shy greeting to the handsome couple standing across from them.

"What is it that you are carrying, Yendelela?"

Respectfully, Yendelela stepped forward and handed the soft robe to Cassandra. "I feared for the lady's life. I think this belongs to you, mamzelle."

Smiling into the soft eyes of the exotic black woman, Cassandra took her robe from Yendelela, but the woman stepped forward to place it around Cassandra's shoulders. Yendelela bowed humbly. "It is my wish to serve you, mamzelle." Then she backed up to stand beside Goliath once again.

"And you shall," Sylvestre said. "You will be personal maid to my wife, along with another young woman named Dulcie. Now, Goliath, let's see what we can do about this mess." He averted his eyes as he looked across Harlan Kirby's corpse.

"I'll take care of buryin' him, Mistah Sy, on his own property way out back."

"Yes . . . and after a few days have lapsed, I shall notify the Kirbys that the shallow grave of their son has been found. Goliath, do not hang your head—you saved two people's lives here today."

Cassandra said nothing, for she was feeling very weak at the moment and was afraid she might faint. She had weathered the violent storm thus far . . . she only had to get through the remainder of the day. But she would . . . oh yes, with her love beside her, she could do anything.

Before Goliath turned with Yendelela, his eyes lit up and he reached around to the back of his trousers and pulled something out. "I plumb forgot. This here must be yours, Missa Cassa. I found it when I was helpin' Mistah Sy out of the burnin' house, and slipped it in my trousers for safekeepin'."

Cassandra reached out for the smoke-darkened book. "Oh, Goliath, it is Emmaline's journal. Thank you . . . thank you so much!" The wedding dress was gone, but they were alive and she had the precious green leather book!

Out back, Yendelela and Cassandra waited in the buggy while Sylvestre and Goliath disposed of the odious corpse of Harlan Kirby. Yendelela sat back after staring out the window for a moment, saying softly, "That man was evil. It is good he is gone, mistress, for if he would have remained on this earth we would have all suffered."

"You suffered at his hands," Cassandra said, softly nodding her head.

"Yes. I did. But no more, mistress."

Just as the sun rose into the glorious heavens, the buggy pulled away from Kirby Plantation. Cassandra looked ahead to greeting her guests at Diamondhead, guests that must be excitedly awaiting their arrival.

They would all be there. All the folks she loved most in the world. Dulcie; Madame Nanette; Valerie; Jared; Camille; Goliath; Yendelela—

She hugged the precious journal to her breast—

And her child to come—

And her most cherished beloved . . . Sy—


Later that day, after everything had settled down and everyone had wished the newlyweds well, Sylvestre and Cassandra sat in the porch swing in the beautiful dusk of evening. Sylvestre took his beloved bride's slim hand in his own.

"I love you, Cassa."

A beautiful awareness enfolded her. Her friends had wished Sy and her a beautiful future filled with golden promise—as many lovely wishes as a woman's heart could hold as an offering to the glorious future.

The late-afternoon shadows lengthened and the tree branches ceased to sway. A bird crooned a lullaby to his nesting mate. An oriole perched on the topmost twig of a magnolia tree in a corner of the yard and opened his golden throat in a rapture of eventide song. It was almost as if spring had come to Diamondhead early.

In the sunset's red glow Cassandra held up her hand with its ring finger, held the diamond's multicolored brilliance before her for a moment, then lowered her hand back to her lap. Her lacy lashes lifted to reveal her shining blue eyes.

"I love you, Sy, and with all my heart I trust in you."

Sylvestre smiled.

*Knowing is all.*

# *Epilogue*

*Journal entry*
December 25, 1850

*The snowflakes are lightly falling outside. My heart goes home at Christmas and I guess it always will. I see the presents wrapped and topped with jewel-colored bows. Christmas at home was always a cheerful occasion. Melantha was always her most happy at these times. I will never outgrow Christmas, the sweet anticipation I feel on that Eve. But now I see it through the simple vision of a little child once again, never doubting or questioning, trusting all the time. Her name is Emmaline. She was born almost two years ago. She has golden hair with eyes the same color.*

*Things have not always been this wonderful since Sy and I became man and wife. There was the trusting I had to learn. But I promised Sy on the*

473

*nights following the wedding honeymoon that I would hold back nothing. I tried so hard to please him. He said my lovely, rounded body was so achingly sweet to him at night and he was certain that I loved him, otherwise why would I have given of myself so tenderly aboard the* River Minx *that first night. My only answer was "I loved you." Indeed I did and still do.*

*The touchy subject of infidelities never once arose in our marriage. I discovered long before ever encountering Miki Rhea and Sherri on the street in St. Louis that my husband was being true to me. However, it was a day I will never forget. The woman named Sherri was just coming out of the* Red Petticoat *with her friend Miki Rhea. Of course Miki Rhea never looks me straight in the eyes. It must be her shame over sharing her stateroom with Monte that night; now to learn that Monte has passed away. Also Sy believes it was Miki Rhea who delivered the hamper to our honeymoon cottage that fateful night. I do not know if we will ever know the truth about that, if it was truly her. But Sherri enlightened me to a few facts about my beloved Sy. She stated that he never bats an eyelash at the "ladies." In fact, she said he never had looked at any woman much. She said he must always have been in love, for even when he was younger he would pass up many lively flirtations. Yes, I told Sherri, he has always been in love. With* me. *The look she gave me was not one I expected. She actually smiled and shook my hand before sashaying off* down the street with her fiery-haired friend in tow.

The next encounter was not as satisfying, but it had a happy ending. Oscar Kirby swooped back into my life like a vampire bat. Bent on revenge, he boldly confronted me in the garden at Diamondhead while Sy was away on business. He had grinned vengefully, showing me bills of lading from one of his boats. I had been puzzled, true, but I believed Sy had only purchased lumber to build a shop for my new line of fashions. By the way, Valerie lost her shop, but she has no care because she and Jared are to be married next week and she will come to work at my boutique.

Oscar told me the "place" Sy was building was for Miki Rhea, and others of "her kind." Well, I almost laughed in Oscar Kirby's fat face. I questioned him as to who had gotten together those bills of lading for him. He had slyly informed me that it was none other than Jared Casey. I almost laughed again. I had left it there and walked away from the odious gentleman. He had walked, too, I suppose extremely pleased with his shrewdness. I went on to question my dear friend Jared, begging to learn exactly what kind of "place" was being built on the waterfront. He told me it was a "whorehouse." I almost fell over. When my golden Sy, my beloved, walked into the restaurant where I had met Jared and Valerie for lunch, I did not even consider questioning him about the "establishment." Be-

*sides, dear journal, I discovered that Oscar's vengeful act failed miserably. My dear Sy was indeed building me—I should say "us"—a beautiful boutique. It will be called LeBeau II. Valerie and, yes, Camille, she's still alive and in good enough health, will work there with me. And which two handsome gentlemen do you think will conduct our business for us ladies . . .?*

Going to her desk in filmy nightgown and soft robe, Cassandra read with shining eyes and smiling lips the last lines written in her journal. She dipped her pen to write further.

*Journal entry*
February 6, 1851

*Emmaline is having her second birthday tomorrow. Already she is talking up a storm and getting into great mischief as most two-year-olds do. She is beautiful, with her soft golden hair curling almost to the middle of her back. She loves dolls, as much as I did at that age. Grandma spoils Emmaline dreadfully. She gets everything she asks for. She has a kind heart, too, and never squirms in our pew at church, but sits still like a little lady. I love you, Emmaline, always know that. I will never give cause to make you unhappy, and you may choose the direction in life that you wish to take, although I pray we give you a strong rudder to steer by and a star to lead you. Just like the Christmas star we stared at out the window last Christmas Eve. Perhaps in years to come you*

*will remember as we held you, your Father and
I, our Beautiful Angel Emmaline. I will be back
soon—*

Arising from their marriage bed, leaving Sylvestre
asleep and satiated, Cassandra slipped quietly to her
desk, and, with pen hesitating, she looked thoughtful
for a moment as she remembered the loving hours just
shared with her husband. Then she wrote:

*That is too sacred to entrust even to you, dear
journal. I shall keep that locked in my own heart
always.*

UNTIL TOMORROW

Then she closed the book.

"Love is a distant laughter in the spirit.
It is a wild assault that hushes you to
your awakening.
It is a new dawn upon the earth,
A day not yet achieved in your eyes or mine,
But already achieved in its own greater heart
having heard."

—*Kahlil Gibran*
*The Earth Gods*